CW00549601

Praise for *Let These T...*

'With this lyrical blend of sch...
Fiona Whyte has conjured a story or immense depth and
power, and helps to lift the veil on a dark and mysterious
period of the early medieval Christian world'
Peter Benson, winner of the Somerset Maugham Award

'Authentic, immersive, compelling – as the novel neared its
ending, I read it more slowly, reluctant to be parted from
this vividly created world'
Martina Devlin, author of *The House Where it Happened*

'The coming of age of a seventh-century monk may seem
like distant emotional territory but *Let These Things Be
Written* thrums with urgent life while tackling the big
themes of belief and doubt. Like the best historical fiction,
the novel uncannily chimes with contemporary experiences
and Fiona Whyte's elegant, stately prose makes it an
unalloyed joy to read'
Mary Morrissy, winner of the Hennessy Award

'A captivating tale woven from wind and waves, from the
whispers of God and of demons, from the prayers of saints
and the power of kings, this novel shines'
Hilary Taylor, author of *Sea Defences*

'Original, clear-eyed and moving, *Let These Things Be
Written* holds the reader from the very beginning and never
misses a beat'
Eibhear Walshe, author of *The Diary of Mary Travers*

FIONA WHYTE has a PhD in creative writing from University College, Cork. Her short fiction has appeared in a wide variety of anthologies. *Let These Things Be Written* is her first novel.

Let These Things Be Written

Fiona Whyte

Published in 2024
by Lightning
Imprint of Eye Books Ltd
29A Barrow Street
Much Wenlock
Shropshire
TF13 6EN

www.eye-books.com

ISBN: 9781785633362

Copyright © Fiona Whyte 2024

Cover design by Ifan Bates
Image of St Cuthbert sailing to the land of the Picts is taken from
Bede's *Life of St Cuthbert*, courtesy of the British Library

Typeset in Georgia and Enchanted Land

The moral right of the author has been asserted. All rights reserved.
No part of this publication may be reproduced, stored in a retrieval
system, or transmitted, in any form or by any means without
the prior written permission of the publisher, nor be otherwise
circulated in any form of binding or cover other than that in which
it is published and without a similar condition being imposed on
the subsequent purchaser.

British Library Cataloguing in Publication Data.
A catalogue record for this book is available from the British
Library.

For Seamus,
whose gift from Durham started all this

This is a great task for me, and my powers of understanding are small

Life of St Cuthbert,
Book I, Chapter I

Anonymous Author

Prologue

AD 721

A s a scholar, he had rarely come across such ugly, misshapen lettering. He was shocked to find it here on Lindisfarne, of all places: a work crafted in so ragged a scrawl, so infested with inkblots, that some savage bird might have pranced with inky talons across its pages.

He had to admit that the clumsiness of the hand was in marked contrast to the quality of the words. The Latin was plain and solid, the structure was sound, rooted in the exemplars of the venerable fathers, and the investigation of the facts was rigorous, demonstrably based on trustworthy sources; indeed this writer had had the supreme fortune of having been a direct witness to the deeds of the blessed Bishop Cuthbert.

Still, it would not do. It would not do at all.

When first they had sent word to him at Jarrow, he hesitated. He was a poor traveller and horses made him nervous; the prospect of a two-day ride to Lindisfarne filled him with dread. Moreover, he was mired in his own latest undertaking, an ecclesiastical history of the English people, which would take years to complete, even if his attention were not diverted to a new project; the very thought of being parted from his monastery library made him queasy. Should he agree to this request, the necessary inspection of documents, the examination of witnesses, would require days, if not weeks. Then he must write the thing and read it before the elders of Lindisfarne for their approval. God alone knew when he might return to Jarrow.

And yet something in the subtle allusions of the letter the emissary had brought intrigued him. It appeared that one of the monks on Lindisfarne had already composed a *Vita* of their beloved saint. Its essential veracity was not to be doubted. But a careful reading of the work would, the letter suggested, uncover shortcomings: omissions, indelicacies of emphasis with regard to certain controversies, which must be corrected, preferably by one whose commitment to the unity of the Church was steadfast and avowed. There was none so suited to the task as he, the letter said, appealing to his sense of brotherly duty – and, he was well aware, his vanity. Surely the glorious life of Cuthbert of Lindisfarne, beloved of God, was worthy of the pen of the great Father Bede himself?

Now that he held the narrative in his hands, he understood those concerns. An unfortunate tendency to emphasise the man rather than the saint. Worse, somehow the text whispered between the lines that Bishop Cuthbert had been equivocal on the issue that had rent the Church asunder: the Easter question. The merest hint of such a position must be eradicated. A new Life was undoubtedly required to ensure that Cuthbert of Lindisfarne be remembered as a man who preached and upheld the practices laid down by Rome.

Bede tried to calculate how long the task would take. He must interview those in the community and any others who might bear first-hand witness, of course; but this document would steer him steadily in his endeavour – he could copy whole passages from it without compromising his own purpose – and the task might be completed sooner than he had first anticipated. Who could say? Perhaps if his humble testament was pleasing to its subject, St Cuthbert himself might intercede with God for the success of his other project.

He laid the manuscript on the desk in front of him in the island's scriptorium. Yes, despite its lamentable appearance it was a fine work, and no doubt its author would be gratified to have planted the seeds from which a whole new book would spring.

Father Bede fetched a pot of ink, prepared a quire of parchment, and sharpened his quill. He made the sign of the cross, prayed God to aid his hand, and began.

Part One

AD 675

One

THEY CAME FOR HIM at twilight. He spied them –
two shadows skimming down Wulfstan's Hill.
He thought at first they might be heading west,
beyond the village, but instead, they crossed the river
and continued on towards the hedgerow which was the
northward mark of his father's land. Wilfrid's heart
beat fast as the two figures, no longer distant shadows,
but darkly cloaked and hooded beings, passed through
the gap in the hedgerow. It seemed to him as they
advanced towards the village that the whole land was
filled with their presence.

Oswine, the servant, met the riders at the outer wall
and directed them towards the house while the villagers
looked on, nudging each other and muttering. Wilfrid
swung down from the branch of the tree he had been

sitting on and followed at a distance. He picked up the hazelwood stick he usually carried with him and busied himself drawing patterns on the ground, glancing up every few moments to see what was happening. The men had dismounted, and Oswine was leading their horses to the stable. Wilfrid's parents stood at the door of the house. He noticed how his father pulled back his shoulders and lifted his head. He had been carrying himself with a hunched gait recently. His mother stood a little behind her husband, holding a small, tightly swaddled bundle close to her chest.

One of the men stepped forward, and it was to him that his father first extended greeting. They exchanged brief words that Wilfrid did not catch. His mother did not speak. Neither did the second man, who stood back and kept his head down. But when they went to enter the house, this man, going in last, turned around, looked back at Wilfrid and stared. He had not drawn back his hood, and Wilfrid could not see his expression clearly, but something in that look made him shiver.

It was late when Oswine came to fetch him. The servant led Wilfrid out of the house and across the yard to the Great Hall. It was dark now, and quiet. A trail of cooking odours – parsnips flavoured with rosemary and garlic – lingered in the air. Oswine and Kendra, the slave girl, had hurriedly prepared a meal for the travellers. Wilfrid had eaten alone though, wondering why there was no music, why no laughter or chatter spilled over from the hall. There hadn't even been storytelling to entertain the guests. He had seen how Godric the Scop, harp in hand, had been dismissed from the door, his services not required. In fact, it had been some time since he had heard Godric sing, and lately Godric's stories had lost their flavour. Like butter without salt, they failed to satisfy, left Wilfrid with a dull and flat aftertaste.

Wilfrid stood at the hall door beside Oswine, waiting to be admitted. Voices carried from within. A man was speaking in a strange accent with words that sounded odd and malformed.

'Yes, yes, your son...' the man was saying, '...some other boys on our island, you see. The prior thinks...'

The other man spoke too. He did not sound as strange as the first man.

'Is the boy at least well-versed in the True Faith?' he asked. 'I've heard that some in your village still follow the old gods.'

'My family serves only the Christ god,' Wilfrid's father said stiffly.

The first man spoke again. Wilfrid had to listen hard to decipher his words.

'Look, the prior wishes only to help. But you must be clear about what this decision demands of you and him. This boy. He's your eldest son.'

Wilfrid's father interrupted. The sound of a goblet landing too hard on the table accompanied him.

'See the child at Rowena's breast. Yes, he is small. He came early, to bring comfort, no doubt. But look at how he kicks, thrashes in her arms. A warrior, for sure. And Rowena is young and strong, of good breeding. We will have more sons.' He coughed. 'By God's grace,' he added.

'Right then. Bid the boy enter.'

Wilfrid's mother opened the door. The light from the wall-torch shone harshly on her face so that her skin seemed unnaturally pale. Her eyes were dull and empty, the shadows beneath them deep. Wilfrid could not tell if she was looking at him or somewhere beyond him, though she held the bundle in her arms fiercely, as if someone was trying to wrest it from her. He wasn't sure which he feared most, this ghost of a mother or the strange men in the hall.

The two strangers stood with his father by the fire in the centre of the Great Hall. They were dressed in identical brown robes, girded by a rope, and both were almost completely bald save for a narrow ring of dark hair forming a perfect circle around the base of their heads. Wilfrid felt them observe him keenly. Once more he was gripped with a desire to flee, but Oswine was right behind him, nudging and prodding him into the room. Eventually, the taller man stepped forward. He bent over and peered at Wilfrid with pale watery eyes.

'You have heard, then, the Almighty calling,' he said to Wilfrid. 'You are eager to enter His service?'

Wilfrid glanced at his father. The Almighty? His service? Did they mean to bring him to the king? Wilfrid's father, Raymund, was a reeve of Ecgfrith King, but these men did not look like warriors. His father answered for him.

'The boy has already reached eight winters. He is of age. He is baptised in the faith, by Bishop Wilfrid himself, for whom he is named. He knows the stories of the Christ god. I have lately engaged the services of a renowned scop who has taught him much about the faith.'

'A scop?'

'I could not get a priest, but this scop, Godric, has much learning and...'

'And your letters?' interrupted the man. 'You have not yet progressed to learning letters?' He moved closer; Wilfrid could smell the wine and garlic on his breath.

'Well then? Do you know Latin?'

Wilfrid shook his head. He didn't know what letters were and he had never heard of anyone called Latin.

'He will learn,' Wilfrid's mother said. 'It is as my husband told you. There is no one in our village who has these letter skills you speak of. But they cannot be too difficult, I'm sure.'

'It's a matter of suitability,' the man said. 'I would like to hear him speak for himself.'

He was interrupted by a cough from behind him. The other man stepped away from the fire. His was the voice with the strange accent.

'The boy is young and slightly afraid of us, I think,' he said. 'It's natural.' He looked directly at Wilfrid. 'You'll be a bit homesick at first, of course, but I'm sure you'll fit in well into our little community. Just remember to be obedient at all times. Place your trust in the prior and in the Lord, and all will be well. Now, let's take our rest. We have a full day riding tomorrow. We start with the sun.'

He made as if to leave, and then stopped.

'Ah, we've been remiss,' he said. 'We haven't given you our names. This is Brother Dunstan and I'm Brother Fergus.'

Wilfrid wasn't sure whether he should give his name also, but the brother called Fergus had already turned away from him and was speaking to his parents.

'Raymund, Rowena, good night. We're grateful for your generous hospitality. The prior, too, extends his blessings in the Lord. And, look, have no further concerns about the boy. He'll grow wisely and well with us.'

Brother Fergus motioned to Brother Dunstan, who followed him out of the hall. As he shut the door, Brother Dunstan glanced again at Wilfrid. Wilfrid was sure now that those glimmering eyes were spewing out a curse.

Alone with his parents, Wilfrid tried to order the questions that darted about in his head. The meaning of the visitors' words held no sense for him. The men were brothers, though they did not look or speak alike. Tomorrow they would continue their journey, and they spoke as if they meant to take him with them. But to where and for how long? How did they know his parents? Wilfrid did not wish to leave his home – not even for one night. Certainly not with strangers. He must tell his father so. Right now. His father was strong, a warrior with gold rings on his arm. He could battle ten of these strangely-shorn men. Wilfrid must simply find the right words, words with weight and force, to persuade his father. And if his mother would lend support all would be well.

He glanced at her. She was gently rubbing the tiny head that had worked its way free of the swaddling. Her eyes, though, were drawn to the bowl of water on the table for the guests to wash their hands. A thought suddenly struck him, as keenly as a blow to the back of the head. He couldn't remember the last time his mother had looked at him or spoken properly to him. The realisation drove out all ideas of making a fine speech. It set something shifting in his head, a worm of a thought, writhing and wriggling but unable to dig its way out.

His father spoke.

'Wilfrid, these men who have come – Fergus and Dunstan – they are men of God. They come from a community of brothers north of here. When I say brothers, of course, I mean brothers in the sense of...'

'He means monks,' his mother said. She was still looking vacantly at the bowl of water. 'Holy men. They are from a monastery, a place called Lindisfarne. It lies north of here, close to the Royal City.'

'It is the way now,' his father said, as he paced up and down in front of the fire, 'in families such as ours to give a son to the Church. It is the new way and it is good. A monastery is a good place for a boy, they say. He leaves all else behind – all cares, all badness. They say he quickly becomes a man, and a good and holy man at that. There will be much for you to do and to learn there. You will soon become accustomed to the ways of the monks, and you need not fear; it is the right place for you.'

Wilfrid felt as though a winter's wind had blown right through him. His whole body trembled; he could almost feel his bones rattling.

'No,' he said. 'No.'

His father must not have heard, for if he had he

surely would have been minded to thrash Wilfrid for his disobedience. Instead, he carried on.

'You have had expectations of a different life. You must put them aside. That life is gone, swallowed up. If it weren't for your mother...well, you are lucky that you have been accepted. The holy men will take care of you.'

Wilfrid turned to his mother.

'Please, Mama,' he said. 'Please. I don't want to go. Why are you sending me away?'

Why would she not hear him? Why would she not appeal to his father? It occurred to him now that they rarely spoke to each other these days. He rubbed his fists against his temples. The worm in his head was still wriggling, unearthing misty images and setting off a humming in his ears, echoes of questions and accusations he couldn't quite hear. Then his mother looked at him. Finally. And he knew there was no point in further arguing.

'It has been decided, Wilfrid. And it's for the best. You must surely understand? You leave tomorrow at first light. Oswine will pack what you need for the journey.'

She reached out her hand, as if she would run her fingers through his hair, but then the baby at her breast started to cry. She turned her back to Wilfrid and withdrew.

He slept fretfully. In his dreams he saw his mother staring at her reflection in a dish of water. She watched as the water swirled and foamed, then spilled over into a great river. And Wilfrid saw how the river changed his mother's reflection to the face of a young, dark-haired boy with a wolf-like nose whose mouth opened out into a giant howl.

He woke with a start, his heart beating fast. A glint of moonlight lit up the empty pallet next to him. He turned away, curled his knees to his chest and shut his eyes very tight. He reached for the little knife in his tunic pocket and gripped it hard. It was small, gleaming silver, its blade strong and sharp, with runes carved along the handle below an etching of a wolf's head. He rubbed his thumb along its grooves and etchings and listened to the sound he'd heard every night for weeks now. From somewhere outside, beyond the hazel tree and the village boundary, came the howl of a tormented creature. A forlorn lost cry. A lone wolf on Wulfstan's Hill. He lay down again, still listening. It seemed to him the wolf cried all night long.

Two

THEY LEFT AT DAWN. Wilfrid was given Alvar to ride. He had wanted Blackeye, the old mare, but his father insisted on Alvar.

'A gift for the prior,' his father said. 'The finest horse in Medilwong and beyond.'

Wilfrid wriggled about, trying to find a comfortable position; Alvar was too large for him.

'When can I come back?' he asked.

'You won't be coming back, Wilfrid.'

'After the winter?'

'No.'

'What about the baby? Is he coming too?'

'Don't be foolish, Wilfrid.'

'But that's not fair! Mama?'

'Heed your father,' his mother said. 'And do

everything the prior requires of you.' She held his gaze for just a moment. 'Take care.'

'We must go now,' Fergus said. 'It's a two-day journey to Lindisfarne.'

He and Dunstan urged their horses forward. Wilfrid froze. He looked at his mother beseechingly, but she was once more soothing the mewling infant swaddled about her. Then his father slapped Alvar's hind quarters, and the horse started off so quickly that in the end Wilfrid didn't have time to say goodbye.

They rode up Wulfstan's Hill, taking the path near the blackberry bushes, Fergus in the lead, with Dunstan and Wilfrid behind. It was late in the season; the women and children had already plucked the bushes bare. Wilfrid had wanted to take his turn at the picking, but had been shooed away, first by the blacksmith's boy, who told him he wasn't wanted, and then by a woman who muttered something darkly about putting him out.

Put him out. Out on Wulfstan's Hill.

He had heard the words before, at the time of his mother's confinement. So loud were her wails and laments he thought the baby must be deformed or dead. But no; Oswine said little Sigehelm had come fighting into the world. Still, there were no celebrations in the Great Hall, the villagers kept their distance, and all around him Wilfrid sensed whispers and murmurs – *put him out*. Then a long great silence that had been broken only by the arrival of the two men he travelled with now.

They continued up the hill, past the standing stones,

then turned east and rode towards the morning sun. As they approached a river, Wilfrid felt a terrible quickening in his heart. The river could be passed easily enough, though the water flowed fast, gushing over stones and racing down the hill. He pulled on Alvar's reins and halted. He watched as Fergus and Dunstan spurred their horses across the river and onto the other side of the bank. Wilfrid knew he must follow, but his hands were trembling, and he could not bring himself to urge Alvar forward. Dunstan turned around. Within seconds he was back at Wilfrid's side.

'What are you waiting for, boy? Tired already? Ha! You won't know the meaning of tired till we reach the monastery tomorrow night, *if* we reach it tomorrow night. Well? What are you waiting for?'

'I...I don't want to cross.'

'Is that so? Afraid of water sprites, is it? Perhaps one is lurking there waiting to pull you in? Well?' Dunstan brought his horse closer, so close he could lean over and grip Wilfrid's chin, pinching him with calloused fingers. 'Believe me, there are things worse than sprites. There is the demon within. He is the one you must fear and battle at all times.'

Wilfrid shook himself free of Dunstan's grasp, but he couldn't escape the monk's gleaming eyes.

'You talk of river sprites and forest wights,' Dunstan said. 'Stories your mama told you to keep you close when you should have been out learning to hunt and fight.'

Wilfrid wanted to say that he hadn't mentioned sprites at all, that he could hunt and fight, though not as well as the other boys of the village, and that his mother did not keep him close, but no words came. He could never find a way of explaining himself, and even when he tried there was always someone ready to wave a dismissive hand and jump in before he could speak, as though he were some tiresome halfwit who must be silenced or shunted away.

Soon Fergus came riding up to them.

'What's happening, Brother Dunstan?' he said. 'Surely the horse isn't lame?'

'There is no difficulty with the horse, Brother Fergus. Only its rider. He fears sprites, if you don't mind. Sprites that live in the stream.'

'Sprites? What manner of foolishness is this? You've been listening to too many of the old tales, Wilfrid. Come here. Tell me what you see.'

Wilfrid curled his fingers tightly around the reins, his nails biting into his palms, and edged his horse closer to the stream. An image rose and rippled over the surface of the water.

'Well?' Fergus said. 'Any sprites, Wilfrid? Or any creature at all?'

Wilfrid hung his head. Fergus spoke more kindly.

'You see, Wilfrid, the old tales had their uses. Sure, no small child who feared water sprites would dare cross this stream and enter the wood. They protected the child from the real dangers of getting lost or attacked by wolves. But the old ways are done. You must wipe those tales clean from your thoughts. When you're afraid, think of Our Lord in Gethsemane, his agony so great it caused his body to emit sweat like drops of blood. And yet, didn't he still go forth to face his ordeal?'

Wilfrid knew the story. Godric the Scop had told it to him. He had it from a travelling priest. The Christ on a hill at night. Enemies, led by a traitor, creep through the line of sleeping thegns and take the Christ king, who does not even resist and allows himself to be captured and brought to his death. It was not a tale of honour, Godric had said sadly, not a tale for a scop to sing in the Hall, and then he brightened up and told Wilfrid a story of warriors and gold hoards and sea monsters. Wilfrid's father struck Godric a blow of his fist when he discovered the tales Godric had been telling.

'I do not pay you beer and bread to tell him tales he can hear any night in the Great Hall. You must teach him stories of the Christ. It's for his own good.'

Godric had wiped the blood from his swollen lip, promised to do better and told Wilfrid other tales he had learned from Christ's priests. But right now Wilfrid did not see how any story, least of all one about a god being overpowered, could help him.

'Right so,' Fergus said. 'We'll ride through the river together. It's quite shallow. Look, you can see the stones on the bed.'

Wilfrid hesitated as a shadow glided over the water, but on Fergus' signal he rode through.

'There, Wilfrid, no sprites,' Fergus said.

'No,' Wilfrid said.

His hands shook. He did not say that the shadow he had seen as they crossed had taken the dark form of a wolf.

They followed a path over the hill and into a valley, stopping to eat when the sun reached its highest point.

Wilfrid's stomach growled with hunger, but when he made to snatch at the food, Dunstan wagged a forbidding finger. Wilfrid waited as the monks bowed their heads and Fergus stretched his hand over the food, chanting words in a strange language whose meaning Wilfrid could not discern. When finally he passed Wilfrid some bread, Wilfrid nibbled at it uneasily, fearful of somehow doing something out of step.

Afterwards, they headed northeast into the hills where the wind grew strong and whipped through their cloaks. Clouds gathered. The first raindrops were light as mist, then grew heavy and fat. The travellers tried to keep their hoods up, but the wind fought them, the rain smacked their faces spitefully, and soon they were soaked to the bone.

Eventually they came to a wood. There was some cover here, though occasionally sheets of water spilled down from the treetops. Low-lying branches swiped at them as they rode. Falling leaves ripped past. The trail grew narrower and darker, and the sky blackened.

'We won't make it to Holburn tonight,' Dunstan said. 'We should seek shelter here.'

'Maybe,' Fergus said. 'It's not yet dark though. We'll press on and please God we'll find shelter if we don't reach Holburn by nightfall.'

They drove on, into the rain, into the dimming light, their cloaks and tunics sodden. As the wood became less dense, the ground grew more rocky and uneven. Fergus warned they must be careful as they were quite high in the hills, and there were sudden dips in the terrain. They went on foot now, leading the horses by ropes tied to their halters. Alvar was uneasy and tugged away from Wilfrid. Wilfrid tried to slow him, but the horse resisted and moved urgently forward. Wilfrid followed blindly, pulling at the rope, trying to keep his balance, unable to heed the shouts from behind. Something caught at his foot – a tree root – and he fell heavily, losing his grip on the rope. He pulled himself up and gave chase, calling desperately. *Alvar, Alvar!* He must not lose his father's best horse. He flung himself forward, and just as he caught up with Alvar the horse kicked and reared. Wilfrid hurled himself out of the way. Suddenly the ground was no longer beneath him. He was falling, falling from a height. Something wet and soft caught him but let him go again, and he landed hard on the ground. He tried to move, but the ground was spinning. Everything was spinning. A sickening sleepiness came over him.

Eventually he opened his eyes, thinking an age must have passed. Somewhere above him he could hear Dunstan and Fergus shouting and calling through the rain. He took a deep breath and called back. Soon there was rustling in the bushes nearby and then Fergus was kneeling next to him.

'Don't move. Do you feel any pain?'

'No.'

No pain, just the damp softness of the grass beneath him and the desire to sleep for a long time. Fergus examined him, gently pressing his hands along Wilfrid's arms, legs and ribs.

'I think you're just winded. I'm going to help you sit up now. Slowly does it; that's it. Take your time. When you're ready we'll get you to stand.' He put his arms around Wilfrid and helped him up. 'Can you go on, Wilfrid? Brother Dunstan is right. It's too late to reach Holburn. We must find shelter.'

Wilfrid looked around to see where he had fallen from. Above him was a huge crag. In the failing light he must have stumbled off it and landed on the bushes below. He was lucky not to have been badly hurt, or worse.

'Come,' Dunstan said. 'This time, stay close and do as you are told.'

Wilfrid drew away from him. He was seized by dizziness, as though he was still falling. A strange buzzing rang in his ears. He thought he could hear water, rushing, roaring. He wanted to get away from it. Now. He walked towards the crag face, stretched out his arms, tried to find purchase against the hard stone of the crag. There was nothing there. He lurched forward into hollow blackness.

And suddenly the rain stopped falling. The wind died behind him. He knelt down, felt the dry earth beneath him.

A cave.

He got up to run out, but Fergus and Dunstan stood in his way.

'Look!' Fergus said. 'The boy's found shelter. We can rest here tonight. It's a miracle he wasn't killed by his fall. Praise God who protected him and led us here.'

Dunstan said nothing. Neither did Wilfrid. He hadn't meant to lead them to a cave, of all places. Caves were the abode of giants and monsters, and he would rather venture back out again into the rain and dark than spend the night here. But he had no choice. Fergus and Dunstan went to fetch the horses. When they returned they stripped off their wet clothing, took blankets from their satchels and drew them around their shoulders. Dunstan worked with a flint from his tinderbox and eventually got a lamp going.

The sense of dizziness, the buzzing in Wilfrid's ears, wouldn't ease. He reached for his belt and removed the knife from its sheath. He lay down on the cave's cold earth, cradling the knife, watching as the lamplight cast strange shadows onto the wall of the cave: creatures, wraiths, dancing and writhing, and then a wolf staring at him open-mouthed. And he felt that worm of a memory wriggle inside his head again while the buzzing sound grew louder and louder, and for one terrible moment he thought that the wolf had let out a long howl. He clutched at the knife, ready to swipe, and then he realised the sound was not a wolf at all.

Fergus and Dunstan were kneeling in front of a large flat rock, speaking words in that peculiar tongue again. Only it wasn't quite speaking. It was more a strange form of singing, with Fergus intoning a strain and Dunstan echoing a response. Each man had his hands joined, as if in supplication, and Wilfrid guessed this must be their way of praying to their god. The singing went on for a long time, Fergus' rich voice drowning out Dunstan's, and Wilfrid was sure that the brothers were imploring their god's protection against whatever malevolent creatures might assail them.

The dancing shadows on the wall receded. Wilfrid drifted slowly into sleep, listening to the music of their invocations – their powerful god-words – fill up the cave, build a wall of protection against the evil spirits. Later he wondered if the brothers had prayed all night, for when he woke the next morning the sun was spilling into the cave and they were still praying, one after the other, back and forth, rising and falling, until they both reached Amen.

Three

THE JOURNEY WAS EASIER the second day, though Wilfrid's heart sank deeper with each step farther away from home. By late afternoon they had emerged from the mountain trails and arrived at a wide and well-trodden path.

'At last,' Fergus said. 'The Roman road. Not too far now, Wilfrid.'

But something other than the road demanded Wilfrid's attention. As they had descended through the wooded hills, every now and then a hazy mass of blue in the distance would come into view. A lake, he had thought, or some great river. No, he realised now. This massive expanse of water that stretched out until it met the sky was no lake. This must be the sea, the mighty whale-road Godric the Scop had sung of.

The sea could swallow ships and men as swiftly as a frog catches a fly. Spirits and demons lived there, and creatures monstrous and marvellous. Wilfrid gripped Alvar's reins tightly. He hoped this Roman road would not lead them too close to the water.

Fergus and Dunstan had halted their horses and were looking intently southwards. Wilfrid glanced in the same direction and immediately saw what had caught their interest. Some way down the coast, set atop a high rock, was a stronghold. Banked by two sets of high walls, with a tower at each corner of the inner ramparts, it gazed boldly out over the sea and all the surrounding land.

'What is that place?' Wilfrid said.

'That, boy, is the Royal City,' Dunstan said. 'I believe your father spends much time there in the service of Ecgfrith King.'

So this was Bamburgh, seat of the kings of Northumbria. Wilfrid peered at it closely. He could just make out a standard flying from the tallest tower, though from this distance he could not see the weaponed men who, his father said, marched along the ramparts, keeping guard over the city day and night.

'See the smoke,' Fergus said. 'The fires of celebration are lit. There'll be mighty feasting tonight, now Ecgfrith has achieved his aim.'

'A king must have a wife,' Dunstan said. 'And a kingdom must have an *ætheling*. We should pray that this new wife will be more...accommodating than the last. And fruitful.'

'Well, the Lord may grant him better fortune this time, though we should not forget, God has not left the

37

kingdom entirely bereft of an heir.' Fergus lowered his voice. 'There's always the king's half-brother.'

'You don't mean Aldfrith? Of Iona? Ha! He is older than Ecgfrith, not to mention the other matter.' Dunstan leaned towards Fergus. 'Doubtful parentage.'

Fergus shrugged.

'Well, I understand that Oswiu King himself acknowledged Aldfrith, and in the event that it become necessary...'

'Then we'll have to pray it *doesn't* become necessary. Beyond his questionable lineage lies the graver danger of false practices and heresy. We must ever battle to keep those at bay.'

Wilfrid wasn't sure what Fergus and Dunstan were talking about. He was so tired he could hardly sit upright on his horse. He wished that instead of going to Lindisfarne they might ride up to Bamburgh and overnight there, take part in the feast, but Fergus turned his back on the Royal City and led them north, along the wide Roman road that ran parallel to the sea.

At dusk they reached a fork in the road and took a winding path that brought them closer and closer to the water. The wind blew strong against them. Damp air licked their cheeks. Eventually the path petered out, and the fields to either side gave way to a sweep of muddy sand riven with streamlets. A series of wooden stakes seemed to mark a crossing over the sands to a long narrow stretch of land. In the fading light Wilfrid spied a high craggy mound of rock rising from the land's southern point. A small distance from the crag were speckles of torch-flame that he guessed were from a settlement, but beyond the lights lay a vast dark mass that he knew must be the sea.

'Come on, boy,' Dunstan said. 'Unless you want the sea to swallow yourself and that fine horse of yours.'

Wilfrid frowned. Surely the sea was some distance away, on the far side of the land mass? But Dunstan's words frightened him, and he spurred Alvar on, following the two monks over the wet and muddy sand until they reached a bank of dry sand and grasses.

They climbed up the dunes and followed a well-worn trail. It was almost fully dark. Wilfrid could barely see the track and kept close to Fergus and Dunstan, who seemed to know every twist and mound in the path. Eventually they came to the settlement, which was set behind a low earthen wall. Exhaustion swept over Wilfrid now, and he had barely the energy to tug at the reins to halt his horse.

Someone came hurrying forward. A small figure carrying a torch and wearing a tunic like Fergus' and Dunstan's greeted them, making a sign with his right hand, cutting through the air vertically and then horizontally. Fergus and Dunstan returned his greeting in kind.

'I've been watching for you,' the young monk said. 'The prior has asked that you bring the boy to his cell before the Silence begins.'

They tethered the horses at a trough of water and walked past a long dwelling, across an open square and towards some small huts. The monk who had greeted them was young, much younger than Fergus and Dunstan – about eleven or twelve, only a few winters older than Wilfrid himself – and his head was not shaven. He walked quickly. Wilfrid struggled to keep up. Every limb in his body ached, hunger gnawed at his insides, and he hoped the prior, whoever he was, would provide a generous serving of food.

'Slow down, Tydi,' Fergus said to the young monk. 'How many times must you be told? Walk with the care of a monk, not the giddiness of a foolish boy.'

They stopped outside one of the little huts. Fergus knocked on the door, and after a moment, someone bade them enter. Inside, a man was kneeling on the ground before a very low table on which a single candle was lit. Another flickered on the window ledge, and the air was thick with a smoky scent of beeswax, herbs and spices. The man stood up slowly, making the cross sign with his hand. Wilfrid held back, suddenly nervous of this figure who towered over him and seemed to require all the space the tiny cell could provide.

The man was tall – taller than Dunstan and Fergus – and very thin. His head too was shaven, though, unlike Fergus and Dunstan, he had a few stray strands which seemed to reach longingly towards his neck. His face and neck were long, and his cheekbones protruded out from his face, so hollow were his cheeks. He was more bone than skin, and his robe hung from him like a rag draped over a stick. He looked down at Wilfrid through large, pale blue eyes, leaning his head from one side to the other, as if examining him for something.

'So, this is the boy.'

His voice was soft and seemed to carry a strain of music.

'This is Wilfrid,' Fergus confirmed, urging him forward to make space for Dunstan. There was no room for the younger monk, Tydi, who had to remain outside.

'Wilfrid, yes,' the tall man said. 'You were named, I think, for Bishop Wilfrid, onetime of our community here, and a man greatly favoured by the Pope?'

Wilfrid shrugged his shoulders. His father had mentioned a bishop called Wilfrid when Fergus and Dunstan had come to fetch him, but until then he had never heard of anyone else of that name. Still, he was sorry he could not answer. Something about the way this man stood, the way he looked at him, his eyes so blue and vivid, made it seem as if there was no one else on the earth, except himself and Wilfrid, and Wilfrid found he could not turn his head from the man's gaze.

'I understand he was baptised as a baby by the bishop,' Dunstan said. 'Though I have heard it said his father was content to follow the old gods until Ecgfrith King made him a reeve.'

'Still, he follows Christ's path now,' Fergus said. 'As I believe Wilfrid does also. We had no shelter last night and feared for our safety in the forest, but God saw fit to lead the boy to a cave which protected us until morning.'

'A cave? A holy place, perhaps?'

The tall man spoke sharply. He looked at Wilfrid so intensely that Wilfrid thought his eyes burned like coals into his flesh. He couldn't remember anyone looking at him so keenly before. Usually people darted sideways glances at him and then looked away.

'I believe it was a holy place,' Fergus said. 'A cross had been carved onto the centre of a flat stone facing east within the cave. It must have been used as an altar.

When we sang the offices I felt our voices were joining those who had gone before us.'

The man stroked his beard thoughtfully.

'You've had a long journey,' he said. 'Go now, Brother Fergus, Brother Dunstan. Get some rest. You are both excused the Night Office. But let the boy stay a moment longer. Brother Tydi may wait for him outside.'

Wilfrid was left alone with the tall, thin man.

'I am Prior Cuthbert,' the man said. 'You are welcome to our community. It will take you a little time to get used to our ways, but young Tydi will assist you with everything you need to know. And since God has favoured you in directing you to the holy cave, I am certain now your place is with us. Kneel and pray with me awhile.'

Wilfrid began to wish he could have gone with Fergus and Dunstan. He was so hungry and tired he thought he might fall to the ground in a weakness. He was a little frightened of the man who loomed over him like an evening shadow. And yet, somehow, he knew that he must stay, that even if he commanded his legs to run they would disobey him and be guided by this man, the prior, instead.

Cuthbert laid his hands on Wilfrid's head. The strength of the palms, the weight of his long fingers, pressed down on Wilfrid's scalp, sending waves of warmth flooding through him. He closed his eyes, breathed in the sweet smell that drenched the air. He remembered how just two nights ago in Medilwong – was it really only two nights? – his mother had reached out as if to pat his head but had not quite reached him, and he had sensed a great absence hovering above him.

Now he felt Cuthbert's hands laid on him so firmly he thought they must leave an imprint on his head.

Cuthbert began to sing in that strange language that Wilfrid had heard Fergus and Dunstan use in the cave. As Cuthbert's voice gradually rose, Wilfrid knew he must be composing some great prayer. Twice he heard his own name invoked. He wondered why Cuthbert should name him in his prayer and why his Christ god must be addressed in a foreign tongue. He listened to the words Cuthbert was chanting – strong words, he was sure, and powerful – and thought that whatever it was Cuthbert was praying for, the Christ would surely be too afraid to ignore him.

A bell rang. Loudly. Cuthbert stopped singing and put a quieting finger to his mouth. He made the sign of the cross over Wilfrid again and gestured to him to leave.

Tydi led Wilfrid swiftly and silently down the hill towards a group of small dwellings.

'Where are we going now?' Wilfrid asked, struggling to keep pace with his companion. 'To get food?'

Tydi turned around and shushed him so sternly that Wilfrid was too afraid to ask anything else. Soon they arrived at another hut. There was just enough light from the torch outside for Wilfrid to make out that there were quite a few beds in the room, though none was occupied. Tydi pointed to the pallet closest to the door.

Wilfrid slumped onto the bed. Every bone in his body ached with stiffness and weariness. His stomach growled like an angry dog. Though Cuthbert had welcomed him, had even treated him with some warmth, Wilfrid sensed that something had passed between them that was beyond his understanding. Everything was beyond his understanding. He didn't want to be here. He didn't want to be in this dark, shadowy place with strange people who prayed to their god in a foreign tongue and then went suddenly silent at the sound of a bell. A tear rolled down his cheek. He was too tired to wipe it away. Tydi fished something out of his pocket and handed it to him. Bread. A small scrap.

'Don't tell anyone I gave it to you,' Tydi whispered. 'Or that I spoke to you during the Great Silence. Now, sleep well tonight, while you can.'

Alone in the dark Wilfrid chewed at the crust of bread. From somewhere outside he heard voices singing together. He thought about Cuthbert's song, a powerful, plaintive incantation. It echoed loudly in his head.

Four

ILFRID TRIED TO KEEP up as Tydi showed him around the settlement the following morning. His legs were stiff and aching. Large welts had bubbled up on the palms of his hands where he had been holding the horse's reins. He wanted to ask where Alvar was, and if he had been fed, but Tydi was speaking so rapidly that Wilfrid couldn't get a word in.

'See the building with the cross on top? That's St Peter's Church. It's where we sing the offices. The small huts are for the tonsured monks. There's thirty of them, and they get to have their own cells. We novices have to make do with the dormitory where the Novice Master keeps an eye over us. Over there is the kitchen. That long building? That's the refectory, where we eat, the most important place in the monastery. But don't let on I said that. Brother Dunstan says the devil will have the last laugh with me if I'm not careful.'

They walked beyond the settlement, climbing a steep path that led to a rocky outcrop overlooking the sea. Across the channel the great fortress of Bamburgh stood mounted on the cliff. It seemed much closer than it had felt when they were travelling the previous day. In the foreground, much nearer to Lindisfarne, lay an island, not much bigger than a large rock. Someone was out there: a tall figure, arms outstretched.

'That's the Holy Rock,' Tydi said. 'The prior goes there to be alone and pray.'

But Wilfrid paid the figure no heed. Instead, he looked around desperately, sensing that something was very wrong. He turned about, trying to spy the muddy trail he had travelled on to Lindisfarne the previous evening. There was no sign of it. On all sides water surrounded the land. Somehow, the sea had swallowed up the path, penning him in like the swine in his father's yard.

'But what's happened to the path?' he said.

'Path?' Tydi said. 'Oh, you mean to the mainland. Tide's in; that's all. You know, the way the sea comes in and goes out again?'

Wilfrid didn't understand half of what Tydi was telling him. Tides and disappearing paths, holy rocks, tonsured monks and novices. This place frightened him. He watched as the prior, Cuthbert, stood on his rock, his arms reaching towards the sea as though he spoke to it, commanded it.

Godric the Scop had told Wilfrid of a man with such powers. In ancient times, one of the Christ God's ealdormen had parted the sea in two, making a dry path so God's people could escape their captors. They were pursued by the enemy, but the ealdorman ordered the sea to repel the evil persecutors. A wall of water, a fierce swirl of waves, bore down on them, pulled them into the darkness of the flood and swallowed them up. But God's people, they walked clean and dry as barley seeds, along the whale-road, back to their own land. And Wilfrid wondered if Cuthbert, too, had the means to bid the sea to move; if he had turned land into island to keep Wilfrid there forever.

Tydi guided him back to the settlement, still chattering on.

'The abbot is the head of the monastery. We never see him though, as he's also the bishop and is based at Hexham. So really, Prior Cuthbert is in charge. You'd better watch out and remember to be obedient, especially to the older brothers, and most especially to Brother Dunstan. He loves reporting us to the prior for even the smallest thing. Then the prior has to give a punishment, and there's as many punishments as psalms in a psalter.' He counted out on his fingers. 'Extra prayers, extra duties – the nasty ones, like cleaning the privy or picking mussels in winter – whipping, fasting...'

Wilfrid's stomach grumbled loudly.

'Don't worry,' Tydi said. We eat at midday.'

Wilfrid looked up to the cloud-filled sky, trying to gauge the position of the sun. It wasn't high.

Outside a large building a group of boys hunched over small sloping tables, scratching at boards with twigs of some sort. One of them whispered something as Tydi and Wilfrid passed. Another whistled. Ignoring them, Tydi knocked at the door of the building. Silence from within. The boys sitting at the desks murmured to each other and giggled, and eventually Wilfrid began to think that Tydi must have brought him to the wrong place or...or perhaps he was playing a trick, just like the boys back in Medilwong. Home. The thought was a blow to his chest, so strong he could hardly breathe. He wanted to go home. Now. Leave this wind-whipped sea-gripped place. Even if it meant going back to being the target stump at which all the village jokes were fired.

The jokes. The tricks. Wilfrid had never really understood them. He supposed it was meant to be that way. He laughed with the boys when they let his father's pigs out of the pen and he blamed the slave girl like they told him to. His father whipped him hard all the same, for being a fool as well as a liar, and for days it was too uncomfortable to sit down. The boys made him show them the welts on his backside and again they all laughed. Wilfrid laughed too, loud and strong, and then they shared the apples the blacksmith's boy had persuaded him to steal from the kitchen store. He felt sorry about the slave girl sometimes. Kendra. A quiet, mouse-like creature, not much older than himself. She had been whipped too. The pigs were her responsibility.

Eventually the door opened a crack. Dunstan stood half-hidden behind the door.

'Well?'

Tydi answered.

'New lad needs his robes and things, Brother

Dunstan.'

'Then bring him to Brother Herefrith. It's the Novice Master's task to take care of such matters. How dare you come here and disrupt the work of God, the transcription of His Holy Word?'

'I'm sorry, Brother Dunstan,' Tydi said. 'Brother Herefrith has just gone on an errand to Bamburgh. He told me to bring Wilfrid to you after I showed him around.'

Dunstan scowled.

'Wait there,' he said to Wilfrid. 'And you, Tydi, get back to work.'

Dunstan disappeared, leaving the door slightly ajar. Wilfrid peered in. He could see the edge of a table on which some unfamiliar-looking implements were placed. He edged the door open a little further. Light streamed in through narrow windows, making the room airy and quite bright. Several tables, some flat, some with sloping surfaces, were laid out in rows. Sheets of cream-coloured material and feathers with stems sharpened to a point lay on the flat tables. Some of the sheets had signs inscribed on them, and Wilfrid guessed it must be the secret language the monks used, the strange tongue that Cuthbert had sung in. He wondered if its powers were even stronger when it was written down. A sudden thrill ran through him; he wanted to see more.

He stepped inside and looked around. Each wall of the room was lined from top to bottom with shelves, and each shelf was filled with wads of the cream-coloured material, some of which were bound in leather. Books. Godric had told him about them. They were made of goatskin and were small as Wilfrid's hand, he said. They fitted easily into a tunic pocket and were filled with tales of the Christ God etched into them in tiny tiny script. The monks carried these books about with them in the way ordinary men carried knives. But some of these books were large and thick, and Wilfrid wondered how many stories they held, what it must be like to inscribe them onto the skins. He wished Godric was here to see all these great books, and for a moment he missed Godric and his stories so much that he wanted to throw himself to the ground and howl.

A sudden movement from behind disturbed him.

'Out! Out!' Dunstan's cheeks were the colour of holly berries, his eyes wide and burning. 'You will never enter this building without permission. All it takes is one fool to knock over a candle. And you, you have no idea. The scriptorium holds all that is sacred in the monastery.'

Dunstan was breathing like a rabid dog. He flapped his free hand towards the open door, and Wilfrid noticed only now that he held a bundle of cloth under the other arm.

'You will learn obedience or suffer the consequences. You are no longer some village boy who may wander where he sees fit. Here you will be subject to the Rule and to the precepts set by your elders. Come with me.'

Wilfrid followed Dunstan out of the scriptorium, past the boys at the desks, across the open space to one of the small huts shaped like beehives that nestled in the shadow of the cliff, the same one, if Wilfrid was not mistaken, they had come to the previous night. Dunstan knocked at the door.

'Brother Dunstan?'

A voice from behind. Wilfrid started and bumped against Dunstan as he turned to see Fergus standing there.

'I'm looking for the prior,' Dunstan said. 'A disciplinary matter. The boy entered the scriptorium without permission, notwithstanding the order I had given him to remain outside. Already he has shown himself to be dangerously disobedient. He could have damaged a script, or caused a disaster, had he knocked over a candle.'

Fergus frowned.

'Surely there was no candle lit?' he said. 'The day is very bright.'

Dunstan pursed his lips.

'I was working on a very tiny interlace detail and needed more light. Forgive me, Brother Fergus, but perhaps you are not best-placed to judge matters of candles in the scriptorium, having been granted gifts of a different nature.'

'Certainly Wilfrid should not have entered the scriptorium,' Fergus said. 'But as it is not one full day since his arrival, his mistake is understandable. In any event, as you can see, the prior isn't here in his cell. He's making a retreat out on the Rock, you see. I'll deal with the boy for now. I'm sure an opportunity will arise for you to let the prior know your concerns at a later stage.'

Dunstan looked as if he was about to object, but he handed Fergus the bundle he had been carrying and, cheeks still glowing, left.

'Come with me, Wilfrid,' Fergus said. He walked more slowly than Wilfrid was used to, and at a very even pace. 'It will take time for you to learn our ways. Be guided by the older brothers. Follow their example and, above all, follow the Rule.'

Wilfrid was about to ask what the rule was – it seemed strange that there was only one – but Fergus was leading him back to the novices' dormitory.

'These are your robes and belongings,' he said. From now on they're all you will ever own. And in truth, you will not own them, because they belong to the monastery and will be passed to another brother after your death.'

Death? Why was Fergus talking about death? Suddenly Wilfrid was talking very loudly, screeching like the gulls outside.

'But I don't want to die here! I want to go home. When am I going home?'

Fergus caught him firmly by the arms. Wilfrid tried to wriggle away, but Fergus' hands were large and strong, and he held Wilfrid tightly until he stopped writhing and squirming.

'Wilfrid, do you know what *oblatus* means?'

'No.'

'It means someone who has been offered. You are *oblatus*. Your parents have offered you, gifted you to the monastery. It is a solemn and holy undertaking, and the gift cannot be taken away.'

'No, that's not fair. I'm not a gift. I can't be. You have to be a slave or a hostage to be a gift.'

'We're all slaves here, Wilfrid, willing slaves of Christ. I know it's difficult, but surely you must know that boys of your age and status do not live with their fathers and mothers? Had things been otherwise you would be with foster parents. Your father consecrated you to God under our care here at Lindisfarne, you see. God guided him in his decision, and you cannot undo his vow.'

'But...but *I* didn't vow.'

Fergus relaxed his grip on Wilfrid's arms and patted him on the shoulder.

'I know. Please God, in a few weeks' time you yourself will confirm your father's vow, but you must understand; it is unbreakable. You will be cared for here. You'll receive learning and knowledge of God's law which you never could have had back in your village. There may be times when you'll be permitted to travel beyond our holy island, but your life will always be here. You're blessed that God has revealed this plan for you, and you must accept His plan and follow the path He has set out for you.'

Wilfrid didn't know anything about God's plan or God's path. He liked some of the things he'd been told, that the Christ himself was a great scop, and people came from many leagues away just to hear his stories; that Christ had many useful powers, such as the power to turn water into wine and make five small loaves of bread increase into hundreds.

But Wilfrid also remembered that even the Christ was visited by devils. To be sure, Christ had defeated them once, but who could say that the devils would not return and defeat him? Where would all the Christ followers be then? But he didn't know how to say this to Fergus.

He could never find the right words to explain himself, clever words, that opened the ears of those around him. His thoughts just wouldn't take shape on his tongue. And now he was weary again, his belly moaned piteously, and all he could think about was food. He would think about how to get God to find him another path later, when his stomach was full and his mind was clear.

'Now, your clothing,' Fergus said. 'Take off everything you are wearing and put these on.'

Wilfrid undid his belt and removed his tunic and undershirt. The pouch containing his knife made a soft thud when it hit the floor. He replaced his own undershirt and hose with the ones Fergus had given him and then pulled on the monk's robe. The robe was threadbare, patched in places, and made of a rougher wool than his own tunic. Even through the undershirt it prickled his skin. It was too long, and he had to tuck it up under the rope belt, which he tied tightly.

Fergus eyed Wilfrid up and down.

'There's one last thing you need. It's in your right pocket. Take it out.'

Wilfrid reached deep into the pocket for the thing hiding there and ran his fingers over it. It was small, no bigger than the size of his hand, soft and leather-bound.

'A book,' he said.

'A psalter,' Fergus corrected. 'And the Rule. It contains all the psalms and our Rule laid down by Prior Cuthbert himself. Over time you will learn each and every one of the psalms and every section of the Rule, until the words are to be found not written on the page, but etched in your heart. When you no longer need your psalter it will be passed on to another novice.'

'So this belonged to someone else before me?'

It must have. The leather cover was thin and frayed – a shoe that had walked too many leagues – and the pages were dirty in places.

Fergus hesitated.

'As I've said, we own nothing, but hold everything in common. In fact, I believe, this psalter may have been used by the prior himself. You'll begin lessons in Latin with Brother Herefrith as soon as he returns and you will learn how to read. If you're obedient and diligent, in time you'll be able to read every word in that book. For now, I want you to find Tydi. He'll teach you how to make the sign of the cross. Repeat the words until you can speak them without hesitating. Then go to Brother Dunstan, make the sign, beg his forgiveness and ask for his blessing. Do it before sunset and the Great Silence. Now gather your old belongings and leave them with me.'

A sudden shout caused Fergus to turn and step outside. Wilfrid picked up his clothes. Glancing around, he quickly snatched the knife from his old belt, slid it into the pocket of his robe and went out. Fergus was looking over at the open area in front of the scriptorium. Dunstan appeared to be scolding a boy of about Wilfrid's age, bending over him and wagging his finger. Fergus sighed.

'I hope you'll be of a quieter disposition than young Hadwald there,' he told Wilfrid. 'Silence is one of the foundations of our life here, as is obedience. These are the tools you will need to forge your path from now on.'

Wilfrid thought of the knife in his pocket, nestling close to the psalter. Obedience was hard. There were times when he simply could not be obedient, not even to his father. Some dancing spirit or laughing boy would draw him away, plunge him into a mischief that was not of his making or desire. But he could be silent. Sometimes silence was the only way.

Five

THE LAST OF THE DAYLIGHT was creeping from St Peter's Church, and the flickering candles cast a patchwork of honeyed glow and shadows about the altar. Silence hung in the air. Not even a cough or murmur from the brethren. Only the long mournful howl of the wind outside. Wilfrid lay face down on the floor, the rushes scratching at his face. Just inches from his outstretched hands he could see the ragged hem of Cuthbert's robe and the frayed tips of his leather boots.

'The verse, Wilfrid,' Cuthbert said.

Wilfrid cleared his throat. His chest was tight. Brother Herefrith, the novice master, had taught him the words – he had spent days learning them – but now he couldn't remember a thing.

'With me, Wilfrid,' Cuthbert said. '*Suscipe...*'

Suscipe. That was it. He tried again.

'*Su...suscipe me secundum eloquium tuum, et...et...*'

'*Et vivam...*'

'*Et vivam, et non confundas me ab expectatione mea.*'

There was a moment for Wilfrid to get his breath back while the brethren repeated the verse. Then he felt the weight of expectant silence again.

'*Orate pro me,*' he said.

Cuthbert made the sign of the cross above him.

'From this hour you are a member of this community, bound to us by vows of obedience, stability and fidelity. Pray for us as we pray for you.'

Wilfrid got to his feet.

'*Kyrie eleison.*'

Cuthbert sang out, his voice high and strong, like the call of the blackbird.

'*Kyrie eleison.*'

Wilfrid answered, the notes surprisingly clean and strong.

'*Christe eleison.*'

The wind cried louder. Wilfrid sang over the wind.

'*Christe eleison.*'

'*Kyrie eleison,*' Cuthbert called again. Wilfrid followed. As his own voice filled the church, he felt light. The tightness in his chest uncoiled; a trapped bird was released from inside him. When the monks joined in Wilfrid sang on, reaching for higher purer notes that danced in the air. When the singing finally stopped he felt suddenly exhausted. He closed his eyes several times during the readings, and twice the *circator* waved his lantern in front of him to wake him up. Wilfrid sat at the edge of the seat and tried to concentrate. There would be time for rest between Compline and the Night Office. He felt he would sleep a deep sleep.

He slept that night and the nights that followed, though always his last waking thoughts were of home. He lay in his cot, knees tucked into his chest, the blanket pulled over his head, the knife hidden in a tangle of weeds in the bracken bedding. He listened to the sounds of the island – the whine of the wind, the crash of rain, the sea pounding against the rocks – and let their rhythm lull him to sleep.

When the bell for the Night Office rang he shuffled along in the line of monks, eyes half-closed, only waking to sing the responses. And though he felt he would never become accustomed to rising in the dead of night, when he sang the psalms his whole body was released from the cold, and his heart was warmed and filled with light until it was time to rise again and face the daily drudgery of chores and the task of learning to read and write.

Lessons took place every morning in the cloister beneath a wooden canopy which provided shelter from the rain. Only on *Sunnandæg*, the Lord's Day, was there relief from the incessant learning, the constant repetition of strange words and prayers, the never-ending drawing and redrawing of letters that were the invention of Romans, men who lived at the centre of the world in a place where the sun warmed and nourished the hands of scribes working in leafy cloisters. Here, on Lindisfarne, the wind sliced through the novices' bones, whipping the hoods from their heads, numbing their fingers so they could barely grip the stylus. When winter arrived the lessons moved indoors, yet still the cold sought out the boys as they recited Latin verbs and nouns – Wilfrid was never quite sure which were which – and scraped shivering letters onto their wax tablets.

One of the novices complained. Hadwald, the boy Wilfrid had heard shouting the day after he arrived. Brother Herefrith, the novice master, was stern. He made the offender stand in front of the community at Chapter and confess his sin of grumbling. When, a few days later, the same boy sighed loudly and shivered ostentatiously on his way to Lauds he was whipped – five strokes on his left arm. He was lucky, Tydi said to Wilfrid. Herefrith wasn't like Dunstan, mean and forceful with the whip, and he didn't usually make the miscreants fast. Better a sore arm than an empty stomach. Besides, Hadwald was asking for it. Grumbling was an evil to be shown neither in word nor sign – the prior had laid it down in their Rule. At best it produced a strong reprimand, at worst excommunication. Tydi didn't want to talk about excommunication. It was low and loathsome, and the shame marked the offending brother with scars worse than from any whip.

Wilfrid wasn't sure about that. He had received a few blows from Herefrith's cane when he had snuck away from his desk to visit Alvar, his father's horse, in the stable. And though the strokes were slight, administered without malice, he had felt the sting of each one for hours afterwards, as if they had left a mark on his skin as ugly and blighted as the marks he made on his own wax tablet.

'*Tibi soli peccavi et malum coram te feci.* Write that,' Herefrith would say. 'Take care with the grip of your stylus. Look at each letter in your exemplar. Observe that the *S* is steady and round, not stretched out as a dead serpent. No, no, that is hopeless, beyond redemption. It will not do at all. I do not know what will become of you.'

Wilfrid didn't know either. As much as he longed to learn to write, his stylus simply refused to shape the letters correctly. Some imp had control of his writing. Just as he seemed about to produce a satisfactory shape, the imp would nudge his hand, causing the stylus to slip and form the unsightly straggles that populated his work like worms in the earth. Eventually Tydi took Wilfrid aside and showed him how the letters worked.

'See, you have the letter *I*, across, then down. Good. Now, if you want to form the letter *J*, just bring your stylus below the line in a curve, thus. And the *O*. Start at the top, curve around to the bottom, then back to the top, the same thing in the opposite direction. A letter *C*? Why that's just half an *O*...'

But no matter how much care Wilfrid took, how much he observed the text in the exemplar, how much he tried to keep his lines straight and his curves even, he could not form the clean lines and shapely bows that were required. He wondered if a time would ever come when he would produce letters like Tydi's, *S*s as graceful as a swan's neck and *O*s as elegant as the shell of a snail, unlike his own miserable efforts, so crooked and misshapen they were an affront to God.

He told himself sometimes that he should not care

about keeping his ascenders and descenders even and uniform, or learning each syllable of the Rule. Because he could not rid himself of the thought that he might yet leave the monastery and go home. As the days slipped into months, whenever an opportunity arose – if he was sent to clean out the latrines or gather herbs – he would go to the top of the cliff facing the Royal City. He would look to the mainland and dream of crossing over to the other side. But though a route across was marked out by a series of wooden poles, the path, trailing alongside sinking sands and deep pools of water, was still dangerous for anyone unused to it, not to mention the risk that the sea might come sweeping in and swallow him.

Occasionally he imagined someone coming to fetch him. Oswine, perhaps. But the image of Oswine, like all the pictures of his old life, was beginning to ebb away. Wilfrid could no longer easily summon up an impression of his mother weaving or his father holding court in the Great Hall. He tried to recall his mother's touch, her smile, but his head had been scoured, like the dishes he and Tydi had scoured with sand in preparation for the celebration of Christ's Mass. All he saw was the vague outline of a distant figure, her face turned from him. And he wondered if he too had been washed clean out of his parents' minds.

At least he had Tydi. The other boys kept their distance from Wilfrid, as though they had sniffed out some distasteful peculiarity in him. But Tydi was different, always on hand with a ready explanation or piece of advice. How else would Wilfrid have known that the terrible moans he heard from the sandspits in the channel were merely the singing of the seals, that at table he must not use his own spoon in the common dish, or that the best place to gather grass and bracken for fresh bedding was close to the crag on the north shore?

Tydi had a store of information larger than a dragon's hoard. He seemed to know all the tales of the island. Whenever there was a brief chance to talk, between lessons and chores and silences, he tossed snippets of stories to Wilfrid like stolen pieces of honeycake. The monastery was founded by St Aidan, he said, way back in the time of Oswald King. Oswald was a saint now too, of course, and his head was buried with Aidan's remains here on Lindisfarne, in the church. The church was dedicated to St Peter, the greatest of the saints, since he was chosen by the Lord to be the first Pope, though some said St John was greater, since he was the beloved disciple, and it was he who composed the greatest and most holy gospel.

Once, many years ago, Tydi said, there had been a mighty row between the monks about it because some wanted to follow St Peter in the matter of Easter and the tonsure, and others wanted to follow St John, and in the end the followers of St Peter won out, and the followers of St John packed up and left for the wildest parts of Ireland.

Wilfrid wasn't sure which saint he should favour. There were so many he could hardly keep track. The tonsure, he learned, was the strange manner in which the monks shaved their heads, leaving only a thin circle of hair looping around their scalps like a crown – a crown of thorns, Tydi said.

Wilfrid had no idea why the way monks wore their hair should cause such bitter disagreement, still less how *Eostermonað*, the month for celebrating the arrival of spring, could provoke an argument strong enough to cause monks to desert their brothers. But he thought about those fugitive brothers, and sometimes at night, just like the wolf, they too came prowling into his dreams, with hooded heads and whispering tongues, and he wondered how they had managed to flee, to follow their own path as far as the westernmost isles of the world. And surely if they had escaped, then he might too?

The days grew very short, and the time they called *Adventus* came. Food portions were smaller, and some of the brothers hardly seemed to eat at all as they denied their bodies in order to fill their souls. And though Wilfrid's heart was heavy with the thought of fasting, at least the music of *Adventus* was sweet and alluring.

When at the offices Cuthbert signalled to him to intone the antiphon, he sang it fervently, his voice ringing out notes that were clean and bright as the morning frost that rippled across the island. Unlike his writing, his singing was pure and true. And it kept everything else at bay, the wailing wind and shrieking birds, the wolfish keening which thrummed in his ears and head and which he could never decide if it came from outside or not.

On *Modranect* they celebrated Christ's Mass. There were two meals that day, an evening feast before Compline, as well as the usual midday meal. They had wine and mead, sweet bread, fish, carrots and parsnips and apples from the larder. The apples were soft and wrinkled after some months in storage, but Wilfrid thought he had never tasted anything as sweet – not the apples or the berries or even the plums which grew back home. He tried to recall the taste of Yule celebrations in Medilwong, roast pig bathed in apple slices and beer, mead spiced with cinnamon, but everything from his old life – the old ways – was fading, drifting out with the mist along the channel, past Bamburgh and out to sea.

He concentrated on listening to the reading instead. Here, even on *Modranect*, they ate in silence while one of the brothers read from holy scripture. Wilfrid had become accustomed to the silence and to the array of signs the monks used to communicate, the nods, the twitches, the twirls of a thumb to signify a request to pass the cheese or beer. He had almost stopped hearing the sounds of gums gnawing on a hunk of bread or the *pfft* of fish bones spat back onto the plate or the clinking of a knife against a plate. But he could not get used to hearing a lector who lacked the gift of storytelling – the power of the rise and fall of the voice at just the right moment, the cunning way a scop could tease his listeners along a certain path, only to steer them off on another track to reveal marvels and monsters and unexpected treasures.

Tonight it was Dunstan's turn to read. He spoke slowly, his voice flat and unvarying, almost a mumble, and Wilfrid, his eyes heavy, his belly full, had to swallow the deep yawn opening up in his throat. Dunstan read in Latin, of course, but Herefrith had explained to the novices that it was a story about the time when Christ was born in the middle of the night in a stable. Wilfrid thought this was an unbecoming and shameful thing for a king, but Herefrith had said that Christ was a man too – a humble man – and Wilfrid supposed there were worse places to be born. A stable was warm and dry, probably warmer and drier than the dormitory of the novices on Lindisfarne in fact, with the ox and the donkey and the lambs all breathing on the Christ Child to keep Him warm, and His mother wrapping Him up in swaddling clothes, made, no doubt, of the finest softest wool.

Suddenly Wilfrid's mother was standing before him. They were in a stable back in Medilwong. Alvar was standing on one side of a straw-and-feather-filled bed, with Blackeye, the mare, on the other. His mother stretched out her arms and came forward to embrace him, but as she did, someone punched him hard and knocked him out of her way. A little black-haired boy with dark eyes and a long nose like a wolf's. He punched again, and when Wilfrid opened his eyes he saw that Hadwald was nudging him with his elbow and Dunstan was scowling from the lectern.

Dunstan was not scowling at Wilfrid, however. Something had interrupted his reading: the gate bell, ringing loudly. Sometimes guests arrived at the monastery, but never at night-time. Cuthbert nodded to the guest master, who left his place and went out.

Later the brothers filed out of the refectory. Wilfrid, being the most recent novice, was in his usual place at the end of the line. As he closed the door he heard murmuring from a few paces away, though the Great

Silence had already begun. Cuthbert and Fergus stood in the torchlight with another man, not a monk, but someone dressed in a heavy twill-woven cloak and rich green hose. When he saw Wilfrid, Cuthbert beckoned to him.

'I'll take the boy with me,' Cuthbert said to Fergus. 'I will need an assistant.'

Fergus hesitated.

'Perhaps someone a little older? Tydi, for instance?' He turned his back to Wilfrid and spoke more urgently. 'Is it not too soon?'

Cuthbert shook his head.

'It's time I got to know the boy. He is my responsibility, after all.'

'Please, may I intervene? I fear I may be trespassing on your charity too much.' The stranger spoke with the air of a man used to giving instructions, but he kept wringing his hands and moving about nervously. 'I'm sure it's not necessary for the prior himself to come. Only let me have a cure from your infirmary, blessed by your hands, Prior Cuthbert, and perhaps there is a relic which would strengthen the cure, and might not that suffice?'

Fergus spoke again.

'Let me go,' he said to Cuthbert. 'Brother Laurence could assume my duties in the infirmary while I'm gone – he's skilled in medicine – and you can make a retreat on the Rock as you intended.'

Cuthbert shook his head.

'No, no, it is my duty and not another's. Wilfrid, you are coming with me. We're called to do God's work.'

Wilfrid pressed his fist against his chest. He was

sure the fast thump-thump-thump of his heart would be heard. It was as if God had sent him the dream as a sign. With Cuthbert guiding him he could make his way safely to the mainland. Once there, he would escape, find his way home. His chance, finally, had come.

Six

WILFRID WAS SURPRISED that Cuthbert hadn't chosen to ride Alvar. There had been no sign of his father's horse in the stable. Outside, Cuthbert stretched a lantern tied to a pole in front of his mount. The light fell on the stranger. Wisps of grey hair blew about his balding head. His face glowed yellow in the lamplight, and a purple bruise on his left cheekbone bulged gruesomely through his skin.

'As I say, I would not for anything trespass on your favour,' he said. 'I would not have come at all but that she is sick, almost to death, moaning and crying out as if in childbirth.'

'And as *I* say, Hildmer, It is my duty to attend to your wife,' Cuthbert said. 'You must pray for her as we ride.'

They rode the winding path down to the sands and

began to cross, accompanied by the swish and swirl of the approaching tide. A shade of doubt passed over Wilfrid. He had not reckoned on this – that they would be pursued by the relentless flow of the sea. The horses kicked up showers of spray that ran down Wilfrid's face and stung his lips. The splash was heavy and Wilfrid feared that Cuthbert's lantern would be extinguished and they would be lost in the darkness, with the sea rising and whirling about them. He glanced at the water. Just beneath the surface was a dark shadow. A shadow with wolf's eyes, glowing yellow in the dark.

His stomach churned. He hadn't thought this through, hadn't realised he would have to ride through the waves. Worse, he hadn't even had a chance to retrieve his knife from its hiding place. He would never recover it now. He looked behind, saw the light from the watch tower on the cliff. But the sea was closing in behind them; even if he wanted to, it was too late to return. He swallowed down the sour taste of bile in his mouth. He must keep going. All he could do was stay close to Cuthbert and hope that Christ would not permit the sea to drown them.

They reached the shore safely and took a path that twisted away from the coast. Wilfrid had no idea in which direction they were travelling, let alone, he now realised, how and when he would make his escape. When they came to a fork in the path he halted. Bright fires whirled in the sky, wheeling like dragon breath: the glow of torches in the turrets of the Royal City of Bamburgh.

He faced the direction of the city. In the Great Hall of the fortress Ecgfrith King and his guests would be feasting and celebrating Christ's Mass. The king's reeves and thegns from far and wide would be there. He could picture the scene just as his father and Godric had described: the queen bearing a great cup of mead to the king, men drinking beer and wine, women carrying in platters of cheese and sweet bread, wild boar and hare in honey, warriors toasting their lord and speaking loudly of his valour, a scop singing a tale of the great deeds of Ecgfrith King.

His father would be there, seated at the high table.

A quickening pulsed through Wilfrid's chest. He must go. Now. Find his father, convince him somehow that he must come home.

'Wilfrid, this is the way.'

Cuthbert's voice sounded clearly from the distance.

Wilfrid tightened his grip on the reins. He mustn't look back. All he had to do was head towards the flames, and soon he would be in Bamburgh. But Cuthbert was suddenly beside him.

'There is nothing for you there, Wilfrid.'

'My father is there.'

'Possibly so, but that is not your path.'

Paths again. That was what Fergus had said. He must follow God's path. But maybe God's path led to the Royal City?

'I want to go to my father. I want to go home.'

'What's happening?' Hildmer called.

'All will be well, Hildmer,' Cuthbert said. 'There is simply a small matter I must explain to our young companion.'

'Of course, Prior.' Hildmer scratched his head vigorously. 'Perhaps you might explain as we ride?'

'Please wait for us quietly, Hildmer. At a little distance, if you please. We will all ride on together in a few moments.'

Hildmer muttered something as Cuthbert drew closer to Wilfrid.

'Wilfrid, you know the story, I suppose, of Oswiu King and his daughter?'

Oswiu King. Everyone knew of him. The scops still sang tales of the famous battle of the Winwæd when he defeated that vicious pagan king, Penda of Mercia. Oswiu was the father of Ecgfrith King, but Wilfrid had never heard anything of a daughter.

'After God saw fit to grant him a great victory over Penda, Oswiu dedicated his daughter Ælfflæd to perpetual virginity at the abbey of Hartlepool in thanksgiving for God's aid in battle. She was a mere baby then, of course, unaware of her vocation, but you know, Wilfrid, God was guiding Oswiu's hand. Ælfflæd is abbess of Whitby now. A most wise and learned lady, she leads a great community of holy men as well as holy women, and is a dear friend and counsellor of my own. So you see, she was lucky, luckier than her brother Ecgfrith, blessed in the decision made by her father, as I believe you are blessed too.'

Wilfrid's head was heavy. How could this Ælfflæd have been luckier than Ecgfrith who was lord of all Northumbria, the greatest kingdom in the land? And blessed? But there was no time for questions. Hildmer was moving about impatiently, his horse turning this way and that. Cuthbert spoke again.

'God guided your parents to gift you to the monastery. Do you doubt God's ways, Wilfrid, you who were led safely to Lindisfarne through the dangers of the storm, who were chosen to find the sanctuary of the holy cave?'

Wilfrid sat still in the saddle. The fires in the turrets sparked embers into the sky, tiny orange imps flitting across the moon. Had God led him to Lindisfarne? How could he tell? God did not speak to him as he seemed to speak to the older monks. But four full moons had passed since he arrived at the monastery. His parents had not sent for him, just as Fergus had said they would not. He recalled the baby swaddled at his mother's breast. They didn't need him any more, he supposed, now they had another son to take his place. Why should he go where he was not wanted?

Wilfrid bit his lip to prevent himself from crying. He looked away from Bamburgh. He saw the yellow glow of the lamp, Cuthbert's arm reaching out to him from the shadows. He turned. Slowly he guided his horse to the lamp.

Progress was not quick after all. They took a narrow path along the coast and rode in single file, following Cuthbert's light. Wilfrid counted the paces to keep himself awake. The cold slipped in under his habit and coiled around him until he could barely feel the reins in his fingers. But at least the wind had died away. It was strangely still, no movement about them, not the rustle of a mouse or a rat in the grass; no owl or night bird called; no fox crossed their path. Wilfrid listened, straining to hear something, but the only sounds were the horses' hooves, following each other pace for pace. Clouds gathered. The moon retreated. One by one the stars fell away. The whole world was swollen with darkness. Wilfrid stared up into the blackness of the sky.

Cuthbert pulled up his horse.

'What is it, Wilfrid? Do you see something there?'

Wilfrid shivered. It had become suddenly deathly cold; his bones were sticks of ice.

'No,' he said.

'We must keep going,' Cuthbert said. 'We will pray as we ride.'

Cuthbert sang clear and strong, like a herald in the silence of the night.

> *In scapulis suis obumbrabit te,*
> *et sub pinnis eius sperabis.*
> *Scuto circumdabit te veritas eius.*

Wilfrid joined in. His voice was small at first, each note quivering with the cold, but after a while he found himself singing out loud. He sang through the cold and dark, until eventually a blade of light cut through the sky and revealed more clearly the path before them. They followed it down into a valley where a soft mist curled around a large enclosure like a cat's tail. Hildmer announced that at last they were upon his village.

A man greeted them at the boundary fence.

'Well?' Hildmer said.

'She is weak,' the man answered. 'She hasn't risen from bed.'

They dismounted. Wilfrid's fingers were so numb he could barely let go of the reins, and he had to be helped to the ground. A noise distracted him. A cry, the tortured cry of a wounded animal, a dog, perhaps, or a fox. Then shouts: 'Where is she?' 'Take hold of her.' Now another scream, higher and shriller, and a figure dressed in a woollen shift came running through the mist. Hildmer rushed forward and tried to grab hold of her, but she screamed and kicked and spat and tore herself free. She wasn't free for long though. Wilfrid moved quickly out of the way as a group of villagers surrounded her and pinned her to the ground. She lay there lay sobbing, her body drawn into a ball, her arms holding her knees tight into her chest, her head pressed against her knees, her hair loose, wild and matted, splayed out around her.

Hildmer turned to Cuthbert. His face was purple-red, and he spoke through gritted teeth.

'So then, you see how it is with her. Can you help?'

'I will try,' Cuthbert said. 'Leave her now. Go inside, all of you.'

Hildmer nodded to the others. They released the woman and walked with Hildmer towards the houses. Wilfrid made to follow, but Cuthbert called him back.

'Stay here, Wilfrid,' he said.

Cuthbert sat on the ground a few paces from Hildmer's wife. Wilfrid did likewise. Reluctantly. The ground was cold and hard, and despite being stiff and sore he suddenly missed the feel of the horse's skin against his legs and the saddle warming him from underneath. Hildmer's wife continued to weep, but more quietly now until gradually the sobs died into silent shivers in her thin body. Eventually she looked up.

Hildmer's wife was much younger than her husband; she couldn't have been more than fourteen winters.

Her face and arms were streaked with dirt and badly scratched, as though she had been attacked by wild cats. Still she made no effort to move, and Wilfrid wondered if they would have to remain there all day. Every bone in his body ached, his head was heavy as a sack of grain, and sleep called like a ghost through the mist.

Cuthbert moved a pace closer to the girl.

'How many of them are there?' he said. 'One? More than one?'

The girl curled into an even tighter ball.

'You need not be afraid,' Cuthbert said. 'I promise you, no further harm will come to you.'

The girl covered her face with her hands. Her whole body shook as if there was a creature shifting and rattling inside her. Cuthbert eased closer. He removed his cloak and leaned towards her. She raised her hands as if to throw him off, but he lowered the cloak gently over her and then moved back again.

'It is a most grievous trial when demons assail us,' he said. 'I have had to fight many. Sometimes they come singly; sometimes they are legion. The Lord asks us to do battle with them. He defends us and aids us in victory. Remember, He only makes demands on the strong and holy. A wise friend said that to me once, many years ago. I was young and troubled as you are now. I believe my friend was right.'

The girl – Hildmer's wife – pulled the cloak tightly about her. She looked no more than a child huddled underneath it. Still, Wilfrid envied her the warmth of the cloak and wondered how much longer they must endure sitting on the damp ground, the cold steeping into their bones while they waited for her to get up. The terrible tremors in her body had eased off, he noticed, but she sounded very shaken and spoke in a whisper.

'I thought it would go away after. I tried to fight it, but it crawled into me during the night, like a worm. Sometimes it lies like a stone in the pit of my belly, and I think it must be dead it's so still, but it's not dead.'

'When is it still?' Cuthbert asked.

'I don't know. I can't remember. I want to go home.'

'This is your home,' Cuthbert said gently. 'Shall I bring you inside?'

'No,' she shouted. 'I won't go in. I don't belong here. I want to go away – anywhere. It might leave me if I get away from here.'

'Tell me when it is still.'

She looked away.

'It fears my bleeding. It's still then. In the last cycle it was quieted for seven days but it returned after.'

'Does it speak to you?'

The girl pulled herself into a sitting position. She held Cuthbert's cloak tightly around her and wrapped her arms around her knees.

'It says things without speaking.'

'What does it say?'

'Nothing. I cannot tell exactly.'

'But you understand it?'

The girl looked over at Wilfrid.

'Who is that?'

'That is Wilfrid. He is one of the novice brothers from our island.'

'He's a child.'

Wilfrid stood up. He took a step closer to the girl.

77

Her face was even more dirty and scratched than he had first realised. Some of the wounds were scabbed, some were bright red and others were yellowing. Her hair was so matted he couldn't imagine anyone being able to drag a comb through it. This degraded creature was the reason they had ridden all night long? The reason they were sitting outside in the wet and biting air? For this he had abandoned his chance of escape? She reminded Wilfrid of Kendra, the slave girl who tended the pigs in his father's house, dirty, scowling, looking at him as if he was little better than she was. He wanted to slap her hard across her ruined face.

'Some of our brothers are chosen at a young age,' Cuthbert said. 'He is cold and tired and hungry. He'd like you to bring him inside.'

The girl locked her arms about her knees and rocked back and forth, whimpering.

Cuthbert kneeled next to her.

'Take my hand,' he said. 'Take it.'

She ignored him, pressed her head harder into her knees and continued to rock. Cuthbert held out his right hand, his long fingers stretched above her head. Wilfrid watched for a long time as she shook and rocked while Cuthbert kept his hand outstretched. After a while her movements became less agitated. Wilfrid wasn't sure in the end who moved first, but somehow her right hand was held in Cuthbert's left. Cuthbert edged closer to her, taking both her hands in his.

'You said you thought the demon would go away after. After what?'

She sighed. Her face was swollen from crying, and her eyes were half-closed.

'After the thing – the child – after it came out.'

'You had a child?'

'Not a child. Only half-formed. It came dead at six months.'

'And then the demon entered?'

'I think it was always there, with the child creature. Only that part of it died and its spirit did not.'

'But it is quiet at times, when you bleed for instance?'

'Yes, I've told you.'

'And it is angry at other times? When?'

'I don't know. Often. It does not like certain things, it does not like me to eat sometimes, or...or to have my husband too close by.'

'Will it let you lie with him?'

She tried to pull away from Cuthbert, but he held on to her.

'Please, let me be,' she said.

Cuthbert spoke firmly. 'Look at me.' He put his hand under her chin and turned her face to his. 'You must let this demon go. It demands that which you must never relinquish – your very soul. I promise you I will battle it with you, and it will have no more power, but you must let it go or it will destroy you. For now, go inside. Bring Wilfrid with you. Eat and rest. I will speak with your husband.'

He pulled the girl gently to her feet and led her towards Wilfrid. She didn't look at him. Her head hung. She walked falteringly to the house, each step the hobble of a lame dog.

Seven

HILDMER'S HOUSE WAS LIKE a smaller version of Wilfrid's home. A couple of chests stood on the floor beneath some shelves stocked with cups and dishes. A cauldron was suspended over a fire in the centre of the room, a strong smell wafting from it. Hildmer sat on a bench at a table. He reached out his arm to his wife, but she withdrew, head still bent, to an alcove enclosed behind a woollen drape. Wilfrid guessed her bed must be there. Hildmer dropped his outstretched hand and curled it into a fist.

'Sit,' he said to Wilfrid. 'I'll fetch you something to drink. When the prior comes in we'll have the broth.'

Wilfrid slumped onto the bench. He was so weary he hardly knew whether he wanted to eat or sleep, but the smell from the cauldron roused him, and the thought of eating food prepared by someone outside the monastery made his belly ache. Hildmer landed a jug of beer on the table and filled a cup for Wilfrid.

'The prior?' Hildmer said. 'He *is* coming in?'

'Oh, I forgot. The prior is outside. He wants to speak with you.'

'Forgot!'

Hildmer spat on the ground and hurried out.

Wilfrid swallowed down the beer. It was stronger than the monastery's and tasted faintly of bog myrtle. He refilled his cup and drew close to the fire. A dark broth simmered inside the cauldron. He picked up a ladle and stirred it. Small chunks of carrot and turnip swam around in the liquid, surrounded by shreds of a dark sinewy meat which he guessed must be hare. He stood still and listened. No sound from outside, not a murmur or footstep. No movement from behind the drape in the alcove. He took a bowl from the shelf and filled it with broth. The steam curled about his face as he drank. The broth scalded his lips and tongue, but the vegetables were juicy and tender. Slivers of hare slipped down his throat, heating his belly like draughts of fire. He hadn't eaten meat since leaving his home. Wilfrid had heard that if one of the brethren was very sick he might be allowed some – a portion of boiled fowl, perhaps – but only with the permission of the prior; otherwise it was strictly forbidden.

Quickly he drained the bowl and wiped it clean with the underside of his tunic. When he turned around he noticed a slight flutter in the curtain around Hildmer's wife's bed. Just the wind coming through the window, perhaps. Or was she watching him? If she was, she might report him. He would be brought before the entire community in Chapter to lay himself prostrate on the ground and confess his terrible gluttony. He might be whipped or excluded from table or, worse, forbidden to sing the antiphons at the offices.

The curtain twitched again. She *was* watching him. Fingers appeared at the edge of the drape; a chink opened up. Wilfrid clenched his fists. He could deny it. Who would believe a word she said? He could say it was the demon talking, the spirit that caused her to moan and thrash and spit as if she was some wild creature, stained and polluted. She *was* polluted, with spittle, filth, blood, and there she was, watching him from behind those curtains, with the demon twitching and twisting inside her, filling her with malign thoughts and impulses. For all Wilfrid knew, she had sent the creature out to tempt him to eat the forbidden food, and who knew what else she might do? He was frightened now. There was still no sound from outside, and he didn't know where Cuthbert was.

The chink in the curtains widened. The girl's scratched face peered through the gap. She glanced from Wilfrid to the door and finally came out. She stood before him, holding her hands to her mouth, biting her knuckles. Her lips were very red and cracked, and there was a sore at the corner of her mouth. Still watching the door, she spoke.

'Will they come inside soon?'

Wilfrid took a step back.

'They?'

'Him, Hildmer, I mean, and that man with you.'

'The prior? He said you were to get some rest and

show me where to rest too, while he speaks to your husband. Don't you remember?'

Wilfrid wondered if she hadn't heard what Cuthbert said. Or perhaps the demon was causing her to forget. It didn't matter. As long as she kept the demon to herself. He took another step back and knocked against the shelf behind him.

'I remember.' The girl looked at him directly. Her eyes were blue and wide, and she had the longest, darkest eyelashes Wilfrid had ever seen. 'I'm not a halfwit,' she said.

'Oh.'

'I want to know when they will come in. What are they doing out there?'

'I don't know. Talking. Maybe praying.'

'That might take some time, then. I've heard that in the monasteries they pray from dawn to dusk, and their knees are worn to the bone from being pressed against the hard floor.'

Wilfrid shrugged.

'But I think there are worse things,' she said.

She seemed quite calm now, less the living cell of a demon and more like a proper girl, though not one a young man might choose to marry, with hair like strangled briars and a face like the scratching post of a wild cat. But Hildmer was an old man, more than forty winters, and the girl might have brought horses and family connections with her.

'Do you really live in the monastery?' she said. 'A boy like you?'

'Yes.'

'I've heard there are monasteries for women.'

She brought her hand to her lip and began to pick at the sore. Wilfrid wondered if Fergus had included any salve in the pouch of medicaments he had given to Cuthbert.

'I think so,' he said.

He remembered what Cuthbert had said earlier about Abbess Ælfflæd. Tydi had mentioned this too. He said there were monasteries teeming with women, mostly from important families, and they lived in the same way as the monks, and made altar cloths and vestments and even copied out sacred manuscripts.

The girl ran her tongue around her lips and winced. They really were very dry and cracked. She was thin, thinner even than Cuthbert; she looked like a starveling. Wilfrid poured another bowl of broth from the cauldron and held it out to her. She hesitated, then stepped forward with hands outstretched. As she sipped at the broth he saw how chewed her fingernails were, how red and raw the skin about them was. She returned the bowl to Wilfrid. He drank the remaining liquid, scooping up the last scraps of hare with his fingers.

Just as he was finishing the door opened, and they both jumped. Hildmer came in first, followed by Cuthbert, who had to bend his head to avoid hitting the lintel. The girl scuttled backwards. Hildmer cleared his throat loudly. In the brief instant that his wife met his gaze he jerked his head towards the cauldron of broth and then towards Cuthbert, but she just fixed her eyes on her feet. Hildmer smacked his right fist into the palm of his left hand, then quickly smiled.

'I see you have eaten,' he said, looking at Wilfrid's

empty bowl. 'Good, good. I'm glad my wife has been ministering to you.' He turned to Cuthbert and spoke loudly. 'Of course my wife will offer you her welcome too, Prior. We have broth and bread, cheese and beer.'

Still the girl did not shift her eyes from her feet.

'Your hospitality is gracious, Hildmer,' Cuthbert said, 'but I think it's better if we fast – all of us.'

He looked at the bowl that Wilfrid was hugging tight to his chest. Wilfrid reddened. He only hoped that Cuthbert wouldn't discover that the broth contained meat, but he was glad he had taken the opportunity to eat when he could, unlike Hildmer, who was shifting from one foot to the other and throwing glances at the steaming cauldron on the fire.

'We will fast,' Cuthbert said, 'and pray God to deliver this woman from the hands of the foul demon that torments her and show us how we may sustain her safely on His path. Hildmer, you and I will find a quiet spot to go to. These two may stay here and rest awhile. Then they too must give themselves over to prayer. I'm certain that God will hear us and show us the way to defeat the devil.'

Light was fading when Wilfrid finally woke. He listened for sounds of breathing and movement from behind the drapes surrounding the girl's bed, but all was silent. He got up and went out. Though smaller than Medilwong, Hildmer's village was a familiar scene: wooden houses with thatched roofs, a large wooden fence around the perimeter, a blacksmith's forge next to what must be the carpenter's house – there was a man outside it, mending a cart. The hills to the north were covered with trees like the ones near Medilwong, hazel, oak, ash and beech, and there were fields for farming just beyond the fence. But to the east was the massive sweep of the grey sea, which swelled out until it met the sky.

Some children were running about. They were just like the children Wilfrid knew at home, shouting and laughing, teasing and taunting, pushing and shoving. There was no sign of either Cuthbert or Hildmer. Then he remembered that they had gone off somewhere to pray, and he was supposed to be praying too. He should go back to the house; it was warm there, and quiet. Then again, he might be disturbed, and he didn't want to be seen praying by anyone. It was alright in the monastery; everyone prayed. At home, they prayed before a feast or the planting and harvesting of crops, but he didn't know the customs here, and he didn't want to appear foolish – not with that girl watching him. Besides, there was the temptation of the hare broth – he surely wouldn't get away with it a second time.

He walked towards the sea. Cuthbert often went to the sea to pray. He would spend a few days out on the Rock, fasting and praying. If the Rock was cut off by the tide he would go down to the shore, and stay for hours, lifting his voice up to Christ so intensely he seemed not to notice the bitter sting of wind or cold or rain. He was praying not just with his mouth, Tydi said, but with his entire body.

'Boy!'

Wilfrid was startled by the voice behind him. Hildmer looked even more old and tired than he had that morning, his eyes more grim, his face more ashen grey.

'My wife – is she still in the house?'

'I'm not sure.'

'Did she go out? Is she alone?'

'I don't know.'

'Christ, she'd better not have escaped again! Give her solitude, your prior says. Ha! He says I shouldn't... Well, she must retain all her strength in order to keep the...that *thing* away. But we'll see.'

Hildmer marched back towards the house. Darkness was settling in with a rising wind, and still there was no sign of Cuthbert. Wilfrid knew that he too should return to the house lest he become lost in this strange place. And yet, now that he had foregone his chance to escape, who knew when he would again be able to explore anywhere beyond the monastery? The moon appeared from behind a cloud and spilled silver light on the sea. He walked to the grass mound surrounding the village, climbed over and followed the path that led down to the shore.

The wind grew stronger as he approached the beach. The waves hissed as they broke on the shore, and the wind cried in Wilfrid's ears, lilting high, wavering notes like a sprite's song. The sounds grew louder and faded, then rose again in sustained familiar notes. He shivered. A tall figure walked into the spread of the moonlight. Wilfrid could just make out the words being sung.

Non timebis a timore nocturno.
A sagitta volante in die a negotio perambulante
in tenebris ab incursu et daemonio meridiano.

Wilfrid climbed into the sand dunes and crouched among the grasses. He watched as Cuthbert removed his cloak and tunic and slowly, his arms outstretched so his body took the form of a cross, walked naked into the water. The waves crashed against him. He sang on.

Cadent a latere tuo mille et decem milia
a dextris tuis ad te autem non adpropinquabit.

Some of the waves were high and reached as far as his armpits. Wilfrid thought the prior must surely turn around now and come back out. It was not safe, even for a servant of God, and Cuthbert, though tall, was thin as a reed. The sea could consume him like a whale swallowing a minnow. Wilfrid wanted to go to him, but his legs refused to move towards the great mass of rolling water. He sank deeper among the sand and grasses, watching Cuthbert standing like a cross in the sea. He listened hard to hear Cuthbert's voice and sang timid, shivery verses with him in time to the swell and breaking of the waves.

Non timebis a timore nocturno.
Non timebis a timore nocturno.

It seemed to go on all night. Every time the moon went in, and Wilfrid could no longer see Cuthbert, he feared that he would be looking at an empty sea when the moon reappeared, but each time Cuthbert was still there in the same position. Sometimes Wilfrid saw shadows rise above the water and then disappear again, and this made him even more fearful. Yet Cuthbert seemed completely unaware of anything. It was like that when he prayed and sang: as if the words were laden with some tremendous spirit, and he drenched himself in their power. His spirit-soaked prayers called out to the monks, filled their hearts. And Wilfrid wondered if the shadows in the water, whatever they were, felt that too.

Eventually Cuthbert seemed to sway. A wave surged forward and almost knocked him over. He turned and struggled out of the water, stumbling from side to side like a man filled to the brim with beer, and collapsed when he reached the place where he had left his clothes.

Wilfrid waited, unsure what to do. If he went to him now he would have to admit he had been spying. Then he saw something slink out of the sea. Two shadows slithering along the sand. They were formless, or Wilfrid couldn't say what form they took, but surely no good creature would emerge from the sea at night to creep after a weakened holy man? They reached the spot where Cuthbert was lying and crouched down next to him.

Wilfrid wanted to rush to him, but the thought of coming close to the creatures, the demons – they must be demons – filled him with terror. And if Cuthbert was too weak to fight them, how would he himself withstand them? They would devour him, possess him like they did that poor mad girl, and who would free him if they had also taken Cuthbert? He waited, willing Cuthbert to move, but everything was still; even the creatures seemed to lie inert on the sand.

The tide was ebbing now and the wind dying down. Cuthbert lay on the shore with the two sea shadows by his side, still as the rocks that dotted the shore. Wilfrid went slowly towards them. The moon dripped silver light onto Cuthbert and the sea creatures. Their grey fur glistened in the moonlight. A momentary rush of relief flooded through Wilfrid. Seals. That was all. Just like the seals he had so often caught glimpses of in the sea at Lindisfarne. Still. He hesitated. He had never come so close to a seal, never seen their gigantic forms splayed out across the sand. They lay almost on top of Cuthbert, pressing in against him, rubbing their sides along his back. Their heads turned in towards his shoulders, the steam from their breath curling in about him. He crept closer, knelt down, stretched his hand onto Cuthbert's shoulder. Cuthbert's skin was warm.

'Prior,' he whispered. 'Wake up.'

One of the sea creatures moved, raising itself and turning its head. It let out a long, mournful cry. Wilfrid jumped back. The other one lifted its head and sang in response. Wilfrid fell back further, his heart thumping as though it wanted to leap from his body. Then the seals turned and crawled away, slipping easily over the sand and disappearing back into the sea.

'Prior,' Wilfrid called.

Cuthbert stirred and slowly hauled himself up into a sitting position.

'My robe,' he said.

Wilfrid pulled the robe over his head and wrapped his cloak around him. Cuthbert remained sitting, breathing heavily.

'Why are you here, Wilfrid? Did you come to spy?'

'No. I mean...'

'Did I not leave you with specific instructions to stay

with the girl, and to fast and pray once you were fully rested? Do you not trust me, Wilfrid?'

'Yes, Prior, but...'

Cuthbert waved the reply away with his hand. He staggered to a standing position. Wilfrid almost put his arms out to catch him.

'There are demons everywhere. No one is impervious. The only way to defeat them is by prayer and fasting. And cunning. The servants of the Lord must be always at the ready, standing guard at the watch tower, because it is easier to prevent the ancient enemy from storming the citadel than to expel it once it has gained entry. I tried to explain this to Hildmer... Hildmer, where is he?' Cuthbert leaned heavily on Wilfrid's shoulder. 'We must return to the village straightaway.'

When Wilfrid and Cuthbert entered the house they found Hildmer sitting hunched at the table, his head in his hands.

'Where is your wife?' Cuthbert said.

Hildmer pointed to the alcove.

'I haven't disturbed her. As you told me.'

Cuthbert seemed relieved.

'Good. Tell her to come out.'

Hildmer threw back the alcove curtain and prodded the girl with his forefinger. She let out a small cry and crossed her arms over her face and chest.

'Quiet!' Hildmer hissed. 'Come out now. The Prior wishes to speak to you."

The girl came out, slowly. Cuthbert gestured to her to sit at the table next to Wilfrid.

'I have asked the Lord for guidance,' Cuthbert said. 'I

believe he has given it to me.'

He reached across the table and took the girl's hands in his. He pushed up the sleeve of her shift and ran his fingers along the scars that crisscrossed her arm. Some were red and angry, Wilfrid noticed, though perhaps not fresh. He felt her leg tremble next to his.

'I promised you the demon would not return while I was here,' Cuthbert said. And he hasn't, has he?'

'No, but...'

Cuthbert raised a hand to silence her. He opened his satchel and took out a small, thick plank of oak and placed it on the floor. The oak had a long central panel with two short sides that folded out as legs. He lit a candle from the fire and placed it on the panel. In the glow, Wilfrid saw that a cross was carved into its centre, with four smaller crosses etched into each corner. There was some writing too: *IN HONOREM S PETRV*. He recognised the letters but didn't know their meaning. Cuthbert knelt in front of the tiny altar. He reached into the satchel again and fetched a flask and a tiny silver bowl, into which he poured a little water.

'Kneel down, please,' he said to the girl. 'You too,' he said to Wilfrid and Hildmer.

He blessed the water while chanting a psalm.

Exsurgat Deus, et dissipentur inimici eius,
et fugiant qui oderunt eum a facie eius!

He dipped his thumb in the water, made the sign of the cross on the girl's forehead, then raised his voice.

'Everlasting God, Who consigned that fallen and apostate tyrant to the flames of hell, hasten to our call for help and snatch from ruination, and from the clutches of the noonday devil, this woman made in Your image and likeness. Fill Your servants with courage to battle the reprobate devil.'

He blessed the girl again and sprinkled her with more water. She flinched as the droplets spattered on her, and let out a tiny cry, but didn't attempt to get up.

'I adjure you, ancient serpent,' Cuthbert went on, 'by the Judge of the living and the dead, by your Creator and the Creator of everything that is, by Him who has the power to consign you to hell, to depart forthwith in fear from this servant of God and to desist from further molesting her.'

He blessed the girl a final time and helped her up.

'He is gone now,' he said. 'I believe for good. Nevertheless, you must guard against his return.' He looked at Hildmer. 'Both of you.'

The girl looked up. Her eyes were wide and bright, Wilfrid noticed, and her eyelashes seemed even longer than they had before.

'A monastery,' she said. 'A demon would never enter a monastery. He wouldn't be so bold. And I know there are monasteries for women. That boy told me so.'

She pointed at Wilfrid.

Cuthbert shook his head.

'That is not the way. You have a husband to minister to. You are bound to him for as long as he lives. And a monastery is not a refuge – from demons or anything else.' He stopped. Wilfrid thought Cuthbert might have glanced at him, but in the dim light he couldn't be sure. 'A monastery is for those without earthly ties who can devote themselves wholly to God.'

'But surely there is a way.' The girl twisted her wild hair around her fingers. 'Can a married woman not take holy vows?'

'Only on the death of her husband. You have a husband who lives.'

'But, but...' The girl pulled at her hair wildly. 'There are cases. I'm sure. Like...like the king's first wife. I heard *him* say it.' She jerked her head in Hildmer's direction. 'I heard him say the king's first wife took holy vows.'

Wilfrid had also heard that. The king's first wife had taken a nun's vows, and now Ecgfrith had remarried, and everyone expected that one day soon an announcement would be made about the new queen carrying a child in her belly. Surely Cuthbert could arrange for the girl to enter a monastery if that's what she wanted? But Hildmer stepped forward, stood between his wife and the prior and leaned towards him, whispering urgently though he hissed louder than a snake, and Wilfrid could hear every word.

'That was completely different. The former queen had taken a vow of chastity even before her marriage, as the world well knows. And *she* had wealth and land enough to repay Ecgfrith King when he finally permitted her to enter the holy house. And even then, it was a...a...' he spat out the word, '...*humiliation*. The king should never have permitted it.'

Cuthbert waved him away. He took the girl's hands in his.

'Now listen. I promise you, you have the strength to defeat the demon, should he return, but we will take steps to ensure that this will not happen. Your husband will assist in this.'

Hildmer grimaced. Cuthbert, still holding the girl's hands, turned to him.

'Your wife is young and innocent, but sometimes the Evil One seeks out those who are most pure and holy for his prey. To guard against his onslaught, you must both pray daily, mornings and evenings, and fast once a week, on Friday, the day the Lord died to redeem us.'

Hildmer nodded, vigorously. Wilfrid frowned. He knew it was not such a simple matter to keep demons at bay. Merely to pray twice a day and fast once a week?

'There is one more thing,' Cuthbert said. 'It's best if the marital bed is not shared, not for some time – at least two winters, I would say.'

Hildmer stood up to face Cuthbert, his cheeks bright red.

'That is outrageous. Two winters! It goes against the law of nature. I will be shamed, unmanned. Surely the Lord cannot require this?'

'It's necessary, I believe, to prevent re-entry of the malevolent creature. It has been said...well, that the female body is more vulnerable at such moments, and it's your duty as husband to protect your wife.'

'Protect her? No man could do more. I have her watched constantly. She has everything she needs, and more, and I assure you I beat her only when she's at her worst, spitting and scratching and spewing out language more foul than the devil's own.'

'Hildmer, you came to me on the night of Christ's Mass, pleading for a cure for your wife. The Lord has heard your prayers. Is this how you repay Him who has shown you such mercy? Do you run the risk of the demon's return? Do you think Ecgfrith King would readily forgive one of his reeves who wittingly risks the entry of a demon into his household?' Cuthbert let go the girl's hand, stepped very close to Hildmer and spoke softly. 'Or who uses intemperate language against him.'

Hildmer's eyes flashed with fear. Then he bowed his head and sat down wearily at the table.

'I ask for your pardon. I'm weary. It has been a struggle. I...'

'We will speak no more of it. Now, the sun will soon rise. We have fasted long enough, and Wilfrid and I must eat before we depart.'

He looked directly at Hildmer's wife. She stared back at him, narrowed her eyes and pressed her lips tightly together. Then she turned around abruptly, pushing against Wilfrid as she did so. She fetched bread and cheese from the shelf and landed them roughly on the table. Cuthbert beckoned her to sit down, and when she did Wilfrid saw her long eyelashes were shining wet.

'Let us thank God for the food He has provided,' Cuthbert said.

In the morning they saddled their horses and left. Hildmer rushed about, shouting instructions to the stable boy. One of the shoes on Cuthbert's horse was loose, and he had to be reshod. Wilfrid thought again of Alvar and wondered where he was. Eventually, Hildmer saw them off in a flurry of God speeds and thank yous. Wilfrid looked back as they came to the gate of the village. The girl was standing in the doorway of the house. She didn't return his wave. He thought about calling out to her, but he had forgotten to ask her name.

'You must be wondering about many things, Wilfrid,' Cuthbert said after a while.

Wilfrid started to reply. He was going to ask about the girl's name. Then he remembered something more important.

'Where is my father's horse?' he said.

'Your father's horse? How should I...?' Cuthbert laughed. 'The horse. Of course. I remember now. A generous gift, a very fine animal I am told, a little too fine for our humble monastery. He was sold, in exchange for calfskins and other implements for the scriptorium, I believe.'

Implements for the scriptorium. Wilfrid clenched his teeth. Dunstan must have been delighted. They rode on in silence, retreading the path they had taken two days previously. When they came to a fork in the path, they stopped. Wilfrid stared upwards. He felt he recognised where they were, though it had been night when they passed this way before. He remembered the terrible sense of the world being swallowed up by darkness and how Cuthbert had asked him if he had seen something in the sky. Perhaps he should have told Cuthbert then about what he had seen that night. It was just an instant, as short as the blink of an eye, but in that instant Wilfrid had seen a racing shadow, lean and sleek with glowing yellow eyes. Wolf's eyes.

Eight

ILFRID PUT DOWN his stylus and blew away the wax residue from the tablet. It floated to the ground of the cloister close to two starlings hopping about by the novices' feet. Since *Eostermonað* they had been working in the open. The sun had finally found its way out of the grey skies, drying out the earth and grass and whitening the thatched roofs of the monastery buildings. It shone on the novices at their desks and warmed them so their hands were no longer stiff and buckled from the cold. Suddenly, scratching out words again and again on their tablets seemed less of a tiresome chore, and they found it easier to make the letters form in obedience to their intentions, to stay within the prescribed lines and margins.

Two long winters had passed since Wilfrid had begun

his learning, but although he could read quite well, and he knew the Rule and many of the psalms by heart, his writing was still clumsy. The curl on the stems of his *B*s was satisfactory, he thought, and even his *O*s were fairly evenly shaped. But the spines of his *S*s were still unshapely, tending to stagger forward as though they had been pushed, and his *E*s suffered from the opposite malady of appearing to fall over backwards. Tydi sat at the desk in front of him. Like Wilfrid, Tydi was copying out verses from his psalter, but, unlike Wilfrid, his script was uniform and elegant, matching exactly the form and character of the writing in his exemplar.

Wilfrid sighed and stretched out his arms. A small ache was winding its way around his shoulders and up his neck. He was about to get back to work when he noticed the door of the scriptorium opening. Dunstan came out, nodded briefly to Herefrith, the novice master, and made his way towards the desks. He walked slowly down the rows, examining each novice's work, bringing the tablet close to his face, clicking his tongue every now and then, or sighing grimly.

Wilfrid handed his tablet to Dunstan. Within an instant Dunstan threw the tablet back onto Wilfrid's desk. It landed with a bang that echoed around the cloister, and the two starlings that had been pecking at the ground rose up, beating their wings furiously. One of them flew off, leaving its companion flitting about aimlessly from desk to desk.

Dunstan returned to Herefrith's desk and began to speak.

'You have all heard the words of the venerable St Augustine: "to sing is to pray twice." Indeed, it is a favoured phrase of our prior.'

Some of the boys sighed. Cuthbert was fond of repeating that phrase in Chapter when he had occasion to scold the brethren for their failure to sing out the responses in the offices, or if they produced sounds that were lazily discordant and tainted the purity of prayers that might otherwise have joined with the unceasing chanting of the angels in heaven. No one wanted to hear this lecture again, least of all from Dunstan, who, as Tydi was wont to point out, sang the offices like an injured crow, trying to seek cover next to the strong voice of Brother Edberht, the monastery's cantor, though sometimes not even Edberht could mask the pitiful squawks issuing from Dunstan's throat.

'Well,' Dunstan continued, 'how much more true is that of the written word? The spoken word, even when sung, is soon lost to men. Who can say how long it remains transcribed in their hearts? But words inscribed on parchment – they are fixed, forever giving glory to God, an unceasing prayer.'

The novices were sitting up straight now. Wilfrid remembered the day in the scriptorium soon after he had arrived on Lindisfarne, the rolls of parchment, the jars of ink, knives and quills, row upon row of books bound in leather covers. He imagined himself working in the scriptorium, dipping a quill into ink and setting it to parchment, perhaps even observing Brother Eadfrith in the midst of his glorious work. Eadfrith was the head of the scriptorium, and his lettering and illuminations were said to be so sublime that he had to deliberately insert a mistake on each page lest God think the scribe was trying to emulate Him.

But Dunstan hadn't finished.

'Sacred words must be well-formed, in letters carefully wrought to be made worthy of offering to God, not like some of the misshapen monstrosities I've seen here today – slovenly scrawls fit only for the dung heap.'

He glared at the novices, then turned to Herefrith and muttered something. Herefrith nodded. He rapped the desk with his stick.

'Leofric, Osgar, Tydi, you will go with Brother Dunstan to the scriptorium, please. Leave your tablets.'

The three stood up. Tydi glanced back at Wilfrid. Dunstan was already striding across the cloister to the scriptorium, with the two other novices scuttling behind him.

'I suggest you follow your fellow novices now, Tydi,' Herefrith said, 'before Brother Dunstan regrets his decision.'

Tydi hurried after the others, knocking against Herefrith's desk as he went. He reached his companions just as they were entering the scriptorium and followed them in. The door closed behind them with a loud creak.

Tydi and the others didn't come to class again. Hadwald said that Dunstan was keeping them prisoner and that he didn't care a sparrow's tail that they were the chosen ones; he would rather do battle with twenty devils than endure Dunstan hovering over him like the hooded crow he was, watching with his beady eyes and stretching his claws, waiting to pounce at the first sign of a mistake. Wilfrid supposed Hadwald was right, yet thoughts of working in the scriptorium niggled at him. He dreamed of writing on parchment, maybe even setting down stories that would be compiled in a book. No one other than Tydi listened to him or allowed him time to finish a sentence. He could never find the words to say what he meant; they were tied and twisted in his head and couldn't find their way to his tongue. But perhaps...perhaps if he could write them down he could somehow make them make sense.

He missed Tydi. He missed his stories. Tydi had more stories about monks than a scop had of warriors. He knew that Brother Herefrith had once been married and that his wife had died in childbirth; that Brother Laurence disliked his position as cellarer and wished to spend more time studying the healing properties of herbs and plants in the infirmary; that Brother Edberht harboured ambitions and hoped to be prior – or even bishop – one day.

Now, without Tydi, Wilfrid felt alone and friendless. He had been cast adrift like the pilgrims Cuthbert had talked about in one of his sermons, who set out on the seas without steer or paddle. But they trusted in God to deliver them to His appointed place, whereas Wilfrid merely drifted along without sign or destination.

He tried to find a way to talk to Tydi. After class one day he collected the tablets for return to the scriptorium. Passing by Tydi, he nudged him and pointed through the open door towards the beach.

'After the meal,' he whispered. 'Sneak away.'

He had just enough time to register the look of alarm on Tydi's face and he quickly looked around to see if Dunstan had spotted him speaking, but Dunstan was busy examining one of the novices' scripts. Wilfrid slipped away, skipped across the cloister and then reminded himself to walk as a monk should: thoughtfully, with deliberate footsteps, each one acknowledging its contact with God's holy earth. But once he was beyond the cloister he ran to the kitchen where Brother Laurence was busy preparing the midday meal. Laurence sighed when he saw Wilfrid, handed him a knife and pointed to a bunch of parsnips on the table.

'Don't cut yourself like you did the last time.'

Wilfrid nodded. He hated kitchen duty. The kitchen was a den of mishap and calamity. No matter how careful he tried to be, dishes slipped off shelves, seemingly of their own accord, vegetables slid onto the floor, and basins of water were liable to overturn at the slightest touch. He started to chop the parsnips and pile them into the cauldron of broth. Some of the boiling broth splashed onto his hands, but he hardly noticed. Soon he would speak to Tydi, find out about what it was like to be a scribe, ask him how terrible it was to work under Dunstan's glare and if he ever managed to get a glimpse of Eadfrith at work. He reached up to the shelf to get a jug but somehow, instead of locking in around the handle, his fingers knocked against the jug and sent it crashing to the floor. Laurence groaned.

'Not again! Look, I have everything in hand here.' He picked up the jug and sent Wilfrid out to help in the fields. 'You'll do less harm there,' he said.

Wilfrid's cheeks burned. It wasn't his fault the shelf was too high, or that Brother Laurence was so ill-humoured. Instead of going to the fields, he headed towards the beach. He crouched down by a grassy slope and hoped no one would notice he was missing. Out on the Rock, Cuthbert was standing in his usual position with his arms outstretched, facing south, as if there was something beyond the shore calling to him, loud as the black-beaked gulls that shrieked in the skies.

'Wilfrid!'

Wilfrid jumped. Tydi crouched next to him.

'I saw you coming this way,' Tydi said. 'Brother Dunstan is busy assisting Brother Eadfrith, but I'll have to go back before he notices I'm gone.' He looked out to the Rock and pulled his hood over his head. 'If the prior sees us...'

Wilfrid didn't care. He'd gladly risk a punishment for one of Tydi's jokes or a funny story about one of the brethren.

'You mustn't come and speak to me like that,' Tydi said. 'You'll bring trouble on both of us. You were lucky Brother Dunstan didn't notice you.'

Wilfrid nodded. Tydi was right. After all, Tydi was the one who had to spend his days under Dunstan's watch, beneath those glinting eyes, always seeking to find fault.

'I'll be more careful next time.'

Tydi slapped the sand with his fist.

'Next time! Wilfrid, what demon has taken hold of your head? There is no next time. I can't come and meet you. I'm a scribe now. The prior says I might even take the tonsure soon. I can't be...' Tydi looked out at Cuthbert on the rock again. 'I must go,' he said. 'Brother Dunstan may have noticed I'm missing.'

'But...' Wilfrid said.

The wind took his words away. Tydi was already scrambling over the sands and running across the field back to the cloister. Wilfrid sank back against the slope. The bitter cries of the birds rang overhead.

Wilfrid tried harder at his work. He took greater care to examine the letters in his psalter, tracing over them with his finger before copying them. He held the stylus closer to the tip and found it gave him a fraction more control. He learned to slow down his hand without breaking up the flow and paid more attention to measuring the space between each letter. Gradually the letters began to take on a certain uniformity and were less likely to look as though they had been scattered onto the tablet like seeds in the ground.

Herefrith remarked on the improvement, though he noted that Wilfrid still sometimes strayed outside the margins with the curve of a tail or a descender that was too long, and he despaired of the length of time it took Wilfrid to copy out a single verse. One afternoon, as summer drew to a close, Herefrith picked up Wilfrid's slate and looked at it closely. 'Hmmm,' he said, before moving onto Hadwald and berating him for his poorly drawn As, not to mention the fact that he had omitted to copy several words from the text.

It was Wilfrid's turn again to gather up the tablets at the end of the lesson. He didn't erase his own tablet but placed it at the bottom of the pile and crossed the cloister to the scriptorium. Dunstan had stretched a long roll of parchment across a table and was showing the scribes how to smoothen it with a pumice stone and pare away the stray goat hairs, without causing any damage. He glanced up.

'Well?' he asked.

'Brother Herefrith sent me to put away the tablets,' Wilfrid said.

'Leave them for one of the novice scribes to take care of,' Dunstan said. 'And don't interrupt the work done here.'

'Yes,' Wilfrid said. He paused. 'I'm sorry for interrupting.' His voice faltered as he felt the gaze of the novices on him. He was sure a chain of giggles was about to form. He tried again. 'Brother Herefrith says the most important work of the monastery, outside of prayer, is done in the scriptorium.'

Dunstan stared at him.

'Did you want something else, boy? Be quick about it.'

Wilfrid heard a definite wave of smothered laughs from the novices. He took his tablet from the pile and handed it to Dunstan. Dunstan peered at it. He brought it to the door and held it to the light then said something under his breath that sounded like a curse.

'Come here,' he said. 'Here! Do you see? The lines are not clean, not steady. The curves are not consistent; there is no flourish in the tails. There is some neatness but no skill, to say nothing of flair. This, this is merely the scratchings of a raven's claw.'

He flung the tablet back, slapping it into Wilfrid's chest.

'And then there is character,' he said. 'The great work of God requires men who are skilled and dedicated; who can sit from dawn to dusk with the freezing air biting at their fingers; who can know pain in every muscle and sinew of the body; who can fix the eye steadily and constantly on the work to ensure that not a single word, not a single letter is lost; who can keep their hands steady through cold and cramp and still form letters which are pure and true. Can you claim to be able to do this?'

Wilfrid clutched the tablet close to his chest. He tried to nod his head, but it twitched and turned into a shake instead.

'Then I suggest you confess your sin of pride in Chapter tonight,' Dunstan said.

He let out a long, deep breath and returned to examining the parchment. Wilfrid looked at his tablet again. He placed his fingers on the wax surface and clawed his way across it, from corner to corner, carving lines that crossed each other like the slashes of a knife. Then he slammed it onto the table and left.

Nine

WILFRID WOKE TO THE CRY of a wolf. Howling. As though it wanted to fill up the whole earth and sky with its anguish. He sat up and looked out of the window. There was no moon. The sky was heavy and black. He listened. One of the novices grunted in his sleep. Another coughed. Tydi's snores wafted over from the far corner of the room. Outside, the wind whistled mournfully, and Wilfrid could hear the rustle and murmur of the sea. But the howling had stopped. There were no wolves on Lindisfarne – wolves didn't leave the shelter of the forests and hills. Perhaps it had been a fox, or the wind, or a dream.

He lay down again, closed his eyes and tried to grasp the shadows of his dreams. There had been whitethorn, he thought, a field full of it, a hill, rocks and white gushing water. And something else he couldn't see. He opened his eyes, kept them open, lay awake until the bell sounded for Lauds.

Brother Laurence handed Wilfrid two pails and sent him to the shore to gather mussels.

'Fill one pail with mussels and the other with seawater,' he said. 'I'll need to rinse the mussels in the water to keep them fresh.'

Wilfrid tried to think of an excuse, but as usual his mind was too slow.

'Go on,' Laurence said. 'And be back before Vespers.'

Down at the beach the sea was yet a distance away, but the tide was turning. Mounds of mussel shells stretched across the shore like a cloak woven in shimmering black and blue threads. He walked over them, wincing as they cracked beneath his bare feet and cut into his skin. At Cuthbert's Rock the cloak of shells gave way to clammy sands. He prised the mussels off the lower part of the Rock, scratching his fingers in the process. It was slow cold work, and his hands were raw by the time he had filled the first pail, but now all he needed to do was fill the second one with water.

The tide had wormed its way toward him. The water bit at him like frost, and the sands tugged at his feet, sucking them down as the water ebbed. He stumbled, almost fell, as the sea rushed at him again, snapping at him with wolfish teeth. He tried to recall the psalm that Cuthbert had recited that night two winters ago in the sea. *In scapulis...in scapulis suis...* That was it. *In scapulis suis obumbrabit te.* He stepped heavily forward, feeling the water swirling about him, drawing him in deeper. It splashed the ends of his hitched-up robe. He needed to move forward only a few more paces to be able to fill the pail. *In scapulis suis obumbrabit te, et sub pinnis eius sperabis.*

He lowered the pail into the water. The words of the psalm caught in his throat. Beneath him he saw not the sea but the stream on Wulfstan's Hill. From somewhere he heard a thundering roar, and it seemed to him that the stream had burst free and was making for him. He cried out loud and turned, dropping both pails as he surged forward, but the water was following. The knot in his girdle became undone, and his robe tumbled into the water, slowing him as he tried to press ahead. He reached Cuthbert's Rock, clambered up, clung to the solid earth, lay down and felt the grass soft and moist against his face. He closed his eyes. When he opened them again he saw two boots, scuffed and scratched, the right sole peeling away from the toe. Above the boots, a brown robe with a torn hem flapped in the breeze. It brushed lightly against Wilfrid's face.

'What happened?' Cuthbert asked. 'Wilfrid? Are you ill?'

Cuthbert knelt down and put his hand on Wilfrid's forehead. His palm was cool and dry, and his long fingers pressed gently into his temples. Wilfrid couldn't remember the last time anyone had touched him. He lay there feeling the coolness of Cuthbert's palm. It sank into him like melting snow, spreading down his face and neck and through to the rest of his body.

'Do you know what happened?' Cuthbert asked.

'I think...I think I felt faint,' Wilfrid said.

'Have you been fasting?'

'No.'

'Have you been unwell recently? A fever?'

'No.'

Cuthbert took a flask from his cloak and blessed it.

'Here,' he said. 'Take small sips.'

Water, cold and fresh.

'Wilfrid, why did you come onto the Rock? You must understand that this is a hermitage, a holy place. It is not to be desecrated by young novices wishing to satisfy their curiosity.'

'I didn't mean to,' Wilfrid said. 'The water – I was gathering mussels – it was coming too fast. I thought, I thought it would...' He sat up. 'The pails! The sea took them.'

'Then, you must pray that the sea will return them.'

'Brother Laurence will be angry.'

'His anger will soften. Eventually.' Cuthbert leaned back next to Wilfrid. 'How are your lessons progressing these days?'

'Well enough, I suppose.'

'Your Latin? No difficulties?'

'No. Well, sometimes.'

'Reading?'

'Alright, mostly. I think.'

'And your writing?'

'Brother Herefrith says it has improved, but...'

'Brother Dunstan does not.'

Wilfrid sighed.

'Not everyone is called to be a scribe, Wilfrid, or a scholar. You serve the Lord well enough in prayer and labour.'

'Brother Laurence says I am clumsy.'

'Perhaps so, though there is nothing clumsy in your voice when you sing the psalms. You think you are more simple than the other novices, Wilfrid, but you are not. God has granted you a great gift, not given to many others, in order to serve Him. Let that be your shield-wall against doubt and despair. Perhaps one day, when you are older, you may take Brother Edberht's place as cantor. He is, I believe, called to greater things.'

Cantor. Perhaps then the other boys would stop laughing at him. The brothers would no longer see him as a weakwit. He would have responsibility for teaching the monks the antiphons, the responses, the different chants for the psalms. He would... Wilfrid closed his eyes. He felt he was pleasantly sinking into the grass.

They fell silent for a while. A sparrow landed on Cuthbert's boot and rested there.

'What happened to the demon?' Wilfrid asked.

'The demon?'

'The one in that girl, Hildmer's wife. Where did it go?'

Cuthbert paused.

'Ah, yes. Hildmer's wife. She was sorely tormented. I pray for her often, Wilfrid – you should too – but I believe news would have reached us had the demon returned.'

'But where did the demon go?'

'Who knows?' Cuthbert said. 'None can understand the precise nature of demons, even those who have battled them. Some find another host or lodge in wild places where they seek out their own kind and regain strength and purpose.'

Something shifted in Wilfrid. That worm again,

wriggling.

'A host?'

'Another person to live in.'

'That demon – it made the girl shake, didn't it, and spit and speak foully?'

'Yes.'

'And it made her fall.'

'That demon,' Cuthbert said, 'was a globe of anger, a rage more venomous than a serpent's spit. I recognised it at once.'

'You recognised it?'

'Yes, yes. I've encountered ones like it, before.'

'When?'

'Oh, many times. Even as a child, soon after they took me from my parents.'

'They took you from your parents? Brought you to a monastery?'

'No. To a foster family, as is our way. I was blessed, really. My foster mother, Kenswith, was a holy woman and devoted herself to my care.'

'But she had a demon in her! Just like Hildmer's wife.'

'No, no.' Cuthbert laughed. 'I don't believe Kenswith was ever troubled by the Evil One – except in so far as she was troubled by me.'

Cuthbert shifted his position a little. The sparrow flew up from his boot and settled about two paces away.

'Our friend doesn't want to leave,' Cuthbert said. 'Perhaps it senses bad weather coming.'

'Perhaps it wants to hear the story.'

Cuthbert sighed.

'I'm not a scop, Wilfrid. I have no stories to entertain

you or please your curiosity.'

He said nothing for a while, but twisted a long blade of grass around his finger, all the while keeping his gaze out to the sea. Then he spoke again.

'I was blessed, you know,' he said eventually. 'But I could not see it, would not see it. I was a child, of course; I had no understanding of the ways of the Enemy. But I see now a devil had entered me and blinded my heart to that good woman. It would not let me heed her, much less love her. I disobeyed every instruction she gave me. I spent my time cavorting with boys of the village, drawing them away from their work, playing foolish games and tricks when I should have been tending to the sheep. I refused to speak to Kenswith, cursed her when she came near. I chewed her food and spat it on the ground while the devil chewed all the harder on my heart.'

Wilfrid frowned. He couldn't imagine the prior as a child, let alone as one possessed by a demon, but it must have been a demon that made Cuthbert behave like that.

'The devil tormented me with physical ailments,' Cuthbert went on. 'I was breathless at times, often to the point of falling away in a faint. I couldn't eat. I vomited up bile. Then my knee swelled, my sinews contracted, and I became so lame that one foot was unable to touch the ground.'

'But how did you get the devil out?' Wilfrid asked.

'God sent assistance. One day they put me sitting outside by the village wall. It was summer, and the sun was shining strong. They thought the heat would ease the swelling in my knee. I lay there all day, watching the women at their work, weaving and sewing and cooking, nursing their babies. Towards evening they began to drift inside, but no one came for me. I was tired and thirsty, my head hurt from the sun, and my knee was throbbing as if the devil himself was boiling his foul brew inside it. Then I saw a man riding from the west toward the village. His tunic was light in colour and seemed to shimmer white in the sun. He rode with his back straight and his head high, and his horse was decked with a rich cloth. He stopped when he saw me and asked if I would be so good as to treat him as a guest for the Lord Jesus Christ's sake.'

Wilfrid let out a deep breath. A man of noble bearing dressed in white on a magnificently caparisoned horse. Perhaps it was an angel of God.

Cuthbert sighed.

'The devil stirred in me. I answered the stranger with harsh and unwelcoming words. I told him I would be only too happy to minister to guests in the name of the Lord had the same cruel Lord not seen fit to afflict me with the bonds of infirmity.'

'What happened then?'

'Instead of being offended, the man dismounted and examined my knee. He carried me to Kenswith and bade her cook wheat flour with milk and anoint my knee with it while it was hot.'

'And that drew the devil out?'

'The man prayed over me all night long. He frequently blessed my knee, but more often he blessed my heart, for that was where the demon was resident. When the sun rose I fell asleep and slept right into the following day. I woke to the smell of oats cooking over the fire.

Kenswith helped me eat. I did not curse or spit out the food.'

'And the stranger?' Wilfrid said. 'Was he an angel, or...what?'

Cuthbert looked out to sea.

'He was gone when I woke. I found out later that he gave his horse to a boy who had been exiled from his village on account of some misdemeanour and was begging for alms. But the stranger had given me far more than he gave that boy. That is why I wanted to go to Hildmer's wife, to see if I could help, though the world out there, beyond our little monastery, with its snares of power and earthly authority – that is not where God calls me.'

Cuthbert stretched his arm out.

'There. Do you see it?'

Wilfrid looked out across the grey water to where Cuthbert was pointing.

'You mean the island?' he said.

'Yes. Aidan's island.'

Wilfrid had heard of Aidan, of course, Aidan of Iona, the founder of the monastery at Lindisfarne.

'But that's not Iona, is it?' he said.

'Oh no,' Cuthbert said. 'Iona is far from here. On the west coast of our land, the edge of our world. It is our sister house, despite...well...despite certain divisions, and it is the home of many good monks whom we still call our brethren, including the king's own half-brother, you know. Aldfrith. He was sent there as a child.'

'Then what is that island?'

'That is the Farne, a place far more desolate and wretched than Iona and nothing like our blessed island.

Aidan made it his hermitage.'

Wilfrid wanted to ask why Aidan would want to make a hermitage somewhere desolate and wretched, but he sensed that Cuthbert would hush that question almost before it could come out of his mouth. Besides, there was something else he needed to know.

'Did you ever see the stranger again?'

Cuthbert hesitated. The bell for Vespers sounded from Lindisfarne. He seemed not to hear it, kept looking to the Farne.

'Yes. I saw him. I heard him. I heard his voice calling me to God's service. I saw his soul, Wilfrid.' He stood up, took a final look out at the Farne. 'Sometimes I think I hear him still.'

The last peal of the bell died away. 'Pray for me, Wilfrid.' He gestured to the oratory. 'You will have to stay here tonight.'

The oratory was tiny and bare except for the same little portable altar Cuthbert had used in Hildmer's house. Wilfrid wondered why Cuthbert needed his prayers and who that stranger might have been or what Cuthbert meant by seeing his soul. It niggled him even as he slept, like an insect flying about his head. Cuthbert woke him for the Night Office. He sang the office with Cuthbert. Outside, the sea and the wind sang too.

Ten

THE BRETHREN GATHERED at first light on the shore. Out on the sandflats, clusters of seals lined up in rows, as if they too were waiting for something to happen. The boats were packed with supplies: waxed sheets for a tent, blankets, flagons of water and beer, bread, cheese, grain, nuts and dried berries. These boats were called currachs, Wilfrid knew – small round vessels with wickerwork frames over which layers of cow hides had been stretched. He couldn't imagine ever setting sail in one of these little crafts.

He looked back to the monastery. Two figures were making their way down to the beach: Fergus and Herefrith, both carrying large bags on their shoulders. As soon as they arrived Brother Laurence spoke to them.

'Where is the prior?'

'Still in the church,' Herefrith said. 'He's been there since Lauds.'

Laurence's eyes brightened.

'Perhaps...'

Herefrith shook his head.

'His prayers are in preparation for the journey.'

Small sighs rose into the wind as the wave of hope broke and died away. Wilfrid himself had not felt hopeful. Ever since the night with Cuthbert on the Rock, he had been sure that Cuthbert was drawn to the Farne Island as the tide was drawn to the shore.

'Our entreaties have failed then,' Laurence said.

'Our entreaties were selfish,' Brother Edberht said sharply. 'The prior is called to make this *peregrinatio*, his exile for Christ, like others before him. He has explained this in Chapter. When God breathes the greatest calling into a man's ear the man does not answer "no".'

'I recall well what the prior said.' Laurence's voice was tight. 'I recall also that Ecgfrith King is less happy with the decision than you seem to be.'

'Brother Laurence!' Fergus' cry rang out. 'You will apologise to Brother Edberht and fast for three days as penance.'

Laurence kept his eyes on Edberht, his lips tightly closed.

'No, Brother Fergus,' Edberht said. He held Laurence's gaze. 'I have been chosen to assume the duties of prior, and I will decide on matters of discipline. But I have no wish to start off by issuing punishments and penance. Brother Laurence is heart-sore at prior

Cuthbert's departure, as are we all. We must learn to bear our sorrow in silence.'

Edberht smiled weakly and looked around at the monks. Some nodded. Others looked at their feet. Laurence seemed unconcerned, but his cheekbones were tinged red.

'I apologise, Brother Edberht,' he said loudly. 'I pray your forgiveness and will undertake any penance you see fit.'

Edberht clicked his tongue.

'As I have said, there will be no punishment. The prior's departure should not be tainted with shadows of bitterness or quarrel.'

There was silence after that. Wilfrid shivered. It was not very cold, but it seemed as though a bitter wind had cut through the brothers, and he sensed that something had passed between Laurence and Edberht that he did not quite understand. He knew that Ecgfrith King had initially opposed Cuthbert's desire to leave the monastery and become a holy hermit – though he didn't see why Ecgfrith should care one way or another – and that the king's objections had become the stuff of whisperings among the brethren.

'He's fearful,' Wilfrid had overheard Herefrith say. 'Three winters have passed since this marriage, and still God does not deliver him what he craves. He believes the prior will forget to pray for him once he is anchored in his hermitage.'

'The prior's prayers will increase in strength when they are delivered from the island of Blessed Aidan,' Fergus had replied. 'That must surely sway Ecgfrith. Though God's ways are not our ways. You see, it may be that the Lord favours another. Have you forgotten Aldfrith?'

'Ah, the supposed brother.' Herefrith laughed. 'Irish, I believe. Well, it's natural you would support the claims of one of your own, Brother Fergus, but...'

They moved out of Wilfrid's earshot, leaving him still confused.

Now Wilfrid waited and watched as Cuthbert emerged from the church and made his way to the beach where the monks parted into two lines to let him through.

'Everything is ready?' Cuthbert asked.

'Yes,' Fergus said.

Wilfrid shivered again. He drew his cloak around him and tried to shelter between the other monks. They gathered close to Cuthbert – old men and young, tonsured monks and novices, oblates, workers and scribes. Brother Eadfrith had suffered himself to be drawn from his work in the scriptorium, though he shuffled about impatiently, rubbing his ink-stained fingers together. They were all there, Wilfrid noticed – everyone except Dunstan.

Cuthbert nodded to the audience gathered around him.

'Well, brothers,' he said. 'Who would have thought all those years ago when I first came here as prior that any of you would be glum to see me go?' He offered a weak smile. 'Who can remember the arguments we had night after night in Chapter about the Rule, about the old ways and the new ways, tonsures and Easter?'

Wilfrid couldn't imagine anyone arguing with Cuthbert, or why he was bringing it up now.

'Well, they were different times,' Cuthbert said, 'and stormy times too. And though we were cast adrift from some of our beloved brethren, God steered us through, and I trust that one day we will all be reunited in Him. So there is no need for low spirits. If God calls me into exile it is for a reason, and I must obey. It may be that my exile, my ever-deepening prayers, will sometime bring about the reconciliation we all desire. But, in any event, I am merely following our blessed Aidan's footsteps to the place where he did not fear to go.' He paused. 'Or perhaps he did fear it, but he did not let fear bind him. He trusted in the Lord's protection and succour, and I will too.'

Cuthbert looked around at each monk in turn and then for a final time back at the monastery. Or, Wilfrid wondered, was he searching for Dunstan? Someone near Wilfrid sniffled loudly. Another did likewise. Laurence was openly wiping his eyes with his sleeve.

'Pray for me,' Cuthbert said.

He raised his arm and blessed them all, and as he did so Wilfrid felt Cuthbert's glance fall directly on him. He trembled. Something was prickling at his eyes. He blinked and felt the salt water at his cheek bones. Some said that Cuthbert would welcome visitors from time to time, that he would need to be kept supplied with provisions, for what manner of crop would grow on that demon-swept island? But Wilfrid didn't think that an untonsured novice such as himself would be permitted to visit the prior on the Farne, and besides, nothing could persuade him to set foot in a currach and brave the sea.

Cuthbert took off his cloak and boots and hitched up

his tunic. The monks pulled the boats over the sand and into the water.

'Wait! Wait!'

They all turned at the sound of shouting. Dunstan was running down the path to the shore, waving something in his right hand. He ran over the sand and into the water without removing his boots or lifting up his tunic. He held the object high above the water. A book. Pocket-sized and bound in brown leather.

'St John's Gospel,' he said. 'I...I've been working on it for some time. It's not illuminated, but I believe – I hope – the work is fair.'

Cuthbert reached out his hand for the Gospel and pressed it to his heart. Dunstan bowed his head. The water had soaked his robe up to his knees, but he appeared not to notice. Cuthbert blessed the gathering for a final time, and the brothers pushed the boats off. They watched as the sea drew Cuthbert away. They watched as, out on the sandflats, the seals slid into the water and swam in the same direction as the boats. Edberht sang: *Elavaverunt flumina, Domine.*

The others joined in:

> *Elavaverunt flumina vocem suam.*
> *Elavaverunt flumina fluctos suos*
> *a vocibus aquarum multarum.*

Their voices were quiet at first but rose with every stroke of the oars, so that the last sounds of Lindisfarne Cuthbert would hear would be the psalm singing, and he would carry their voices with him over the sea.

Eleven

WILFRID COULDN'T SLEEP that night. His throat was dry, and a dull ache had settled into the pit of his stomach. He lay in his pallet, listening to the seal-song as it sounded across the water. It seemed to him they were singing a lament. He thought of Cuthbert on the Farne. How would the prior make shelter out in that fearful domain, surrounded by water on all sides? Everyone said that the Farne, for all that it had been Aidan's hermitage, was a hive of devils. In Chapter Cuthbert said he had been called to defeat demons. This could only be achieved in a place of complete solitude, where there were no barriers between him and God. But Wilfrid feared there might be too many demons to overcome. Defeating one – that terrible creature that had invaded Hildmer's wife – had required all Cuthbert's strength. What if this time it weakened him, left him tired and hungry, flailing about on that tiny island like an injured seal cub, defenceless against the gulls and sea ravens who came to pick at it?

He felt suddenly hot. The scratch in his throat was getting rougher, and his whole mouth felt constricted. He threw off the blanket and lay restlessly on his bed. After a while he started to shiver. He reached for his cloak, wrapped himself in it and pulled the blanket about him again. But it felt as though he was bound in a coverlet of ice while hot coals burned in his throat.

When the bell sounded for the Night Office he dragged himself from his bed and was immediately seized by a fit of coughing. He tried to stop and take a breath, but it seemed to him that something was pressing down on his chest and squeezing the air out of it as though it were a bladder pipe. He fell back on the bed and tried to suck in some air, breathing in loud and desperate gasps.

There was movement about him. Two of the novices – was it Tydi and Hadwald? – made a stretcher of his blanket and carried him to the infirmary where Fergus – no, not Fergus, of course; it was Laurence – quickly set to mixing herbs and boiled them in a pot over the fire. A sweet sickly smell rose. The cloying smell, along with the bouts of coughing and rawness in his throat, all combined forces to torment Wilfrid. Even the dim candlelight pained his eyes, and his head was as heavy as a boulder.

Laurence brought a cup to him and helped him drink. The liquid was thick and sweet, but still it scrawled at his throat like cat's claws, and Laurence's palm against his forehead was a slab of ice. As he lay down, Wilfrid was aware of a sudden cramp in his stomach which swelled up inside him but died again as something stronger, the softness of the straw pallet or the lightness in his head, drew him finally to sleep.

He slept in fits and starts. Often he was wakened by long coughing fits which threatened to tear out the whole of his insides. The coughing would ease after a while, and he would slip back into a honeyed sleep where his body was light as air, floating above the pallet in some other world. But soon the coughing would start again, his throat closing in on itself like a clam. Sometimes he woke to the stink of his own piss and soil. Then someone would drag him from the bed, fetch a pail so he could relieve himself and rub his body down with wet cloths. They gave him drinks, some sweet, some bitter, some so foul-smelling they caused him to retch.

He was never sure who was tending to him or speaking to him, who was in the infirmary with him and who was merely a spirit in his dreams. He saw Cuthbert standing upright in his boat, arms spread wide into the wind as he was tossed about by the waves. He saw his father once, his mother more often, and some of the children from his village. Once he saw a little dark-haired boy waving at him. The child was laughing at first, but as Wilfrid drew closer, he realised he was standing knee-deep in water, and as the child reached out to grab him Wilfrid saw it wasn't a child at all but a terrible fish that wanted to pull him down into the deep. Then Laurence was rubbing some oil onto his forehead and whispering Latin words into his ear.

*

Wilfrid woke one morning and realised something had changed. It wasn't a coughing fit that had stirred him but the sounds of voices speaking in low tones. His throat was dry but no longer raw, and the boulder weighing down his head was gone.

'He's well enough, I believe,' a voice said. 'I hope. The first night and the second, God help him, he was sorely afflicted – the Old Enemy.'

The Old Enemy. Wilfrid flinched. The devil? Had the devil entered him? Is that what was making him sick?

'I worry for him,' a second voice said. 'We all do. Can he withstand it?'

'Please God, he will,' the first voice said. 'But yes, I worry too. He's never been strong, you see, not since the plague that time, and yet he endures more than is possible for any of us healthier men.'

The plague? He had plague?

'But we shouldn't doubt,' the voice went on. 'You heard what the prior said. God called him to exile. God and St Aidan. They'll protect him. And besides, the plague, that terrible time, sure it was years ago.'

Wilfrid uncurled his fists. The men weren't talking about him. He knew that voice: Fergus.

'Still, I worry for the prior.' Now Wilfrid recognised Laurence's solemn tones. 'They say Aidan himself was at times hard-pressed to endure the wretchedness of his hermitage, so beset was he by the foul creatures that dwelt there. What's it like, Brother Fergus? Is it as bad as they say?'

'It's...it's not like this island. There is – how can I put

it? – a presence, a wildness, as if there is something alive in the very air.'

'You mean evil?' Laurence said. 'An evil presence?'

There was a brief silence, and Wilfrid wondered if the brothers suspected he was awake. He was terribly thirsty and longed for a drink – any drink – even some of that bitter potion Laurence had been spooning into him.

Fergus continued.

'No, not evil exactly. Desolation. Desolation as profound as any I have experienced. Though the seas were quiet as we journeyed out, we found it almost impossible to beach the boat. It was as though the sea itself was trying to hold us back and prevent us from landing. Then, when we did eventually land, we were attacked by the swarms of terns that live there, who swept down on us, beat us with their wings, pecked at us viciously and despoiled our heads and garments with their filth.'

'And the prior?'

Fergus gave a low laugh.

'The prior, for whatever reason, remained unscathed. It was Brother Herefrith and I who bore the brunt of their attack. I don't think I will ever remove the stench from my cloak. In any event, other than reassuring the terns that we had not come to harm their young, the prior said little. Herefrith and I set up the tents in the most sheltered spot we could find, though in truth there is more shelter on the outer ridges of our own cliff than there is anywhere on that wind-filled spot. We gathered stones to make a sturdier shelter and a break against the wind, but we had only the timber we brought with us and a few rotting logs left over from the hut that Blessed Aidan had made, long since collapsed, and there are no trees on the island.

'The prior walked and blessed the land. He blessed every pace of it, sprinkling it with water from our own well here. He slept alone, fasting, of course; he didn't eat in the few days we were there. Then yesterday morning he bade us be gone, one to each boat, while the winds were fair.'

Fergus paused.

'He wouldn't permit us to leave him one of the boats, you see, lest he be tempted to return. Already the demons were troubling him, their old taunt – about the Whitby synod, schism, betrayal.'

Wilfrid swallowed a cough. He knew what a synod was, though he had no idea what they meant about schism and betrayal. He wondered who might have betrayed Cuthbert, and why demons still taunted him about it.

'So you obeyed?' Laurence said.

'Of course we obeyed!' Fergus sounded shocked. 'But my heart was heavy as we rowed away from that woeful place. I prayed for him with every stroke, though it seemed to me that some demon had planted its seed of doubt in me. I must weed it out.' He sighed. 'Well, we'll see how the prior truly fares when we return.'

'When you return?'

'He'll signal when he needs more supplies. But tell me about Wilfrid. You say he was almost lost?'

'Yes,' Laurence said. 'Several times I heard the death rattle from his chest and expected him to expire. I anointed him, of course. His whole body has at times been on fire and at other times plunged into ice, and the dysentery has been...well...extreme.'

Death. Wilfrid clutched the blanket. A cold sensation ran through him.

'He's keeping down fluids?' Fergus said.

'Since last night, yes,' Laurence said. 'Look, he's moving.'

'Let's sit him up,' Fergus said. 'And fetch some of that medicine.'

Wilfrid opened his eyes. The coughing returned immediately though this time it was short-lived. Fergus helped him to drink the medicine. It burned his throat but eased the thirst.

'Easy now,' Fergus said. 'Small sips.'

Wilfrid wanted to explain about his great thirst, but the only that sounds he could make were tiny whines that pulled on his throat.

'Don't speak yet,' Fergus said. 'You've been very ill.' He motioned to Laurence. 'Fetch him the pail, and then boil some ginger in water.' He put his hand to Wilfrid's forehead. 'Still a little feverish, but not badly so. You say none of the other brothers have been afflicted.'

'None,' Laurence said, bringing the pail. 'It's a blessing.'

'It's a wonder,' Fergus muttered.

He sat Wilfrid forward and pulled the robe above his waist just as Wilfrid was seized by a sudden burning in his insides. Fergus and Laurence got him to the pail just in time, and all he could do was cover his face with his hands as his bowels noisily emptied.

The fever continued to come and go, but mostly it

went. The cough eased, troubling him only at night. His throat was no longer sore, though the scratching sensation remained and could be relieved only by drinking one of Fergus' many concoctions. At least his voice was recovering, though he could not speak at any length without it being reduced to a rasping whine. The dysentery, too, attacked him less frequently, though twice he had woken up during the night covered in his own filth. Fergus made no fuss. He helped him wash and prepared a fresh pallet with clean straw and warned him it was a condition that was apt to return to sufferers at intervals over a lifetime. For now, though, it no longer overtook him with sudden vehemence. He learned to watch for the signs of the approaching enemy, the feeling of air rising in his stomach, the cramp which came like a punch in the belly, and he would run outside and deal with the attack there.

As he became stronger he was allowed to assist Fergus in the infirmary, tending the fire, cleaning the hut, fetching fresh straw and sometimes with brewing remedies. He watched Fergus weigh and measure the ingredients exactly and wondered if he was working to a scheme or merely experimenting, but Wilfrid said nothing, happy to be assigned these light duties rather than the more arduous tasks in the fields and kitchen. In any case, Fergus had told him he should rest his voice as much as possible and ensure that no further strain was put on it. Wilfrid obeyed. Eventually, though, he asked Fergus the question that had lingered in his head since the night Fergus had returned from the Farne. He asked what the Whitby synod was.

Fergus looked at him sharply.

'Does it not say in our Rule that a monk should forbid his tongue from pointless speech or questioning? Silence is the key that unlocks the doorway to the Spirit.'

Wilfrid reddened. He had become used to working silently with Fergus and had almost forgotten what it was like to be scolded. Fergus continued to grind the compound he was preparing, leaning heavily on the pestle and vigorously crushing the ingredients beneath it to a fine powder. Eventually he spoke again.

'I suppose it's as well you should have some understanding of that time.' He put the pestle down. 'You know, of course, how Easter is calculated.'

Wilfrid nodded. It had been explained by Brother Herefrith, though in truth he could not comprehend the calculations system at all. He just knew it had something to do with cycles of the moon, and that Easter must always be celebrated on a *Sunnandæg*, the day the Lord rose from the dead.

'Well then,' Fergus said. 'You know that the brethren of Northumbria and Pictland, Brega and Armagh employed a different method to calculate Easter to that used by the brethren in southern parts of these lands, and even in Francia and Saxony and Rome itself. Our way was the way laid down by John, the beloved disciple, and observed by our fathers on these islands, St Columba and Blessed Aidan. But the pope sent Bishop Wilfrid, for whom you were named, to convey the message that we must all convert to the Roman way, the true way, *he* said, ordained by St Peter himself, and that also we must adopt the St Peter's tonsure, the crown of thorns.'

Fergus bowed his head slightly to indicate the circle of grey hair surrounding the large bald patch at the centre of his scalp. Wilfrid noticed a few thin stray tufts of hair – the weekly shaving of the monks' heads would take place the following day.

'Well, the arguments continued back and forth. You see, some believed that to abandon the way of St John was to betray the very saints that guarded us, while others said that to disdain the way of St Peter was a terrible heresy. At last Oswiu King, the father of Ecgfrith King, you know, called a great synod of all the brethren and bishops and holy sisters to be held at the holy house at Whitby, and after hearing all the arguments Oswiu decided in favour of Bishop Wilfrid and Rome. And so we took St Peter's tonsure, and St Peter's precepts for calculating Easter.'

'Is that what Prior Cuthbert meant when he said there were divisions?' Wilfrid said.

'The real divisions came afterwards. Many of our brethren left, went to monasteries in Ireland rather than accept the new ways, and the monasteries at Iona and in Pictland continue to follow the ways of our Irish saints. It is a festering sore.'

'But why would they not obey the pope?' Wilfrid asked.

Fergus hesitated.

'Sometimes a belief is so strong no man can disabuse you of it. God chose the time for Easter, they said, not the pope, and certainly not Oswiu King. They would rather incur the pope's wrath – even the fracture of our entire community – than abandon their faith.'

'But didn't Prior Cuthbert favour the new ways?

Surely his faith is stronger than any man's. Would they not heed him?'

Fergus returned to his mortar and pestle.

'There's no more to be said. Those days are in the past and best left there. Go and rest a while now.'

Wilfrid lay down. He still didn't understand how Easter was calculated, or why one manner of tonsure was deemed more sacred than another, or why any of it should cause division; still less why those errant monks – they must be the same ones Tydi had mentioned – had betrayed Cuthbert and the brethren. Fergus must be right when he said those days were best left in the past. Still, as Wilfrid fell asleep he couldn't rid his head of the image of a sore – a great black boil breaking open and oozing yellow pus in a slowly meandering trail.

At last Fergus told Wilfrid he was well enough to return to the monastery. The prospect of rising in the night for the offices was not welcome, but at least he could finally sing again. More than the coughing had torn at his chest and the rawness had torn at his throat, not being able to sing had torn at his heart. A small irritation persisted in his throat, but Fergus said he was hopeful it would soon dissipate fully.

After the morning lessons Wilfrid proceeded to the oratory for the Midday Office. He held his psalter in his hand. He had lost count of the days and had no idea where they were in the cycle of prayer, but he would soon figure it out. All he need do was listen to the antiphon, let the note enter him and as soon as he sounded it the words would come and float in the air about him, and while he sang he would be floating too.

Edberht began. Wilfrid opened his mouth. Air filled his lungs. He closed his eyes and sang out.

Domine, labia mea aperies,
et os meum adnuntiabit laudem tuam.

Or tried to sing out. The only sounds he could make were pitiful squeaks, as raspy and reedy as anything Dunstan might produce. He tried again, but it seemed a serpent had wrapped itself around his throat. He looked up at Fergus, wanting a nod of reassurance, but Fergus was frowning. Eventually, Edberht sang the verse as Wilfrid hurried from the church in a fit of coughing. A cold feeling streamed through him. He thought of Cuthbert alone on the Farne, of the evil spirits lurking there, of Cuthbert's dread of loneliness. He thought of himself on Lindisfarne and feared he would be no less lonely, that he too was beset by spirits, one of whom had stolen his only gift. He feared he would never sing again.

Twelve

WILFRID SAT ALONE on the beach looking out towards Cuthbert's Rock. A half-moon dripped silver light over the incoming sea. Out on the sandflats the seals sang, a low hum gradually rising and ringing out into the skies, then falling back to a plaintive echo. He was bone-and-soul weary. Weeks had passed. Weeks of remedies, ointments and infusions, blessings and prayers. Still he could not sing. Fergus was clear. This was not the breaking of the voice that marked the passage from boy to man. This was something else, a lingering malady in the throat that caused his voice to be raspy and hoarse. It might eventually heal. Or it might not. The exertions of singing were not advisable lest they wreak even more damage.

Something broke within Wilfrid. He had no means

of explaining his loss to anyone else, to tell them that when he sang he stepped from darkness into sunrise, that only when he sang could he find a sense of purpose or joy, that not being able to sing had plunged him into a deep pit out of which he could not climb. No one would have understood. Or cared.

He crawled into himself, curled up in his misery. Speaking with the other novices became an effort he could no longer make, and in any case they maintained the distance they had always kept. Even Hadwald, who has happy to talk to anyone as long as they would listen to his grumbling, had stopped bothering with him. Tydi was so preoccupied with his scribing and studies that he barely gave Wilfrid the customary blessing as he passed. And Cuthbert. Cuthbert was gone to that devil-ridden island out in the sea, and Wilfrid did not suppose he would ever return.

He looked out to Cuthbert's Rock now and saw how the moon shone a path over the sands towards it. He remembered the night he spent there with Cuthbert, the sense of release from the monastery it had given him. He reached into his pocket for something. The knife. He had taken to carrying it with him lately, not caring if he was caught. Its wolf-head glistened in the moonlight. He felt the smart of the blade, the cool silver handle in his palm. He wrapped his fingers tightly around it and walked to the moonlit path.

He kept going until he reached the Rock. He went into the oratory, lay down on the floor and listened to the low rumble of the sea as it drew nearer, sucked and splashed its way around the Rock. As the sea closed in and cut him off from the monastery he heard shouting and calling, his name ringing out over the water. He closed his ears. He closed his mind. He held his knife and fell into a deep sleep.

They took him to the infirmary when they found him. Herefrith and Fergus, each taking an arm and dragging him along. His limbs were heavy as stone. He wasn't sick, he wanted to say – just tired – but his tongue was as listless as his legs. They sat him down on a pallet. He turned his face from them and looked into the darkest corner of the building. A huge maggot was crawling over the straw.

'What were you thinking of?' Herefrith said. 'The whole community has been out searching for you. Didn't you hear us calling? Prior Edberht had to give special permission to break the Great Silence.'

'Answer Brother Herefrith,' Fergus said. He took Wilfrid's chin between his forefinger and thumb and looked directly into his eyes. 'What made you enter the retreat on the Rock? None but the prior may go there.'

Wilfrid pulled away from Fergus and leaned back against the wall. He watched the maggot crawl under a stone.

'Wilfrid, you must speak,' Fergus said. 'If you're ill, say so. You'll have to answer for your actions in Chapter, you know. If you cannot give Prior Edberht a satisfactory explanation, I fear the punishment will be...grave. Wilfrid?'

Wilfrid shrugged. He would be whipped again. Well, he would bear it. He would not cry out this time, not even if the whip left welts on his backside the length of a snake. He put his hand into his robe pocket and felt the knife nestling there. He closed his eyes. All he wanted was sleep.

Edberht opened the Chapter meeting with the blessing. Wilfrid sat in his usual position, vaguely recalling Fergus' advice: repentance, reparation, remorse. The words ran into each other and swirled around like vegetables in a stewing pot. The monks sang a hymn. Wilfrid kept his mouth closed, didn't even mime the words. His psalter hung limply in his hand, opened on the wrong page. After a while Hadwald nudged him. Edberht was standing at the top of the hall, looking directly at him. Slowly Wilfrid stood up. He stepped into the centre of the hall, alone in a vast space, it seemed to him, with Edberht and scores of monks bearing down.

'Wilfrid,' Edberht said. 'Do you have anything to say for yourself?'

Wilfrid kept quiet. He pressed his fingers into his arms, making spiral patterns about his wrist bones.

'Perhaps,' Edberht said softly, 'you can explain your actions, your disappearance.'

It was colder than usual in the hall; darker. There must be fewer candles burning, though the smell of beeswax was intense. The air was filled with it, its sickly sweetness mingling with the stink of the monks – the sweat, the lingering odour of onions and stale fish on their breath.

'We're waiting, Wilfrid.'

Wilfrid glanced at the rows of monks on either side. They seemed to lurch closer than before. Edberht, too, seemed to have advanced a little nearer to him and was now looming above him, his arms raised, the sleeves of his robe like the wings of a hunting hawk. Wilfrid closed his eyes, put his hand into his pocket and clasped the knife.

'Then let me summarise,' Edberht said. 'You fled your community. You trespassed on a sacred place. You abandoned your duty, your Rule and your God. You caused grief and worry and disruption to your brothers, and yet you've expressed no repentance, no remorse.'

Wilfrid flinched as at the crack of a whip. He wished they *would* whip him. Just get it over with.

Someone to his right coughed politely.

'If I may intervene at this point, Prior Edberht.'

'Brother Fergus, you have something to say?'

'With your leave,' Fergus said. 'We all know of Wilfrid's recent illness, and though by the hand of the Lord he was saved, still it has left him with certain debilitations, debilitations which have pressed him sorely, brought his spirit down.'

'You think he is soul-sick?'

'Yes. The foul expulsions of the body, the strain on his voice, have caused his spirit to be cast into a dark place where my medicaments cannot reach.'

Wilfrid wondered how much longer this would go on. He should lie down on the floor and confess something, anything – it didn't matter what. Even Fergus had admitted that he was beyond help. But Edberht had begun to speak again.

'Well, he is not the first of us to be subject to the black humours which feed on the soul. And Brother Dunstan has informed me of certain other weaknesses the boy is subject to, laziness and vanity, which have hitherto gone uncorrected. The solution to spiritual frailty is prayer and more prayer, fasting, and above all the discipline of the Rule. Or are you suggesting, Brother Fergus, that Wilfrid's disobedience should go unpunished on account of a weary spirit? If I were to apply that to all, the monastery would descend into chaos.'

Herefrith stood up.

'I'm sure that is not what Brother Fergus is suggesting,' he said. 'Of course Wilfrid should be punished, but punishment must be tempered with mercy, as Prior Cuthbert has laid down in his Rule. As novice master, I suggest a whipping – five strokes which I will administer myself – and daily recital of the Rule which I will oversee.'

Edberht stepped suddenly forward. He stood just a single step away from Wilfrid.

'You forget, Brother Herefrith,' he said, keeping his eyes set on Wilfrid. 'I am prior now. I will decide what the punishment is to be.'

When Fergus passed Wilfrid in the cloister the following morning he withheld his blessing. He didn't even look at Wilfrid but hurried off towards the infirmary as if one of the brothers was lying there *in extremis*. The pattern repeated itself all that day and the days following. No one spoke to him; no one looked at him if they could avoid it. Even Tydi kept his hands in his sleeves and his eyes to the ground. Worst of all, like Fergus, no one gave him the blessing as they passed. Even his food, which he ate alone in the kitchen, was unblessed.

He overheard Laurence and Herefrith talking outside.

'Excommunication is too severe a punishment in this case,' Laurence said. 'Did the boy even receive a second warning? And Prior Cuthbert's Rule is explicit: those who are intellectually inferior should be scolded merely and subject to light corporal punishment.'

Herefrith said something Wilfrid couldn't catch. Laurence grunted.

'If you ask me, there's too much change going on about here – and not for the better.'

'Take care, Brother Laurence,' Herefrith said. 'Mind you do not find that you are subject to sanction also. Ensure the boy finishes his meal and then give him some work. Work will distract him from the darkness of the soul.'

Days passed. Wilfrid didn't know how long the period of excommunication was to continue. He knew he was expected to go to Edberht, confess and repent, but every time he considered it, his legs grew heavy, and his bowels churned. It didn't matter in any case. Nothing mattered. His spirit was dead. Sometimes it felt as if his body was dying too. Each movement he forced it to make bled him of energy. Herefrith had to drag him from his bed each morning and again for the Night Office. He did so wordlessly, without looking at him. Laurence stood over him in the kitchen, sighing and clicking his tongue as Wilfrid took an age to chop a single carrot. Once, he tripped over the leg of the table and lay on the ground, unable to command his legs to move. Laurence pulled him up.

'Pointless,' he said.

He took Wilfrid by the shoulders, brought him outside and turned him in the direction of the church. Wilfrid walked slowly towards it. But instead of entering and praying, as he supposed Laurence had meant him to, he stopped. Something was lurking there, a dark wolfish shape prowling in circles by the door. It flicked its tail, moved off stealthily and headed to the beach. Wilfrid followed.

A fog was drifting in, curling its way across the water. It quieted everything. The seagulls and geese stopped screeching. The seals were silent. The wolf padded noiselessly away. Laurence was right. It was all pointless. He wanted to let the silence of the fog creep up on him and take him. He was dead anyway. He felt nothing any more – not the bite of the wind, not the caress of the sun, the sting of the rain. But he did feel the knife, the leather sheath lying next to his thigh. He felt the curve of the handle and the point of the blade. He held it in his hand. He felt it mark his arm. He felt it pierce his skin. He held his breath, held his nerve, his knife. He sliced in. Felt the bite. The sting. The raw life.

Thirteen

IN THE END IT WAS TYDI who discovered him. Wilfrid had been so careful with his knife, making sure to use it only when completely alone, sometimes slipping out from the dormitory at night to feel the thrill of the blade against his skin, the relief of the pain bleeding out of him. He thought of Hildmer's wife, her ruined face. She was brazen, but not clever. She seemed not to realise there were parts of the body where the marks were easily hidden: the upper arms and legs, even the belly.

The excommunication period had come to an end, but still he felt the brothers were skirting around him, keeping a polite distance, as though he were a dog of unreliable temper. But it didn't matter. Nothing mattered. All he wanted was his knife, the knowledge of it resting next to his skin. It had become part of him, another limb.

One afternoon he was sent to assist Tydi with preparing lime mix for washing calfskins. He watched as Tydi plunged a skin into a basin of lime and stirred it around with a stick.

'Now you try,' Tydi said. 'Careful. Don't get that mix on your robe. Roll your sleeves up to your shoulder. No, higher. Honestly, Wilfrid! Here, let me.'

Wilfrid tried to push Tydi away, but was too late; Tydi was staring at the scars that etched Wilfrid's arms like runes.

'It's nothing,' Wilfrid said. 'Just scratches, that's all. It's...you know...self-mortification, like the prior does – Prior Cuthbert, I mean – fasting and all that. It's the same thing.'

Tydi shook his head. He stirred the lime mix, around and around, slowly at first, then faster and faster. He stopped and stared into the swirling liquid. Then he headed off in the direction of Prior Edberht's cell.

A day or two later, or was it more? He woke to find Fergus leaning over him.

'This has gone on long enough.' Fergus put his hand on Wilfrid's shoulder and shook him. 'Wilfrid, are you listening?'

Wilfrid pulled away. He didn't want to hear what Fergus had to say. Some new punishment, he supposed. He wondered what could be more severe than excommunication. Expulsion, perhaps. Would they send him home? Even that thought failed to give him heart. At least they hadn't found his knife. They had assumed that the cuts on his body had been made with the ordinary paring knife that all monks carried, which they had duly confiscated. The wolf-knife nestled safely in his robe pocket. He curled in towards the wall and pulled the blanket over his head. Fergus snatched at it.

'Get up, Wilfrid! I mean it.'

He hauled Wilfrid to his feet, and tied an oiled cloak about him. Then he stuffed the blanket and Wilfrid's spare habit into a leather satchel, pulled him out of the dormitory and led him to the beach. Dunstan stood in a currach on the shore, rolling up the sail and securing it to a pole that stretched across the top of the mast.

'There,' he said. 'That should hold fast.'

'You've checked everything?' Fergus said. 'Ropes, mast, yard, sail?'

'Everything's in order.'

'Good,' Fergus said. He looked skywards, frowning. 'Hmm. Mackerel sky since dawn.'

'Let's go quickly then,' Dunstan said firmly, 'while the weather's fair. With the wind in our favour we should be there in less than two hours.'

Wilfrid stepped back – surely they didn't mean to bring him out to sea? But that was exactly what Fergus and Dunstan intended. They each removed their boots, hitched up their robes and heaved the boat to the water's edge.

'In you get, Wilfrid,' Fergus said. 'Right now! We've no time to waste. Don't make me lift you in!'

Miserably Wilfrid clambered into the little boat. Dunstan pushed them off, then he and Fergus each took position on the two boards that stretched across either end of the currach and rowed together, drawing the oars through the water as to the beat of a drum. Wilfrid sat on a small chest of supplies situated between the two monks. He grasped tightly to the edge of the box, breathing fast as they pulled out into the channel between Lindisfarne and the mainland, passing the Royal City and heading out towards the open sea. Fergus said something to him – something about where they were going, Wilfrid thought – but at that moment Dunstan unfurled the sail; it dropped from the yard with a loud slap, and Wilfrid missed what Fergus had said.

Dunstan secured the sail, passing a line through two iron rings attached to the rim on either side of the craft. The wind filled the sail, and they ploughed swiftly out to sea, with Dunstan at the helm, directing the boat with a steering oar, and Fergus, no longer rowing, seated at the bow. Soon the wind grew stronger. It lashed at Wilfrid, striking him with a force meaner and crueller than even Edberht's whip. The boat swayed from side to side, and every now and then a rush of water would leap up and lunge at Wilfrid, spraying him from head to foot, the salt stinging his hands and cheeks, his stomach heaving with every roll of the waves.

'Look to the horizon, Wilfrid,' Fergus shouted as he bailed the water out with a bowl. 'It will help ease the seasickness.'

Wilfrid tried to look to the horizon, but the vast wall of grey only made him feel more sick. He leaned over the side of the boat and vomited.

Over the next two hours he vomited again and again until his stomach had emptied, yet still the sea demanded that he give more. He retched and spat out bile.

'Keep south-west,' Fergus shouted to Dunstan. 'Look, Wilfrid, there's the island. Not too long now and we'll come ashore.'

But Wilfrid couldn't look. All he knew was that everything about him was swirling grey and black, the skies and seas in a frenzied dance. He crouched down in the bottom of the boat and wished himself dead.

It started to rain, lightly at first – it seemed no more than sea spray – but soon it fell more heavily. The wind drew strength from the darkening sky. The waves rose, tossing the boat around.

'Time to furl the sail,' Fergus shouted to Dunstan.

But Dunstan appeared not to hear. He was shouting himself now, and pointing.

'We're there, almost there! Isn't that the island's landing point?'

Wilfrid made himself raise his head. Cliffs loomed out of the sea, black speckled with white, pounded by the waves. Teems of birds circled about the rocks. Fergus called back.

'Yes it is. And look! Up there. It's him. He must have seen our signal from the watchtower last evening.'

And there, standing at the edge of the cliff was a man, his cloak flapping behind him. Cuthbert. Wilfrid gripped the side of the boat and kept his eyes on Cuthbert. The sea continued to toss them about mercilessly, but they were almost there. Fergus took the oars again to help steady the course.

'Right, furl the sail,' he repeated. 'The wind is too strong. Brother Dunstan, stay at the helm for now.

Wilfrid, see that rope there on the starboard gunwale? There, on the side of the boat. Your right side, Wilfrid! Good. I need you to let it go. Don't move position. Just undo the knot. Quickly now.'

Wilfrid reached over to the ring where the line attaching the sail to the side of the boat was secured. He tugged and fumbled at the knot, trying to undo it, but it refused to give. 'Hurry, for God's sake,' Dunstan shouted. 'The wind is pushing us off course.'

Wilfrid continued to scramble at the knot. Uselessly.

'My fingers...too cold... I can't...'

The boat spun as a sudden gust lashed at it. Fergus stopped rowing.

'Right. Let me. Now listen, Wilfrid. Just ease yourself a little to the left. Carefully. That's it. Stay down, don't move. Brother Dunstan, keep watch and hold us steady.'

Fergus pulled in the oars. He looked quickly about and then half-walking, half-crouching, began to move towards Wilfrid's place. The boat pitched. Dunstan cried out as another gust of wind whipped through the currach and drove it into a rolling wave. Fergus stumbled as the little craft spun. He flung his arms wide and tried to hurl himself towards the mast, but another wave lurched at them, he fell backwards, and then, suddenly, he was gone.

'Wilfrid!' Dunstan yelled. 'Cut the rope.'

Wilfrid hesitated. Just an instant. Or was it more? Dunstan threw a knife to him.

'Use this, Wilfrid! Cut the damned rope!'

Wilfrid caught the knife and sliced through the rope. Then he leaned over to the other side of the vessel and cut the line there too. Immediately the sail slacked, flapping helplessly, and the boat slowed.

Dunstan shouted again.

'The halyard, Wilfrid! That rope there. Release it. Haul down the sail.' He drew in the steering oar and leaned over the starboard side of the boat. 'Fergus, Fergus!'

Somehow Wilfrid managed to lower and roll the sail.

'The wave,' Dunstan cried. 'It came from nowhere, knocked him over.' He looked about him wildly. 'Fergus!' he called again, and this time his voice was a shriek, louder than the cries of the gulls whirling above them. 'Dear God. Help us. Wilfrid, can you see anything?'

But all Wilfrid could see was rolling black water, edged with grey scum, thundering towards them. Suddenly he spotted something riding the waves.

'There!' he said. 'His cloak. It must be him!'

Dunstan grabbed the oars. He rowed, his every stroke a prayer. 'Dear God, dear God. Let him live. Dear God.'

He continued to pull on the oars with all his might until they reached the spot Wilfrid had pointed to. 'Pull him in, Wilfrid. We must pull him in. Dear God, dear God.'

Wilfrid stretched his hand out over the side of the boat, grasped at the cloak and hauled it in. He stared overboard, his eyes searching the rolling water.

'It's...it's just his cloak. He's not here,' he cried. 'I can't see him.'

'Keep looking,' Dunstan roared.

Wilfrid shouted with Dunstan, one after the other – *Fergus, Fergus!* He plunged his hands into the black water again and again, and prayed hard to Christ that they would find Fergus, that they would heave him back into the boat and strike for safety, that he would live. But he knew. He knew.

He wasn't sure how long they went on calling and searching. He was so cold now he could barely feel his limbs. The clouds blackened, and it rained harder. The boat moved about, and Wilfrid no longer had any idea of where Fergus had fallen in, but he saw that they were drifting away from the island and further out into the jaws of the open sea. He looked back to the island, saw Cuthbert, still on the cliff, waving, beckoning.

'B...Brother Dunstan,' he said, and he could hardly get the words out, his teeth chattering harder than the rain. 'P...Prior Cuthbert. I s...saw him. He was waving.'

Dunstan looked vaguely in the direction Wilfrid was pointing to.

'I see nothing,' he said. 'I see nothing. We must...'

'I think,' and Wilfrid's teeth shook so violently now, he thought they must fall out of his mouth, 'I think he is c...calling us in.'

Dunstan stopped rowing. The boat tossed and rolled with the waves and almost turned over, and still he didn't row.

A final effort.

'M...must we not obey the prior, Brother Dunstan?

Dunstan took one last look at the sea around them. Then he turned the boat and rowed for the Farne.

Cuthbert led them to a ramshackle pile of stones, wood and heather that hid a hollow dug into the earth. They climbed in. It was dark and dank, the air was thick with smoke. The only light came from a small opening in the roof and the smouldering fire at the centre of the room. A bracken bed was laid against the earthen wall next to a wicker basket. The ground was covered with a mean layer of rushes. Cuthbert took some sticks from a woodpile and threw them onto the fire.

'Take off your wet things,' he said. 'There are blankets in the basket.'

Slowly they prised their wet cloaks from their bodies, shivering so fiercely it seemed the earth itself was shaking beneath them. Wilfrid pulled his spare habit out of his satchel, but even the heavily greased leather had been unable to protect the garment from the sea, and it was as wet as the one he was wearing. Dunstan didn't attempt to get his spare habit. He stood naked before the fire, shuddering as if in a fit. He seemed shrunken, suddenly old, his stick-thin legs barely capable of supporting his frame, his head almost completely bald, spittle dribbling down his chin as he moaned to himself. *Dear God, dear God.*

Cuthbert covered him with a blanket.

'Wilfrid, you must take off your habit too. It's soaked through.'

Wilfrid turned away. He peeled the robe from his skin, tugged it over his head and reached for the blanket. Suddenly Dunstan appeared behind him, grabbed him by the arms and turned him around.

'Show him why we're here,' he said.

Wilfrid tried to break free. He folded his arms into his chest.

'Look!' Dunstan said.

Cuthbert pulled Dunstan off. He took Wilfrid's left

arm and looked at it closely. He drew his fingers over the scars. Wilfrid winced and turned his face away, waiting for words of reproach, but Cuthbert just draped the blanket over him and made him sit down. Dunstan sat too, rocking back and forth, his breath coming in shallow quick gasps.

'Been going on for months. Lying in bed, has to be dragged to the offices, won't speak, won't carry out a simple task. Then this.' Dunstan shook his fist in the direction of Wilfrid's arm. 'Making a mockery of... It's not self-mortification, not that, not prayer with the body, not prayer... A defilement of prayer.'

Cuthbert knelt down in front of Dunstan and tried to hush him, but Dunstan waved him away.

'Brother Fergus, he didn't want the boy punished any further. Insisted...fought with Prior Edberht. Fergus – his heart is soft as a woman's sometimes – he wanted... He said bring the boy to you, here, to this place, that was the only solution. You would cure him, Fergus said... Fergus.'

He sank his head into his knees and pointed a shivering finger at Wilfrid.

'He, he has let the devil in. I always said it. And now Fergus is lost because of him.'

'That's enough, Brother Dunstan,' Cuthbert said. He took Dunstan's hand and spoke more softly. 'You will not blame Wilfrid for this. We cannot know the ways of Providence. And Fergus is not lost, not to God.'

Wilfrid covered his head with the blanket and wrapped it tightly around him. He couldn't stop shaking. He felt as if he was still on the sea being rocked about. Silence fell. Heavy and dark, it prowled the little hollow like a wolf. Eventually Cuthbert spoke.

'I'll warm some wine and prepare something to eat. Then we'll pray for our brother Fergus, for his blessed soul, that even now at this very moment it may be received by Christ's angels into Paradise.'

They crouched side by side, praying for Fergus. Cuthbert prayed that Christ would welcome Fergus to His side, that his sins would be forgiven, that his good deeds, not his bad, would be reckoned. He knelt in front of his low altar – the one he had taken with him to Hildmer's village.

Wilfrid remembered how carefully Cuthbert had unwrapped it from its casing and opened it out, how he had touched it and prayed for the souls of those who had made it and consecrated it. In the candlelight he could see how much older Cuthbert looked now. The skin below his eyes sagged like empty sacks. His beard was long, and his wispy hair had outgrown the crown shape on his head and was beginning to trail down his neck.

Wilfrid prayed for Fergus too. He entreated St Peter to unlock the gates to Paradise and bid Fergus enter. But each time he closed his eyes he saw Fergus' spirit emerge from the sea and come in pursuit of him. He heard Fergus' voice. *Just undo the knot. Just undo the knot.*

Dunstan was right. Wilfrid was the reason they had come to the Farne. Wilfrid was the reason Fergus was lost. He couldn't untie a simple knot. His fingers had been too cold, too weak, too...too clumsy. Fergus had been forced to move position to undo the rope and that was when the wave had slammed into the boat, making him lose his balance and fall overboard. Wilfrid lay listening to the sounds of the island, and they were all Fergus: the seals' endless drone was a lament for the dead, the waves lashing against the rocks was God's anger, and the wind howling was Fergus himself, crying for vengeance.

Fourteen

A SMALL STREAM OF LIGHT through the gap in the
roof announced the morning. It was only now
that Wilfrid noticed how deeply cut into the
ground Cuthbert's little dwelling was – almost to the
height of a man – though it was not high enough for a
man as tall as Cuthbert to stand up straight, and it was
not large enough to allow the three of them to lie down;
they had slept sitting up. It gave some shelter from the
ravaging winds, Wilfrid supposed, but it was cramped
and dark – little better than a pig's hovel.

Cuthbert sang the office of Lauds. Dunstan made
some feeble efforts to join in, only occasionally meeting
Cuthbert's note. Wilfrid was silent. The last time he
had heard Cuthbert sing, he had been able to sing with
him. Now he couldn't even attempt it. He wondered if

Cuthbert would admonish him, but when it was over Cuthbert merely beckoned to him and Dunstan to follow. They crawled through the entrance and looked around.

The island was small, much smaller than Lindisfarne. Wilfrid thought he might walk the length of it in a matter of minutes, though he would have to battle his way through the heather and low-lying bushes, as there were no clear pathways. And he would have to fight through the noise too. The island was seething with sound. Hundreds...no...thousands of birds of all kinds – kites, kittiwakes, redwings, sea ravens, gulls and gannets – all swarmed in the sky, calling and shrieking, beating down the hiss of the winds and waves with their cries.

The brothers stood on the cliff, high above the sea, looking out. The sea was even wilder than the day before, the damp air heavy with salt.

'I keep thinking,' Dunstan said, 'I keep thinking that perhaps, perhaps he has somehow swum to safety, reached the rocks. He knows the sea. No one knows the ways of the sea as well as Fergus.'

Cuthbert shook his head.

'Fergus was a skilled oarsman, not a swimmer, and the sea is greedy. Besides, I think...' Cuthbert pressed his fingers against his temples. 'God forgive my pride, I think if God had rescued him, I would know. I would feel it, Brother Dunstan, as strong as my own heartbeat. I would see it. I've seen things before. You know that.'

Dunstan's face was white, his mouth pinched into a thin, straight line, his eyes watering. The sting of the wind, Wilfrid thought, the salty air.

'Then we must watch,' Dunstan said. 'And pray, pray that the sea will at least return his body.'

They kept constant watch, willing the sea to deliver up Fergus' body. Wilfrid stayed close to Cuthbert, fearing to be alone with the spirits and demons that hovered nearby. He jumped at every rustle in the bushes, at each squawk of a gull or gannet overhead, at the wails of the seals on the rocks. Dunstan too kept vigil, wringing his hands and muttering disparate prayers into the wind.

Tu scis insipientiam meam...
Delicta mea...non sunt abscondita.

Once he shouted out. 'There, there, I see something. It's him! I think it's him.'

Wilfrid and Cuthbert ran to him and looked at where he was pointing.

'There! I saw something coming towards the rocks. I'm sure of it.'

They watched and waited, and after a few moments a black shape was propelled onto the landing point by a strong wave. Dunstan trembled.

'Is it...? Is he...?'

Cuthbert took his arm.

'It's a timber, Brother Dunstan, just a large timber. From a boat, I imagine.'

Dunstan stared at it, narrowing his eyes. He strode down towards the landing cove. A little later he reappeared, carrying the timber, which he deposited next to Cuthbert's dwelling. Then he went and began to gather some stones.

'Let's help him, Wilfrid,' Cuthbert said.

All day long they gathered stones and boulders. They built up the walls of Cuthbert's cell, piling the stones together and compacting them with earth and bracken. Every now and then Cuthbert would break into prayer or sing a psalm if the boulder he was carrying was particularly heavy – he seemed to be able to bear almost any weight – but neither Wilfrid nor Dunstan spoke. They worked through the wind and rain until dusk approached and then they rebuilt the roof, pasting rough-hewn timber planks with heather and mud, leaving only a small gap for smoke from the fire to escape through. Now the walls had been built up, the little dwelling seemed even deeper and darker than before, the gloom barely alleviated by the patch of grey sky visible through the hole in the roof. Still, Cuthbert seemed pleased with it. God had delivered them the timber for a reason. Now he could stand fully upright and pray without distraction, he said.

The storm lasted for days. The sun was invisible behind the wall of grey sky, and the light changed from moment to moment, being sometimes as dark as evenfall when they ate their midday meal. Wilfrid tried not to think about returning to the monastery. He couldn't bear to think of putting out to sea again. Yet the thought of remaining on the Farne, where in every direction the sea churned and pounded against the rocks, where every stone and bush was inhabited by malign spirits, made him feel ill.

The dysentery returned. Cuthbert gave him boiled water and ginger to drink, but it didn't help. Each time he had to struggle out of the hut in the night he did not know if he would find his way safely to the latrine that Cuthbert had built. If there was a moon it darted in and out of clouds like a sprite casting misguiding light, and the wind clawed at his cloak trying to tear it from him. When he drank the boiled water that Cuthbert prepared, Dunstan would watch him drink it, and then check the supply of water left in the barrel.

'We must leave tomorrow,' Dunstan said. 'The sea has calmed. I will send Brother Herefrith and Brother Laurence back immediately with more supplies of food and water, and wood for the fire.'

'Go and check the boat,' Cuthbert said. 'See if it needs any repairs. Wilfrid, you stay here with me.'

They watched as Dunstan made his way down the path to the cove. Wilfrid trembled. The notion that he must brave the sea again, alone with Dunstan, and return to the monastery, filled him with a sick dread. He caught hold of a spade lying near Cuthbert's cell and leaned heavily on it, his breath was coming in short gasps, like a wriggling fish snatched from the water.

'This island is a desert,' Cuthbert said. 'Not like our own Lindisfarne. Barren, no well of fresh water, only the seals and birds to talk to. To be a hermit here...well, it's a difficult calling. I fail. I keep failing.' He laughed, a small lonely laugh. 'Sometimes when the seals are singing I go and sing with them and tell myself I am singing the psalms with my brethren in the monastery. I watch for ships, and if one passes I wave. I imagine the seafarers waving back to me, though they are never close enough for me to see.'

Wilfrid struck the ground with the spade. He dug

and dug, not knowing why, turning up clods of stony earth.

'So you mustn't think it's your fault,' Cuthbert went on. 'What happened to Fergus, I mean. I told them they should bring supplies from time to time. And I told Fergus he might come if there was any serious trouble or illness back at the monastery. Fergus was a good monk. He obeyed his prior's instructions.'

Wilfrid flung the spade to the ground and sat down. He wanted to release the burden, let Cuthbert take it on his back, but it clung to him like a limpet to a rock. He didn't know how to explain this to Cuthbert. He didn't know how to talk to him at all. Several times over the last few days Cuthbert had tried to raise the topic of his scarred arms, but Wilfrid had remained silent, unable to voice any explanations or put words to the desolation that besieged him and could be relieved only by his knife. He dug into the earth again, scratching at it with his fingers now, trying to find something to cling to. The earth was hard, the pebbles cut his fingers and broke his nails, but he kept at it, boring into the hollow, till his hands ached and bled.

'I tempted him, I suppose,' Cuthbert said. 'I knew Fergus would worry; he wouldn't let me starve. And I knew too that sooner or later someone would need help. They would come then, and I wouldn't always be alone.'

Wilfrid kept scratching at the soil. It felt colder, damper. He wanted his knife. He could feel it resting against his thigh in the pocket of his habit. He shut his eyes to try and calm himself. Something was simmering inside him, bubbling up; he must not let it boil over, but it was like the sea, beyond his control.

'I hate him,' he said.

'Hate?' Cuthbert's tone was sharp. 'Brother Dunstan, you mean? Wilfrid, hate is sewn in our hearts by the Evil One and must be uprooted like...'

'No, not Brother Dunstan,' Wilfrid said. He stopped digging and made tight fists of his hands.

'Ah,' Cuthbert said after a moment. 'Then you must mean Brother Fergus.'

'He lied to me,' Wilfrid said. 'He said I would get better, and I didn't. He made me get in the boat, and it just made me sicker. And then, then he fell in the sea, and he made it my fault, and now I have no one, and everything's even worse.'

'Wilfrid, look at me.'

Wilfrid shook his head.

'I can't. It's all black, everywhere I look. I have to...'

He needed his knife. He didn't know if he could resist it for another moment. He wanted to scratch, to dig, to scrawl. Cuthbert took his hands. He opened them out and rubbed the dirt away. He pushed up Wilfrid's right sleeve and traced his fingers over the marks on Wilfrid's arm.

'This darkness,' he said. 'It's found its way inside you, crawled into your heart. You must let it out.'

'I've tried. I... It keeps coming back.'

'Then you must let God's light in. The light always defeats darkness.'

Wilfrid pulled his hands away. He didn't understand why Cuthbert couldn't help. He had expelled the demon from Hildmer's wife. Why not from him? It must have grown strong, too strong, even for Cuthbert.

He scratched at the earth again. It was wet.

'There is no light,' he whispered.

'Wilfrid, if you don't pray, if you don't attend the offices, how can you...?'

'I can't.'

'Wilfrid, listen to me. Just sing the psalms. Sing them over and over. They will carve God's word into your heart and let His light in.'

'I can't!' Wilfrid shouted. It hurt his throat. 'Didn't they tell you? I can't sing any more, not since I was sick – not a note. I can't let God's light in.'

Cuthbert took Wilfrid's hands again and wiped the dirt from them. He held them over the little pit that Wilfrid had dug and looked into it. A pool of water had formed there. Cuthbert frowned. He dipped his finger into the water and tasted it.

'Fresh,' he said. 'Like a spring. A miracle.' He dipped his fingers into the water and sprinkled it over Wilfrid's hands. He traced the sign of the cross over his palms.

'If you cannot sing, then you must write,' he said.

Part Two

AD 684

One

ILFRID WROTE. He wrote until his fingers stiffened and could not be clawed away from the quill. He wrote until every bone in his body was rigid with cold and cramp gripped him like a crab's pincers. He must write, Cuthbert had said. He must write until the words of the Gospels, of every psalm, were carved not only on the page before him but in his head and heart as well. Devils and darkness were stayed by the Lord's Word, and writing His Word would bind Wilfrid in His protection as leather binds a book. He buried the knife. He carried an ordinary knife now, used it to sharpen his quill. The quill was his knife and buckler, his sword and shield.

When he wasn't writing he was preparing parchment. His hands became red and raw from soaking and rinsing calf hides, and his skin peeled away like the shavings from the hides when he scraped them clean. Still, Cuthbert was right. The devils had been stayed – mostly. Sometimes at night he would sense the blackness creep up on him again, cold as ice, slithering under his skin. He would hear voices crying, Fergus's spirit out on the sandflats, moaning and wailing with the seals. Then with his fingertips he would trace all the words he had written that day onto his skin, trace them over the thin white scars, the remembrances of his wolf-knife, until the spirit-sound receded, the words sank into his bones and lulled him to sleep.

The season of darkening days had crept up on the brothers again, bringing with it stinging cold and damp. Rumours of plague in southern parts of the kingdom had reached the monastery, and Brother Laurence, who had taken over as infirmarian, was busy preparing a host of tinctures and salves. The younger monks, though, were more preoccupied with the present menace of cold. The scribes huddled at their desks, breathing onto their frozen hands to keep numbness at bay. Wilfrid stretched and rubbed his fingers, grinding life back into them that they might grip the quill steadily. He caught a glimpse of Eadfrith sitting at his own desk at the far end of the scriptorium. He'd been there since Prime, hunched over his manuscript, surrounded by quills and cloths, knives and pumice stones and at least a dozen pots of ink. There were whispers that he was illustrating a Book of Hours commissioned by Ecgfrith King himself as a present for his wife, Queen Iurminburgh.

Eadfrith was a monk apart. His large desk was set in a spacious alcove away from the other scribes. No one other than Dunstan might approach him without permission. Wilfrid knew what the other brothers said: that God worked through Eadfrith's hands, whispered to Eadfrith's fingers, made them to move with the lightness of an angel so that each page, each letter, was filled with God's breath, God's light, God's grace.

Wilfrid pared his quill. He took his measuring stick and pricked tiny holes in the parchment to mark the margins. As he applied the quill to the page a nasty blob of ink gathered in a pool at the top of his letter *B*, while the stem refused to settle into a clean, straight line, but shivered nervously like a blade of grass in the wind. A small *tsk* sounded from above him – Dunstan on patrol again. He saw the twitch in Dunstan's hand, the fingers curving into a fist. Wilfrid took the blotter and knife, cleaned the page and started again.

Again and again he started. That was his pattern. Ink was as difficult to navigate as the sea. It had its own will and would not be mastered. It ran wherever whim took it, above the lines and below, in and out of margins, curling capriciously in wayward streamlets away from the letter it was supposed to form. Sometimes he would get to the end of a page without a single flaw, and just then the quill would tremble, and the ink would gush away from him, plotting its own course, or the tail of a letter would sprout tiny growths just like the pimples that pocked his own chin.

The light was fading now, and soon it would be time for Vespers. The other scribes tidied away their materials. Wilfrid kept writing, hoping to bring the section he was working on to a close. Eadfrith and Dunstan were in the alcove.

'It's ready for binding,' he heard Eadfrith say. 'The illumination is perfectly dry. See the design here. The four crosses must be uniform and evenly spaced so the eye may note an invisible circle surrounding them. Other than that, the cover needs no fine detail, no embellishment. Do you understand? The embellishment will be on the pages inside.'

Wilfrid finished his work and placed his writing implements on a shelf near the door.

'I will see that the binding is carried out as soon as possible,' Dunstan said.

'I suggest you make a beginning at first light,' Eadfrith said. 'The manuscript is expected within days. The king will not tolerate a delay.'

'I do understand the importance of this particular book, Brother Eadfrith.'

'Then you understand more than me, Brother Dunstan, but I have no wish to comprehend the ways of kings and their consorts.'

Wilfrid finished tidying. From outside came the sounds of horses' hooves clomping over the ground and men shouting and laughing. The brothers looked at each other. Dunstan paled.

'Guests, on horseback. Wilfrid, go and see who it is. Quickly.'

Wilfrid hurried to the door. He started. A group of five men, all with swords in their belts. Brother Laurence came running across the cloister, panting and almost tripping over.

'I will fetch Prior Edberht,' he said. 'He will...'

'It's not Prior Edberht I wish to see.'

The man who spoke wore a thick fur cloak. He jumped down from his horse and tossed Laurence the reins.

'Now where is this famed scriptorium that men up and down the kingdom speak of?'

Wilfrid backed into the room.

'It's men,' he said to the two monks. 'With swords. I think it's...'

Dunstan's face was even paler now. Eadfrith grimaced. He stood very straight, head up, his long chin jutting out. The man in the fur cloak swept into the room, followed by two of his retinue who stood guarding the door.

'Well, where is it?'

Eadfrith bowed stiffly.

'Lord, it's not ready yet. We were led to believe we had another week.'

'Show it to me.'

Lord. Only one man other than Christ could be addressed as lord. Wilfrid tried to quell the shake in his knees. Eadfrith stood very straight while Dunstan pointed a trembling finger to the manuscript on the table. The man picked up two quires of the manuscript, one in each hand, glancing from each to the other and frowning and wrinkling his large and very crooked nose.

'Some light for Christ's sake. It's darker than a cave in here.'

'Fetch a candle,' Dunstan said to Wilfrid. 'Quick!'

Wilfrid brought a candle and placed it on the table at a safe distance from the manuscript. The man, the lord, squinting at the parchment, breathed heavily. His breath was beer-filled and crumbs of food nested in his red beard. A long deep scar ran from the side of his broken nose across his cheek. So this was Ecgfrith King, feared throughout Northumbria, the whole land and even lands across the sea. Only that summer he had sent an army across to Ireland, to Brega, and had mercilessly sacked their monasteries and seized many slaves and hostages.

'Closer!' the king said.

Wilfrid edged the candle closer. The light fell over Eadfrith's manuscript, like the early morning sun casting a glint of gold on buttercups. Wilfrid gasped. He knew that Eadfrith worked with inks of all hues, azure and vermillion and even gold leaf. He had caught glimpses of his manuscripts before but had never been this close; close enough to see letters crafted into glorious forms, their spaces filled with colour and light, and worked with such cunning that sometimes the letters deviously shape-shifted to take the head of a snake or some wondrous beast such as Wilfrid had never seen or even heard tell of.

Ecgfrith King snorted and belched loudly.

'Hmm. This then, this writing, it is...colour-filled; quite charming.' He belched again. 'Yes, it may well please the queen but will it bring her what she seeks?'

'It is Holy Writ, lord,' Eadfrith said. 'It brings us all what we seek, if we seek Christ's truth.'

'I know what it is!' The king landed his fist on top of the manuscript. 'You dare presume me ignorant?' He caught Eadfrith by the neck of his habit. 'I may not have my so-called brother's learning and book devotion, but those are not the concerns of a king. Those are the ways of monkish men who have retreated from the business of the world. So my queen will be pleased with this pretty little thing of yours, but I ask you, will it bring her what she seeks?'

He continued to hold Eadfrith, his knuckles pressing hard into his neck. Eadfrith didn't answer. His face was very red; his breathing came in tiny gasps.

'Lord.' A voice from the doorway. Prior Edberht bowed. 'Ecgfrith King is welcome to our holy island. Forgive us. Had we received word of your arrival, we would have been more prepared. Nevertheless, our cellarer is at this moment in the kitchen roasting salmon and onions. We have bread and cheese, and of wine and beer there is plenty.'

The king released Eadfrith. He wiped his hand on his cloak.

'I haven't left the Royal City in search of fish and onions.'

'I understand, lord.' Edberht bowed his head again. 'The manuscript is finished; the binding will not take long. I will ensure it is delivered the moment it is ready.'

The king sat down at the table. He put his head in his hands.

'Tell these others to leave.' He looked at his thegns. 'You too. Wait outside.'

Wilfrid moved the candle away from the manuscript and made to go. The king called him.

'You, fetch some wine, and plenty of it. Now!'

Wilfrid hurried out, took a flagon of wine and a cup from the kitchen and crossed the cloister back to the scriptorium. The king's thegns stood a short distance away, laughing and talking.

'I still don't see how prayer is the solution,' one of them said. 'If you ask me, all that's needed is more pleasing, fresher meat. It's all very well that Iurminburgh is the daughter of some Kentish lord, but she's no spring chicken, and she has a face like a pig's arse.'

The men's laughter trailed after Wilfrid as he went inside, taking care not to spill the wine. The king was seated at the table, his head in his hands.

'Tell me, priest. When will God answer my prayers?'

'Our prayers are continually raised to heaven,' Edberht said. 'But God's time is not our time. We cannot know when...'

The king banged his fist on the table again.

'Then tell me this. How much land have I granted you brothers for the building of your monasteries? Hmm? Who provided you with the lead to replace that miserable straw roof on your church? How many hides of cattle have I had stripped to fatten your scriptorium?'

'The king has been most generous.'

'Then where is my reward from God? Where is my *ætheling*, my heir? The queen spends her days in prayer. She sleeps at night with holy relics tied to her stomach, yet still she fails to quicken. She asks for a holy book that she might be accompanied by prayers at all times, and when I come to fetch it, it is not ready.'

'Forgive us, lord. As I've said...'

Wilfrid stepped forward slowly, as if he were treading barefoot over briars, and placed the wine on the table.

'I have listened to you monks long enough,' the king said. 'And given you enough of what is mine. Even my first wife I put aside at the behest of the church. Who knows? She might not have proved barren, had I put her to the test, but no, no, I paid heed to that pompous bishop of yours and his decree that her vow of perpetual virginity be honoured.'

'I believe Bishop Wilfrid was concerned lest a...a coerced concession of chastity would draw down divine retribution.'

The king spat on the floor.

'Well, your erstwhile bishop failed to reckon with my retribution.'

The king stood up suddenly, and with the speed of a hare turned around and drew his sword, making whirling movements with it in the air. Wilfrid shrieked and ducked as the king affected to bring the sword down on his head.

'I could have killed you then,' he said. 'It's easily known you monks have no training in battle, sneaking up in such a clumsy fashion. Well, what are you waiting for?' The king's sword glinted in the candlelight and for an instant the scar on his cheek seemed to flash. 'Pour me some wine.'

Wilfrid shook as he poured out a large measure of wine. The jug almost slipped from his sweating hands, but he managed not to spill any. The king laughed as he sat down again, his legs splayed either side of the bench.

'A little girl would have done better, but I suppose those are in short supply on this holy island.' He drank deeply, gulping loudly. He banged the cup on the table. 'More!'

Wilfrid poured again. The king leaned towards him and grinned.

'I don't suppose I can persuade you to leave all this behind, eh? What do you say, come and be a warrior in the service of Ecgfrith King?' He leaned closer. The gaps between his teeth were deep pits in his mouth. 'Ever seen the painted body of a Pict? You monks like to battle devils, don't you? Well, I'll tell you, you haven't battled a devil till you've skewered a Pict on your sword.'

Wilfrid froze. A warrior. Like...like his father, fighting the enemy and listening to the songs of the scop in the mead hall. He hadn't thought of his father in a long time, and it unsettled something in him now.

Edberht coughed.

'This is Wilfrid, lord. He is an oblate, gifted by his father, you know, Raymund of Medilwong. He is bound to the monastery.'

The king laughed. Heartily.

'You didn't think I was serious? I need strong warriors, not trembling wraiths. Wait, Raymund's boy, you said?' He pulled at his beard. 'But I thought... Mmm, I remember now. Perhaps children don't always bring the solace they should. Better off where he is. More wine! Still, to think that a king's thegn should have an heir while the king does not.'

Wilfrid refilled the cup. An heir. Was he his father's heir? He remembered now the child swaddled at his mother's breast, though he could not call up his mother's face. That whole other life seemed a distant and unlikely dream.

'God will not leave the kingdom without a king,' Edberht said.

The king banged his fist on the table again.

'You put your life in peril, priest, if you are referring to that...that book-loving, quill-wielding, monkish impostor on Iona. Aldfrith!' He spat again. 'I'd wager my fortress that not even his own mother could say for certain who his father was.'

'No, lord.' Edberht shuffled from one foot to the other. 'I merely meant...'

'What more does God ask of me?' the king said. 'I have endowed monasteries, built churches and worshipped at the shrines of the saints, and still, nothing.' He gazed into the cup. 'Not even with a slave girl.'

'My lord has been generous,' Edberht said.

'And will be more generous,' the king said. 'You'll see. Once the queen is fat with child, I'll bestow more gifts. Your hermit may not be a hermit for much longer.'

'Lord?'

'A bishopric in return for his powerful prayers.'

'Father Cuthbert does not demand reward for his prayers, and would not seek the episcopacy, even if there were a vacancy, which there is not.'

'But you'll agree it's in your interest that one of your own be made bishop?'

'Well...'

'And you'll agree that Cuthbert is a man to whom certain people, certain stubborn people, beyond our borders, might listen?'

Edberht didn't answer. He took the jug from Wilfrid and poured the last of the wine. The king finished it in one gulp.

'You see, perhaps there is something more that God requires of me: to complete the task my father began, to succeed where he failed.'

'I see.' Edberht frowned. 'And Father Cuthbert?'

'Is needed as bishop. My sister, Abbess Ælfflæd, will send him word. She is desirous of holy converse – you know the sort of thing. She may be an abbess, but she's also daughter and sister to a king. She'll surely persuade him. Still, no harm to send one of your own as well. Whom does he listen to?'

'Father Cuthbert listens to all who entreat him, but...'

'No buts, priest. Whom does he favour? Whom will he hear?'

Edberht shook his head.

'None, lord. There is no one, not since we lost Brother Fergus.'

The king snatched the cup from the table and hurled it across the room. It hit a shelf and sent some scraps of parchment scattering to the floor.

'Find someone!'

'Yes, yes, lord,' Edberht said.

'And ensure the queen has her book before two days have passed.'

'Yes, lord.'

The king banged the door behind him. Edberht looked at Wilfrid strangely. Wilfrid picked up the scraps of parchment from the ground. When he had finished tidying them away, Edberht was still looking at him, tugging at his beard thoughtfully, as though an idea had occurred to him.

Two

FATHER CUTHBERT, *most reverend brother and servant of God, from Ælfflæd, unworthy servant of the house of Whitby, greetings in our Lord.*

I hear you still persevere in devotion to Christ in your hermitage, that island desert, where, like your forefathers in dry deserts, you fight the good fight and battle with the demons of darkness, drawing nearer each day to the Source of all light, wisdom and truth. My prayers and the prayers of all the holy men and women of Whitby are with you constantly, that you may be sustained by God's grace.

Yet circumstances compel me to disturb your holy and solemn contemplation. There are matters of great consequence, spiritual and temporal, on which I would speak with you. These are difficult times. Plague and pestilence have arrived yet again on our shores and stalk the villages, like wolves circling a lamb. The people are bereft of a shepherd, with one bishop in exile and the other, alas, incapacitated by those ravages which age may sometimes inflict on the mind. Some fear another war, as well as famine. And there are other matters of state which stir anxiety in the hearts of those who wish to see a peaceful and prosperous future secured.

I entreat you most earnestly to cross the sea and meet me on Coquet Island, which lies at an equal distance from my abbey and your Farne retreat. Though the season is turning I would not let these matters rest until spring. God willing, we will keep vigil together on All Hallows' Eve. I have sent word to the abbot on Coquet Island and trust in Him who is All-Powerful to deliver us safely there.

May the grace of heaven wrap you in its protection, dear friend,

Ælfflæd, Abbess of Whitby

Wilfrid read the abbess' letter aloud, just as Edberht had instructed. Cuthbert stood immobile, a tall, thin shadow, his face grey as the gloom of his cell. Wilfrid was sure his own face was grey too. The crossing to the Farne had been turbulent, but at least the sea had not threatened to take them, to swallow them whole as it had swallowed Fergus six years before. Wilfrid had taken his turn at rowing, together with Herefrith and Laurence, thinking of Fergus with every stroke. Fergus was with the saints now, of course, with God, in Paradise. But Wilfrid could not rid himself of the sense of a presence, some shadow beneath the surface of the water, swimming alongside them.

He still wondered why he'd been chosen for the task. He had overheard Edberht muttering to Herefrith, just before they set out. 'This may be the chance for the lad to prove himself. We shall see if the ties between the two can play a part.'

Herefrith had looked as if he might object, but Edberht added, 'Wilfrid is to tell him that *all* of our community on Lindisfarne wishes him to heed the entreaties of the abbess. You will say nothing to cast doubt on that.'

After Wilfrid had read the letter, Cuthbert knelt at his altar and prayed for a time. Then he turned to the monks and spoke wearily.

'Very well. We will set sail for Coquet Island at first light.'

They were exhausted when they reached Coquet Island. Wilfrid's hands were blistered from the oars. His back ached, and his legs were so cramped he could hardly climb out of the boat. Herefrith and Laurence seemed equally worn, and only managed the barest response to the guest master's greeting.

'The abbess arrived yesterday with one of her holy women,' the guest master said. 'She would speak with you before Vespers if you are willing.'

Cuthbert shook his head.

'We are in need of rest after our journey, and I must spend some time in prayer before I speak with her.'

'Certainly,' the guest master said. 'But you will surely take some food before you retire?'

'My brothers will eat,' Cuthbert said. 'They are weary from rowing and are in need of nourishment. Brother Herefrith and Brother Laurence go to the mainland tomorrow to preach in the villages and seek out those in need of healing. I will fast. There is much to think on.'

They slept in two small cells, Herefrith and Laurence in one, Cuthbert and Wilfrid in the other. Cuthbert's breathing was heavy and tight. Wilfrid shifted about on his pallet. Despite his exhaustion, sleep would not come. He had not left Lindisfarne in over six years, and lying in a bed that was not his own, away from the rhythms of his own monastery, made him feel as though he was standing in shifting sands, unable to pull himself to solid ground. He wondered how long they would spend here, what the abbess might have to say, and why Edberht had thought he should be the one to deliver her letter to Cuthbert. He listened to the sounds of the island, the whirling of the wind and sea, the cry of an owl as it swooped on its prey. The last thing he heard was music – not the chanting of the monks, but the strains of a lyre, the beating of a drum, though surely that must have been the singing of the wind, or a dream as sleep claimed him at last.

The following morning Wilfrid walked the island. He had expected Coquet to be like the Farne. Indeed, birds of all kinds teemed through the air, and seals popped up from beneath the water – he saw a mother and a baby pup on the rocks at the shore – but though they were surrounded at all times by the sea, the mainland was very close. He could just make out the beach market with people coming and going, gathering around small fires, selling and bartering their wares.

He thought he could hear music, the lilt of a harp, the singing of a scop. He listened for a while, trying to make out the words, but as soon as he felt he could grasp something, the sound of the waves crashing on the shore drowned it out. Occasionally he heard applause and bursts of laughter. At other times he seemed to hear a song lilt and fade away mournfully, and he remembered how a skilful scop could draw tears from the eyes of the most hardened warrior, or could cause the whole company to hold their bellies in fits of guffawing, though often Wilfrid had had no understanding of what they were laughing at.

When he pulled his eyes away from the mainland he saw her. A woman in a dark cloak with a long, white veil waving about in the wind. She stood by the rocks, watching the seal pup suckling on its mother, its small white body pressed into her huge mass of grey. She was too close, this woman – this nun. The mother seal had surely seen her. Yes, the mother shook off her pup, lifted her head, then her entire expanse, and cried out. The nun started back and turned.

She was a young woman, Wilfrid saw, a little older them him, certainly, but not old enough to be an abbess. She must be the companion. As she walked towards him he raised his arm to give the customary blessing, uncertain if holy women observed such a custom or had practices of their own. She glanced at him, a sudden piercing glance, and then, with barely a nod, she was gone. There was a sting in that look, like a slap across the face. Wilfrid rubbed his cheek and tried to remember where he had felt it before.

They gathered in the refectory for the midday meal. Wilfrid and Cuthbert stood with the monks behind long benches at either side of the hall, waiting for the other guests to arrive. It was a dark day. Lighted candles were scattered over the table, illuminating loaves of bread, freshly baked with steam wafting about them, platters of cheese and eggs, dishes of onions and parsnips, slices of apple and cubes of honey, jugs of beer and wine.

Eventually the door opened, and the guest master led the nuns in. The older of the two wore a large gold cross studded with garnets, hanging from a thick gold chain. She walked stiffly, her back very straight. The younger nun, the one Wilfrid had seen earlier, kept her head down. As she took her place at the table a trace of a scowl crossed her face, and she seemed to chew the inside of her lip.

The abbot said a long Grace, giving thanks for the food and for the clement weather which had ensured the safe arrival of their esteemed guests, Abbess Ælfflæd and Sister Meredith of the great abbey at Whitby, and Father Cuthbert and Brother Wilfrid of the Holy Island of Lindisfarne, who honoured the brethren with their presence, and who, he hoped, would find the humble hospitality of Coquet Island to their satisfaction.

They ate in silence, listening to a reading from the

Book of Samuel. The lector had a strong, melodious voice, and when he spoke the words of God's call to Samuel, the hall was filled with his cries. The abbess helped herself liberally to food and wine, but Cuthbert declined everything. The other nun, Sister Meredith, her eyes firmly downcast, sat very still. Her face was pale, with some thin white lines across both cheeks.

'You are even leaner than when we last met,' the abbess said to Cuthbert when the meal was finished and the dishes had been cleared away. 'I had not thought such a thing possible.' She looked at his tonsure. Wispy strands of hair curled below his ears and down his neck. 'And, you'll forgive me for saying so, just a little unkempt for the former prior of the greatest monastery in the north-east and the spiritual descendant of Bishop Aidan.'

Cuthbert smiled, a small smile through cracked lips and worn eyes.

'It's true we both served the brethren of Lindisfarne and both made our dwelling on that lonesome island for love of Christ, but where Blessed Aidan succeeded, I fail. God has made known the greatness of Aidan's merits, and I am but an insect in his shadow.'

'False humility does not become you, Father Cuthbert,' the abbess said sharply. 'The many wonders that Aidan of blessed memory worked are well known, but still more have been attributed to you.'

Cuthbert shook his head and waved his hand. His nails had grown very long, Wilfrid noticed, and were brittle as shells.

'Brother Herefrith and Brother Laurence send their greetings,' Cuthbert said. 'They were sorry to have missed you. They left at first light.'

'I understand they have gone to preach in the villages,' the abbess said. 'The people are in need of God's Word and healing hands. This plague has taken many. They come to our monastery for help. Some I can heal with herbs and cures; most I cannot.'

'Brother Laurence has medicaments with him,' Cuthbert said. 'He learned much from Brother Fergus and has made careful study of the medicine books in our library.'

'But the people need soul comfort too. They fear the Lord has deserted them. They need a guide, someone who can bring comfort and healing, who will restore their faith. I'm right, am I not, Wilfrid?'

'Yes, yes,' Wilfrid said, startled.

He had not expected the abbess to address him. He knew this was his opportunity to say more, but he couldn't think of anything.

'Bishop Tunberht...' Cuthbert said.

'Is stricken by the ailments of an aged mind,' the abbess said. 'He cannot minister.'

'I don't believe Bishop Tunberht is much older than me,' Cuthbert said.

The abbess leaned back a little.

'The king tells me the bishop himself acknowledges his weakness. The king says Tunberht wishes to retire.'

Cuthbert was silent for a while. Wilfrid glanced over at the young nun. She flashed a look back at him, quick as lightning spark, then gazed downwards again. But Wilfrid's memory had been ignited. Those startlingly blue eyes, the long dark eyelashes, the scars. He was sure he recognised her.

'There is news from Armagh,' the abbess said, jolting Wilfrid from his thoughts.

'Oh?' Cuthbert said.

'The church there is willing to conform to the true practice of Easter at long last, praise God for it.'

'Well, that was a victory won at a terrible cost. I'm told the war in Ireland was vicious and blood-soaked. And uncalled for.' Cuthbert tapped the table with his fingers. 'Is it true the king has made noise about an assault on the North?'

'So I believe,' the abbess said. 'Of course, they too continue to rebel against the ways of the Church, with particular regard to the celebration of Easter at the time appointed by the pope. My brother would wish to bring them into the Roman fold.'

'But it ought not be done violently. Persuasion worked in the past, for the most part. And even then, the divisions it caused – brother against brother...'

'Sister against sister. The wounds are not yet healed.' The abbess leaned forward and spoke more quietly. 'The king needs a steady hand and a wise counsellor. I have often urged restraint, but Whitby is some distance from Bamburgh, and, of course, he does not pay heed to the exhortations of a mere woman.'

'There are surely others in the *Witan* who can advise, as well as the brethren at Lindisfarne,' Cuthbert said.

'He listens to Raymund only. He made him warmaster for the campaign in Ireland, and since the successes there he has heard no other voices.'

Wilfrid started. Raymund. She must mean his father. Had his father become the king's warmaster, his chief advisor? For a brief moment he saw his father again, out in the yard demonstrating his battle skills: plunge with the scramasax, slice with the spear, trick your opponent into moving the wrong way, fell them and gut them. A warrior, and yet he had gifted his son to the monastery. Wilfrid blinked the memory away and listened again to the abbess. She had reached across the table and cupped Cuthbert's hand in both of hers.

'Hear me, Father Cuthbert. Many years ago you fought alongside my father, Oswiu King. You defended him in the shield-wall.'

'That was in another life, Ælfflæd.'

Wilfrid frowned. Cuthbert a warrior? It hardly seemed possible.

'There were certain tasks he entrusted to you,' the abbess said. 'Delicate negotiations only you could bring to fruition. Ecgfrith knows that. And when finally you set aside the service to the earthly king in favour of the High King of Heaven, you steered away from that conflict that rent asunder the family of Christ; you forged a middle path, accepting the new ways without condemning those who adhered to the old. Even now you have the ears of those who practise the Roman ways and those who still follow old ways. And so Ecgfrith wishes you to be bishop. He believes the stubborn brethren of the north will listen to you. More importantly, I believe, *he* will listen to you.'

Cuthbert shook his head.

'I was called hence from all that, to the hermitage, away from the worldly ways of men and kings. I dare not repudiate the voice of the Lord.'

The abbess pursed her lips. She released Cuthbert's hand.

'Then perhaps you will at least seek God's guidance on what He requires of you now.' She sighed. 'We have kept our brother and sister here for too long. They are young and ought not be burdened with these tedious affairs.'

She signalled to her companion, who stood up and left. After a moment Wilfrid too got up. Before he reached the door the abbess had begun to speak again.

'There is one other matter,' he heard her say softly.

He left the door slightly ajar when he went out. There was no sign of Abbess Ælfflæd's companion. He stood at the door and listened, wondering if the abbess would mention his father again. He could just make out her low tones, speaking urgently now.

'My brother has a proud heart. He believes as king he is favoured by God, that God will aid his hand, whether in battle or...or elsewhere. Even now. But this second marriage is in its tenth year. The queen, as you must know, wears a girdle with hairs from the head of St Oswald about her waist. Around her neck is the reliquary taken from Bishop Wilfrid with holy relics from Rome. She carries a Book of Hours made by Brother Eadfrith, though she cannot read. A wise woman and priest attend to her daily. She eats stinging nettle and red clover, yet...'

Wilfrid turned around quickly. He thought he heard something, the swish of a cloak, but no one was there. He leaned to the door again.

'I have wondered about God's plan in this matter,' the abbess said. 'About how He wishes to order the future of our earthly kingdom, about how He wishes us to help.'

'Us?'

'The king has seen over forty winters,' she went on. 'He has fought battles, some bravely and gloriously, and others – perhaps less so. What I mean is, if he were less fortunate the next time...well...I fear the consequences.'

'A campaign such as the one he led in Ireland would surely bring down God's judgement.'

'Again, I say we must discover what God asks of us, how we may ensure that the future of the kingdom follows God's path. I have had many anxious nights. I have prayed. I have asked Him Who knows everything to reveal to me an answer, to show me who might lead us along His path, and then I remembered, though I know there are those who cast crooked comments on his lineage, and others who damn him for his constancy to the old ways, but, but I remembered...'

There was another sound, this time of boots crunching over stones. Wilfrid turned and saw the younger nun moving swiftly away. The last words he caught were Cuthbert's.

'You remembered that you have another brother,' he said to the abbess. 'A brother no less than the other.'

Wilfrid followed the nun to the beach. He was thinking about her face, the scars. She stood close to the water, looking out to sea. At least he knew her name now. Meredith. He stopped a few paces from her, unsure whether she remembered him or not. The wind whipped up a few stray raindrops onto her face. They trailed down over the pale white marks which stretched across her cheeks. She had changed a little, was older, of course. The wild, matted hair was pressed firmly beneath her veil. The filth on her hands and face had long been washed away. The writhing creature was stilled, the wounds healed. But the hardness was still there, set like stone on her face.

'You've been following me,' she said.

'No, I haven't.'

He heard his raised tone, a defiant child who knows he has been discovered.

'You've been watching me and following me, spying, like you were spying on the abbess and prior.'

'I don't know what you think you saw, but if you saw me, then you must have been spying yourself.' Wilfrid sat down on a rock. He picked up a stick and started to write in the sand. 'I remember you,' he said.

She said nothing for a moment. He thought she might leave, but she stayed there next to him looking out towards the mainland.

'You're no scribe, then,' she said after a while. 'The tail on that *L* is far too long, the curve on the *E* is crooked.'

Wilfrid felt the heat rise in his cheeks. She was as bad as Dunstan. He stood up straight. He was taller than her – just.

'I work in the scriptorium. I copy psalms and letters. I even copied out the letter your Abbess Ælfflæd sent the prior.'

She smiled. Or was it a sneer?

'I remember you,' he said again. 'I remember the prior said you were bound to your husband.'

'I have no husband but Christ.'

'And your other husband?'

She stood before him, her blue eyes flashing like tongues of fire.

'I see you are still no more than a stupid boy, asking stupid questions about matters you will never understand.'

'Perhaps I understand more than you think. Perhaps I understand why the abbess chose you as her companion.'

She frowned.

'Per...perhaps she thinks you need to see the prior,' he said. 'That you need to be healed again. Why else would she bring you here?'

She stepped forward. The scars on her face glowed white through her red cheeks. She came to him. She slapped him hard across the face.

'I didn't ask to be healed,' she said.

She walked away quickly, her veil flapping like a sail behind her. Wilfrid put his hand to his cheek, felt the stinging heat seep into his fingers. It was like drinking warm wine in the winter snow.

Three

ALL HALLOWS' EVE CAME. The day was dark and cloud-filled. The sea battered the rocks and spat up all manner of things onto the shore: rotting driftwood, torn segments of fishing nets, a sailor's boot, a dead seal pup. Cuthbert and Abbess Ælfflæd spent the day together in discussion. Wilfrid went to look at the manuscripts in the monastery's library. A rustling noise in a corner of the room disturbed him. He thought at first it must be a rat and looked around to see if there was a broom with which he might kill it, but then he heard a frustrated sigh and the sound of a veil being swept back. She stood in front of him. Meredith.

'It's too dark to read here,' she said. 'And there are no candles.'

Wilfrid hesitated.

'I'll fetch one. If you like.'

He ran to the guesthouse and returned with a lighted candle, holding his hand close to the flame to prevent it from going out. As he passed her the light his hand brushed against hers. Her skin was rough, like parchment.

'Perhaps they don't keep candles here,' he said. 'For fear of fire. Brother Dunstan says there can be no forgiveness for starting a fire in a library. Setting fire to a holy manuscript is like setting fire to a thousand prayers. The devil would greatly rejoice to have a foolish brother with a candle do his work for him.'

'Then I must be careful not to let the devil near my hands,' she said. She took the candle and went over to one of the shelves.

'Oh, I didn't mean,' Wilfrid said. 'Brother Dunstan – he has a great fear of candles – I only meant...'

She walked along the bookshelf, one hand lifting up manuscripts, the other holding the candle. Every now and then she let out a click of annoyance through her teeth.

'I'm sorry,' Wilfrid said eventually. 'For my words to you. I... The devil entered my mouth. He... I mean, I let him in.'

She gave a barely perceptible nod and held the candle towards him.

'Will you hold it?' she said. 'So I may search for the volume I need. Your Brother Dunstan is right. It would be a great sin to destroy a manuscript.'

He followed her, holding the candle as she searched among the piles of books and documents. Eventually she pulled an unbound manuscript from a pile.

'Here it is.'

Wilfrid read the words on the title page.

Vita Sancti Martini

Sulpicius Severus

'The abbess has asked for permission to borrow it,' she said. 'So I may make a copy. Do you know it?'

Wilfrid shook his head.

'I've read St Patrick's *Confessio*,' he said. 'And Pope Gregory's *Dialogi*.'

'Mmm. The *Dialogues* are fine writing.'

She sat at a table and gestured for him to sit next to her. She opened the book, and they read a section together.

'He is dead, I believe,' she said after a while.

'St Martin?'

'*Him.*' She turned over the page carefully. 'Hildmer. My *other* husband. In that barbaric war in Ireland last year. A fitting end.' She sighed heavily. 'Abbess Ælfflæd says bitterness is a sin beloved of the Devil, for it was his first sin and caused his heart to become heavy with jealous rage and full of evil design. Still, I am not sorry he is dead.'

'I suppose then you were able to go to a holy house, as you wished.'

She didn't answer. He watched her finger move slowly across the page, as if caressing each word.

'What's that word?' Wilfrid asked.

He put his finger next to hers. She laughed softly.

'It's a mistake. That's what it is. Poor scribe. He's written *camydem* instead of *chlamydem*. It means cloak. Perhaps he was tired or half-blind from copying.'

'Or it could be a manuscript demon,' Wilfrid said. 'Brother Dunstan says they are legion. He says they inhabit my hand as if it were the bowels of hell itself.'

They both laughed.

'I have a good hand,' she said. 'But I write too quickly. I am forever leaving words out and having to insert them above the line afterwards. It's so...so ugly.'

'There were some insertions in Abbess Ælfflæd's letter to Father Cuthbert,' Wilfrid said.

'Yes. The abbess suffers from attacks of ague. It cramps her fingers and she cannot write, so she dictates the work to be done.'

'Then you wrote the letter?'

'Yes. I do much of her writing, and other tasks. She trusts me.' She looked up. 'You're not stupid, you know. I shouldn't have said that.'

Wilfrid was glad of the dim light. He hoped it would conceal the rush of heat in his face.

'Oh, look. There's another mistake,' he said, pointing to the page, and again their fingers brushed. 'But you learned to write very quickly. You've been in the convent for only a year.'

She shook her head.

'It's been longer than that. He put me aside.'

'I see. Like Ecgfrith King and his first wife. But Father Cuthbert said...'

'I could not be...pleasing to him. I could not, and he hated me for it. Then word came that Cuthbert had gone into exile on the Farne. So, he put me aside, gave out that I was barren and sent me to Whitby. He said I was as much a wife to him as a dead dog.' She made no effort to conceal the bitterness clinging to her tongue.

'Your Father Cuthbert should have listened to me back then, but men must ever believe they know what's best. At least now I may do things which are pleasing to *me*: copying, writing. One day I'll write a *Vita* myself. You'll see.'

'Then, I'm not sorry either,' Wilfrid said. 'I'm not sorry your husband is dead.'

She took her hand away from the book and brought it lightly to his cheek. He turned his face and pressed his lips against her palm, but barely had time to register the taste of her skin. She jumped up, snatching her hand away as though she had been bitten. Then she grabbed the manuscript, pressed it to her breast and ran out.

That evening they kept vigil in honour of the saints and holy dead. They prayed for all the blessed departed, kings, queens, bishops, brothers, sisters, priests; the lector read from a list that went on and on. Wilfrid shifted from foot to foot. His stomach pained him, his bowels strained. When the name Fergus was called he could bear it no longer and rushed out to relieve himself.

He was returning to the church when he saw Cuthbert coming towards him. They walked in silence to the beach. The moon was bright; Wilfrid could see over to the shore on the mainland. Cuthbert removed his clothes and went into the water.

Wilfrid waited, listening for footsteps, for the flapping of a cloak or veil, but the only sounds were of the wind and sea and Cuthbert singing the psalm.

Salvum me fac Deus quoniam intraverunt aquae

usque ad animam meam.

After a while he came out, shivering and trembling. Wilfrid helped him dress. He tied Cuthbert's cloak tightly and pulled the hood over his head. Cuthbert sat down heavily on the sand.

'God has not answered me,' he said. 'He sends me dreams, visions. I have seen devils dancing in a fire around a great throne. I have seen the pustule-ridden bodies of the sick and the souls of the dying. I have seen war and famine, pestilence and death.'

Wilfrid took off his own cloak and wrapped it around Cuthbert's shoulders.

'Perhaps the Farne has clouded your vision,' he said. 'Perhaps God called you to this island so you might see things differently.'

Cuthbert smiled, a small, grim smile.

'Did they tell you to say that?'

Wilfrid sighed.

'Well, yes. Prior Edberht told me what to say. I'm not good with words of my own.'

'God called me into exile. He called me to be a hermit.'

'But everyone wants you to be bishop. The abbess, Prior Edberht, the brethren, the people, even Ecgfrith King. They say God is calling you back.'

Cuthbert shook his head.

'On the Farne every moment is a prayer, the psalms falling like water from my lips day and night. I have enclosed myself in the cell. The air is thin there. The veil that covers the spirit world falls away, and I know God's presence in a way I cannot know it elsewhere. These days I keep even the shutters closed, keep all else out, but, but...'

'But what?'

'Sometimes there are voices. From outside.'

'Voices? You mean visitors' voices?'

'No. Other voices.'

'What do they say?'

'They call me from my cell, to look out towards Lindisfarne, towards Bamburgh. Once, at sunset, I looked over to the fortress of the Royal City, shining purple, pink and gold. The Temple of Jerusalem was not so splendid, nor the gardens of Paradise, nor the gates of heaven itself. I saw it as it was back in the time of my service to Oswiu King, when we plotted stratagems in the Great Hall and debated treaties with the enemy. The sight of Bamburgh was a picture painted by the arch-fiend himself, I believe. I shut myself back in my cell, implored the protection of God and St Aidan.'

'But what if the voices are right? What if it's not the devil? What if God is calling you back?'

'What do you say, Wilfrid?'

The moon went in and the sky darkened. Wilfrid stood up. He was seized by night and cold. He no longer cared about this mission that Prior Edberht had sent him on, about Cuthbert returning, about the future of the monastery. He couldn't stop himself from looking to the mainland, couldn't stop himself from listening for her, watching for her, waiting for her.

'I don't hear God's voice,' he said. 'I don't know what He wants. For you or me.'

'Wilfrid, He wants what He has always wanted for you – to be a monk, to give your life to Him. You were chosen for this purpose; dedicated for it. How often must I say this?'

Wilfrid shook his head.

'I don't hear God's voice. I pray, I meditate, I write, I would sing if I could. But I don't hear His voice. I don't know if He really chose me. I don't know what brought me to Lindisfarne.'

Wilfrid closed his eyes. He tried to picture his home. Medilwong. He could scarcely remember it now, though he could recall the furze and heather, purple and yellow, on Wulfstan's Hill, and a wide gushing river that raced down towards the village. It had been nine winters and more since they had come for him – Fergus and Dunstan, like eagles swooping out of the sky to snatch a mouse – and he had never quite fathomed what had brought them. He opened his eyes again. Cuthbert was trying to get up but was shivering so much that he almost fell forward into the sand. Wilfrid caught him.

'It was God's plan,' Cuthbert said. 'You must realise that. As soon as I heard, I knew – I must help poor Rowena – and God showed me the way.'

Rowena. His mother's name. Something in Wilfrid shifted. A worm, wriggling, squirming, trying to dig its way out.

'I think perhaps it is this place that has clouded my vision,' Cuthbert said. 'I believe I must return to the Farne, shut myself away in my cell and listen to what God wants.'

Wilfrid pulled at the neck of his habit. It was scratching his skin. He wanted to tear it off.

'What do you mean you knew you must help poor Rowena? What did God show you?'

Cuthbert sighed.

'Why, He showed me my very own circumstance, of course – opened my memory. Just as Blessed Aidan was sent to me as a child, I must now send for you.'

'Aidan?'

'Yes,' Cuthbert said. 'When the devil had infected me, body and soul, Aidan healed me. I remember telling you that before.'

Wilfrid remembered now too. The man on the magnificently caparisoned horse, the figure in dazzling white, the angel who made a poultice for Cuthbert's wounded body and who comforted his suffering soul. Blessed Aidan. But he couldn't see what that had to do with him or his mother.

Cuthbert gestured towards the monastery.

'We must go back now, Wilfrid. It's as I've always told you. You were gifted to the monastery, like others before you; like the abbess, in fact. I remember telling you that once too. Come now.'

Wilfrid stepped forward. He stood in front of Cuthbert, his back to the monastery. His voice shook.

'But it was my parents who dedicated me. And you said God showed *you* what must be done. What was done?'

Cuthbert stretched out his hand to Wilfrid.

'Let me have your arm, Wilfrid. I have need of a staff.'

Wilfrid gave him his arm, tried not to flinch.

'Will you answer me?' he said.

Cuthbert nodded, though he did not meet Wilfrid's eye. They moved slowly towards the monastery.

'Rowena sent word to me after the trouble. It was simple, as I said. God showed me the way. You must come to us, not just for old times' sake but for your own sake. And so I sent for you.'

'Wait.' Wilfrid stopped. Too many thoughts were chasing around his head, like a bucketful of eels, and he could not catch them all. He was only now beginning to realise what Cuthbert meant. 'You *sent* for me? It was *your* idea that I should be brought to the monastery?'

Cuthbert pressed his fingers tightly around Wilfrid's arm.

'It was God's idea. I was merely the vessel through which He communicated, and it saved...'

'And my mother? Old times' sake?'

'But surely you knew already?' He held onto Wilfrid even more tightly. 'Rowena is my sister, my family.'

Wilfrid stopped. He wanted to shake Cuthbert's hand off, wanted to run, to breathe. Cuthbert was drinking in all the air around him.

'No,' he said. 'No. That doesn't make sense.'

'Rowena is much younger than me, of course, and since I was brought up with foster parents I could never be a brother to her as I would have wanted, but I had a responsibility to her, and to you. We are kin, Wilfrid. Of course, it would not do to dwell on this in the monastery where all brothers are equal – indeed, I feared the other boys, even some of the monks, would resent it were I seen to show you favouritism based on family ties. But surely your mother must have explained this to you?'

'No,' Wilfrid said again.

Nobody had explained anything. All he could remember were long silences and empty eyes and heads turning away from him as he approached, as if there was something unspeakable in the air.

Cuthbert leaned even more heavily on Wilfrid, but Wilfrid shook him off.

'Then it was your idea, not God's, not my parents'. Yours. You thinking you know what's best. And no one spoke to me of...of anything – not even you. You didn't give a second thought to me, to what I wanted. Nothing mattered to you except getting more recruits, more *slaves* for your precious monastery!'

Cuthbert tried to stand fully straight, but he seemed to bend like a tree in the wind.

'Wilfrid, you are losing your reason. Don't you remember?'

'I never wanted to be a monk. I wasn't called. I don't understand things, I can't sing, can't do anything right, not even as a scribe, and...and I don't want to try any more.'

Somewhere behind him the loud groan of a door opening sounded across the field. The monks were filing out of the church. The two nuns came out first. He stared at Meredith, willed her to look at him, prayed that she would see him, that she would walk towards him. He kept praying, even while her head remained bent, her back to him as she headed to the guesthouse. When he saw the door close he turned to face Cuthbert.

Cuthbert had raised his hand. He pointed a long, bony finger at Wilfrid, the fingernail brittle and yellowing.

'Wilfrid, you will never speak like this again. You have been redeemed, blessed by God, yet you throw His blessings away like soiled water. When you return to Lindisfarne you will lie prostrate before the community, confess your sin and accept the punishment Prior

Edberht imposes on you.'

Cuthbert seemed suddenly taller, his back more straight. He removed Wilfrid's cloak from his shoulders and slapped it into Wilfrid's hands. Wilfrid tied the cloak roughly about him. A cold wind flapped at it, threatening to tear it away, but Wilfrid was hot. He could feel fire in his cheeks, his belly, his feet. It raged through him. He turned from Cuthbert and ran to the beach.

A pale dawn was rising. He looked across to the mainland. Somewhere over there, hidden in the hills, was Medilwong, his family. The longing for home surged in him, drove him forward, brought him to the monks' currach. Behind him a voice shouted his name. He kept his eye on the mainland, didn't look back. It wasn't very far, and the sea was very calm. He would count out the strokes of the oars as he rowed. He would keep counting and ignore Cuthbert calling across the water. He would not fall prey to the spirits of the sea. He dragged the boat into the water and pushed off. He wrapped his hands around the rough grainy oars. He rowed.

Four

ULFSTAN'S HILL. The river in full flood. Deep and black, swelling like the sea, it raced down the slope, a maddened creature. Wilfrid was tired, and hunger beset him like a wild dog. His limbs ached with cold, with stiffness; his feet were blistered and covered in sores. Still, it could not be far off now. He imagined his mother looking up to Wulfstan's Hill. She would spy him from a long way off and come running to greet him, arms outstretched. There would be a blazing fire, a pig roasting on a spit, steam from freshly baked bread, a mattress, thick and straw-filled.

These thoughts had kept him company as he'd journeyed over the last few days, stumbling from village to settlement, trying to find his way. When people saw his monk's habit they offered him food – even shelter for the night – and told him of their ailments: a child's club foot, a brother's fever, a poxed mother-in-law who had been sent to die in a hut some distance away. In one village he had been set upon, and men had raked through his pockets, looking for tinctures and cures, cursing him for a false priest when they found none. He had been lucky to get away.

He climbed upstream now, looking for a safe place to cross, and came to a point where the stream narrowed. Removing his boots and hitching up his cloak and robe, he stepped in. The water lashed at him, gripping him with icy tentacles, and there, in the swirling rush, staring up at him, was the wolf's face. He threw himself onto the bank at the other side and when he looked back the wolf was gone.

Halfway down the hill and it came into sight. Smoke from fires curled into the cloud-laden sky. Medilwong. He climbed down towards the village, his bones aching, his feet burning. He reached the ford, the gateposts at the village fence, the boundary stones to his father's holding. Dusk was settling in. Everything seemed smaller than before. Some children ran by. One stopped and then ran after the others shouting *stranger, stranger*. He reached his father's house, the largest in the village, rebuilt, he thought, its roof freshly thatched. He had the sense of being in a dream, where everything familiar was changed, unsettling and somehow wrong.

He heard that child again. *Stranger, stranger*. The boy pointed at Wilfrid.

'See, Mama? I told you – a stranger.'

A woman appeared at the door. Her dress was rich

green velvet, embroidered with blue and yellow flowers at the neckline, hem and cuffs. Her hair was dark, streaked with silver. She looked Wilfrid up and down.

'Are you looking for someone?' she said.

Wilfrid swallowed. Where was the great speech he had prepared? He hadn't considered this – that she wouldn't recognise him.

'I...I've come back,' he said.

The woman, his mother, narrowed her eyes.

'My husband is at Bamburgh,' she said. 'But a servant of the Lord is always welcome in his house.

'It's me. Wilfrid.'

The woman opened her mouth slightly, but no sound came. She pulled the child close to her. His brother, Wilfrid realised suddenly, little Sigehelm, the baby Rowena was nursing when Fergus and Dunstan had come to take Wilfrid away. He must be nine winters now.

Rowena found her voice.

'Oswine,' she called. 'Oswine!'

Oswine came hurrying from the stable. He had changed little though his hair had thinned and was now completely grey. He glanced at Wilfrid and frowned.

'Take the boy in,' Rowena said to him. She nodded to Wilfrid. 'You'd better come in too.'

The fire was lively and hot, hissed and spat like an angry cat. They sat beside it, Wilfrid, his mother and his brother, eating a stew of vegetables with slivers of salted hare. Wilfrid remembered suddenly the last time he had eaten meat, at Hildmer's house, sneaking up to the pot, glancing around to check if *she* was watching him. He drew his hand hard across his forehead as though it might wipe the memory away. Rowena, his mother, narrowed her eyes.

'Your head aches?'

'No, no,' Wilfrid said. 'Though I suppose I would hardly notice if it did.' He attempted a laugh. 'My feet are so sore, I'm insensible to the rest of my body.'

He hoped that she might bring a bowl of water, offer to wash his feet. She must have done that for him as a child.

'Mmm,' she said. 'My husband will be sorry to have missed you. He spends much time at Bamburgh now. The king has need of his counsel.'

'My father is a thegn of Ecgfrith King,' the boy said. 'Soon I'm going to go and live in the Royal City too and learn to be a king's warrior, aren't I, Mama?'

'Yes, Sigi,' Rowena said.

The boy rolled his eyes and pointed his thumb at her.

'My father named me Sigehelm, but she calls me Sigi.'

Sigi was restless. He ran around the room, took a knife from the pouch on his belt and pretended it was a spear. He thrust to the right, dodged to the left and held up an invisible shield to block the attack of his foe. He swung himself around to face a second attack from the rear, and his hair, long and dark, swished about his shoulders. He put Wilfrid in mind of someone. A face began to emerge in his head, but it quickly dissolved again. Rowena was speaking.

'If the monastery is looking for more gifts, I believe my husband will do his duty, though he was most generous in the past, and we were led to understand...'

'Gifts?'

'Isn't that why you've come?'

A worm of doubt shifted in his brain, gnawed at him. He shook his head.

'Then, why?'

Why.

'I...I wanted, I needed to come home,' he said.

Rowena stared at him. Her fingers tugged at the embroidered neck of her dress, as if she wanted to pluck out the stitches one by one.

'I didn't think they allowed monks to visit their families,' she said. 'We were told...'

The boy left off his battling and came back to the table.

'Is he family, Mama?'

'Hush, Sigi,' Rowena said. She turned back to Wilfrid. 'Of course, you are welcome to stay a while, to rest before you return to the monastery.'

The boy put his knife on the table. It was small, silver-handled, engraved with a warrior's helmet.

'Mama, is he...?'

'Hush, Sigi. You mustn't interrupt.' Rowena ruffled his hair. He squirmed and wriggled free. 'You're hot. Take a drink and sit still.'

But Sigi couldn't sit still. He played with his knife again, twisting it deftly between his fingers. Wilfrid tried to catch his attention.

'Sigi, I'm your...'

'Sigi! Don't do that!' Rowena's voice rose over Wilfrid's. 'How many times must I tell you?'

Sigi scowled and put the knife back in his pocket.

'Go on then,' his mother said. 'Off to bed with you.

Now. A warrior needs his rest.'

She made to kiss him, but the boy dodged her lips with a deft jerk of his head and ran off. Wilfrid waited for her to speak again. Words tumbled about his head, sentences he had been preparing on his journey, but they were stuck, like fish caught in a net, flapping and flailing together, unable to set themselves free. His mother served him some more stew, without looking at him. A tide of silence surged in and swelled until it had filled the entire room.

Wilfrid woke early. He'd slept badly. The demons of the flesh had haunted him through the night, stoking his foolish imaginings, urging him to touch himself as they showed him Meredith, her veil coming undone, her hair, strand by strand, falling loose. He threw a log on the fire and went outside. The air was frozen and still. Soon the snows would come. They would change the aspect of the land so that even a man who knew the hills as well as the shape of his own hand might easily go astray. The village would be cut off, for a time at least, and no one could come looking for him, though he doubted anyone would want to look for him. He imagined Herefrith shaking his head, Tydi shrugging his shoulders. Edberht would wash his hands of him, Dunstan would denounce him as irretrievably damned, and Cuthbert, Cuthbert would... Would he pray for him, stand in the frozen sea and offer petitions for his lost soul? Or would he too condemn him, call for his expulsion from the community? It didn't matter. He would never forgive Cuthbert. He would never return. He was here now, back with his family, and soon the snows would come.

On his way to the stables he saw a woman by the pigpen. The slave girl, he supposed. She seemed to be muttering something to the pigs inside the shelter. When she saw Wilfrid she coloured and hurried away. Wilfrid continued to the stables, where he found Oswine. He took a spade and began to help, shovelling the dung into buckets to be brought to the midden heap. Oswine brushed down the largest horse.

'I don't recognise these horses,' Wilfrid said. 'Where's Blackeye?'

'Blackeye? She's gone long since, bartered for this fine specimen here. He belongs to Sigi. Your father had to trade three lambs as well to make the deal.'

The horse whinnied and jerked its head.

'I'll exercise him,' Wilfrid said.

'No, lad, I mean, Brother. Begging your pardon, but the master is very particular about the horse. Only myself and young Sigi may ride him. I'm surprised Sigi isn't here this minute, pestering me to take him out.'

'The horse wants exercise now,' Wilfrid said. 'See how restless he is.'

'I'm sorry. I can't go against your father's instructions. The horse needs special handling – good training – since it's supposed to go to Bamburgh with the boy. But perhaps if you asked your mother?'

Wilfrid turned away.

'I haven't seen my mother this morning,' he said.

He walked out to Wulfstan's Hill, the boots pinching his feet, chafing his sores. He passed the blackberry bushes, places where he had played and fought with other boys in the village. He remembered wooden swords carved to a point sharp as a knife. He remembered punches thrown, fists swung through the air, slingshots that pelted stones with the fury of a devil, a swollen eye, black, closed, the pain spreading across his forehead, and the blow to the back of the head from his father for letting a young lad barely weaned from his mother's skirt best him. He pictured the lad now, a cloudy image, dark-haired, dark-eyed, fast on his feet and laughing, laughing. He pushed the image away. He wondered about the other boys, the blacksmith's boy; all men now; farmers, hunters; married, probably. Some would have gone to battle for the king, perhaps had found glory and returned, perhaps had found glory and died.

He took off his boots. It was more comfortable to walk without them. He must get some more leather and make a new pair. His feet had outgrown these. He returned to the village, looking for the tanner. The villagers stared at him. A woman outside the blacksmith's called to him.

'Father, are you going to do one of those Masses for us?'

'I'm not a priest,' he said.

A young man, vaguely familiar, came out. He was tall and despite the cold wore only hose. He was muscular, sweating, his skin smeared with black. He winked at the woman.

'Them's right peculiar clothes you're wearing for a man who's not a priest,' he said.

'I'm a brother, not a priest,' Wilfrid said. 'I can't say Mass.'

'What about a baptism then?' the man said. He grabbed the woman, kissed her and slapped her backside. 'Maybe I'll get lucky tonight.'

The woman pulled from him and turned her face away. He gripped her more tightly and puckered his lips. She tried to claw his hands away from her, but he had her pinned to him. Wilfrid wondered if he should try and pull the man off, berate him for his behaviour, polluting the woman and himself. He just wanted to run away.

'Get off, you fool!' the woman said.

'She's a wild one, really,' the man said. He slapped her once more, harder this time, and let go. She called him a fool again. 'In front of the priest,' Wilfrid heard her hiss as he left.

'Priest, my arse,' the man said. 'I remember him alright. That's the halfwit lad was sent away that time. Looks like he found his way back.'

His mother and Sigi were in the kitchen. Sigi jumped up when he entered.

'Mama says you're a brother,' he said. 'She says you've come for a short visit.'

'Here, Sigi, have a honey cake,' Rowena said. 'Take it to the stables and tell Oswine to bring you out for a ride. Go on.'

Sigi made a face, but he went out.

Wilfrid sat down.

'Will you be staying for long?' Rowena said.

'Mama.'

The word was a trespasser on his tongue.

'Mother,' he said instead.

'It cannot be for that long, I'm afraid.' Rowena said. She ran her fingers up and down the thick gold chain that hung from her neck. 'The snows will come soon. We could be cut off for weeks, even months.'

'Mother,' he tried again. 'I wonder if I might stay a little longer, perhaps even winter here?'

Rowena dropped the chain from her fingers. It fell heavily against her breast.

'But the winter is long. What would you do here? Won't your people be expecting you?'

'My people?'

'The monks, the monastery people.'

Wilfrid scratched at his ankle.

'I could help in the stables, tend the animals, farm, like the other men.'

'I have Oswine for that, and the slave girl. Besides, you're not like the other men. You're a monk.'

'I can read and write, keep accounts.'

'Accounts? Who needs to read and write to keep accounts? You think I can't keep every strand of cloth, every barrel of beer, each ounce of flour and salt in my head? You... What's wrong with your feet?'

'They're sore, blistered. I walked for days. And these boots don't fit any more.'

Rowena frowned.

'There's some water in the pail there if you want to wash them.'

The boy came back in.

'That was quick,' Rowena said to him. 'Did you not find Oswine?'

'I'm tired,' he said. 'I don't want to ride.'

'Look at me,' Rowena said. She took the boy's face

214

in her hands. 'You're flushed.' She lay her palm against his forehead, then opened the button on his tunic and checked his arms and neck. 'Nothing,' she murmured. 'Though you are a little hot. Too much running around, I think. Best let Mama take care of you. Some nettle soup will make you feel better.'

'You could give him some chamomile and honey,' Wilfrid said. 'Lavender if he has a headache. That's what Brother Fergus gave me when I was ill.'

'Go and rest, Sigi,' Rowena said. 'I'll be with you in a while.' She waited until he was gone, then turned to Wilfrid. 'Go back to the monastery,' she said. 'There is nothing for you here.'

He was wakened by footsteps, the rustle of the fire being stoked, the clank of a pot and the swish of liquid spilling into it.

'Not too much,' someone hissed. 'It will never boil.'

Wilfrid sat up. In the glow of the firelight he saw Oswine and the woman he had noticed at the pigpen earlier. She was spooning some honey into a cup, while he was filling a basin with water.

'Get that drink made up, quick as you can,' Oswine said. 'And then boil up some more water. I'll ride out at first light. I'll find a medicine woman and get word to the master.'

'What's happened?' Wilfrid asked.

Oswine spat out an audible *tsk*.

'Nothing to be concerned about,' he said.

He took the basin of water and hurried out. Wilfrid looked at the woman, the slave girl who used to tend the pigs. He tried to remember her name – Coelwyn?

Cynegyth? She was still small and very slight – the thin purple veins in her arms looked like they might break through her skin – but she was no longer pale as she had once been. Her face was bright red, probably from the heat of the fire. She stirred the water over the flames, keeping her eyes firmly on the pot.

'Stirring won't make it boil any faster,' Wilfrid said. 'Tell me, what's happened?'

'It's your brother,' she said after a moment. 'He's not well.'

'The fever? It's worse?

She shrugged.

'You must know something.'

She glared at him.

'Why should I know anything? All I know is they told me to make a drink of honey and lavender and to fetch ingredients for a poultice the mistress will make.'

Wilfrid went out to the Great Hall where his mother and brother slept. Rowena was kneeling on the floor, leaning over Sigi's bed, wiping him down with the cloth while Oswine looked on.

'About time,' she said without turning around. 'Give me that drink. Oswine, help me sit Sigi up.' She glanced over her shoulder and saw Wilfrid. 'You,' she said. 'Where is that damned woman? I sent her to fetch a drink an age ago. Kendra!'

Kendra. That was her name. Wilfrid remembered now.

'She'll be just another moment, Mistress,' Oswine said.

He helped Rowena to sit Sigi up. The boy was naked from the waist up and sweating. He panted and gasped and coughed. Sores, red and pus-filled, had sprouted across his chest. Wilfrid stepped back. He wanted to step back further, slowly, in his bare feet, keep stepping back until he was out of the fever-filled room, out of the plague-drenched air.

Kendra came in with a cup of steaming liquid. Rowena poured some of the liquid onto a spoon, blew on it and spooned it into the side of Sigi's mouth. He coughed and spluttered it back. She tried again. Again the drink was spat back.

'Dear Christ, Thunor, Friga, help me,' she said.

Kendra flinched, Wilfrid noticed, her face still red. She backed away, a shadow slipping from the room. Wilfrid breathed deeply. He tightened his muscles and walked forward.

'Let me help,' he said.

Rowena looked up.

'You?'

'Mistress,' Oswine said. 'Perhaps Wilfrid knows a cure. They say the monks and nuns study physic and medicaments and are great healers.'

'Well, I know what Brother Fergus gave me when I was sick,' Wilfrid said. 'Chamomile, lavender, honey, garlic, and...and I'm not sure what else.'

'Chamomile? Honey? That's it?'

Rowena hung her head in her hands.

'Then you haven't learned of any cures at the monastery?' Oswine said.

'I don't work in the infirmary,' Wilfrid said. 'I'm a scribe. I write.'

'Writing,' his mother spat. 'What use is that?'

Wilfrid reeled. He wanted to tell her. How writing

had steadied him, given him a sense of purpose, his quill a single blade of light that steered him through the darkness of his life. How he had abandoned the one thing that made his life meaningful to return home to her. But this was not the time, and it was not how he would prove himself to her.

'I can be of use,' he insisted.

Rowena came towards Wilfrid, her frame crooked, bent with grief. She raised her fist, and for a moment Wilfrid thought it would come driving into his face, but instead she extended a long finger towards him.

'You,' she said. 'You bring death. You carry death with you like an amulet and now you bring it back, back to my house, to my other son.'

Her words felled Wilfrid, struck him like a knife-blow to the breast. He didn't know whether to run or hit back.

'What?' he said. 'What?'

'You bring death. First...' Her mouth trembled and she made a choking sound. She pointed at Wilfrid's feet and gestured back to Sigi. 'And now...' She started to cry but immediately composed herself. She knelt by Sigi again.

Wilfrid looked at the sores on his feet. They were still large and ugly but less angry than before. He almost laughed.

'No,' he said. 'You're wrong. My feet are sore from walking. I told you. I need new boots. That's all. Look, the blisters are starting to heal. Look!'

Oswine looked.

'My lady,' he said.

Rowena wasn't listening. She tried again to get the

boy to drink, failed again and then turned back to Wilfrid. He saw her tremble and shiver, her whole body a hive of hate.

'I had a dream,' she said. 'Just before you were born. In this dream I saw a ball of darkness bite at the moon and eat it up. Then the darkness fell into my mouth and I swallowed it, and it filled my belly, filled it to tearing point. Do you know what that dream meant?'

Wilfrid shook his head.

'Well, I knew what it meant. It meant the child in my womb would bring death. But your father said no, no we must ask the priest – that fool priest Wilfrid, the one we named you for, the same one Ecgfrith King expelled years later.'

'What did the priest say?'

He wanted to hear everything. He didn't care anymore. He hated her. Let her strike at him, each word a slash across his heart. It didn't matter. He hated her more than she hated him.

'He said my dream was sent as a warning. Some of the villagers had gone back to the old ways, the old gods. Your father had tolerated it, was sympathetic even. The dream, the priest said, was meant for Raymund, to tell him the darkness of hell would swallow us all up if he did not persuade the villagers to return to Christ's path. And he assured him of Ecgfrith King's favour if he stamped out the noxious spread of idolatry. And Raymund listened, of course.'

Rowena steadied herself. She dipped her finger in the drink and put it into the side of Sigi's mouth.

'There. Just a little, my darling, just a little, for Mama.'

Wilfrid shuddered. He shouldn't have come here. It was worse than the monastery. The place was infected with sickness, madness. His mother was mad. Dreams, visions. She made less sense than Cuthbert. It would serve her right if the boy died. She just wanted someone to accuse because she had failed to notice how sick Sigi was, hadn't listened to him when he spoke of Fergus' remedies.

Fergus.

Wilfrid leaned heavily against the wall. *You bring death.* Fergus was dead, drowned because of him. Back then, Cuthbert had said it wasn't his fault. God had called Fergus for His own reasons, he said, and no man understood the mind of God, but the more Wilfrid thought about it now, the more he began to wonder if his mother might be right. He had always sensed a presence, saw it sometimes, as he had in the river the previous day – that dark shape, the wolf. Now his brother had plague, and the thought grew and swelled in his mind that somehow, somehow he had carried the plague with him without becoming ill himself.

'Fergus,' he said.

'Who is this Fergus?' Oswine asked. 'Can he help?'

'No,' Wilfrid said. He reached into his pocket, ran the tips of his fingers along the psalter that still nestled there. Cuthbert's psalter, given to him by Fergus when first he arrived on Lindisfarne. 'Not Fergus. But there is someone else. I told you, I can be of use. I can bring help.'

Five

WILFRID RODE HARD. Through icy winds in stone-grey light he drove the horse over hills and streams, on tracks hardened with frost. Oswine had prepared him well for the journey, packed food and blankets and found him a pair of strong boots and a wolfskin cloak to wear over his own monk's cloak. The cloak was hooded with an iron clasp shaped like a sword and shield that tied tightly at Wilfrid's shoulder. Still, the cold gnawed at him like a ravenous dog. He longed to stop and find shelter, but as long as there was the faintest trace of light he must keep going.

He rode hard and prayed hard, prayed the boy might yet live, that God would ride with him, aid his plan. Cuthbert must have returned to his hermitage by now, so first Wilfrid must get to his father in Bamburgh.

His father would find a way, hire a fisherman, a trader, anyone who would take them out to the Farne. Together, somehow, they would persuade Cuthbert to go to Sigi and heal him. Wilfrid would prove himself to his family. Even his mother would accept him. Perhaps he might return home. And in saving Sigi he might finally atone for his role in Fergus' death. He spurred his horse on and prayed the psalm.

Non timebis a timore nocturno;
a sagitta volante in die,
a negotio perambulante in tenebris.

At noon of the second day he halted. He had expected to reach the coast by now and was unsure whether to ride north or south. Neither Lindisfarne nor Bamburgh was visible from his vantage point, and there were no recognisable landmarks. Some way down the hill a thin trail of smoke snaked to the sky. A man was foraging about the scrub at the edge of a settlement, searching, no doubt, for nuts or berries, though the season had turned. He was thin, more shadow than man, his face grey as the sky. He wore no cloak, and his tattered tunic revealed limp sagging flesh. He looked up when he saw Wilfrid, his hand edging to the pouch hanging from his belt.

Wilfrid raised his hand in greeting.

'I'm a monk of Lindisfarne,' he said.

'You're too late,' the man said.

'Late?'

'Dead'. The man nodded in the direction of the settlement. 'All of them. Or as good as. Unless you're a wonder-worker as well as a priest.'

'I'm not a wonder-worker,' Wilfrid said. 'Just a monk. I need to find the path to Bamburgh. It's urgent.'

The man edged closer, teetering a little.

'They say one of your monks has healing powers,' he said. 'They say his powers are stronger than any medicine. But I've heard he's locked himself away on some devil's island, spends his days with demons and dark spirits and refuses to come forth and help the people.'

'Please,' Wilfrid said. 'Show me the path towards Bamburgh. You must know the way.'

The man snatched a knife from his pouch and pointed it at Wilfrid.

'Give me your cloak,' he said. 'And that bag.'

Wilfrid held the reins tightly.

'First tell me the way.'

The man moved towards him. He raised his arm and lunged clumsily with the knife. Wilfrid dug his heels into the mare's flanks, she bolted forward, and the man stumbled to the ground.

'Which way?' Wilfrid said.

The man seemed not to hear. He lay there curled up on the ground. Wilfrid sighed. He shook the reins to urge the mare on but then halted her again. He unclasped the wolfskin cloak that Oswine had given him from his shoulders, took a hunk of cheese and a piece of bread from his bag and threw them with the cloak to the ground. The man clawed at the food and gnawed into it with red, toothless gums. Then he wrapped himself in the cloak and slowly stretched out his hand and pointed.

Wilfrid steered his horse in the direction the man had indicated. Beyond the settlement there was a trail, narrow and overgrown, barely wide enough to fit a horse, but a trail nonetheless. It brought him to a wider path and then to a wider path again. The Roman road. Along it stretched a line of hoofprints and footprints, the track marks of a cart; a large contingent had come this way. He spurred the horse on. As he rounded a bend he saw it, still a great distance away, but unmistakably the mighty rock, the Royal City looming into the sky.

It was dusk when he reached the outer gates. A watchman shouted to him from the parapet.

'You there, what do you want?'

'I've come...'

Wilfrid tried to shout back, but his voice was weary.

'What do you bloody want?' the watchman roared at him.

He took his sword from his scabbard and waved it about. Wilfrid was reminded of Sigi, dancing across the kitchen, thrusting his knife at imaginary foes lurking behind chests and underneath the table.

'Be still, you fool!'

A second watchman caught the first by the hair and shook him.

'Learn to hold your beer, and look with your eyes not your sword. See, it's another monk.' He called down to Wilfrid. 'Where have you come from, Brother?'

'I...I'm a monk of Lindisfarne.'

'Wait there,' the second watchman said.

A moment later a small door to the side of the gates was unlocked and Wilfrid was let through.

'You're another one come for the synod then?' the

watchman said cheerfully.

'Synod?'

The watchman grabbed Wilfrid suddenly, twisting his arm behind his back, patting him roughly, shaking out his cloak and digging into his pockets.

'Sorry about this, Brother. Have to check everyone. Can't be too careful with so many important folk about.' He called up to the first watchman. 'Nothing. Just a small knife. Wouldn't cut honey. He's here for the synod.'

'He's a bit young for all that carry-on,' his companion said. He belched loudly. 'Looks like he should be back in his cell, saying his bedtime prayers.'

'Shut your trap, I've told you, or you'll find yourself in a cell of your own, along with those Irish bastards. See how they'll take to you.'

'Please,' Wilfrid said. 'I'm in a hurry.'

'Yes, Brother, of course. Come with me. I'm Cerdic, by the way.'

Cerdic beckoned to a young girl of about eleven who was carrying two large pails of water. She was barefoot, thin as a spindle and wore a frayed woollen tunic that didn't reach her knees.

'Put those down,' Cerdic said, pointing to the pails.

The girl landed the pails heavily on the ground, and some water spilled on Cerdic's foot.

'Watch what you're doing, fool!'

He shook his fist, and the girl scrambled backwards, her arms crossed over her face. Cerdic pointed to Wilfrid's horse and made eating and drinking gestures with his hands.

'See it's fed and watered.'

The girl moved slowly, making sure not to come too close to the watchman's fist, and took the reins from Wilfrid's hand.

'Irish,' Cerdic said. 'She'll catch on. Eventually.'

He led the way across the outer courtyard, through another guarded gate into an inner enclosure. Men and women hurried by, bearing pitchers of drink and platters of food. Smoke from the fires drifted past them, oozing smells of roast meats. Pig, Wilfrid thought, and maybe duck or goose. One woman, wrapped in a thick cape, was overseeing the activity, snapping orders and occasionally stopping the servants to rearrange the food on the dishes. She paced up and down, clutching something hanging from her girdle.

'Best stay out of the mistress' path,' Cerdic said in a low voice. 'She's jumpy as a sack of kittens lately. This way now. The synod is in the Great Hall. The king and bishops and your brethren are there already.'

'Bishops?'

'Yes. A few of them, even that bigwig from down south.'

'Theodore? The Archbishop of Canterbury is here?'

'That's the one, with some of his followers. All shouting and arguing. It's worse than a war council in there.'

Wilfrid frowned. A synod. It must have been organised months ago, before Edberht had sent him to bring Cuthbert to Coquet Island.

'And Bishop Tunberht? Is he there?'

'Tunberht? Don't think so. Isn't he the one they got rid of?'

Cerdic led Wilfrid through a passageway. Wilfrid

grimaced. The stench was vile, akin to the reek of a midden heap, though why anyone would put a midden heap in the interior of a building was beyond him. Cerdic laughed.

'That's Irish shit you're smelling. Nasty sort. Almost as bad as Pict shit. Down there.'

He pointed to a pit in the ground covered with an iron grille. Wilfrid bent down, peered through the grille and immediately pulled back. The stink of a thousand demons had gathered and congealed there: putrid flesh, shit, piss, bile, vomit. He covered his mouth and nose with his cloak and looked into the pit again. It was very dark; there was no candle. Someone shouted from below in a foreign tongue.

'Shut your stinking gob, Irish bastard,' the watchman shouted back. He gestured to Wilfrid to keep moving.

'What are they doing there?' Wilfrid asked.

'Doing? They're prisoners, hostages. They'll be exchanged or ransomed – if they're lucky – or conscripted to fight the Picts, the ones that don't die off, that is.'

'Then, there is a war coming.'

'Not for me to say.' He patted his sword. 'But if you were looking for the opinion of a warrior loyal and true to Ecgfrith King, I would say those Picts will soon be taught a lesson about following the ways of the true Church and keeping the true Easter – though, of course, you'd know more than me about that, Brother.'

'But, surely these hostages should be well treated, as we would expect the enemy to treat ours?'

'Not for me to say. Happen things are changing. Besides,' he laughed, 'they didn't get any of ours, did they? Ecgfrith King and the warmaster saw to that. Wish I'd been let go. But I'll have my chance next time. You'll see.'

They reached the innermost point of the fortress where the long, thickly thatched Great Hall stood, its heavy wooden doors guarded by sentries on each side.

'Here we are,' Cerdic said. He nodded to the sentries. 'This is Brother...'

'Wilfrid,' Wilfrid said.

'Here for the synod,' Cerdic said. 'No weapons, just a small paring knife.' He gave a parting salute. 'Best get back to my post before that other fool lets in an army of marauding foreigners.'

'I have a message for Raymund,' Wilfrid said to the sentries.

'Raymund?' one of them said. 'The king's warmaster? I thought you were here for the synod?'

'First, I must speak with Raymund,' Wilfrid said. 'Tell him Brother Wilfrid of Lindisfarne would speak with him urgently.'

The sentries looked at each other, shrugging their shoulders.

'Wait there,' one of them said.

The sentry entered the Great Hall. Loud noise burst forth from within as the sentry entered: many voices talking at once; groans; a fist banged on a table; a staff hammered on the floor. After a few moments he returned with another man.

Raymund.

His father had changed but little in appearance. His beard was greyer, longer, his hair thinner and his belly fatter. Something in his demeanour had altered though; the mouth was grimmer, the eyes harder. Two thick gold rings gleamed on his right arm. Wilfrid noticed how the two sentries now stood straight as gateposts, looking ahead, not meeting the warmaster's eye. Raymund looked hard at Wilfrid. He nodded, grimly. Then he grabbed Wilfrid by the arm pulled him up a sloping path to the parapet and pressed him against the wall.

'What are you doing here?' he said. 'You should be in the monastery. You're not supposed to leave.'

Wilfrid tried to edge to one side, but his father's grip didn't loosen.

'I know,' Wilfrid said. 'But, but sometimes you can leave, to go forth to bring God's Word to the people and...'

'You've come to bring me God's Word? Christ! Is that what you think we need? Do you not think we have enough priests and bishops in that hall back there?'

'No, yes. I didn't know they'd be here.'

'Didn't know?' He wiped his mouth with one hand, kept the other firmly on Wilfrid's shoulder. 'Devil halfwit,' he muttered.

Wilfrid wrestled himself free of Raymund's grip.

'I've come from Medilwong. It's Sigi. He's sick.'

'Medilwong?' Raymund caught hold of Wilfrid again. 'How sick?'

'It's plague.'

Raymund dug his fingers into Wilfrid's flesh. His voice trembled.

'You're certain?'

'I saw the marks.'

'How long?'

'Two days; perhaps three.'

Raymund let Wilfrid go. He beat his fist against the wall and breathed heavily.'What of Rowena?' he said, eventually.

'She is well.'

'She'll not survive this,' Raymund said. 'Not this time.' He leaned against the wall, his body slack and heavy. 'I should have sent for him. Had him fostered here. I even thought the queen might...but it would have called attention to her lack.' He slumped even lower against the wall. 'And now he's gone.'

'No!' Wilfrid said. 'Listen to me, that's why I've come. Sigi can be saved. I know it. Father Cuthbert can help. He can perform wonders. I have seen it.'

'Cuthbert? That madman is back out on that damned desert rock convening with spirits and angels and Christ knows what else. What does he care for some child he's never met?'

Wilfrid shook off the misgivings running through him. He must not let his father's doubt infect him.

'He will care. He cared for me. And Sigi is his kin too. We must persuade him to leave the island and journey to Medilwong and...'

Raymund put his head in his hands and groaned.

'Why does God see fit to take only worthy sons and leave fools to walk this earth? Even if the plague has not yet taken him, even if Cuthbert is willing, it's too late. The snows are coming. And besides, the king has other plans.'

'Raymund!' A shout came from below. 'Raymund! Where the devil is he?'

A man in a fur cloak, a flask in his hand, was striding

up the slope towards them. Wilfrid recognised him immediately.

'I'm here.' Raymund pulled his body straight. 'I beg pardon, lord. A messenger arrived.'

Ecgfrith King looked at Wilfrid. He frowned and took a swig from his flask.

'From Lindisfarne? You bring word of Father Cuthbert?'

'No. Yes, that is...'

'Well, which is it? We've had our work cut out for us trying to persuade him to accept the bishopric. It seems my sister hasn't quite managed to persuade him. Still, never send a woman to do a man's work.' He spat on the ground. 'Well? What message?'

Wilfrid looked at his father. Raymund sighed and took a deep breath.

'It appears our messenger has not come from Lindisfarne, lord. He has...'

'Wait,' Ecgfrith said. He pointed at Wilfrid. 'I've seen him before, at the monastery, you know, in that place where they keep their writings and books and so on. Yes, I remember now. They told me he's your...'

'Lord,' Raymund said. 'This is Wilfrid. But he has come from Medilwong, not the monastery. He brings news from Rowena. It seems my, my...' He cleared his throat. 'My son, Sigehelm, my boy, he is...'

Raymund faltered, swallowing hard.

'Sigi is dying,' Wilfrid said.

'He is most likely, most likely gone,' Raymund said.

Ecgfrith put his hand on Raymund's shoulder.

'Dear Christ. Dear Christ.' He rummaged in the pouch on his belt and found a key. 'Here, this way,' he said, and led them to a storeroom at the side of the Great Hall.

Inside the air was heavy with the scent of onions, herbs, fruit, flour and yeast. There were rows of sacks and barrels against one wall, and locked chests against another. Ecgfrith found some cups and filled them from one of the barrels. He and Raymund drained their cups in one go. Wilfrid drank too. It was wine, rich and strong, not beer as he had expected.

They sat on the floor, leaning against sacks of grain. Wilfrid slumped against the sack, then straightened himself up. He must keep himself steady.

'The loss of sons is a heavy burden, Raymund,' Ecgfrith said. 'But the king and those close to the king cannot let themselves be distracted by family sorrows. We have pressing matters at hand.'

Raymund nodded. 'I understand, lord.'

'Good.' Ecgfrith patted Raymund's shoulder. 'Drink up,' he said to Wilfrid. 'You, at least, have something to celebrate. Drink.'

Wilfrid drank. From the Great Hall nearby he could hear shouting and laughing. He could not imagine what he might have to celebrate, what anyone might have to celebrate here in Bamburgh, where men were kept like animals in pits, where little girls were half-starved and worked to the point of collapse, and all around they waited for the call to war. He drank again.

'That's more like it,' Ecgfrith said. 'Drink to the elevation of your holy hermit to the bishopric.'

Some wine dribbled down Wilfrid's chin.

'Father Cuthbert? But I thought you said he had not been persuaded?'

'Yet.' Ecgfrith winked. 'He hasn't been persuaded yet. But then how much persuasion does he need? Perhaps he'd like a taste of exile or prison to help him reach his decision.'

Wilfrid thought of the pit and shivered.

Ecgfrith grinned, took Wilfrid's cup and refilled it.'

But, lord,' Wilfrid said. 'He's already in exile. He has made a prison of his cell. It's not much better than the place you keep those Irish. He believes God has called him there.'

'And I believe God has called him to be bishop.' Ecgfrith waved his arms in the air, spilling some wine as he did so. 'I have explained this over and over to you monks. With Cuthbert as bishop, the Picts and all the men of the North, even those schismatics on Iona, will more readily come over to the ways of the true Church. They will remember that he was ever their friend, even after they refused to accept the proper calculation of Easter as ordained by my father, Oswiu King. Well, now the time is ripe for them to renounce their stubborn errors, come over to the ways of Northumbria.' He drank again. 'And when they have come over, when I have achieved what even my father could not, God will reward me.'

He laughed softly, patted his stomach and thrust his pelvis forward.

Wilfrid thought back to Coquet Island. He remembered what the abbess had said about Queen Iurminburgh – about the holy relics she wore attached to her girdle, the Book of Hours Eadfrith had made for her, yet still her belly remained flat and empty. Did Ecgfrith believe that if he delivered God a people converted to the true Easter then God would deliver him a child?

'Drink up,' Ecgfrith said to Raymund, 'and then prepare the ship. You'll sail for the Farne at first light. Give Cuthbert the decision of the synod and tell him that Ecgfrith King invites and constrains him to come and serve as Bishop of Lindisfarne. Some of the brethren will accompany you. The investiture takes place at York as soon as Archbishop Theodore can organise it.'

He stood up to go. Wilfrid's head was spinning. They would take Cuthbert from the Farne, bring him to York, imprison him if he refused. And now the light of his plan which had shone with such clarity was dimmed. A fog had snaked around it, and he could no longer see a way to bring it to fruition.

'And if he refuses again?' Raymund said.

The king spat on the ground. 'You,' he said to Wilfrid. 'Do you think Cuthbert will dare refuse the king?'

'I...I...' Wilfrid staggered to his feet. He closed his eyes, tried to see the light again. 'Lord,' he said. 'God called Father Cuthbert to be a hermit, to go to the Farne, to fight devils and battle for Christ, to make his entire life a prayer for the souls of others.'

'I've heard enough of that talk,' Ecgfrith said. 'Mostly from those brethren of Bishop Tunberht, whose minds are almost as eaten by age and infirmity as his. There are devils enough here for Cuthbert to fight and prayers enough to pray.'

'You don't understand, lord. I know him. I have spent time with him, been on his island, listened to his stories.'

Ecgfrith stepped closer to Wilfrid and gripped his

chin. He took the cup from Wilfrid's hand and, without taking his eyes off Wilfrid, passed it to Raymund.

'More wine for your son,' he said. 'Now, what did you say your name was? Wilfrid? You say you know Cuthbert, you know his stories.'

'Yes.' Wilfrid looked the king in the eye, trying not to flinch as Ecgfrith still held his chin, pinched between his thumb and forefinger.

'Then you know his weaknesses also,' Ecgfrith said.

'Yes,' Wilfrid said again.

Raymund refilled Wilfrid's cup.

'Drink,' he said.

Wilfrid drank, and the light of his plan began to gleam through the fog.

'He's lonely,' Wilfrid said. 'He fasts and prays all the time but he cannot be sure that the voices he hears, the visions he sees...he cannot be sure they are from God. He fears the call from this world, the world beyond the Farne. He fears it is the devil calling, not God.'

Ecgfrith threw his arms in the air.

'What is wrong with the man? I am Ecgfrith King, son of Oswiu, grandson of Edwin himself, who brought the religion of Christ to our kingdom. How can I be the voice of the devil?'

Wilfrid closed his eyes. He thought of Cuthbert on Coquet Island, how frail he had seemed, like a starved fox, tempted by a morsel of meat put its way, edging closer to a trap.

'You can't, lord, but he fears, I suppose, that being a bishop would lead him away from God, not closer to Him, that he would be caught up with things of men's world, with power and battle and...'

Wilfrid pictured Cuthbert again, his ribs protruding from his skin, his toenails long and grotesquely yellow, his hands chapped and his mouth blistered. Perhaps in the long run what Wilfrid was doing now would help him. Besides, what did he owe Cuthbert, the man who had torn him from his family? No, Cuthbert had been a hermit long enough.

'He needs a sign,' Wilfrid continued. 'Give him a sign. He has forgotten that he can heal bodies as well as souls. It will be a sign to him that God is calling him to be bishop if he must heal someone. Tell him he is needed, not by the king but by the people, by his family. Sigi is his kin. Let my father plead with him for Sigi's life. Bring Father Cuthbert to Sigi. He will cure him, I'm sure. And it will make him want to cure others, to comfort them, to be their shepherd. That's what a bishop is, isn't it? A shepherd for the people?'

Ecgfrith looked at Raymund.

'What do you think?'

'This is not my idea, lord,' Raymund said. 'I've told him Sigi must be dead by now, that snow is coming, though...otherwise the idea is not without merit.'

'Yes,' Ecgfrith said. 'And a journey into the hills would take him away from the road to York. Still...' He paused, then spoke to Wilfrid again. 'What else?'

'He does not like to feel that he is being played upon, steered like a ship; only God may steer him. He will want to know that he is called by God, not by men.'

'But he *is* being called by God, through a man, through *me*,' Ecgfrith said.

'Per...perhaps if *you* tell him that, lord? Perhaps Father Cuthbert would obey the king's commands more readily if the king himself were to deliver the message?'

'I?' Ecgfrith laughed. He slapped Wilfrid so hard on the chest that Wilfrid almost fell over. 'Raymund, perhaps this son of yours is not such a weakwit after all. Or then again, perhaps he is so feeble-minded he cannot see the dangerous snare he walks into by presuming to tell his king what to do.'

Raymund glared at Wilfrid. Wilfrid felt his disapproval like the swing of a fist.

'Mmm,' Ecgfrith said. 'But maybe it's quite simple, after all. I will make the wretched journey to the Farne myself so there can be no doubt that God calls Cuthbert to the bishopric through the voice of Ecgfrith King. The boy is right, Raymund. God sent him, I believe, to show us the way to Cuthbert's heart. And who knows, maybe he will save your other son. And if not, it's a long road to York. No doubt there will be other creatures along the way for him to cure.' He pointed his thumb in the direction of the Great Hall. 'They've already begun to bring in the food. Let's hope the holy brethren haven't devoured all the best fare. See that the boats are prepared, Raymund, and then come and eat. We set out at first light. This Wilfrid will come too.'

'No,' Wilfrid said. 'Begging your pardon, lord. It's best that no mention is made of me in regard to the bishopric. I am...well...a little out of favour with Father Cuthbert, and it would not go well if he suspected that I had given you any information.'

Ecgfrith smiled. 'See, I told you, Raymund. Not such a halfwit, after all.'

Raymund nodded. Slowly. They made to go, but Wilfrid called after them.

'Father.'

Raymund turned around.

'I wondered if I might return to Medilwong? Perhaps stay there. I could take things over when you are occupied at Bamburgh.'

Raymund shook his head. He was firm.

'Your place is not at Medilwong. Go back to the monastery.'

Wilfrid struggled to keep upright on the horse as it trudged over the sand path. Darkness was falling, and the wind was like blades of ice, but for now the snow held off. He was bone-weary, heart-weary. It had all been for nothing. His family would never accept him. And now he could not even be sure that the monastery would take him back. All he knew was that he could not relinquish the hope that Sigi would live. He clung to it as a drowning man might cling to a rope thrown to him. Sigi's life as reparation for Fergus' death.

As he approached the monastery gate he saw in the distance the monks heading to the church to keep the office, to keep the faith. There was something more God wanted, Wilfrid realised. He made his pact there and then with Christ. Wilfrid's own life, given freely, willingly this time, to God and the monastery, if only Sigi lived.

Light from the gate torch spread across the long grass on his right. Something gleamed there, yellow and bright. Wolf's eyes. He was surprised. He had not thought to see the wolf again.

Part Three

AD 685

One

Easter Day. Wilfrid stood at the door of the
church. He blinked away the glare of dawn-light
that glinted on the whitened landscape. Slivers
of frost and ice laced the island, as delicate and pretty
as the intricate frills on one of Eadfrith's manuscripts,
but the air was viciously cold and snapped at the
monks with wolves' teeth, causing them to walk with
heads bent and shoulders hunched, barely capable of
raising their hands to give a shivery blessing to another
brother passing by. It had been the longest darkest
winter they had known.

For Wilfrid it had been particularly long, and he had
performed more penances than he could remember, as
reparation for renouncing his vocation and abandoning
the monastery. His fears that he would not be taken

back were assuaged when Edberht announced that justice must be tempered with mercy, particularly since a missive had arrived from the Royal City, naming Wilfrid as a young monk who had earned the favour of the king. Under those circumstances Wilfrid must be given a chance to redeem himself.

Still, doubt had plagued him throughout the last few months. Perhaps he had been wrong to involve himself in the king's machinations, to manipulate Cuthbert into renouncing his calling as a hermit. Yet had Cuthbert not toyed with Wilfrid's life also? And who could say? Perhaps Cuthbert's true vocation lay in being a bishop. Certainly the community on Lindisfarne had rejoiced in the elevation of one of their own. Wilfrid cast his misgivings aside. He had made his decision, and there was no going back. He must not be distracted from his purpose as he prepared, finally, to take the tonsure.

He walked down the aisle towards Edberht, towards the waiting dish of water, shears and blade. He didn't look back, didn't flinch at the scrape of the blade across his scalp. He kept his head still as his hair was shaped in the manner of a crown of thorns, the sacred manner laid down by St Peter, and then, standing before the altar, before the community of his brethren and his God, Wilfrid made his final, irrevocable vows to live a life of obedience and stability in the monastic way of life.

In his silent prayers he remembered Sigi. As yet there had been no word, but it must surely come soon. He brushed his cold, bare scalp, with the tips of his fingers. He had kept his vow to Christ, taken the tonsure. Cuthbert was bishop. He could do no more.

*

A week since Easter Day. Still the land was winter-gripped, but strangely the snows that had threatened for months still did not appear, and surely now that Easter had arrived, they would not come at all. Yet spring seemed as far away as ever; night lingered, the skies remained grey throughout the day. Neither had the swallows and terns made their return. They too were late, and some whispered that perhaps they meant never to come again.

Wilfrid trudged to the well to draw water, then carried it to the rinsing house where the calf skins were prepared. The pail handles chafed his blistered hands. Ecgfrith King had been true to his word. As well as endowments of land, two boatloads of calfskins for the scriptorium had arrived, with the promise of more. Wilfrid had spent the previous day soaking skins in lime and water, and though he had washed himself afterwards, the stink of lime and flesh still clung to him; his hands were so raw that each breath of the wind stung them, and the touch of water was sharp as vinegar.

He would have asked Brother Laurence for a salve, but Laurence was travelling with Cuthbert, as was Tydi; Cuthbert had asked for him. Wilfrid blew fiercely on his sore fingers, swept the thought of Tydi from him like an adder from his foot.

He looked out over the sands where the series of wooden posts marked the safe passage to Bamburgh. If only Cuthbert would return. Finally then there would be news of Sigi, and one way or the other he would know what had happened. Suddenly he wondered if he could bear to know. What if it had all been in vain? Bad enough that his scheming, his treachery toward Cuthbert, had failed to reconcile him with his family. What if it was all wasted effort and Sigi had not survived after all?

In the afternoon he did some work in the scriptorium, making an inventory of gifts sent to mark the occasion of Cuthbert's investiture as bishop. As Wilfrid passed by the open door, Dunstan signalled to him to fetch some more ink and a hot stone. Dunstan was working outside, a blanket wrapped around him. These days, he worked at all times in the open, where the light was best. His own cell had somehow become too dark and gloomy over the years, he said; the scriptorium too busy. He hunched so low over his desk that often when he sat upright again his nose was blotched with ink, and his eyes were red and scaly from being rubbed so much by his calloused fingers. He clutched the stone Wilfrid brought him.

'Do you need anything else, Brother Dunstan?' Wilfrid asked.

'You may fetch me another hot stone in a little while,' Dunstan said. Wilfrid shuffled a little from one foot to the other.

'Well, what are you waiting for?' Dunstan was inspecting his manuscript closely, frowning and grimacing. Wilfrid could see that the descender on a *q* had come too far below the line, and there were a couple of tiny stray ink dots in the right margin.

'I wondered, Brother Dunstan, if you have had word of Bishop Cuthbert? Has there been any news? Does he intend to visit us soon?'

Dunstan sat slowly upright. He put down his quill and rubbed his eyes, leaving a fresh ink stain just above his left eyebrow.

'I do not understand why you, of all people, should ask about the bishop's return,' he said. 'All those years ago, I knew; I warned him. But he took you in – said it was the only way. He blessed you with his love, his protection, and you, all that time were but a viper in his bosom.'

He stood up, pointed his long, stained finger at Wilfrid. He opened his mouth to speak again, as if about to deliver a long-withheld speech, learned by heart, just waiting for an opportune moment to be recited.

Wilfrid didn't wait. Though Dunstan shouted after him, he closed his ears to the words, ran to the rinsing house and plunged a calfskin into fresh water, rinsing it then wringing it until his arms ached and every trace of lime had been expunged from its surface.

The brethren were at table the following day when the door to the refectory opened and Tydi entered. The monks rushed to him, one steering him to a seat, another offering him food and water. Tydi looked worn; his robe was stained, the hem of his cloak frayed. He spoke hesitantly, trouble etched on his face.

'Bishop Cuthbert is at Bamburgh, speaking with Ecgfrith King, making preparations...'

Edberht interrupted him.

'The bishop is to undertake a mission to the Picts?'

'Yes. As the king's emissary. The king insists that the

Picts renounce their disarrangement of the Catholic Easter. He believes that God wishes him to complete the task undertaken by his father Oswiu King, that God will reward him in some way, that...'

'Yes, yes,' Edberht said. 'But when does the bishop set out? He will surely visit us before he departs?'

'He will come to Lindisfarne once the preparations are in place,' Tydi said. 'Perhaps tomorrow.'

'And Brother Laurence?' Herefrith asked. 'He is to accompany the bishop?'

Tydi flushed. He brought the cup to his lips but replaced it on the table without drinking.

'Brother Laurence,' he began. 'Brother Laurence...'

'What of Brother Laurence?' Edberht said, sharply.

'He is...' Was Wilfrid imagining it or did Tydi glance at him? 'He is lost... That is, he is gone to his heavenly reward.'

Silence followed. Then a thud as someone sat heavily onto the bench.

'Plague then,' Dunstan said, his voice bitter as vinegar. 'It was plague that took him?'

'Yes,' Tydi said.

'When?'

'Some months ago. Before the bishop's investiture.'

'We will pray for our departed brother,' Edberht said. His voice trembled. 'He gave his life that others might be healed.'

One by one the monks knelt as Edberht began the prayer. Except for Dunstan. A strangled sound emitted from his throat as he pushed past Wilfrid and lurched through the door.

*

Afterwards, Wilfrid wanted to go to Tydi, who must know about Sigi, but it felt unseemly to pester Tydi with questions when the whole community was grieving for Laurence. And besides, he didn't know how to face him. Tydi must surely despise him for deserting the monastery. Worse, he would not be able to hide his feelings. Tydi, who knew him better than anyone, would see the viper of jealousy that bit at his heart. He went back into the rinsing house, and spent the afternoon there, treating the calfskins, washing and rinsing them in the trough, breathing in the stench of putrid flesh.

Just before Vespers, he heard footsteps.

'God bless you, Brother Wilfrid.' Tydi stood at the door. 'I trust you are well?'

Tydi's voice was sombre, older. He held himself very erect, like Cuthbert. He had a beard now, though it spread unevenly and was thin and fuzzy in patches. His head was freshly shaven, his scalp smooth, gleaming. He had taken time to remove the mud stains from his habit.

'Well, Brother Tydi, and you?'

'Well enough. The loss of Brother Laurence was a sore trial, but God has been gracious to the bishop and me and wrapped us in His protection.'

Us. Wilfrid tasted the word – a sour apple. He wondered how it had been for Tydi really. The plague-ridden villages, ministering to the afflicted as they reached out with sore-laden arms, coughed globules of poisoned phlegm into the air, writhed in death throes... He pushed the thought away, back to the dark lair of his heart from which it had come. Tydi would have watched Cuthbert, done as he was bid, learned quickly. He would be a priest someday; that was certain.

'We travelled to many places,' Tydi went on. 'You should see York. The church there – it's bigger than a fortress and made of stone. And not just the church. The city itself is stone, surrounded by stone walls, but...' He frowned. '...But even the mighty walls of York are no defence against plague. Some places are so afflicted. So many taken. It seems the pestilence has devoured almost entire villages, and those who are left are but shadows of people, living skeletons.'

Wilfrid swallowed hard.

'What of Medilwong?' he said.

Tydi sighed deeply.

'It was badly struck. So many already dead when we got there, some unburied. The blacksmith still at his anvil, his hands ravaged with sores. The contagion had wound its way through the village. Those who survived were angry, bitter. Some of them didn't...well, they didn't welcome us. They said we were the same as the brother who had polluted the village. They spat on us, cursed us, said God – *your* God, they said, *your* Christ – He had turned His face against them, was punishing them for some offence they knew nothing of. One old man said it wasn't Christ at all, but the old gods taking revenge on the village for deserting them, by sending a priest to infect them.'

Wilfrid sat on the edge of the trough. He gripped it tightly.

'It was too late then,' he said.

The words were a whisper. He wasn't sure if Tydi had heard.

'The bishop preached anyway. Some turned away. The old man shouted at him, vile words laced with the devil's bile. Brother Laurence and I went to seek out anyone still suffering from the pestilence. We didn't have far to look. The wife of the warmaster came weeping, wailing. She'd been waiting, she said, didn't believe help would come. Her servant had succumbed, and her son, this poor creature in her arms, his whole body swollen, was already half-dead and breathing his last. The bishop himself took the child, brought him into the house and laid him on a bed. He blessed the boy, over and over, kissed him. I saw a tear fall from his eye. He bade Brother Laurence make a poultice and a drink of yarrow and calendula, though our herbs and medicaments were running low, and it seemed certain this boy could not come back from the threshold of death. But he insisted we stay there all night, sing psalms, keep the offices, and then, just at dawn, the fever began to abate. The boy opened his eyes.'

Wilfrid lifted his head, tried to catch his breath.

'You mean, he lives?'

'Yes, he lives. He opened his eyes, as I've said. He spoke, asked for his mama. The boy lives, but...'

Wilfrid breathed out a long low sigh. The tightness that had gripped his chest for months began to uncoil. It had not been in vain. Everything he had done – it wasn't in vain. Sigi lived. And he had made what atonement he could, carried out every penance asked of him, and more, fulfilled his bargain with Christ, given his life to the monastery in return for Sigi's survival. Yet it wasn't that simple, he knew. He had sold Cuthbert to the king, sold him like Judas sold Christ. Worse, unlike Judas, he did not renounce his sin. How could he, since his actions had led to Sigi's recovery? That sin had wormed deep into his soul, would sit tightly locked there till Judgement Day, when he must answer not only to Cuthbert but to God.

'But...' Tydi hadn't finished. He paced up and down. 'There's something else you should know.'

And suddenly Wilfrid realised. He had been wilfully blind.

'It's Brother Laurence, isn't it? That's when he fell victim. When you were in Medilwong.'

'Yes. In Medilwong.'

Wilfrid leaned against the trough, his face in his hands. He hadn't thought. Hadn't thought of the risks to others. Now Laurence was lost, just like Fergus.

'Our hearts were rent at his loss,' Tydi said. 'But, God be praised, his suffering was not long, and he, at least, went peacefully to the Lord, unlike, unlike the girl...'

'The girl?'

'The slave girl. It was a terrible death,' Tydi said quietly. 'The fever drove her to madness, I think. The bishop did his best, tried to get her to take the last of the yarrow drink, but she could not swallow, or...or else she would not. He kept trying to make her drink, but she pressed her lips together and turned her head from him. Even the droplets of holy water he blessed her with seemed to give her more discomfort than relief.'

He shook his head slowly.

'It seemed to me she wished to be released from this world, that she did not wish to be saved, though I thought it must be a terrible blasphemy to fight against a miracle of the Lord. Sometimes I still see her, her pustule-ridden face, that bitter smile.'

'Kendra,' Wilfrid said. 'Her name was Kendra.'

The bell for Vespers rang. It was time for silence. But Tydi spoke again, hurriedly. 'Wilfrid, I did try. I tried to make them see that it was not you who brought the plague. But they clung to their suspicion. The brother who had come before us had infected them, they said. They said I didn't know what I was talking about, that things had happened before. The bishop told me not to pursue it. They are a people with superstition carved in their hearts.'

'It doesn't matter,' Wilfrid said. 'It doesn't matter.'

'You don't understand,' Tydi said. 'The slave girl. I heard her talking to the bishop. A runaway slave had come to the village, someone known to her – kin, I think. She kept him hidden in an empty pigpen. We found his body after she died. It was putrid, pus-filled, crusted with sores. Don't you see? He must have come to her seeking help, carried the infection to her, and then it spread to the entire village. You have done many things, Wilfrid. Sometimes I don't understand how it is you are still here at this monastery. But you should not carry the blame for this. It is unjust.'

Wilfrid looked at Tydi, saw the boy in him again, the boy who had shown him the ways of the monastery, the one who had taught him the signs to use at table, helped him with his chores, advised him never to cross Herefrith or put a question to Eadfrith, the one who cheered him when he had earned the lash of Dunstan's whip or tongue, a good monk who would make a good priest.

'It doesn't matter,' he said. 'Really. The bishop is

right. It's best left now.'

They walked down the hill to the church. He thought about the slave girl. Kendra. Her face expressionless, her head held down. Had she felt as he did now? That cold terror of knowing she was a death-carrier. Watching Sigi grow ill. Watching the others, Oswine, the blacksmith, his wife, the villagers. He too held responsibility for death. Fergus, and now Laurence, had died because of him. And yet, God had heard his prayer. Sigi lived. Wilfrid took his place in the church. At the office the psalm rang out.

*Confitemini Domino quoniam bonus
quoniam in aeternum Misericordia eius.*

Wilfrid stayed behind in the church when the brethren had left. He knelt before the holy relics of St Aidan, praying for Kendra, prayed that her soul might not be blighted, that she had turned to God and not away from Him as she died. He prayed for Laurence and Fergus too. He felt he would never be acquitted of their deaths. And that was his punishment. To know that he could never make reparation for what had happened.

When he went outside he looked out to Cuthbert's Rock. A sliver of moonlight glinted silver-white on the sea. Out on the sandspits the seals sang a dirge; their mournful song echoed in Wilfrid's ears as he returned to his cell.

Two

THE SUDDEN RINGING of a bell pealed across the island. It rang with such clamour that Wilfrid thought at first some calamity had befallen the monastery, and he ran out from the scriptorium to discover what was happening. From all over the island monks had abandoned their work and were scurrying down to the beach. Even Eadfrith had left his manuscript unattended and was moving quickly to catch up. Only Dunstan moved slowly, picking his way carefully down the path, occasionally reaching out an arm to the hedge at his side. Wilfrid followed, even more slowly than Dunstan, keeping a distance.

A boat drawn by two oarsmen was approaching the shore. A tall man, staff in hand, his cloak billowing behind him, stood erect at the prow. Something hung at his chest, gleaming red and gold as it caught the sun. Several of the brethren flung off their boots, hitched up their robes and pulled the boat into shallow water. Edberht greeted Cuthbert first, kneeling down on the wet sand to receive the bishop's blessing. The other monks followed, Dunstan last of all. He stumbled as he went to kneel, but Cuthbert caught him and held onto him as he knelt.

Wilfrid crouched in the sand behind long grasses. He couldn't bear to approach. Arriving late and alone, all eyes would be drawn to see how the bishop would meet the disgraced and errant monk, the one who had flown from him, abandoned his community, broken the bonds of brotherhood. He clenched his fists, his fingernails digging into the sores in his palms. Cuthbert should surely be glad he had repented of his sins and returned, a prodigal son, ready to make good his errors, to take the tonsure. As bishop, shepherd of the flock, Cuthbert should surely forgive him. But Cuthbert had underestimated the darkness of his heart, did not know to what extent Wilfrid had betrayed him, probably would never suspect. And he wondered which would be the harder to endure, Cuthbert's condemnation or his forgiveness.

He crept back up the path. There was still much work to do with the calfskins, stretching, cutting, plucking out the hairs and impurities. He would lie low. Cuthbert could not be staying long – not if he was on his way to Pictland. He slipped away and set to work. The pealing of the bell echoed after him.

After the midday meal Cuthbert stood to speak. He

was wearing a new robe, Wilfrid noticed, with a white woollen stole. The gleaming object at his chest was a large, golden cross studded with a brilliance of glittering garnets. It must be a weight around his neck. Cuthbert kept rubbing it between his finger and thumb, worrying the garnets so much that Wilfrid would not have been surprised if one of the tiny jewels dislodged.

'Ecce quam bonum et quam iucundum habitare fratres in unum!' Cuthbert said. 'Behold, how good and how pleasant it is for brethren to dwell together in unity! It is like the precious ointment upon the head, that ran down upon the beard, even Aaron's beard: that went down to the skirts of his garments.'

Wilfrid sensed a series of smiles and nods at the familiar text as the monks settled down to listen to the forthcoming sermon.

'How often does the psalmist strike for us the right note?' Cuthbert went on. 'He sings to us of our sorrows and despair. He names our troubles, our desires, lays bare our wretchedness and opens our hearts. He tells us truths our own tongues cannot voice and fills our souls with hope and promise we dare not express.'

Cuthbert's eyes were bright, burning.

'Is it mere happenstance that tonight at Vespers the order of the office will bring us to this particular psalm? Or is the Lord speaking to us now, directing our hearts to look to unity, reconciliation?'

He paused, as if waiting for a response. Wilfrid was aware of a chorus of nodding heads about him.

'Brothers, some twenty years ago the communities in Christ who share these islands at the very edge of the world, were ripped apart. Holy men and women who had joined in fellowship to dedicate themselves to God suddenly found themselves on opposite sides of a battlefield. Whose Easter is the true Easter? Whose tonsure is the true living mark of Christ? One champions St Peter, another St John. One calls on the venerable memories of St Columba and our own St Aidan, another on the authority of the pope, the anointed successor of Peter himself. Thus the saints who guide us are pitted against each other by wily words and disputing tongues.'

So many saints. Wilfrid could barely keep track of them all or which tradition they guarded. He had never understood how the differences in the dating of Easter and the manner of the tonsure caused such rancour that it split the Church.

Cuthbert continued.

'I do not mean, brothers, to call up again the torments of those days, the divisions, the endless arguments. For those of us who lived through them, the memory of bidding farewell to the brethren who departed from us, set sail for Iona and for the shores of Ireland, is an old ache that has never gone away.

'Yet, that these men could not accept the judgement of Oswiu King speaks less of obstinate and obdurate hearts and more of a fervent love for the customs of our most holy forefathers, of their cleaving to a solemn discipline, ancient and holy. And even the fortunate ones among you, too young to conceive of those men as anything other than schismatics, must understand that God's purpose for the world is brought into disorder when there are divisions among his servants.'

Schismatics. That was how Ecgfrith King had

described the Picts and the monks of Iona, Wilfrid remembered. He shivered. The draught coming from the open shutter was an icy gale. He turned his head to the window, half-expecting a flurry of snowflakes, but there was nothing. Cuthbert raised his voice.

'It's time to heal these old wounds which have scarred communities of holy men and women for twenty years. Tomorrow at first light I set sail for the monastery at Arbroath. From there I journey to other monasteries in Pictland and then to the stronghold of Bruide, their king. I trust that with God's help I may find words to persuade those who rejected the judgement of Oswiu King at Whitby to open their hearts now to the rites of the universal Church, to reunite in spirit with their brothers in Northumbria and beyond.

'For if we, the sons of Aidan, can accept the decrees of Rome while still holding to Aidan's order and tradition, then surely others too may reconsider. And so, I beg that your prayers for me, for my mission, will be unceasing. Our Pictish family in Christ may not yet be moved by strong words and apostolic decree, but I trust that the love and prayers of their brethren will not fail.'

Something had changed in Cuthbert's manner, his voice. He spoke to the community almost as a great warrior about to lead men into battle. And Wilfrid remembered that he had once been a warrior in the service of Oswiu King and had earned that king's favour.

The monks looked at their new bishop, full of admiration. Dunstan's eyes were shining. He was of an age with Cuthbert, must remember the Synod of

Whitby at which Oswiu gave his judgement. Perhaps he had been there with Cuthbert, came afterwards to Lindisfarne with him. He and Herefrith were Cuthbert's closest allies, as Fergus had once been.

Edberht stood to address them.

'Our bishop has spoken well. Let the Spirit of the Lord guide all brethren in reconciliation. For who knows? If the Picts can be persuaded, then surely our brethren on Iona and beyond will soon follow? We will pray for the success of this great mission and for the safe return of Bishop Cuthbert. Tonight I will light a fresh candle on the altar. It will remain burning until the bishop returns.'

He said the Grace, and the monks cleared the tables. Cuthbert blessed them all and departed. He didn't look at Wilfrid as he went out.

That afternoon Wilfrid busied himself in the scriptorium. Cuthbert was meeting with Edberht and other senior monks. After Vespers he would go to the Rock and spend the night there in retreat before setting off the following morning. With luck, Wilfrid would not have to face him at all.

He worked steadily, smoothing out a prepared calfskin and cutting it into even quires. A sudden stream of light burst into the room. Edberht stood in the doorway.

'So, this is where you have been hiding,' he said.

Wilfrid made to object but Edberht silenced him.

'Now listen, after nightfall you are to go to the Rock.'

'The Rock?'

'Yes. The bishop wishes to speak with you. Alone.'

Wilfrid's chest tightened. He should have known there would be a reckoning, that he would have to answer for his desertion after all. He returned to his cell and stayed there until evening brought a dark and starless sky.

Three

WILFRID MADE HIS WAY to the Rock, his path lit only by an occasional glint from the half-moon as it drifted in and out of the clouds. He dreaded coming face to face with Cuthbert, but at least this way his chastisement would not take place publicly. The wind whistled about him; the seals sang plaintive, discordant notes. As he clambered onto the Rock the moon retreated behind a cloud. He paused, unsure of his bearings. This wasn't the main island where he knew every path, every ridge, mound and depression as well as the callouses on his hands. It had been years since he had been out here. He should have taken a lantern, but he had been reluctant to draw attention to himself. Now in the darkness he was as helpless as a blind man, groping his way along. *Just like Dunstan,* he thought. He crouched down and waited for the moon to reappear. From somewhere very close by came the sound of a voice, high and urgent.

'I cannot remain silent about my concerns. Ecgfrith should not demand this of you.'

Wilfrid stiffened. That was Herefrith's voice. What was he doing here? Was he to oversee whatever punishment Cuthbert would mete out to him?

'It is not Ecgfrith alone who demands it,' Cuthbert said sharply. 'You do wrong to criticise your bishop. And to come here uninvited.'

So it seemed Cuthbert had not expected Herefrith's visit. Wilfrid wasn't sure what to do now – make a noise, announce his approach? Herefrith spoke again, cautiously.

'Forgive me, Bishop, I know you believe God requires this of you, but hear me as one of your oldest friends: I fear this is an unwise mission, and dangerous also.'

'You insult me, Brother Herefrith! To attempt to reconcile all our brethren, cast old enmities aside, that we may share the same Easter in unity together – this is unwise?'

'You're asking them to break with the faith of their holy fathers, to abandon the holy rites observed by their beloved saints, to betray the very men who showed them how to be monks. And for what? For some whim of a hostile king. That is how they will see it, at any rate.'

Wilfrid heard the sound of pacing back and forth.

'No, no,' Cuthbert said. 'We have observed the new customs on this island for twenty years now. We have prospered. Neither God nor Aidan has cursed us. The brethren in Brega and Armagh have come over to the new ways.'

'Yes, at the point of a sword.'

'Herefrith, that is why our Pictish brothers must consider again. Because if they cannot be made to listen by eloquent words then I fear they too will be made to listen by the thrust of the sword.'

There was silence for a moment. Wilfrid edged a little closer to the oratory.

'I have had word from Iona,' Cuthbert said at last.

Did Wilfrid imagine it or was there a trace of anxiety in Cuthbert's tone? Iona lay in the most western reaches of the world, almost as far as Ireland, and the monks there, Wilfrid knew, were mired in the same stubborn heresies as the Picts.

'Aldfrith has left the monastery there,' Cuthbert continued.

Aldfrith. Wilfrid remembered now. Ecgfrith's half-brother. Aldfrith of Iona, the bastard son of Oswiu King and some Irish princess. *A brother no less than the other.* That was who Cuthbert had been talking about in his discussion with Abbess Ælfflæd.

'I see...' Herefrith sounded as if he did not see at all. 'Where has he gone? Back to Ireland?'

'Possibly,' Cuthbert said. 'I wonder if he is gathering allies?'

'Allies? For what purpose?'

'There is no *ætheling*, no clear successor,' Cuthbert continued. 'Aldfrith, I believe, is ready to step forward.'

Herefrith laughed.

'But he cannot hope to challenge Ecgfrith, surely? He is no warrior. He's a scholar, a monk, older than

Ecgfrith.'

Herefrith was right, Wilfrid thought. After hearing the stories of Ecgfrith's terrible victories in Ireland, Wilfrid doubted anyone could threaten him.

Cuthbert spoke again.

'From what Abbess Ælfflæd told me some months ago, Aldfrith wishes only to be acknowledged as his brother's heir. I have let it be known to him that when the time comes, *if* it comes, he will have my backing. But it may be, if God wills it, that Aldfrith won't be needed in Bamburgh.'

Wilfrid thought he heard a sharp intake of breath.

'There has been a development?'

'The king believes a development is imminent. I blessed the queen in York, blessed her belly, her chamber, her bed. I gave her holy water to drink.'

Another pause, followed by Herefrith clearing his throat.

'Tell me, Bishop, did you bless the king too?'

'The king trusts his...um...endeavours have been successful. I am told that he made several visits to the queen's chamber.'

'And the queen?'

'Keeps her counsel. It has been but a few weeks.'

'And you think that after all these years...'

'I think these are dangerous times, Brother Herefrith. All we can do is pray and work for a peaceful succession.'

There was silence for a moment. Wilfrid saw his opportunity, knocked at the door and entered.

A single stub of a candle illuminated the room. Cuthbert and Herefrith stood to one side, their heads bent for fear of hitting against the low roof.

'You have been long outside, Wilfrid?' Cuthbert said, sharply.

Wilfrid hung his head. He hadn't asked to come here, hadn't meant to listen, and now the speech in his head about penance and reparation was swallowed up in a mire of confusion.

'Answer the bishop when he speaks to you,' Herefrith said.

'I will deal with Wilfrid,' Cuthbert said. 'You needn't worry about him, Brother Herefrith. His eyes and ears are ever alert, but his lips remain tight, his tongue still. Usually.'

Herefrith nodded, grimly, then bowed his head for Cuthbert's blessing and left.

'Well, Wilfrid,' Cuthbert said.

Wilfrid waited for the admonition, the punishment, but only silence followed. He knew he should apologise, beg forgiveness, but the words stuck in his throat.

'Sigi,' he said eventually. If he could not force himself to apologise to Cuthbert he could at least thank him. 'You saved my brother.'

'God saved your brother, Wilfrid – not I.'

'But if you hadn't gone to Medilwong perhaps Brother Laurence might not have died.'

'God took Brother Laurence to himself. We cannot question His reasons. But, yes, his loss will be felt keenly, especially by Brother Dunstan, who, I believe, had come to rely on his assistance more and more of late.' Cuthbert stared intently at Wilfrid. 'You do know what it is that Christ asks of you?'

Wilfrid stared back, in disbelief.

'Wilfrid, you will forgive Brother Dunstan for any wrongs you may perceive he has committed against you. You will remember that he is your brother and you will bind yourself to him as such. You will watch for him as you would a brother of your flesh. You will be his servant and his guide, his hands, his feet, his eyes, and you will do all this silently and discreetly, without expectation of thanks or reward. Do you understand?'

Wilfrid nodded, slowly.

Cuthbert stretched out his hand. Wilfrid hesitated. He had come expecting Cuthbert to curse him, not bless him but slowly, he knelt, bent his head and closed his eyes. Above him he heard the words of the psalm:

Dominus custodit te ab omni malo:
custodit animam tuam Dominus.

Wilfrid breathed out an *Amen*, stood up and turned to go. But Cuthbert called him back.

'Wilfrid, I believe that on your journey from Medilwong back to our monastery you diverted your course to the Royal City. Is this correct?'

Wilfrid's heart pounded. So this was why Cuthbert had summoned him. It wasn't just about Dunstan. Cuthbert must somehow have discovered what had passed between himself and the king and had been waiting for him to confess.

'Yes,' he said, a tiny tremble in his voice.

'Wilfrid, I wonder did you hear any mention at all of Aldfrith when you were in Bamburgh? Or elsewhere on your travels?'

A rush of relief flowed through Wilfrid. It seemed

Cuthbert was more concerned with Aldfrith than with him.

'No, nothing.' Again Wilfrid made to leave, but his curiosity had been aroused now. 'Why?'

'I just wondered. There are some who say that beneath his scholar's cloak Aldfrith hides a worldly ambition.'

Cuthbert sounded weary, not the man whose fire-filled tones had roused the brethren only a few hours before. He blessed Wilfrid again.

'Keep me in your prayers,' Wilfrid heard him say as he closed the oratory door.

Later, Wilfrid lay awake in his cell. Cuthbert couldn't have chosen a worse punishment for him. To be bound to Dunstan, to have to watch out for him at all times. It didn't bear thinking about. He rolled over, his mind turning to Aldfrith – an old man, a monk, a scholar, would-be *ætheling*. Aldfrith King. It didn't make sense. And yet Aldfrith was a king's son too, banished to a monastery while his younger brother sat on the thronestool, claiming a stolen birthright. It was unjust. As Wilfrid drifted into sleep a dark thought whispered to him. Why should Aldfrith be denied?

Four

CUTHBERT LEFT AT FIRST LIGHT. The monks waited for his return. For two weeks they tended the torch which burned in the watchtower to guide him safely back, watched the sea for a currach with the bishop's standard. But the only boats that passed were fishing and trading vessels. The king demanded news of the bishop, but the messenger sent to Lindisfarne was dismissed with empty hands. There had been no report, no rumour, no sign, though the messenger said there were signs enough in the queen's household for anybody to see: it appeared the queen's belly was ripening at last.

'A miracle, if it's true,' Herefrith said later, in Chapter.

'Yes,' Edberht agreed. 'Who knows what mountains may be moved by faith? This, I think, must augur well for the bishop's mission in the North. It is a sign that the Lord is with him. The Lord has worked through Bishop Cuthbert and shown his favour to Ecgfrith King. The Picts will surely concede now, accept Rome's dating of Easter and St Peter's tonsure.'

The brethren knelt and gave thanks for the news. They prayed the queen would be safely delivered of a son and that the bishop's mission in the North would come to a swift and successful conclusion. Wilfrid hoped that Edberht was right. Still, he felt uneasy. Over in Bamburgh, everyone knew, the king was gathering his army; his warriors were training night and day. Wilfrid kept thinking about the conversation he had overheard between Cuthbert and Herefrith that night on the Rock and grew ever more anxious, watching and waiting for Cuthbert to come back.

This must be how Dunstan felt all the time, Wilfrid supposed, staring out over a mist-laden sea one morning. He had been trying to carry out Cuthbert's instructions, to be Dunstan's guide, his servant. He watched for when Dunstan needed more ink, offered assistance in cutting his vellum into quires or tidying his desk when the day's work was finished. At table he passed the food closer to him. But Dunstan pushed all help away with an impatient wave of his hand, and Wilfrid began to think it was pointless even trying. Sometimes he stole a glance at Dunstan's work. It was progressing slowly, and there was an increasing number of blemishes in the manuscript: ink spots, letters with straggling tails and shivery ascenders, margins that undulated like waves instead of standing straight as a sword.

Often during the day, Dunstan made his way to the church, slowly picking his way down the winding path, stabbing at the ground with the staff he now used. Wilfrid watched him now, lumbering towards the church, his robe flailing about him as the wind whipped in from the sea. He was without a cloak.

Wilfrid grimaced and returned to the scriptorium where the other scribes were busy at work. Dunstan's cloak wasn't hanging on the peg where he normally left it. Eventually Wilfrid found it bundled at the back of a shelf next to some rough goatskin parchment the novice scribes used for practising on. Someone giggled. Wilfrid looked around. One of the novices, his cheeks very red, shuffled in his seat. Wilfrid remembered Dunstan thrashing the same boy a few days before for some misdemeanour or other. He rolled the cloak up under his arm and followed Dunstan to the church.

Dunstan was kneeling on a cushion of rushes in front of the altar.

'Who's there?' he asked sharply. He turned around, and Wilfrid noticed that his eyes were now so cloud-filled they hardly seemed to see him at all.

'It's me. Brother Wilfrid.'

'You should be in the scriptorium.' Dunstan leaned on his staff to pull himself up from the floor. 'Didn't I tell you to copy out the accounts of the gifts of calfskin from Bamburgh?'

'I've finished them, Brother Dunstan. I've brought...'

'What is it? A message? Word of Bishop Cuthbert?'

'No, Brother Dunstan.' Wilfrid held out the cloak. 'I thought you would need this.'

Dunstan reached for his cloak with trembling hands,

clutched it to his chest.

'What are you doing with this?' He stepped forward and pointed his finger at Wilfrid, almost stabbing him in the chest. 'It was you. You took it, hid it, didn't you? You know the punishment for thieving. I should see you whipped before the community for this.'

Wilfrid gritted his teeth. He was a fool for coming.

'I found your cloak on the floor,' he said. 'It must have fallen off its peg.'

'Indeed. Tell me, Brother Wilfrid, how is it that when trouble arises you always seem to be standing right next to it? I say you hid my cloak and brought it here to torment me. Why else?'

Wilfrid clenched his fists, tried to quench the simmering fury that was rising from his chest into his mouth; he must keep it from alighting on his tongue. But the taste of vengeance was sweeter than blackberries dipped in honey.

'Because Bishop Cuthbert instructed me to.' He paused to watch the look of confusion, anxiety spreading over Dunstan's face like a rash. 'Before he left for Pictland. He said I must care for you. And forgive you.'

'Forgive me!'

Dunstan's face was mottled red and purple, his Adam's apple pulsing.

'He said you need an assistant; you cannot make do. I must be your eyes, he said – your servant, your guide.'

Dunstan shook his head. He wagged his finger at Wilfrid again.

'It's my punishment you see,' Wilfrid said. 'For running off that time. My punishment is to be bound to you, even though you have always hated me. You hated me before you even knew me. No matter how hard I tried, you never gave me a chance. And still I must forgive you!'

Dunstan dropped his cloak, caught Wilfrid by the arm, brought his face close to Wilfrid's, his mouth so wide open that Wilfrid could see each of his seven yellow teeth. His mouth widened into a smile. A hollow wheeze came from his throat on cabbage-scented breath. Wilfrid pulled away, roughly. He had never heard Dunstan laugh.

'The bishop is great in his wisdom,' Dunstan said. He laughed again, shaking his head. 'God has gifted you with a scribe's keen eye, but has given you the understanding of a mule. Don't you see? The punishment you spoke of – well-deserved, yes, well-deserved – but it's for me as much as for you, and the greater pain of it must be endured by me.'

Dunstan leaned heavily on his staff, so heavily Wilfrid feared it would snap.

'I wronged you, yes, once, and other times also. Too late now, too late, and no reparation to be made, no forgiveness, no matter how sorry I am for it. You know it. The bishop knows it too.'

Dunstan's face clouded again. Wilfrid edged away, the simmering anger cooled, the sweetness of vengeful words a bitter aftertaste in his mouth. He was weary suddenly, tired of the pattern of conflict that repeated itself between them, and this humble sorrowful Dunstan left him queasy. Dunstan advanced slowly towards him, reached for his arm.

'Well then, if the bishop wills it, you may be my eyes,

walk ahead of me, make straight my path. The day is dark.'

Wilfrid gave Dunstan his arm, tried not to flinch at his trembling grip. Slowly he led him down the hill towards the scriptorium.

The understanding of a mule. It had never occurred to him that Cuthbert would find fault with Dunstan, let alone punish him. He didn't understand Cuthbert's reasoning, why he should push himself and Dunstan together. He didn't understand Cuthbert no matter how hard he tried, could see him but through a glass, darkly, as the apostle put it. Dunstan was right. Everything was dark. Wilfrid looked back up the coast. All he could see was the grey and heavy sky, the empty sea.

Five

THE EASTER SEASON was drawing to a close when
the bishop returned. In the ice-dawn light, just
before Lauds, the window in Cuthbert's cell on
the Rock flapped open in the wind. Wilfrid ran from
the watchtower where he had been tending the torch-
fire and made his way across. Cuthbert lay prostrate
in the shadows of the oratory, his arms outstretched
making a cross of his body. He was still, still as a dead
man, and for one terrible moment Wilfrid thought he
was dead, that he had been laid out for the monks of
Lindisfarne to mourn.

'Who is it?'

The words shook Wilfrid out of his imaginings.
Cuthbert's voice was faint, but at least he was alive.

'It's just me. Wilfrid.'

'Just Wilfrid. Good. Come here, Wilfrid. Pray with me.'

Wilfrid walked forward into the gloom. He lay down on the ground next to Cuthbert and prayed, not knowing what he was praying for. Cuthbert was reciting something, disparate whisperings that died away even as the words were formed.

Wilfrid had expected him to pray aloud, to lift his voice to God, as he usually did, and these breathy mutterings seemed not to belong to Cuthbert at all, but to some crook-backed ancient, teetering on the edge of this world and the one to come. He whispered the same verse over and over:

Ne projicias me in tempore senectutis;
cum defecerit virtus mea, derelinquas me.

Wilfrid pulled himself to his knees. There was something foul here, something in Cuthbert's hoarse psalm-whispers that made it seem he had caught a contagion – not the plague, but a disease far worse – and Wilfrid didn't know how to contain it.

'Bishop,' he said. 'The brethren have been waiting. They've been worried. Prior Edberht needs to speak with you.'

Cuthbert continued to pray.

'Bishop, the community needs you. The people need you. The king is preparing for war. He pays no heed to Prior Edberht. You're the bishop, the people's shepherd. You must lead us.'

Cuthbert's whisperings trailed away. He put out his hand to Wilfrid.

'Help me up.'

His fingers were needles of ice.

'And it's the wrong psalm,' Wilfrid said, pulling him up.

'What?'

'At least not that verse. You shouldn't pray that verse. God would never desert you.'

Cuthbert leaned on Wilfrid's shoulder.

'You have studied the scriptures well, Wilfrid. The Lord has armed you with words to teach your elders. And, yes, you are right. God does not desert us.' He clasped his pectoral cross, traced his thumb over it, back and forth. 'It is we who desert Him, close our hearts to His voice, let the devil slip his oiled tongue in our ears instead. The devil's voice is smooth, dripping in the sweetest of honey. Especially sweet to an old man. I've tasted his honey, Wilfrid, swallowed it, let him in.'

'No, Bishop. You're tired. Worn from your journey. That's all. The devil isn't speaking to you.'

'But he did speak to me, Wilfrid. Quite clearly. On the Farne. Oh, he was clever; wily. Used no less than the king himself as his mouth, and worse, Archbishop Theodore and my own brethren. And I listened. I listened to the Evil One, did his bidding, left the Farne, deserted my hermitage and anchored myself instead to a rock of vanity and dream-filled ambition, which must end in failure.'

Wilfrid's cheeks flushed.

'But it wasn't the devil, Bishop. It was the king, the archbishop, the abbess, Prior Edberht, the brethren, everyone...'

'He knew I was weakened by age and infirmity, by whisperings from the old days – the brethren I had betrayed, telling me I should set the past aright. I thought that message about your brother was a sign, and then when God healed him I took it as another sign, that God was with me, that He wanted me to heal other wounds – wounds more deep and vicious than any inflicted on the body: wounds on the souls and hearts of our brethren.'

'You were out on that island long enough. How many demons could there have been left to fight? You were needed elsewhere. The plague, people needed healing, comfort. Have you forgotten all that?'

'Wilfrid, what I forgot is this. God did not call me to the Farne because it was easy. He called me because it was hard. And when the devil sent the most cunning temptation of all I didn't see through its disguise.'

Cuthbert went over to the little window and leaned his head against the wall.

'*Ne projicias me in tempore senectutis.*'

Wilfrid felt an urge to stamp his foot hard on the ground, like a small child.

'God can't have deserted you,' he said.

'He has turned His face from me, on this matter at least, as did Bruide King, as did all the Pictish brethren, one by one. I have failed.'

Failed. So despite the miracles that spoke in favour of the bishop, despite Ecgfrith's threat of war, the Picts had refused to come over.

'Brother Herefrith was right,' Cuthbert continued. 'When I was finally admitted into Bruide's presence he spat at me, said it was perfidious enough that at Whitby

I had turned my back on the saints and brethren of old. Now I was trying to lure his people away from the protection of St Columba, and who but Columba could protect them from the plague that was ravaging all of Northumbria? He said I was a mere emissary of Ecgfrith King, Ecgfrith so-called King – that's how he named him – a king so unmanned he couldn't even provide his kingdom with a girlchild, let alone an *ætheling*, and that it was all a foolish plot, a pretext on which I was to scheme a surrender to Ecgfrith. Soon the envoys would come looking not for a surrender of the true Easter, but of gold, slaves, their best men as hostages. He said I was merely the anvil on which Ecgfrith sharpens his sword and he would not become a lot to be cast in Ecgfrith's bargain with Christ.'

He tugged at the chain of his pectoral cross as though he would wrench it from his neck.

'God has taken my sight. I have seen nothing since I left the Farne. And now there will be war.'

Cuthbert bent his head. He seemed small, crumpled, like an empty sack. Wilfrid thought a world where Cuthbert could not see God's light must be a place darker than any he himself would experience. And if God had taken Cuthbert's sight it was Wilfrid's fault. He was the devil who had shown Ecgfrith how to lure Cuthbert from the Farne, who had caused his mission to fail. He was the one who had summoned the darkness.

'*Signatum est super nos lumen vultus tui, Domine,*' Wilfrid said. '*Signatum est super nos lumen vultus tui.*'

Something caught his eye through the open window behind Cuthbert. A speck of cloth waving and flapping in the distance.

'But perhaps war can be averted,' Wilfrid said. 'The queen is with child. Surely if God gives Ecgfrith an *ætheling*, Ecgfrith can be persuaded to relinquish his plan to convert the Picts to the true Easter. It may be the brethren will remain in disharmony over Easter, but at least war will be prevented.'

Cuthbert shook his head.

'It's not that simple, Wilfrid.' He opened the door of the cell. 'Look.'

Wilfrid went to the door. This time, he clearly saw a large boat out in the bay, its sail flapping in the wind. It was surrounded by other smaller boats, a whole fleet of them, all driving north over the sea.

'Ecgfrith didn't listen to me either,' Cuthbert said. 'I went to him last night. Rage has consumed him. Rage and terror.'

'I don't understand. The boats are sailing to Pictland? But why now, when the queen's belly is ripening, when God has finally answered his prayers, does Ecgfrith want to battle Bruide?'

Cuthbert sat on the edge of the Rock.

'To ensure the child's safe delivery. He is frightened, always looking behind him, fearful of some enemy or conspirator lurking in the shadows. He says God has appointed him protector of the queen's womb. God will deliver him a live son only if he delivers to God a people who observe Easter in the right manner. In that way he will protect his son. He thinks he owes it now to God to punish the Picts for their stubbornness. Or else he will be punished. For what, he does not say. I suppose he means the war in Ireland; the hostages.'

'But surely he will listen to you if you tell him the

war is unjust?'

'I told you, God has turned his face from me. Ecgfrith sees that and turns from me too. Besides, he has other advisors, some who have not love of God in their hearts, nor desire for reconciliation, but harbour a stronger, darker need: to move men, manipulate them like children do the little stick figures they play with.'

The boats were leaving the harbour and sailing out into the wider sea the smaller vessels still flanking the larger ship. Ecgfrith would be on that ship. Wilfrid's father, the warmaster, would be there too.

'You mean my father, don't you? He is one of the men who counsels Ecgfrith against you. Even though you cured Sigi, he counsels against you.'

Cuthbert sighed.

'He is the warmaster. He looks beyond these things. He looks north and sees not the brethren who have been divided from us, not the men who might be our allies, still less the women and children who must ever endure men's thirst for bloodletting. He sees instead Bruide King, the small seedlings of a threat to Ecgfrith. A warmaster will not counsel waiting for the seedlings to grow, or for men to desire peace, for Christ's sake. And then there is the matter of the Irish.'

'What do you mean?'

'Ecgfrith is terrified as well as enraged. The terror is all around him, right in his own fortress. The Irish will not come to the Picts' side while Ecgfrith holds their hostages. That is his gamble, but how long can he hold the Irish at bay? Their hearts are filled with bitter gall since the defeat at Brega, their hostages still held at Bamburgh in conditions that violate every solemn code about the keeping of hostages, conditions that mimic the very pits of hell. And that is Ecgfrith's greatest fear. That one day there will arrive at the gates of Bamburgh a great force of Picts and Irish, clamouring for justice, headed by his brother, and you know, Wilfrid, don't you, how they might enforce that justice? You understand who pays the price?'

Wilfrid supposed Cuthbert must mean the women who would be raped, the children slaughtered or taken as slaves. They would pay the price of a war battled out between men. Children. Ecgfrith's child.

'You see, Wilfrid, Ecgfrith knows more than anyone what happens when a king is defeated. He himself was the price many years ago, and I was one who paid it; I handed him over.'

Wilfrid clung to the edge of the Rock. The stone dug into his palms.

'It was before God called me, when I was in the service of Oswiu King, Ecgfrith's father. It was also the time of Penda of Mercia. I think I told you about him.'

Wilfrid remembered. Cuthbert had told him the story many years ago, the night they journeyed to Hildmer's village. Penda, the fierce pagan king, was defeated and destroyed by a much smaller army led by Oswiu. Afterwards Oswiu gifted his baby daughter Ælfflæd to the abbey at Whitby in thanksgiving to God and to seal the peace. She was lucky, Cuthbert had said. He remembered now exactly. *She was lucky, luckier than her brother*. What had happened to her brother?

Cuthbert seemed to hear his unspoken question.

'You see, in the years before the great battle Penda had been conducting raids in Northumbria, advancing further into our territory each time. His forces were larger than ours; something had to be done. Oswiu sued for peace rather than risk Penda overwhelming the Royal City. The gold tribute was enormous, but not sufficient. Hostages were required.'

Wilfrid began to see.

'You mean a royal hostage. Ecgfrith.'

'It was the only way to prevent Penda from destroying us. I was one of the men who travelled with Ecgfrith to Penda's stronghold and handed him over. I promised that God would protect him, that one day we would return for him, but it was years before anyone did. Penda had to be defeated first. Sometimes I still hear his little boy cries, his pleas to us not to abandon him, his screams for his mama as we left. Ecgfrith does not want that for his own child, will avoid it at all costs. He will seek out every possible enemy, tear up every kingdom rather than risk his child being taken and used as a bargaining token.'

'Was it you who suggested it?' Wilfrid said.

His voice was a knife.

'Suggested what?'

'Handing Ecgfrith over as hostage. Sending him away, like I was.'

A shout distracted them. The monks had come out of the church and had spotted the fleet of ships. One of them must have spotted Cuthbert too, because he was running out to the Rock, followed by some others.

'There was no other way,' Cuthbert said. 'It secured the peace. For then. It secured the peace.'

All the monks were running towards them now. Almost all. Dunstan was making a slow, faltering way across the stone and seaweed-strewn sand. Wilfrid went and guided him to where the bishop and brethren were waiting, their faces grey, their mouths pinched. He looked upwards. He remembered what Dunstan had said. The days are dark. Something landed lightly on his scalp. A drop of rain, cold as ice. It stung. Or perhaps it wasn't rain. He looked to the sky again. Perhaps it was snow.

Six

CUTHBERT DISPATCHED TYDI with missives to Bamburgh and elsewhere and then retired to his retreat on the Rock. He must turn from the cacophony of men, he said, crawl back into a cave of silence and listen for God's voice. For more than a week he remained out there, alone, walled inside the oratory. Word came to Lindisfarne that the plague had reached settlements south of the Royal City. Herefrith and his assistants busied themselves in the infirmary, preparing medicaments. Still Cuthbert did not emerge. Then one morning came a knock at Wilfrid's cell.

'We will go to Bamburgh now,' Cuthbert said.

They were still some distance away when they noticed a rolling cloud of black in the sky. Birds, Wilfrid realised, teeming about the hillside, close to where the fortress stood. As they climbed the path they were assailed by a host of ravens, hooded crows and black-backed gulls, all swooping, diving, shrieking and crying, swirling about each other like warriors in a battle dance. A rancid smell permeated the air. Wilfrid pulled up his hood and tried to keep his face covered, as the torrent of birds plunged so close now that he and Cuthbert had to swipe them away with their hands.

But the birds had not come for the living. Outside the walls of the fortress was a huddle of corpses, clothing ripped, faces, hands, any exposed parts, plucked clean of flesh. One body, that of a long-limbed, gaunt man, lay on its back, mouth open, lips ripped away, bloodied hollows where the eyes should have been. The cloak that was tied at the man's neck was undamaged, though. A thick warm wolfskin cloak, hooded and tied with a shield and sword clasp. Wilfrid shuddered. The cloak Oswine had given him. The one he had passed on to the starved man in the mountains. Just six months ago now. It seemed like years. He swallowed down the bile rising in his throat and made the sign of the cross over the dead man.

A watchman, eyeing Cuthbert's pectoral cross anxiously, admitted them inside the gates.

'Why are these people unburied?' Cuthbert said. 'Why were they not afforded the king's protection within the walls?'

The watchman was not the one Wilfrid had met on his first visit to Bamburgh. This was a small, thin lad, not yet of battle age. A sword, too large for him, hung heavily from his waist.

'They had plague, Bishop. The king said no pestilence carriers were to be admitted to the city. No one was to touch them or come within ten paces of them. They were ordered away time and again, but they kept coming back.'

'It is a violation of every sacred rule and custom to leave their mortal remains here unburied and unblessed. Even under the old gods, respect was accorded to the bones of the dead. This...this is a sacrilege. See that they are buried. I will say the funeral rites myself once I have spoken with the queen.'

The boy watchman shuffled from foot to foot, looked miserably at the ground.

'No one will touch them, Bishop, for if they do, they may not be let back into the fortress. The King says he will keep the plague beyond these walls as surely as he will keep the Picts beyond the boundaries of our territory. The bodies are to be left to the birds of the skies to serve as a warning to others who are plague-ridden from spreading their contagion here. Those are the orders of Ecgfrith King. The queen herself would not go against them.'

Cuthbert put his hand under the boy's chin, lifted it so the boy had no choice but to look at him directly.

'I will bury them myself if I have to,' Cuthbert said. 'But first take me to the queen.'

A guard, a well-built warrior this time, admitted them to the queen's quarters. The sour smell of vomit greeted them. The queen, white-faced, barely stood up when they entered. She was taller than Wilfrid remembered, and older, though he had only seen her in the distance before. She wore a dress of green velvet embroidered with a trail of daisies. Across her belly was a girdle from which hung the Book of Hours Eadfrith had crafted for her. She inclined her head just slightly for Cuthbert's blessing.

'You are welcome, Bishop,' she said. 'Finally. I had expected you some time ago. The king promised me your protection. As you have seen, he left one or two strong warriors here, but they are few in number. The others are little more than children or age-infirmed.'

'I'm sorry I was not able to come immediately. There were matters I had to attend to at the monastery. The Lord required me to set time aside for prayer.'

'Then it seems your prayers are working.' She touched her belly, as if for reassurance. 'Your visit is timely, Bishop, as it happens. A messenger has just come from the North. God has given the king many victories. Villages fall to him, one by one. Bruide's army retreats. Ecgfrith pushes him back further into the hills. It will not be long now.'

'You seem very certain these victories are from God,' Cuthbert said.

The queen laughed, a half-laugh that immediately turned to a frown.

'I hear you did not give the king your blessing when he left. I understand you have misgivings concerning his mission.'

'Mission!'

'That is Ecgfrith's word. He believes he will succeed where...'

'Where I failed.'

Another queenly half-smile.

'And where his father failed. As I've said. Ecgfrith King has been granted many victories. God guides his hand, the thrust of his sword. Much of Pictland is now under his control. Already, some have sent tribute.' She pointed to a small wooden casket and nodded at her serving woman to open it. Gold rings, silver goblets, candlesticks, a bejewelled cross gleamed from within. 'He expects to return within months, God willing, in good time for the birth of his son.'

'God does not guide Ecgfrith to burn villages,' Cuthbert said. 'Nor to murder children or rape their mothers.'

Wilfrid saw a sudden flash in the queen's eyes.

'I know nothing of this,' she said. 'War is played out by men, not women. Perhaps you have information I do not? From your own spies, I suppose?'

'Spies are not needed, Iurminburgh. You know what happens after battle. You know what happened in Ireland. He will do worse in Pictland, especially now that...'

The queen placed her hands on her belly.

'Now that he has something new to protect. Now that God has shown His favour.' She looked at Cuthbert defiantly. 'Well, He has shown favour, hasn't He? On me as well as on the king? But it is well that you have finally come.' She clutched the Book of Hours at her belly. 'I think I will need your protection.'

'You are assured of my prayers,' Cuthbert said. 'And the prayers of the entire community at Lindisfarne. As for the protection of my presence, I think it is of less worth than you imagine. There are others who need my help, and others who can help you more than I can.'

'The king feels the presence of his bishop will ensure that God's grace surrounds his queen and his son.'

She swallowed hard and put her hand to her mouth. Wilfrid wondered if she would be sick.

'Iurminburgh, God's grace is not dispensed through the hands of a bishop alone. And a bishop is pastor for his entire flock, not just those who live within the protection of a fortress. There are others in the plague-ridden villages who need help, on whom I must attend. Just outside these gates there are bodies unburied, unblessed by a priest, whose souls await prayer.'

'They are contaminated! The contagion must not be allowed to spread further.' She put her hand to her mouth again and swayed a little. 'The king promised me your protection. You're a healer. You brought the warmaster's boy back from the very precipice of death. Everyone knows that. I can't eat; can't sleep. My belly is not fattening. My medicine woman tells me I must not worry myself, but, but some demon is whispering worry to me, pouring it into my ears. I cannot get it out. You must take it away. You must help.'

Cuthbert took the queen's arm and bid her sit down. He spoke gently.

'It is true that God has sometimes blessed my hands with His healing, and I have knowledge of the herbs and plants that alleviate ailments, but, as I've said, there are others, chosen by the Lord and better equipped than I am to help you in this.'

Chosen by the Lord. Wilfrid felt a memory stir.

'I've sent for the abbess, the king's sister,' Cuthbert said. 'She has knowledge of the ways of women that I do not. She will bring you God's blessing and comfort.

And I will not be gone for long. I must go out to the villages, but I will return. I promise you.'

The queen stood up and promptly sat down again. Her face was grey.

'Abbess Ælfflæd,' she said. She motioned to Wilfrid. 'Fetch me the slave girl. I'm going to be sick again.'

They buried the corpses in a large, shallow pit which they dug at a short distance from the fortress. Using a spade, Wilfrid pushed the bodies onto a large winding cloth, then, trying not to retch, he dragged them to the pit and dropped them in. The body of the gaunt man was lightest of all, and when he let it fall into the pit the eyeless face of the man stared up at him. Cuthbert sang from the office of the dead, his pure voice wavering in the wind as Wilfrid shovelled earth on top of the corpses, birds flying about in a dark, wild fury. A scattering of snow fell down with the earth.

There was no end to the corpses to be buried. In the nearby villages they helped the women lay the dead in the ground and treated the sick with what medicines they had. At first Wilfrid avoided touching anyone he blessed or buried. He feared the plague would come for him in the dead of night, wrathful and vengeful, desirous of taking him in Sigi's stead. He kept checking his body for sores, but there was nothing – not a mark – and he began to think that Cuthbert's presence was indeed a protection.

Cuthbert had no such qualms. He blessed and nursed the sick, held the hands of the dying and comforted the bereft. He made a game of carrying children on his back and told them stories of Jesus and the daughter of Jairus; Jesus and the loaves and fishes; the prodigal son. At Cuthbert's bidding Wilfrid did likewise. At first he stuttered over his words, but as soon as he was a few sentences into a story he found he could keep going quite easily, the tide of words coming like the flow of an oft-repeated psalm. It was almost like singing again. And it held him, for those moments, kept him from thinking about the abbess coming to Bamburgh, from thinking about her companion. But at night, the dark urges of the flesh tormented him, as they had done for months now. In his dreams Meredith came to him, touched him as he touched himself. In his waking he kept wondering about her, if she would journey with the abbess, if he would ever see her again.

Seven

THEY RETURNED to the Royal City after some days. They feared they would be refused entry on account of their contact with the sick, but it seemed the queen had been calling for the bishop. She was desirous of a blessing, the watchman said; a remedy; anything that might quell the storm in her stomach. When they entered her chamber they found her slumped in bed, her face frost-white, strands of hair, spotted with vomit, straggled across her cheek.

'I'm dying,' she said. 'This sickness is a curse.'

Cuthbert wet a cloth and wiped her face and hair.

'There is no help, not from prayers or relics or remedies. God has cast me off. Unless you can do something, if it's not already too late to save me.'

'I see no reason why our merciful Lord should

reject you,' Cuthbert said. 'This is but a debilitation of motherhood. It will pass.'

He blessed her and sprinkled her with holy water. She shivered at its touch, and Wilfrid noticed a tear roll from the corner of her eye.

'Try to sleep,' Cuthbert said.

Outside they were met by a servant.

'Bishop, there are guests. They wish to speak to you before greeting the queen. You see...'

Her explanations were swept aside by the entrance of a tall, veiled woman with a garnet cross at her breast. Behind her stood another woman. Wilfrid felt the thump of his heart, the tightness in his ribs. The abbess had arrived, and with her was her companion, Meredith.

It was late morning the following day when the queen admitted them to the Great Hall. She was pale as ever, the shadows under her eyes even deeper, but she stood straight, her lips set in a narrow line.

'Your visit is somewhat unexpected, sister,' she said to the abbess. 'Though you are always welcome. As is your companion.'

'Sister Meredith,' the abbess said.

Meredith. Wilfrid had to concentrate to avoid looking at her too much. He longed to check if there was a rebellious strand of hair fluttering out from beneath her veil again but he forced himself to look away.

'You must forgive my delayed greeting,' the queen said, 'but, as you can imagine, with the king away, there is much for me to take care of. I hope your journey in this unseasonable weather was not too difficult. Let me know if there is anything you need. Ah.'

She turned her face away and pressed a linen cloth against her mouth.

'I have a tincture to help with that,' the abbess said.

'Thank you.' The queen dabbed at her mouth with the cloth. 'I will add it to the other remedies I already have to hand. I am assured that this...this little debilitation is to be expected.'

Wilfrid frowned. Only the previous day, the queen had thought she was dying.

'It is the way with boy children, I believe,' she said. 'Girls draw less on their mothers' strength.' She looked at Cuthbert. 'I welcome it as a sign of God's favour.'

'God has given us some means to counter the afflictions that come with your condition,' Cuthbert said. 'The abbess wishes to help you as she has helped countless others. Sister Meredith too has had experience. That is, she is well placed to be of assistance also.'

Wilfrid looked at Meredith. A slight flush washed over her scarred cheeks. The queen waved her hand dismissively.

'I have no desire to be of trouble to Abbess Ælfflæd. She has many duties at Whitby, I know.'

'We are sisters by marriage, Iurminburgh,' the abbess said. 'I have a duty to you too, and to my brother, and your child.' She narrowed her eyes. 'Speaking of the king, I believe you have had word?'

The queen drew herself up very straight.

'I'm sure you do not need to come to me for word of the king. Are there not other informers – emissaries, I suppose you call them – who bring this information to you?'

'It's true the abbeys and monasteries communicate with each other.'

'Spies! You have spies. What of it? You are your brother's sister. It's to be expected.' She shivered and brought the cloth to her mouth again. 'It's so cold, always so cold. Perhaps when Ecgfrith returns from Pictland the spring will finally come.'

Meredith stepped forward.

'Please,' she said. She held out a ginger root. 'Chew on this. It may alleviate the turmoil in your stomach.'

The queen waved the ginger root away.

'Why are you here, really?' she said to the abbess. 'Ecgfrith said the bishop would come. He never mentioned you.'

Wilfrid had been wondering this too. He remembered that the bishop had sent for the abbess almost a week ago now. Before he had known how wretched the queen was in her pregnancy.

'As I've told you,' Cuthbert said. 'I sent for the abbess to be of assistance to you. And also, I – that is, we – we hoped you might assist us.'

'Iurminburgh,' the abbess said gently. 'Both the bishop and I have failed in our efforts to make the king see reason. He is ravaging Pictish lands, burning crops and villages, raping women, slaughtering children. Think of it, sister.' She took the queen's hand in hers and placed it on the queen's belly. 'Babies torn from their mothers' breasts, left for dead or put out for the wolves. Even the monasteries are not safe. At Arbroath his men attacked the monks and forcibly shaved the head of the abbot.'

Wilfrid winced. He thought of what Herefrith had said about the holy devotion of the Pictish monks to the old ways.

'We should have come to you before,' Cuthbert said. 'It was my doing. I believed I could turn the king's bent from war. I believed my mission to the Picts would be successful, that God would make me an instrument to bring His unity and peace. My sight was clouded by a fog of vanity.'

The queen dabbed at her mouth again. A greenish tinge had come over her face.

'What is it you think I can do?'

'Send him word,' the abbess said. 'Appeal to him as a mother. Beg him cease the slaughter and come home, lest he bring down God's wrath on us all.'

The queen laughed.

'Me? Why? Ecgfrith is king. A man. In battle with enemies. This is what men do. Even him.' She pointed at Cuthbert. 'Yes, him! Did he not serve Oswiu King in battle? He knows well enough how to thrust a sword through the enemy's heart when it is required. Besides, what will become of me if I betray my husband, make any noise against his will and purpose?'

'We will speak for you,' Cuthbert said. 'The king will...'

'Will put me aside. He will put me aside and take the child, make a nun of me like that holy fool he was married to before me. Do you think now, after all these years, when God has finally blessed our union, that I will risk being cast out?'

She pressed the cloth to her mouth and hurried from the Hall. They heard a groan and loud retching outside.

The abbess sighed.

'It was worth trying,' she said. 'But Iurminburgh's heart was ever stubborn. She walks in her own counsel.'

'I hoped she might be persuaded by you,' Cuthbert said. 'This place is a snare where men's worldly desires and ambitions grow fat and devour the better part of their inclination towards God. I will be glad when the Lord permits me to leave it. But it's well you are here, Ælfflæd, though I hope the queen isn't right – that I haven't taken you from where you are needed.'

The abbess shook her head.

'There is more than one at the abbey who can take my place.' With a small laugh she nodded in the direction of her companion. 'That is why I have had to bring Sister Meredith with me, for fear I should no longer be abbess when I return!'

Sister Meredith remained expressionless. Cuthbert smiled weakly. He made circles with his thumb over the garnets on his pectoral cross. Wilfrid knew there must be something else troubling him.

'The queen was right,' he said, wearily. 'No matter how many people God has aided me to heal, no matter that I have given my life to His service, it does not restore life to those from whom I took it.'

'That was a time of war,' the abbess said. 'Before you took up the shield of the Holy Word. And even then you had worked ever to secure peace. But it does not do to stoke the flames of the past. Let them be quenched.'

'You are right, as always, Ælfflæd. Still...' Cuthbert shook his head. 'Death. It's so close. I can smell it in my nostrils, taste it on my tongue.'

'God has sent us a long winter of trials,' the abbess

said. 'War, hunger, pestilence. We should pray that the souls of those who have been taken may rest with the Lord.'

They knelt. Wilfrid went to close the door against the onslaught of cold. Outside, finally, the skies were letting go of their long-held burden. Snow – May snow – was falling, thickly, quietly, in sheets. It fell as if it would never stop.

Eight

A HOWLING FROM SOMEWHERE. A desperate cry carried on the wind, through the still falling snow. Wilfrid huddled beneath a sheepskin coverlet, pulled it tightly around him. The straw bedding was thicker than he was used to, the blanket warmer. Still, he shivered. Snow in May was not unheard of, but this snowfall was heavier and more relentless than anyone had ever known. Cuthbert was restless too, his breathing coming in gasps and groans. Wilfrid wondered if he should wake him. It must be near time for the Night Office.

He got out of bed, still wrapped in the coverlet, and walked back and forth to try and warm up. He expected Cuthbert would wake at any moment, his whole body and being so conditioned to the rhythm of prayer that he no longer needed the call of a bell. Another howl. Louder this time. Cuthbert slept on. Fitfully. Wilfrid put on his cloak and stepped outside.

Snow fell in cascades, stars falling from the night sky. It was already piled so high it came to the top of Wilfrid's boots. Sentries with blankets draped around their shoulders had cleared a path and were huddled around a fire. One of the queen's slaves hurried past him, a jug of steaming liquid in her hand. He followed her to the queen's rooms. Two sentries, one very young, the other wrinkled and white-haired, stood outside.

'Is she ill again?' Wilfrid asked.

Another cry from inside, sobbing, followed by the quiet but firm voice of the abbess.

'Looks like it,' the sentry said. 'Or worse.'

The door opened, and Meredith came out.

'Brother Wilfrid. I was on my way to find you. The queen is asking for the bishop.'

'I'll fetch him. Is it very bad?'

'The abbess is making a potion for her now, but that's just to calm her.' Meredith lowered her voice. 'She is bleeding.'

'I'll wake the bishop straightaway.'

'Yes, do. But...Who knows? Perhaps it's for the best.'

Wilfrid trudged back as quickly as he could. Snow was already piling up on the recently cleared path, and when he reached the hut he found the door half-open with snow blowing into the room. Cuthbert's bed was empty. A low moan came from the corner. Cuthbert was on his knees, rocking back and forth, his hands pressed into his forehead.

'Screams.' His words came in gasps. 'Screams across the earth. Everything is falling. Darkness coming down.'

He swayed, and Wilfrid had to hold tight to steady him.

'You've been dreaming, Bishop. There was a scream, but it was the queen. She's unwell. She has sent for you.'

Cuthbert clung to Wilfrid's arm.

'It's ripping apart. This pain is ripping everything apart.'

'Let me get you into bed, Bishop. Then I'll fetch the abbess. She'll have a remedy. She'll help you. Sister Meredith will take care of the queen.'

Wilfrid tried to get Cuthbert to stand, but Cuthbert was a dead weight in his arms.

'The ground has given way; cracked; splintered.'

'Please, Bishop. Try to stand. It's just a step or two to the bed.'

Wilfrid felt a rising swell of fear now. He didn't know what was happening to Cuthbert, or if the abbess would be able to help. He doubted if even Fergus would have had a remedy to counter this malady.

'They sink in deep mire. They are come into deep water.'

Wilfrid placed his arms around Cuthbert's chest and hauled him to the bed. He felt his forehead. It was cold. But Cuthbert was still raving, and Wilfrid remembered Cuthbert saying that demons often seek out the most pious and holy to inhabit. He wondered now if Cuthbert, exhausted from tending the sick, from the failures that had beset him, had fallen prey to some devil.

'See, the dead lie all about us. Bloodied limbs stain the snow.'

'Please, Bishop, please. All will be well. I will fetch the abbess. She will know what to do.'

Cuthbert groaned.

'He is dead. So many dead. All lost.'

His body went completely limp, and he stopped breathing. Wilfrid tried to move. He must get help, fetch the abbess, send to Lindisfarne, but his legs were trembling, the ground beneath him swaying, and all he could do was hold onto Cuthbert's inert body. Then, after an age, a long deep breath, a sigh that seemed to come from another world, Cuthbert's chest was moving, rising and falling. Wilfrid dropped to the ground, crouched by the bed and watched as Cuthbert's breathing steadied, as he opened his eyes. The fever, or whatever malady had seized him, had passed. When Cuthbert spoke again his voice was clear and steady.

'The war is over. Judgement has been given against our people in the battle. We must prepare for what is to come.'

A while later and Cuthbert's words were still beating like a drum in Wilfrid's head. He helped Cuthbert sit up as the abbess handed him a cup of warmed wine.

'I hope it is warm enough,' she said. 'This snowstorm is murderous. I feared the wine would freeze in the few paces from the kitchen to here.'

She fussed about Cuthbert, put her palm to his forehead, patted his hand. Cuthbert handed her back the cup and slumped back against the wall. A few red drops trickled down his beard. She pulled the blanket up about him. Wilfrid wanted to crawl under a blanket too. Unlike the abbess, he didn't want to hear anything more. There was something about Cuthbert that whispered death, as if the aftermath of the lost battle had entered the room and spread its cold wings about them.

'You're certain?' the abbess said eventually. Her face was ashen. 'Certain about the battle? And my brother? Might it have been someone else you saw? Or perhaps there has been a terrible battle, but our men may yet prevail?'

'Ecgfrith is dead,' Cuthbert said. 'And most of his men. I'm certain of it, Ælfflæd.'

His men. There it was. An ice-stab to his chest. The thing Wilfrid had not wanted to hear. Ecgfrith's men. Dead. His father. He tried to catch his breath. His father. He tried to get up. His feet were unsteady. It must be the cold. It was seizing his body up. He needed something to warm him. Wine. Some of the wine the abbess had heated. That would steady him. He must make himself move, breathe. Carefully. Just one step, then another. He moved, shakily, but he moved nonetheless. His feet were frozen. His hands too. He put them in his pocket and felt something there, something warmer than wine. His knife. He stumbled to the door.

'Wilfrid,' Cuthbert called. His voice was weak and distant. 'Wilfrid?'

Wilfrid stepped out into a blaze of white. Cuthbert's voice melted into the snow.

Nine

THE WOLF WAS OUTSIDE. It padded silently across the snowswept courtyard and led him to the kitchen. A fire was lit. Wilfrid moved close to it, tried to think. The abbess hadn't wanted to believe it either. But he heard the waver in her voice, saw the tremble in her hand. She knew. Ecgfrith was dead. And if Ecgfrith was dead and the battle was lost, then his father was surely dead too. The warmaster would have formed part of the shield-wall around his lord, would have defended him against sword and spear, strike and blow, would have guarded his lord's body as long as there was still breath in his own.

Wilfrid knelt next to the fire, tried to draw in some heat. He was shivering, shaking. He hadn't known his father. Not really. Even as a child. All he had was vague memories, fragments floating in his head like grains of sand tossed up by the tide. He saw his father laughing in the mead hall, riding out at the head of a band of men, training the young boys, his face lit by a smile as big as the sun when Wilfrid knocked over a foe. A shadow crossed the picture. No, that wasn't Wilfrid. It was some other boy, that dark-haired one with the wolfish teeth. Wilfrid couldn't remember Raymund ever smiling at him.

He reached into his pocket, felt the knife nestling there. *The wrong knife, he thought. It's the wrong knife.* He had an overwhelming longing to grasp again the right one, the one he had buried on Lindisfarne, to feel its metal burn into his hand. And then for some reason he thought of Sigi. Sigi with a silver knife, prancing around the fire, swiping at imaginary enemies, slaying foes in a single slice. Wilfrid took his knife out, unsheathed it. It didn't have a silver handle or a gleaming blade. No wolf's head or warrior's helmet or runes delicately carved onto it. But it did have a recently sharpened edge. He rolled up the sleeve of his robe, placed the blade against his skin.

A voice, sharp and sudden.

'Does that bring you close to Him?'

The knife fell to the floor. The door banged and now Meredith was kneeling beside him, shivering also, warming her hands at the fire. *Him?* he wanted to say. But he didn't dare look at her, didn't dare retrieve the knife. He wanted to speak, but no words came. He considered picking up the knife, flicking it casually in his hands before settling it back into his pocket, but he didn't trust his hands to stay steady. He thought about the sensation of the knife next to his skin, the warmth of it, the pull of the metal, drawing his arm toward it. He wouldn't have done it, he told himself. It was just a momentary temptation that would have passed. Another instant and she wouldn't have witnessed a thing. Unless...unless she was meant to witness it. Unless God had sent her to stop him.

'It's unnatural,' she said. 'The cold, I mean.'

He took a deep breath, made himself speak.

'Yes, yes, it is. Unnatural.'

She leaned closer to him. Her veil brushed his arm.

'You didn't answer my question.'

'No, I suppose I didn't.'

'Well, does it bring you closer to the Lord?' She nodded toward the knife. 'Piercing your skin, carving it with Christ's wounds?'

He hesitated a moment. He felt ashamed at having been caught and yet he wanted to explain it to her, to have her understand. Maybe then he might understand it himself.

'No. No, I don't think so,' he said. 'Just, I don't know, it brings me close to, to...something.'

'Something deep,' she said. 'A place inside you that you didn't know existed.'

'Yes. It's like you uncover a spring and all the bad blood gushes out and everything is pure again, except...'

'Except it doesn't last.'

'No. Besides...' Suddenly he didn't feel so cold any more. 'I wasn't going to. Probably. I haven't in years.'

'Hmm.' She picked up a log, threw it on the fire and knelt down again. It seemed to him she was kneeling even closer to him now. 'Neither have I, though

305

sometimes I have wanted to, but there are other ways, you know.'

'My father is dead,' he said suddenly.

She stretched her hands close to the fire. He watched how she moved her fingers, spreading them like butterfly wings. If he moved his hand a little closer, her fingers might accidentally flutter against his.

'If the bishop is right,' she said, 'and the war is truly lost, then your father must be among the dead.' She looked at him closely. 'You believe the bishop is right, don't you? That God sent him a vision?'

Wilfrid thought about Cuthbert writhing in pain, how something unearthly seemed to have taken hold of him, a waking dream more real and solid to him than the ground on which he lay. Was it a vision? A presentiment so strong it left no room for doubt?

'I know only that God reaches Bishop Cuthbert in ways I will never understand,' Wilfrid said at last. 'I don't know what he saw, Meredith, or what he felt, but I witnessed something powerful move in him. He is certain there has been some calamity. I fear he is right.'

'I am sorry then, about your father. You will feel his loss deeply.'

She took his right hand in hers, pressed her long fingers into his palm.

'Yes,' he said, though why he should feel it any more deeply now he did not know. He had been living without father and mother for so long now it should not be possible still to miss them. But perhaps that ache would never truly disappear.

'I have no family,' he said. 'Or none that wants to know me, at any rate.'

Meredith frowned.

'But that cannot be true. The abbess told me that you and Bishop Cuthbert were kin. And the brethren. Surely they are your family now?'

He thought about what she said, felt the warmth of her fingers against his flesh. Yes, it was true: he and Cuthbert were of the same blood and bone, and Cuthbert had always looked out for him. He had never been truly alone in the monastery. And the brothers, for all their differences and divisions, were a family of sorts, and he had bound himself to them.

'I was going to say to you,' she said, 'there are other ways of making a mark. On other skin, dead skin. It helps. But I thought you would know this?'

Wilfrid nodded. He kept very still, fearing to move lest she withdraw her hand.

'I do know. The bishop told me years ago. That's why I was trained as a scribe, though I have no real skill, and my hand remains at best a wormish scrawl. Brother Dunstan says I am a festering wound in his soul.'

'What do you write?'

'I copy letters, inventories, some histories that come our way. And psalms. The bishop told me to write out the psalms; they would drive the demons away, he said, would be a shield-wall of holy words.'

'And he was right?'

'Yes, yes, he was. But sometimes...' Despite the dancing fire in front of him, despite his hand in hers, he suddenly felt cold again. 'Sometimes I see things. Or maybe I remember them. I don't know. They are there just for an instant, as if a sprite has just flitted across my path, and then they're gone again, and I worry that even writing out the psalms won't keep the demons away. Some day they will get back inside me.'

She squeezed his hand, and there was a moment when he pressed his fingers against hers, and she didn't pull away. He almost brought her hand to his lips, but a log shifted, collapsed in the fire, spitting out venomous sparks. He let go.

'Have you written something of your own?' she said. She looked at him with her intense gaze. The firelight danced over the faded marks on her cheeks. 'You must write something of your own. I don't know – a prayer or a sermon or something. Maybe a commentary on those psalms you love – how they should be sung.'

Wilfrid almost laughed.

'Me?'

'Why not?'

'Someone must have served you too-strong wine. I can barely copy out a page without creating a trail of ugly errors, let alone craft words of my own.'

'Your hand – that is mere form. You have the learning, the skill. You're not a fool, Wilfrid.' She smiled, leaned forward to the fire, stretching out her hands again. 'I am writing a *Vita*, a Life.'

'A Life? You mean like St Martin's Life?'

She nodded, her eyes gleaming.

'You have no idea of the trouble I had persuading Abbess Ælfflæd to let me do it. She wanted one of the brothers to write it, naturally, but it was my idea. In the end I managed to convince her that it was God who had put the thought into my head. Why shouldn't Whitby produce a great manuscript as they do on Lindisfarne and Jarrow and Iona? It will take me years, most likely, but one day your monastery will be sent a copy of *The Life of Pope St Gregory*, and you will know it was composed by me.'

'Send a copy that is written in your own hand,' he said. 'If you can.'

A noise outside startled them. She stood up quickly and pulled her cloak tightly about her.

'I should return to the queen.'

The queen. He had almost forgotten. He had sat next to Meredith, the space of a sheet of vellum between them, her fingers spread beneath his, and for that moment everything else, the queen, the king, his father, had fallen away.

'Of course,' he said. 'She is still unwell?'

'She is calmer – that cold calm that comes after shock. And the bleeding...' She frowned. 'Well, it seems to have eased. Her serving woman is with her, and she was sleeping when I left, but I must go back. The abbess will be angry with me for leaving her for so long.'

She picked up his knife from the ground and handed it to him. He dropped it deep into his pocket.

'It wasn't that long,' Wilfrid said.

Not long at all.

She opened the door and stepped out into the snow. Wilfrid watched her go. A pale dawn was bleeding through the snow. Somewhere in Pictland, he thought, the same dawn was rising over a bloodied battlefield, over the bodies of warriors, over the body of Ecgfrith King, and over the body of his father.

Ten

The queen was propped up in bed beneath a mound of thick coverlets.

'You have come to accuse me then,' she said to Cuthbert. 'You have your witnesses lined up.'

Her eyes flashed anger through swollen, red eyelids. Wilfrid was puzzled. He didn't understand what the queen meant by accusations. They were meeting with the queen to comfort her and discuss what must come next. He and Cuthbert stood at one side of the bed, with Meredith and the abbess at the other.

'You are sorely troubled, Iurminburgh,' Cuthbert said. 'Now I bring you more affliction and I am sorry for it.'

'The abbess has told me of this new *affliction*. I don't see why I should believe it. For all I know, your visions are the devil's work, not God's.'

'Iurminburgh!'

The abbess pointed a warning finger. The queen sniffed. She reached for a book on a stool beside her bed. Eadfrith's Book of Hours. She turned it over in her hand.

'I'm sorry to tell you of this latest calamity,' Cuthbert repeated. 'I would wait until word comes through, but it may take days or weeks, and we must prepare.'

'I suppose you will accuse me for that too,' she said. 'Well, go on. Go on, all of you. Tell me I have brought destruction on the king and the entire army as well as on my child and myself! You think I don't know it?'

Cuthbert frowned and looked at the abbess. Ælfflæd shook her head and lowered her voice.

'She has been like this since the bleeding last night, blaming herself, talking about God's retribution. I've seen it with women before, but with her it seems particularly acute, and also pointless, since...'

'You!' the queen shouted. 'You talk about me as if I were some weakwit child. As if you had any idea what it is like to have your belly made the whetstone for a gossip's chatter or a scop's filthy song or even a holy man's miracle.'

'That is enough, Iurminburgh! I have told you. You must take care not to do yourself any harm.'

'Iurminburgh,' Cuthbert said firmly. 'The king is dead. I'm sure of it. And even if your child had lived, it would not have been safe.'

'Bishop.'

The abbess tried to interrupt, but Cuthbert held up his hand.

'Aldfrith is coming,' he said. 'Most likely, he has an army prepared. He has waited a long time.'

'Bishop.'

The abbess again. Wilfrid wondered why she was so keen to speak. She and Meredith had been exchanging glances.

'Aldfrith?' the queen said. 'Aldfrith? The king's bastard brother? But he's a monk, an old monk.'

'He would be king,' Cuthbert said. 'And there is no one else. Unless you would have Bruide of the Picts march south, take Bamburgh and do to our people what Ecgfrith did to his.'

'I don't believe you. You've put your faith in some foolish dream. You may yet be wrong.'

'If I'm wrong we will soon hear. I can only tell you of what I'm certain in my heart. But you must know this too. Aldfrith is not on Iona, I believe now he is in Pictland, in league with Bruide King. He will be here soon, and we must be prepared.'

'Aldfrith!'

The queen took the Book of Hours and flung it across the room. It hit the door like a thunderclap and fell heavily, its leaves spread out on the ground. A shocked silence followed. Wilfrid waited for the abbess to strike the queen or at least berate her soundly. But it seemed it was the abbess who had been struck, felled with weariness. She put her head in her hands.

'Bishop,' she said at last. 'I've been trying to tell you. The bleeding last night caused Iurminburgh great terror, naturally, but it was slight and soon ceased. It may not signify anything. I do not know why she will not hear this.'

Cuthbert raised his eyebrows.

'You mean?'

'I mean there is hope; the child may yet live.'

'Then we must pray that the new king will be merciful, but if the child is a boy, I fear...'

Wilfrid understood what Cuthbert left unsaid. Aldfrith, deprived of his birthright, banished from his brother's kingdom for so long, would not now tolerate a rival – even a child rival – behind whom others might unite.

Cuthbert picked up the book that the queen had cast to the floor.

'Eadfrith's work,' he said. 'And God's work too.' He opened it up and ran his finger over the page. *'Ad vesperum demorabitur fletus, et ad matutinum laetitia.'*

'It did nothing,' the queen said. 'Nothing at all. Not that book, nor all the blessings or prayers or masses or holy water and sacred oil. Month after month, year after year, none of these made my belly ripen. How could they?'

'Hush, Iurminburgh,' the abbess said firmly. 'I have warned you not to upset yourself. Your condition may yet be precarious.'

But it seemed to Wilfrid that the queen was unable to keep from speaking. She was like the skies that had gathered a winter's worth of snow, holding it in until it could no longer be retained.

'I listened to the priests, prayed the prayers, but none of them helped, for none of them told me how to make myself as sweet or as pleasing or as young as a slave girl – any slave girl, no matter how thin or

313

unkempt or unwashed, as long as she was little more than a child. You blessed my belly, Bishop, and my bed, and I was glad of it. You sprinkled water from your holy well on the Farne on my blanket, and I thanked God for it. It was necessary to...' – she twisted the corner of the coverlet on her bed – '...to dilute the stain of the sin I was about to commit.'

'Sin?' Cuthbert said. 'There is no sin in lying with your husband. You must know this.'

The queen put her hand to her forehead and disturbed a strand of hair from her headdress. It was white, Wilfrid noticed, as white as her face. She threw back the coverlets and struggled out of the bed.

'And you must know this,' she said to Cuthbert. 'I'm sure it is the talk of all the Royal City; and even on Lindisfarne, no doubt, there are tongues that lick gossip from the plates of travellers and messengers.' She spat into the slop bucket in the corner of the room. 'My husband does not lie with me. That is, he tries at times, not often – when his belly is filled with a barrel of beer or wine – but his *efforts* do not always meet with success.'

A wave of embarrassment wafted through the room. Wilfrid glanced at Meredith again. He thought with shame on the many nights in his cell when the demons of longing had tormented him. He had thought then that the only difficulty with desire lay in quelling it, not in arousing it.

The queen looked at them all in turn, half-pleading, half-scorning.

'Can't you see? He prefers younger flesh. Much younger. What was I to do?'

The abbess gasped.

'Iurminburgh, What did you do? You're not saying you lay with another man?'

'Do you think me a complete fool? Ecgfrith would know the child wasn't his.'

'Well then?'

The queen began to pace the room.

'I told you, I have been prayed over, blessed by priests and bishops, clothed in holy relics, but these did not make me younger or give me the body of a little slave girl, and this was necessary, it seems, so Ecgfrith said – necessary for him, if anything was to happen. So, so, he, we...' – this time it was her hair that she twisted, wound it fiercely around her fingers – '...we took one into the bed with us, one of the Irish, very young. He said it was the only thing that would help.' She leaned against the wall, clutched her stomach and groaned. 'He was right. It did. And I was glad. For nothing else could fill the space in my belly that had been empty for so long.'

The abbess took a step back. She covered her mouth with her hand. Cuthbert's face was crimson. He moved towards the queen, and for a moment Wilfrid thought he might hit her.

'Look at me, Iurminburgh!'

She faced the wall, her hands against her ears as if she would block out the recriminations and condemnations that must surely rain down on her now.

'That is a sin,' Cuthbert said. 'A grievous sin. Not even the pagans would have permitted such a practice. You went along with this. You permitted a hostage, a child, to be used in your foul act. Such a thing is beyond the imagination even of demons.'

'Permitted!' She turned around, eyes glowering. 'When does a queen *permit* a king to do anything? Least of all in his bed? And it had failed, those blessings and sprinklings, everything had failed until finally he suggested the girl, and...and I had no choice.' She raised her voice, wringing her hands. 'Can't you see? I would never have had a child of my own. He would have put me aside. I would be with *them* now in their holy house.'

She jerked her head violently towards the women.

'But you did not object,' Cuthbert said. He was trembling, speaking slowly, as if trying not to let his speech disintegrate into a stuttering mess. 'And you had me bless the bed before this, this *act*?'

Droplets of spittle ran down his chin.

'No. *He* did, not me. And you, of all people, must know Ecgfrith does not suffer objections.' She slumped down on the edge of the bed. 'When my bleeding was late, he said God had favoured me, but that he still must fight the Picts, now more than ever, bring them to the true Easter, to protect our people and our son. It would expiate our sin, he said.'

'Some sins can never be expiated.'

Meredith stepped forward. She pointed a trembling finger at the queen.

'You would have done better to come to our holy house, *Iurminburgh*.' She spat the queen's name. 'Better to have no child of your own than to despoil another.'

'Child! She was at least eleven winters. And who are you – some lowly nun – to preach at me?'

'That's enough, both of you,' the abbess said. She looked suddenly old and worn. 'Sister Meredith, God will judge the queen, not you. Iurminburgh, lie down now and rest while you can. You should have had more patience and faith. If God willed that you and Ecgfrith should have a child, He would have caused it to happen. And if God willed otherwise, not even Ecgfrith should have dared outmanoeuvre Him.'

'Then let God punish me,' the queen said. She lay back into the bed, clutching her stomach. 'He already has.'

'You're in pain again?' the abbess said.

The queen shook her head.

'More bleeding?'

'No.'

'Then your situation remains unaltered. Though I see now why you chose to disbelieve me.' She spoke bitterly. 'I wonder if it had been better that you had lost it after all, though I must not doubt that the Lord has His plan.'

Cuthbert paced back and forth.

'We must hope that Aldfrith may be moved towards mercy, that he will permit the child to live, but if it's a boy, well, I fear the worst. If it's a girl it will be taken once it's born and sent away, probably to Aldfrith's kin. The queen will go to a nunnery.'

The queen lay on her bed, sobbing. Wilfrid almost envied the baby she was carrying. At least its mother did not see it as a curse or a death carrier. Given the chance she would care for the child, never allow it be separated from her. He thought for a moment.

'There may be another way,' he said.

The abbess waved a dismissive hand.

'I will entreat my brother to let the baby live, even if it's a boy. But of course it must be taken from Iurminburgh.'

'But...' Wilfrid said.

Cuthbert nodded.

'Aldfrith will not have the former queen stoking ambition in a son or forging alliances with a daughter.'

'Then we must discover a means to pacify Aldfrith's fears,' Wilfrid said. 'Or...or somehow eliminate them.'

'Wilfrid, be reasonable!' Cuthbert's tone was sharp. 'Aldfrith is not some weakling to be manipulated. We will do well to persuade him to spare the child.'

But something tightened in Wilfrid. He would not let go.

'A child should not be torn from its family.'

'Nonsense!' the abbess snapped. 'This is no time for foolish sentiment. Many a child has fared perfectly well when cared for by others. As I did myself.'

She turned abruptly and fussed about the queen, draping the coverlet over her. Something in the line of the abbess' mouth was too pinched, Wilfrid thought, too firm.

'Truthfully?' he said. 'There was never a time when you yearned for your mother's embrace? Or you?' he said to Cuthbert. 'Did you not tell me once how you longed for your own family, though your foster mother was kind and good?'

'Wilfrid, you mean well, but...'

Meredith intervened.

'We have not yet heard what Brother Wilfrid's suggestion is. Perhaps it has merit. Let him speak.'

'Oh, yes, let him speak.' The queen's voice rang out bitterly. 'You *holy* people stand about my bed, disputing what is to be done with me, with my child, as though we are inconveniences to be rid of. And you.' She looked at Wilfrid. 'Another monk. Another scheme. Why should I listen?'

'Because,' Wilfrid said, 'I think there may be a way for you to keep your child.'

The queen stopped crying. She sat up.

'Very well then,' she said. 'Tell me.'

Eleven

THE SNOW HAD MELTED AWAY when the news finally came. A single horseman on a lumbering beast, staggering up the path to the fortress. The horse was sweating, faltering. The soldier on its back fared little better. He fell as he went to dismount and Wilfrid had to help him up. He almost didn't recognise him at first. He seemed to have aged a dozen winters. Cerdic, the young watchman he had met that first time he entered the Royal City.

'Lean on my shoulder,' Wilfrid said. 'We'll get you something to eat and drink, but first you'd better come to the bishop.'

Cerdic sat beside the fire in the Great Hall, shivering beneath a blanket, though the ice-bite of winter was gone. He drank from a large cup of beer, his hand trembling so much that every time he brought the cup to his mouth, beer spilled over his already filthy, matted beard.

'There were victories at first,' he said. 'Skirmishes, really. Some of the villages were deserted by men – not even a boy left to fight. It was almost too easy, made taking the women less rewarding somehow. Sorry, Bishop. I meant...'

He swallowed hard, as if the beer had a bad taste.

'Anyhow, those men who fought soon surrendered and handed over tribute. Eventually we saw an army across a valley. Bruide's men. Finally. It was late afternoon and bitter cold. The ground was hard, and the frost never melted, and even the water in our flagons iced over. Well, the Picts raised the battle cry and came towards us but when they saw the might of Ecgfrith's army they turned and fled into the hills.'

'They fled? Without giving battle?'

Cuthbert was incredulous.

'Yes. Ecgfrith King gave orders to pursue. The warmaster disagreed. Wait, he said. Send scouts he said. But the king insisted. We must press on, take advantage. The Picts were scattering. We must find Bruide, negotiate a surrender, or kill him. Preferably both.'

'So the king paid no heed to his warmaster?' Wilfrid said.

He imagined his father trying to persuade Ecgfrith to tread cautiously, that something was not right.

'No. He was so certain that God would give us victory. We pushed into the mountains, following the trail of the Picts, but it grew late, and we had to make camp. That was when the trouble started.'

'Trouble?' Cuthbert said.

'Cries of pestilence-carrier went up. A young lad, one of the hostages we made fight, was struck with fever. His body was covered in sores.'

A familiar sense of foreboding ran through Wilfrid.

'What did you do with him?' he asked, though he knew the answer.

'Well, we put him out, of course. No one liked it. I mean he was just a child, really. But that's what has to be done, isn't it?'

Cerdic gulped down some more beer.

'Go on,' Cuthbert said.

'We were quiet that night. In the mountains around us we heard singing. It stopped as soon as it had begun, but we knew they could not be too far off. Ecgfrith King said the Picts were little better than devils anyhow, with their shameless painting of their bodies and their unholy practices of Easter. We would pursue them the next day and we would prevail.'

'But surely Ecgfrith was suspicious?' Cuthbert said. 'And the warmaster? Why would the Picts risk revealing their whereabouts?'

Cerdic shrugged.

'There were whispered consultations in the king's tent. I know that. But we were a strong force, three times the size of the Pict army, the king said, and they were already on the run.'

'So you set out the next day?'

Cerdic nodded.

'At dawn. If you could call it dawn. We could barely

see in front of us, the clouds were that low. Our scouts found the Picts' trail easily though. But then the clouds opened, spilled their guts. Such snow you have never seen. And in May. It blinded us, confused us. The warmaster though, he kept us together, shouted commands, encouragement, never stopping. We would soon have the Picts in our grasp, he said. They could not hide their stupid, painted faces in this snow.

'So we kept going. All morning. Though truth be told we could not tell the hour, so dark was the sky. We came to another valley. Dunachton, I heard it was called. A tight valley, everything hushed and snow still falling.'

He held out a trembling hand for another cup of beer and took a deep draught.

'I was lucky. I was close to the back. They went down, you see, the men ahead of me. They sank.'

'Sank?' Wilfrid asked. 'What do you mean, sank?'

'Ice.' Cerdic let out a sob. 'Ice they were walking on, not solid ground. A frozen lake hidden beneath a shield of snow. But it didn't hold. It cracked. The men at the head of the retinue went first. Some quickly, dragged down by their armour. Others were trapped on sheets of ice and tried to leap to safety, but they landed in the water. Men were scattering and retreating, and the horses were rearing and panicking, and everyone screaming *go back, go back!* The warmaster sounded his horn, and the king called *retreat*, and I ran and ran just like everyone else, and many of us did make it back to the edge of the valley, but it was too late.'

Cuthbert placed his head in his hands. His dream, Wilfrid thought. Is that what he had dreamed or sensed that night? Men sinking, screaming?

'Go on,' Cuthbert said.

Cerdic wiped his eyes with his sleeve and took a deep breath.

'That's when they came. Sprang up from behind the hills. Pict men coming at us from every direction, with sword and spear, arrow and axe. I battled hard. I swear it. I went for a Pict boy with my axe. All he had was a knife and a wooden shield, but he fought me until he stumbled, and then I raised my axe and swung it back and brought it down and sliced into his shoulder. But I didn't have time to finish him off. I was kicked in the head by a rearing horse – one of our own – and down I went, and I couldn't get up again.' He hung his head. 'Or maybe I wouldn't get up again. I didn't want to end up dying like that Pict boy, crying in agony and calling out for his mama. I lay there in the snow, watching our men as the Picts drove them back to the icy lake, and one by one they fell.'

'What of the king?' Cuthbert asked.

'They came for him finally. The thegns, what was left of them, made a shield-wall around him, but the Picts circled them. The warmaster was the last to fall. He shielded Ecgfrith with his body. They sliced through him and then slew the king.'

Cerdic drank again, crying and shaking and spilling his beer.

'They tricked us, those dirty Picts. The devil showed them how. They drew us into the valley with the frozen lake and surrounded us. But they got lucky, those bastards, with the snow and ice. Or maybe the devil sent them the snow. Who knows?'

He held out his cup for more beer, and Wilfrid refilled it.

'That wasn't the end of it. More men went down with the plague. There's almost none of us left. Some said it was because you never came to bless us, Bishop, before we set out, to give us the shield of holy water. But I don't know. Maybe they were the lucky ones, the ones who died, not the few of us who were spared, who failed to protect our lord. It's as if God spared us to show the whole world we're not warriors, not even men at all.'

Cuthbert put a hand on Cerdic's shoulder.

'Where is the king's body?' he asked.

'That was the odd thing,' Cerdic said. 'We feared to see the king's head hung from the gates of Bruide king's stronghold, but they did not dishonour his body at all. They sent it south, with a band of their own men and some of us captives.' He frowned. 'We didn't understand it. We were met at Din Eydin by another man with his own retinue. He gave instructions to bring Ecgfrith's body to Iona. He would not listen to our men's pleas to be allowed take the body to Lindisfarne for burial. He would not have a shrine to the former king out there, he said. But he said Iona was the most sacred place in these islands, and a fitting burial place for a king and for his own brother, and that's where Ecgfrith King would lie.'

'How far away is this man now?' Cuthbert said.

'A day's journey. He sent me ahead. He said I was to tell you that Aldfrith King is coming to the Royal City. He said he comes in peace; that he wishes to be met by his bishop at the gates of the stronghold; that he expects the bishop's blessing; and that in return he pledges an oath to be a king who will serve the Word of God and not the sword and spear.' Cerdic paused. 'He said also he expects to find the queen cared for and guarded. She should not be left unattended at any stage, and he will take custody of her child once it is born.'

'I see,' Cuthbert said. 'Yes, I understand his meaning. Unfortunately, this last part of the new king's message is untimely.'

He coughed, looked as if he might spit out some phlegm, but then swallowed it again. His eyes, Wilfrid saw, were red. Dark hollows pooled beneath them. His hair, always wispish, was thinner and scanter than ever, and he stood bent over like a crookback.

Wilfrid found his voice.

'The queen is being well cared for and guarded,' he said. 'At Whitby Abbey. She requested to retire there, to live out her days as a holy woman. The child was lost.' He looked straight at Cerdic as he spoke. 'I was there, I heard the screams of the queen as she bled, spoke with Abbess Ælfflæd afterwards. If Aldfrith King wishes to speak to a witness to these matters then please send for me.'

Wilfrid went up to the ramparts and looked out. Somewhere to the north the new king was preparing to march on Bamburgh. Further north again, Ecgfrith's men lay dead in a bloodied battlefield, their bodies picked over by crows, or drowned at the bottom of a lake. South of Bamburgh a group of holy women were being welcomed home to Whitby. He doubted he would see the women again, any more than he would see his own father.

The sun was setting on Lindisfarne, and the sky washed a flood of yellow, orange, blue and lilac through a gauze of shifting clouds over the monastery. Further out, the Farne sat lonely as Wilfrid was, gleaming black in the sea.

Part Four

AD 686

One

A SUDDEN CALM on the December sea. The storms that had wracked the island on the eve of Christ's Mass had abated, and today, the feast of St Stephen, promised to be a still enough day, the winds light, a low pale sun bleeding through the clouds. A good day to set sail. If you must set sail.

Cuthbert leaned heavily on his staff and looked on as Herefrith and Tydi loaded up the boat with provisions. An onion fell from a sack and rolled onto the sand near Wilfrid's feet. He bent down to pick it up, careful not to dislodge Dunstan's grip on his arm.

'What's happening now?' Dunstan said.

He tapped Wilfrid with the handle of his staff, a habit he had developed every time he asked a question. Wilfrid had learned to discipline himself, to hold still and not pull free each time he felt the tap of the staff against his wrist, like the smack of a cane he used to receive in the scriptorium as a boy.

'Brother Herefrith and Brother Tydi are putting the supplies in the boat. They're almost ready. The bishop will give his blessing soon.'

'The sail. Have they checked the sail?'

'Yes,' Wilfrid said. 'Everything seems to be in order.'

'And the mast? The mast is strong and secure?'

'Yes, yes, of course.'

Wilfrid fought back the urge to shake Dunstan off his arm as he might a persistent wasp, to leave him just this once to his world of shadows and cloud. He gritted his teeth as Dunstan dug his nails into his wrist. They had grown long. He would have to pare them again, the toenails too, he supposed, this afternoon, when all was quiet, when Cuthbert was gone.

'It's not right,' Dunstan said. 'If he must go, someone should stay there with him, so that he is not alone when...when the time comes.'

'Brother Herefrith will visit as often as he is permitted. The bishop has made all this clear.'

But Dunstan brushed off Wilfrid's reassurance with a strike of his staff into the sand that made one of the novices standing nearby dive out of the way like a frightened fish.

In a sense it was a relief that Dunstan could not see the deterioration in Cuthbert. His obvious pain, his very appearance – an ulcerated skeleton – had become difficult to endure. Cuthbert's old trouble, as it was called, had struck soon after Aldfrith had entered the Royal City, and Wilfrid felt sure it was Cuthbert's visits to the plague-stricken villages that brought it on again. The thought gnawed at him. He tried to push it away, but he knew that had he not intervened with Ecgfrith, shown him the way into Cuthbert's heart, Cuthbert would have remained in his hermitage and not become bishop. He would still be serving God's purpose and would still be well.

Cuthbert faced the monks. Edberht stood just behind him, ready to move in an instant, Wilfrid thought, should Cuthbert sway or stumble. The monks knelt to receive his final blessing. Cuthbert made the sign of the cross over them and recited the verse from the psalm.

Signatum est super nos lumen vultus tui,
Domine ... In pace, in id ipsum,
dormiam, et requiescam, quoniam tu,
Domine, singulariter in spe constituisti me.

He stood for a while, looking at the brethren and over to the monastery, then, refusing Herefrith's arm, turned and limped to the awaiting boat. Herefrith and Tydi hauled the boat into the water, climbed in and began to row. The brethren gathered in a line on the shore, watching as the boat sailed up the channel, beyond the Royal City and out into the open sea towards the Farne. One of the monks began to sing a hymn, but it died away like a falling breeze, and then they all stood silent and still. They looked on, grief etched on their faces, until the white sail of the boat had merged into the grey of the sea.

Wilfrid looked at Dunstan staring wildly out to sea, rubbing his eyes as if somehow that might bring his sight back and enable him to see Cuthbert one last time. And for one uneasy moment Wilfrid saw an image of his own face the summer before last, when another boat with three figures put out to sea, sailing south towards Whitby, and he had watched and felt as though someone had wrapped a hand around his heart and wrenched it from his body. That time too, he had stood watching, waiting, hoping for a backward glance, until the boat disappeared into the horizon. And, like Cuthbert, she had not looked back.

There was still the letter, however. He went to the library sometimes and fished it out from a thick stack of documents pertaining to land endowments and gifts. It had arrived this summer, almost exactly a year after the three women had left for Whitby. The letter, from Abbess Ælfflæd, was written not in the abbess' own hand, but in one that Wilfrid immediately recognised.

To Cuthbert, most reverend father, bishop and servant of God, from Ælfflæd, unworthy servant of the house of Whitby, greetings in our Lord.

I send to you with blessings word of our humble monastery and enquire also of you as to your own matters on Lindisfarne. We are grateful for your prayers, and be assured that the bishop remains ever in the supplications we send to the Lord, for I have received reports that you are beset at times by that old illness which first assailed you in the pestilence which came after the Easter Synod.

I fear also that your tireless ministering and preaching to your flock may inflict further injuries on a body already wracked and worn, and hope the Lord grants you some rest and solitude. I beg Him daily that He show mercy to His servant, though I do not question His ways and know how often it is that those closest to Him must follow a path of sorrow and suffering.

Here at Whitby, our holy house continues to prosper and live peacefully under God's law. My dear brother, Aldfrith King, as generous as he is merciful, has endowed the monastery with hides of land and cattle, and our humble scriptorium thrives, where one of our sisters has recently begun the great task of compiling a record of the Life of St Gregory. Moreover, God continues to send us new sowers for the field of His Word.

As you know, the former queen, Iurminburgh, has taken the veil and, with great humility and tenderness of heart, has dedicated herself to the Lord, and recently we have received into our community a very young girl child, Godgifu, whose venerable mother wished her consecrated to the Lord.

I hear the king has been equally generous, if indeed not more so, to your own monastery at Lindisfarne, and it gives my heart no small joy that my brother has brought peace to our troubled land, and seeks good relations with our brothers and sisters north in Pictland and across the sea at Brega, and that he has negotiated the return of the Irish hostages.

Some discord about the old question remains among the brothers and sisters in Christ, but

I urge you to cease beating your breast about these ancient wounds, for you have done all in your power to heal them. May the Lord who is the Helmsman of our souls steer us to unity in His time, not ours, for we must ever trust in the Lord.

My dearest bishop and friend, may He Whose heart is overflowing in charity and mercy draw you ever to His abundant grace and glorious light.

Ælfflæd, abbess of Whitby

The book the abbess sent had been copied by the same hand that had written the letter: Meredith's. Wilfrid borrowed it often from the library, let his fingers hover over the words, imagined there was a message from her inscribed into the holy text, secreted somewhere in the spaces between the florid loops and the needle-sharp ascenders and descenders.

He remembered her telling him to write something of his own, how it seemed to stir an unvoiced longing in him. But it would never be permitted. Not even Cuthbert would encourage a poor scribe such as himself to compose his own text. Still, the thought of it on this cold and quiet St Stephen's night as he lay in his cell – it kindled something in him, filled his bones and blood like a cup of warmed wine.

Herefrith tended to Cuthbert regularly on the Farne. When the weather was fair he sailed over with provisions, bathed the ulcers which pocked the bishop's legs, refreshed the bracken for his bedding, prepared a nourishing broth, though he reported that Cuthbert sipped barely enough to satisfy a mewling baby, and his pain seemed to have worsened. It was clear he was weakening. He could not move at all now without his staff and could barely summon the strength to leave his cell.

Dunstan grew increasingly restless when these visits took place. He insisted that Wilfrid accompany him to the clifftop and give an account of the boat's progress out to sea. He even questioned the seaworthiness of the vessel, examined it as best he could with his hands, feeling along the hull of the boat, the mast, the oars, for any signs of cracks or rot. He checked the stitching on the sail, rubbing the stitches between his finger and thumb.

Wilfrid supposed it must be his blindness that invoked this new and constant fear, as if in his mind's eye all he could see was that time with Fergus, the rising waves, the malevolent winds, the flapping sail and the emptiness of the sea when they searched for their missing companion.

Wilfrid knew the terror of his own dreams. Fergus holding his ankle, dragging him down. He, kicking out hard, trying to free himself from the fingers clutching at him. White water cascading all around. Dunstan must have suffered similarly, he realised. Perhaps he still did. This bond that chained them together was never acknowledged, but Wilfrid knew Dunstan would never forgive him for Fergus. No matter how often Dunstan prayed for the gift of forgiveness and mercy, his heart would remain a cup of bitter gall.

On a Lenten Wednesday in the middle of *Hreðmonað*,

Herefrith returned from the Farne, weeping. He'd had a difficult crossing and was so exhausted he had to be assisted from the boat and more or less carried to the infirmary by Edberht and Tydi. Dunstan insisted that Wilfrid bring him there too. Edberht gave Herefrith some warmed wine, and Tydi rubbed a salve into his oar-bitten, blistered hands.

'The bishop is weaker,' Herefrith said. 'Legs and feet covered with ulcers. His breathing is like the whine of a seal. Even his eyesight is failing.'

'But he should not be alone,' Dunstan said. 'What were you thinking of, Brother Herefrith, leaving him alone?'

Herefrith drew a deep breath. 'He bade me go. He said he must be alone a short while, on his pilgrimage to Christ, in his final battle for the Lord. I am to return again in two or three days and...and then I may remain.'

The brothers glanced from Herefrith to each other, shadows descending their faces. Dunstan stared into the darkness before him.

'I will accompany you,' Tydi said at last. 'You will not be fit to row, even in two days.'

'No,' Herefrith said. 'You may assist me in preparing medicaments and a salve for his ulcers, but the bishop is clear. When I return I must bring Wilfrid with me. Only Wilfrid.'

Two

CUTHBERT'S CELL WAS COLD and dark, the air laden
with a sour stench. Cuthbert lay crumpled on a
thin, bracken pallet in the corner. A few onions,
one half-eaten, lay next to the bed. He did not get up
when they entered, nor raise his hand in blessing. The
only sign of awareness was a moan, a heaving whine
from his chest. Wilfrid fetched some water from the
spring he had discovered all those years ago. God-
given water, Cuthbert had said; the great sweetness
of its flavour alone bore witness to that. Indeed when
Cuthbert had blessed him with it then, Wilfrid had felt
its calming, stilling powers run through his spirit as
surely as it ran down his face and neck. He hoped it
would bring some relief to Cuthbert now.

Herefrith spooned a little water into Cuthbert's

mouth and wiped his face. He pulled back the coverlet and lifted his robe. The bandages on his legs were stained, and a fresh ulcer, ink-black, had opened up on his right foot. A stream of yellow pus oozed down his heel.

'More water,' Herefrith said. 'And start a fire. We must bathe these ulcers and get some nourishment into him. It seems he has eaten nothing but a couple of onions since I was last here. His mouth is dry, and there is a fever in him.'

Herefrith bathed the ulcers and laid a wet cloth on Cuthbert's forehead. Wilfrid edged morsels of bread soaked in warmed wine into the side of the old man's mouth. He sprinkled drops from a potion that Tydi had prepared onto his tongue. After a while, Cuthbert began to shift about a little and to half-open his eyes. He muttered things – names, mostly. Fergus, he said several times, and Wilfrid felt the old shame burn within him. If it were not for him, they would not have sailed to the island that time. Had he managed to furl the sail, Fergus would not have had to move position in the boat, and the accident would never have happened.

'Dunstan,' Cuthbert said suddenly. He tugged at his coverlet, pulling it over his face, and Herefrith had to set it aright again. He felt Cuthbert's forehead.

'Still feverish. But cooler.'

'Dunstan,' Cuthbert said again.

'He's back at the monastery,' Wilfrid said. 'He would have come, but his eyesight...'

Cuthbert sighed. His breathing was easier now.

'His eyesight. Yes.'

Cuthbert reached out his hand weakly from the bed,

and Wilfrid took it in his. It was cold and clammy, the fingers thin and weak as strands of straw.

'Do not trouble yourself, Bishop,' Herefrith said. 'Brother Dunstan is well, even if the Lord has seen fit to take his sight. Brother Wilfrid serves him faithfully, and while we remain here Brother Tydi acts in Wilfrid's stead.'

Herefrith went to draw some more water and heat it. Cuthbert opened his eyes and whispered something. Wilfrid leaned closer.

'Not just his sight. His heart. Cannot forgive.' Cuthbert sighed a long, low sigh, and it seemed some time before he breathed again. 'Cannot forgive himself. That time with the sail. He couldn't see...didn't see the wave coming, ignored the sky, the warnings...shouldn't have come.'

He coughed and seemed to want to speak again – 'cannot forgive himself,' he said once more – but then fell back into a fitful sleep.

Wilfrid sat with Cuthbert's hand held in his. The sail. Dunstan. Dunstan and Fergus. The journey to the Farne. Fergus hauling him to the boat. *A mackerel sky*, Fergus had said. *Let's go quickly then*, Dunstan had replied. Then later, when Wilfrid had been unable to undo the knot that held the sail – it was Dunstan who had tied that knot. Wilfrid remembered now how desperately he himself had pulled at it, how taut it was. And the wave that rocked the boat as Fergus had left his position at the bow. *It came from nowhere,* he recalled Dunstan saying. But hadn't Fergus warned Dunstan to keep watch? Wasn't Dunstan supposed to steer the boat steady as Fergus moved?

341

Dunstan. For so long he had blamed only himself, had felt responsible for Fergus' drowning as surely as if he had deliberately flung him out of the boat and held his head beneath the water. He hadn't thought of Dunstan – Dunstan who looked on him as if he were a pestilence carrier, infecting others with his poison. Dunstan was to blame! He had ignored the signs in the sky, dismissed Fergus' reservations and calculated that they would reach the Farne before the weather turned. And Dunstan was at the helm; he had failed to see the approaching wave, failed to warn Fergus. Not only that, he had kept his guilt hidden from the brethren, let the blame fall instead on Wilfrid. Though none of them had ever accused him, Wilfrid had always sensed a silent denunciation hovering over him.

He sat still, continued to hold Cuthbert's hand. He should be seething. His heart should beat with the fury of a dozen devils; a score of curses should spew from his tongue. He waited for rage to strike like a storm. The storm. He forced himself to think back, to recall everything about that day. He saw himself again scrambling to untie the knot – how cold and cramped and feeble his fingers had been. He saw Fergus moving position – surely a dangerous thing to do? He remembered the sudden blast of wind, how quickly the wave had approached. Would it really have been possible in that instant for Dunstan to steer them away from it? He saw Fergus flail and reach for the mast only to be thrown again as another wave blasted them and catapulted him overboard.

No, Dunstan did not cause the storm that took Fergus. Dunstan was not the reason Fergus had changed position. Dunstan was not the reason they made the journey to the Farne. And it had not been Dunstan who at last insisted they abandon Fergus to the sea, steer themselves to the Farne and safety.

Wilfrid watched the rise and fall of Cuthbert's chest, listened to his short gasps. What had the old man said? Dunstan could not forgive himself. His heart was twisted in a hatred of himself that was fiercer than any ill-will he bore Wilfrid. He thought of Dunstan alone in his own cell now, praying, waiting for a sign from the Farne, waiting for someone to bring him word of the thing he dreaded most, the thing that would plunge his soul as well as his eyes into darkness from which it would not emerge. Wilfrid pressed Cuthbert's hand. He could not be sure if his own heart was any more forgiving than Dunstan's, but he could will it to be so. He could try.

Wilfrid and Herefrith kept vigil with Cuthbert all night, taking turns to bathe his forehead and hold his hand. They read him passages from St John's Gospel, the book that Dunstan had made for him, and from the psalms. Wilfrid grew more anxious as time wore on, and many times he was struck by his old complaint, his stomach knotted in a cramp. He tried to concentrate on the words of the readings to control the hated urges which must beset him at this of all times, but every now and then they overwhelmed him and he had to rush from the cell to the privy.

At the third hour of the day Cuthbert opened his eyes. His forehead was cool, his breathing more relaxed.

'Brother Herefrith, leave us awhile,' he said.

Herefrith made to object, but Cuthbert dismissed him. 'Don't worry. Wilfrid will call you when the time is at hand.'

Cuthbert pointed to his little portable altar. Wilfrid lit a candle from the fire and placed it on the altar.

'Aidan's holy altar,' Cuthbert said. 'His spirit is with me when I pray at it. He strengthens me. Except...when I have left his spirit behind – abandoned him.'

'You never abandoned him, Bishop,' Wilfrid said. 'You followed his path, made his hermitage your hermitage, preached and healed as he did, became bishop, even.'

'Vanity. Bishop Cuthbert of Lindisfarne. I was trying not to be *like* Aidan, but to be him.'

A sliver of shame ran through Wilfrid. He had cleared the path that made Cuthbert bishop, shown Ecgfrith the means to burrow his way into Cuthbert's heart, and it seemed Cuthbert had never recognised his role in the matter.

'No, Bishop. It wasn't...'

Cuthbert continued speaking. 'I had already abandoned Aidan's ways, and Columba's, long before, followed the king's ways instead. Never worthy to be bishop of Aidan's flock. Betrayed them.'

'But, Bishop, if you are talking about the proper calculation of Easter, the new tonsure – those were the pope's ways too, and the ways of the Church from one end of the world to the next, everywhere except this small corner of the earth. That's what we've been taught.'

But Cuthbert seemed to be beyond the reach of Wilfrid's words.

'Disharmony. Division and disharmony. A broken hymn. One side of the choir takes up a false note. The other gives battle. Eventually both have strayed so far from the true sound that the devil himself rejoices in the discord.'

He closed his eyes and seemed to fall into a half-sleep, but his breathing came in shorter gasps, and Wilfrid began to wonder how he would know when the time had come to fetch Herefrith. He must call Herefrith now. He needed the privy and Cuthbert would need someone to watch over him while he was outside. But Cuthbert spoke again.

'The devils returned when Herefrith left. Have never been as strong...tormenting me... my failings as bishop, as pastor...could not bring unity, prevent war.'

'Bishop, listen. None of that was your fault, not the matter with Easter or being made bishop or anything else that followed. It was...' The cramp in Wilfrid's stomach grew urgent. 'It was my fault, mine... I'll...I'll fetch Brother Herefrith.'

'No.'

Cuthbert took his hand, his grip surprisingly firm, his hand warm. Wilfrid felt the warmth flow into him. The pressure of the cramp died back a little.

'Not yet,' Cuthbert said. 'No. Not that...' His voice was low and rasping. 'That is not what I wanted to say, not...' Cuthbert's eyes closed. The gaps between each breath seemed to be getting longer. Still he held onto Wilfrid's hand. Still the warmth flowed through Wilfrid, and the churning in his bowels ebbed completely away.

'Will I read to you, Bishop?'

'A psalm, Wilfrid. Of comfort.'

Wilfrid read and reread the psalm.

Dominus regit me, et nihil mihi deerit.
In loco pascuae ibi me conlocavit.
Super acquam refectionis educavit me.
Animam meam convertit.

It seemed to calm Cuthbert, though still his breathing was short gasps with long intervals between them.

Nam et si ambulavero in medio umbrae mortis
non timebo mala, quoniam tu mecum es.

Cuthbert stirred.

'Wilfrid?'

'I'm here, Bishop.'

He squeezed Cuthbert's hand. Cuthbert opened his eyes, stared into empty space ahead of him.

'Dark,' he said.

And Wilfrid suspected that indeed the shadows of death had come upon Cuthbert and taken his sight.

'Let me fetch Brother Herefrith.'

'No. Water.'

Wilfrid fetched a fresh cup, but Cuthbert didn't wish to drink. He dipped his fingers in the water, felt for Wilfrid's head and blessed him. He ran his fingers down Wilfrid's face, made the sign of the cross on his forehead and mouth.

'I should have said,' Cuthbert whispered. 'All those years...I should have said, but you did not wish to speak of it, I know.' He coughed. 'Not your fault. That thing with your brother. Not your...'

'Yes, Bishop. I know.'

'And even...even if it was...a demon in you, or...' He coughed again, gasped. 'God has forgiven you.'

He tried to speak again, but nothing came out; the words seemed trapped in his lungs. Wilfrid squeezed Cuthbert's hand. He didn't know why Cuthbert was so concerned with Sigi.

'I know, Bishop, and Sigi is well now. You healed him, remember?'

'Not Sigi.'

Cuthbert was shivering now, and Wilfrid knew he should fetch Herefrith, but Cuthbert held onto him and moaned something, something Wilfrid couldn't quite make out, a single word. Wolf. Was it wolf? Not Sigi, Cuthbert had said. But he must not think. Not yet. He must look away. Cuthbert gasped, a long terrible gasp, and Wilfrid feared it was his last. But Cuthbert rallied a final time.

'Herefrith,' he said.

They sat with him through the night. Herefrith sang the offices, with Wilfrid mumbling along. Neither left his side. Cuthbert slept deeply, gave no recognition of their presence. He was beyond the threshold of their world now. Only once, towards the very end, did he try to speak. As Herefrith intoned the antiphon for Lauds, Cuthbert's hand moved, as if to give a blessing, Wilfrid thought. A sibilant sound fell from his mouth. 'Sing. Sing.'

Herefrith placed the *viaticum* on Cuthbert's tongue, blessed him and took up the psalm.

Deus, reppulisti nos et destruxisti nos;
iratus es et misertus es nobis.

He faltered, the words and notes stuck in his throat. From outside came the high moan of seal-song and the loud cry of nightbirds. Wilfrid clasped Cuthbert's hand tightly. He tried. He raised his voice from a mumble. A note. A single note.

Commovisti terram et turbasti eam;
sana contritiones eius, quia commota est.

Herefrith recovered and sang with him, though his voice trembled and choked.

Ostendisti populo tuo dura;
potasti nos vino conpunctionis.

By the time they reached the end of the psalm Herefrith was weeping more than singing, though Wilfrid managed to sustain a wavering note in this strange voice that seemed his and yet not his. Only then did he look at the face of his bishop. Cuthbert was still, his hand limp. Wilfrid and Herefrith sat together unmoving. Outside, the sea carried the echoes of seals moaning, and the sky filled up with every kind of bird cry. Eventually Herefrith gently removed Wilfrid's hand from Cuthbert's. He fetched an unconsecrated host from a small tin, placed it on Cuthbert's breast, and together he and Wilfrid blessed their bishop and said the final prayer of Lauds.

Three

A GLOWERING DAWN was creeping in over the sea when Wilfrid left the cell. He made two torches of dried bracken, held them aloft on the west side of the island and waved. He sang again the psalm he had read to Cuthbert just a few hours before.

*Et ut inhabitem in domo Domini
in longitudinem dierum.*

His voice was weak, no longer the voice that had once pitched music as pure as a blackbird's. It was perhaps not much better than Dunstan's, but the notes were there, more or less, and the notes, he knew, gave the words power. For once he felt his impoverished prayers might find their way to God. He waved the torches, and it seemed to him that his voice was carried over the sea to the watch tower at Lindisfarne where the brethren awaited his signal.

Across the water a torch waved back at him, shooting red tears into the sky. And Wilfrid knew that though day was dawning, the monastery was plunged into long night, and the brethren's laments would fill Lindisfarne like stars fill the night sky, now that Cuthbert was gone.

He waved the torches until they burned away, then turned to go back to the cell. The wolf was waiting for him. As he had known it would be. Wolf, Cuthbert had said. He must have realised it was there, sensed its presence. And this time Wilfrid must not look away. He must look. He must follow. The wolf led him to the edge of the cliff. Below him, waves beat against the rocks, the sound louder than thunder as they crashed and broke. And through the clamour of the waves he kept hearing Cuthbert's voice, *wolf, wolf, wulfi*. Wilfrid fell to the ground, the noise of the waves roaring in his head, the clouds wheeling above him, the earth spinning beneath him. He dug his fingers into the grass. The wolf came to him, wrapped his mouth around his ankle, and Wilfrid felt the ground widening and opening up, dragging him down, down. He didn't know where the wolf was bringing him. He hoped it was not to hell.

*

Wulfstan's Hill. High on the hill, beyond the village, beyond the standing stones – the marker past which they must never venture. A large pool surrounded by rocks and trees. Water thunders from above, spills furiously over a cliff. His eyes are blinded by the glare of the white cascading torrent – battalions of sprites, he thinks, fighting their way forward to the pool. A huge, flat boulder lies atop the rocks at the point where the river leaps into the pool. Beneath it, a hollow space stretching into blackness behind.

A cave.

That's where they buried Wulfstan. His bones are still there.

He knows that voice. The blacksmith's boy. He has led them here – four of them – prattling about Wulfstan all the way. Everyone in Medilwong knows of Wulfstan. The hill is named for him. Wulfstan was a great warrior from the time of Woden, when men were giants and battles were so fierce they lasted for years instead of days. The blacksmith's boy knows all the stories.

See the pool? Wulfstan dug it out of the rocks with one scoop of his giant hands.

But where did the water come from?

Another boy. Young. Dark-haired. Wolfish teeth.

Well, that's his piss, of course. Giant's piss. Who's first into the piss pool?

Laughter, screeching, pushing, shoving, and suddenly he goes down tumbling into a shock of cold water. He opens his mouth to scream, but it fills with liquid. He hits out wildly with his arms and somehow finds the grass at the edge of the pool. He climbs out, spitting and coughing, his tunic sodden, his mouth stinging with giant piss. The dark-haired boy is laughing at him. They all are. He bites his lip, does not cry, pretends to laugh too.

The dark-haired boy jumps up on a rock.

Look at me. I'm Wulfstan. I'm the greatest warrior giant. See? See the wolf sign on my knife? My knife, my hill, my pool.

The boy holds out his silver knife. It glistens in the sunlight. The others run about him and launch into a chant.

Wulfi, Wulfi, Wulfi.

The blacksmith's boy takes charge.

Come on, warriors. Time to make camp. Up there, in the cave, with the bones of Wulfstan the Warrior.

Yes! Let's race up the side of the hill. We can get at it easily from there.

No, no. We're warriors. We'll climb up the rocks, through the waterfall. Wilfrid will go first. He's the eldest and the bravest.

More laughter, grinning, nudging.

Go on then, Wilfrid.

They stand around him, smirking, waiting. The dark-haired boy leans forward.

You must, Wilfrid. You're the eldest. I'll tell father you wouldn't lead, that you're a coward.

He's not a coward, are you, Wilfrid? He let the pigs out, remember?

A girl could do that.

A girl did do that, according to Wilfrid. Come on, forget him.

He sees them throwing off their clothes, hears the ringing of their screeches as the first cold blast of cascading water hits them. They push each other, splash each other, duck each other's heads under the water. The blacksmith's boy gives the command.

Well, who's first to the cave? On my count.

Suddenly he is running toward them, flinging his boots aside. He is in the pool. White water thunders down on him, heavy as stones, cold as snow. He pushes past his companions. He is first to reach the edge of the rockface.

Hey! Not fair! I haven't given the signal yet. Get back here.

He climbs, ignores the sharpness of the stone underfoot, ignores the shouts from below.

Wait, Wilfrid, wait.

He doesn't wait, climbs higher. The water beats faster, colder. He can hardly feel his fingers, his feet, but he is nearly there. In a moment he will reach the cave, be the first in, the first to discover the bones of the giant. He hesitates. He doesn't really want to see any bones, even if they are those of a great warrior, but then he thinks of how he will tell this story to his father later. He imagines each word. His heart thunders, loud and fast as the waterfall. His left hand grabs the flat rock that forms the entrance to the cave. He almost loses his footing on a slime-covered stone but somehow he steadies himself. Nearly there. He starts to pull himself up.

Wilfrid, wait. It's not fair. You had a head start.

Something grasps his left ankle. Claws that want to wrest his foot from the rock, to hold him back, to deny him. The claws grip tighter. He tries to find a foothold with his right leg, but everything is slippery. The whole rockface has turned into a slippery, wriggling eel. He shakes his left foot. Shakes it hard.

Wilfrid!

He cannot hold on. He shakes even harder. Suddenly he is free. He uses his freed foot to propel himself upwards. He thinks he hears screaming but he isn't sure if it is coming from himself or someone else, and then the thunder of the water drowns it out. He hauls himself over the top and plunges into the cave, the falling water a closed door behind him.

The cave is empty. Just a small hollow in the rocks. No bones. Barely enough room for him to stand up, let alone bury a giant. There won't even be enough space to fit the other boys. The other boys. Where are they? Surely they were just behind him? One of them certainly was just behind him.

He thinks he feels something snatch at his ankle again and he kicks out. But nothing is there. Slowly he crawls out of the cave to the edge of the rock and peers over, the rush of water filling his head.

The boys are no longer climbing up the fall. Two of them are clambering away from the rocks. The blacksmith's boy has made it to the hill and is running down, down towards the pool below where a swirl of red is whirling in the water, spinning and sweeping away downstream, and there, his legs caught between the rocks, his head stuck beneath the water, is the dark-haired boy with the wolfish teeth. Wulfi, his little brother, Wulfi.

When he finally manages to crawl from the cave to the hill and down to the pool, the boys have pulled Wulfi out of the water and onto the grass. The blacksmith's boy is shouting. They are all crying and shouting.

Wilfrid pushed him, kicked him away. I saw it. He was cheating. We all saw it. He did it on purpose. There must be a demon in him.

Wulfi's head is smashed, bloody bits trailing from the side, bones sticking out. He must have hit the rocks as he fell. His mouth hangs open, his tongue lolling. His dark eyes stare up at Wilfrid, not blinking, not moving.

Get up, Wulfi, Wilfrid says, though he cannot hear himself speak the words. *Wulfi, get up.*

Wulfi doesn't hear either. His right ear is torn, half of it ripped away by the jagged rocks. The rest of it must be in the water. Wilfrid goes to find it. Wulfi will need it. Besides, he cannot look at Wulfi's smashed head and open eyes. He cannot look at Wulfi at all. But when he steps into the water he feels the claw on his ankle again, trying to pull him down, down into the black, tangled water where sprites are swimming like eels, and he only just manages to draw back. He limps to where the boys have discarded their clothes. They are still shouting.

It was his fault. He pushed Wulfi deliberately. Just so he could win.

He wants to say something, but his tongue is too soft; a great and terrible silence has entered him. His legs are soft too, soft as honey, and they ooze away from beneath him. He falls onto Wulfi's tunic.

Something is protruding from a pouch on the belt of Wulfi's tunic. It gleams wet, shiny and silver in the sun. The etching on the handle winks at him, a head, a perfectly carved wolf's head. Wulfi. Wilfrid rubs his thumb in circular motions over the etching, presses it hard into the grooves. Then he seals his hand around the knife, draws it to his chest, feels his heart thump next to it. He closes his eyes. The knife is Wulfi's heart. And his own heart. He doesn't want to go back to the other Wulfi, the broken Wulfi. He will never go back. The water roars in his ears and in his head. He keeps his eyes tightly closed. He pushes broken Wulfi away.

*

When he woke the wolf was gone. Sunlight warmed his face. He lay on the ground, listening to the sounds of sea and sky, the waves breaking rhythmically against the rocks, seals singing a mournful song, echoed by hosts of swallows and shags, kittiwakes, kites and sea ravens. He was still – empty – as though a poison had been sucked out of him. Not your fault, Cuthbert had said, though how could it not have been his fault? That was surely the talk of death fever. But the death words of a holy man must have power, truth. Cuthbert had blessed him, and his blessing had power too. Perhaps it was, as Cuthbert said, a demon. And he thought surely the demon had finally been drawn out of him; it was gone now, like the wolf. He prayed it was. He got to his feet, slowly.

Part Five

AD 698

One

THE DEAD WERE WITH HIM AGAIN. Sitting silently by his desk. So often over the years they had kept him company, prowling wolf-like by his side, following him from cell to scriptorium, watching as he stole scraps of goatskin and secretly refilled his inkpot from the barrel. For years he had scratched away at it, this veiled task, scribbling stealthily beneath the blank gaze of poor blind Dunstan. He worked in fits and starts, only when he was seized by the need to do so. It brought him back from dark days when malevolent dreams assailed him, demons took him to the fortress of hell, where he must live again the day Wulfi drowned, see again his broken face, hear the long, loud cry as he fell and the screams of his mother when they brought to her the ruined body of her son. Even now he still sometimes heard the whispers of the village elders, the women who at first comforted his mother, then turned aside, the slaves who skulked in corners and shrank from him as he passed.

There is an evil spirit in that boy.
They say that even when her belly was ripening
with him his mother knew.
Put him out, out on Wulfstan's Hill. The wolves
will take care of him.

He saw Fergus too, Laurence and Cuthbert. He listened again to Cuthbert's deathbed lament, the bishop's failures listed like a litany chanted in the offices, and knew he must rewrite the litany to make atonement. It would serve as atonement even if no one ever set eyes on it. God would see it. And Cuthbert, seated now in his place with the saints in heaven, would surely see it too. And so he used the quill as Meredith had once advised, used it as a ladder to climb out of hell, wrote words of his own.

He wrote down everything Cuthbert had told him, everything he could remember himself, and all of the stories he had heard from the brethren. There was a time when Cuthbert was caught alone, weary and hungry, in a terrible storm. God's angel led him to a deserted hut where, hidden in the roof, was a warm loaf and meat wrapped in a linen cloth. On another occasion he encountered a group of monks adrift on the River Tyne. His prayers caused the wind to turn and delivered the brothers safely to shore. There were so many stories – tales of prophecy, healing, curing those vexed by devils. Writing them down took Wilfrid out of the savage visions that came at him like Picts out of the snow. It brought ease to his spirit, just as Meredith had said it would.

Eventually, when he thought he had no more tales to tell, he wrapped his writings in a leather pouch and hid them in his cell. They were just scraps of tales after all, fragments of the truth, written in a poor hand by a poor scholar. They had served their purpose. Now he let them be.

He had not seen his mother again. He remembered now, or thought he remembered, after they buried Wulfi, the villagers casting accusatory looks in her direction. Had they blamed Rowena for birthing a demonic son? Had his father? Wilfrid hoped that his part in saving Sigi had tempered the bitterness that gnawed into his mother, though nothing, he supposed, could mitigate his guilt over what had happened to Wulfi. Even if a demon had seized hold of him that day, even if he had not intended to do what he did do, he had killed Wulfi as surely as if had planned the whole thing, exactly as those boys had made out.

And Cuthbert had been right. Wilfrid was blessed. Justice had not been meted out to him. He had not been put out for the wolves. He was sent to the monastery and he lived. That must suffice. He must not desire his mother's forgiveness. He had made what atonement he could to her. And he had discovered a way of living, of being. Even if God's love did not burn like a furnace in his soul, even if he did not hear God's voice calling to him on the wind, feel His guiding hand on his shoulder, it was enough that there had been times when he had known kindness and grace, and perhaps even love.

But now the *translatio* and the dead were returned. The brethren had been waiting years for this day. Bishop Edberht was sure the time had been ordained by God, the season of Lent and Easter occurring on exactly the same dates as they had when Cuthbert went to the Lord. And so on the fourth Wednesday of Lent, eleven years to the day since he had been buried, Cuthbert's bones were finally to be elevated and accorded the veneration they deserved. Taken from their resting place, they would be cleansed and blessed, laid in a silver casket and placed to the left of the altar, next to the remains of St Aidan himself.

Wilfrid understood the great honour the *translatio* conferred on the monastery's former bishop and prior, but the thought of interfering with the dead filled his stomach with a sickening unease. His mind drifted as he walked with the brethren in procession to the church. It hardly seemed possible to him that eleven winters had passed since Cuthbert had died, even longer since that storm and snow-filled winter, those murderous days when men bargained and battled with their Creator and lost. The plague had not spared Lindisfarne, and many of the brothers had succumbed. The sudden swoop of memories stopped him dead, plunged him for an instant back into that other time, and Dunstan, who was holding onto his arm, stumbled and disrupted the entire procession behind them. Wilfrid steadied Dunstan and himself, and together they followed Prior Herefrith into the church to the spot where Cuthbert was buried.

The monks formed a circle around the grave. Despite his pronouncement about when the *translatio* should take place, Bishop Edberht was not present. Not even this solemn ceremony could draw Edberht away from his now customary Lenten retreat on Cuthbert's Rock. His belly was swollen with a tumour; pain was his constant companion. He would not see another Lent, and he wished to prepare his soul for its departure to Christ.

Standing next to the tomb, Wilfrid wondered if Edberht, in confronting the imminence of his own death, would truly wish to be present at the unearthing of the bishop's remains, to partake in the cleansing of the corpse, the scraping away of skin residue, worms and maggots, the washing of the bones before they were carefully wrapped in silk and placed in a silver casket. Wilfrid would have wished himself in a small vessel out on the wild sea rather than here. His left arm, held by Dunstan, was shaking like a sail in the wind, and he hoped this was due to the trembling sickness Dunstan had developed and not to his own trepidation. He wished that just for this moment he could be in Dunstan's shadowed world. He did not want to look upon a carcass. He did not want to raise up any more dead bodies or dead spirits. He wanted to let the dead lie dead.

Herefrith sprinkled the sarcophagus with holy water and led the prayers. Then four of the younger, stronger monks set to removing the stone slab that lay atop the sarcophagus, while others sang psalms of praise. Wilfrid felt Dunstan's arm trembling even more fiercely as the monks plied the slab off, the sound of scraping stone ringing out harshly against the psalm singing. The brethren sang with wavering voices now, as the shallow pit of the sarcophagus was revealed. Wilfrid closed his eyes. He kept them closed though Dunstan's fingers dug like cat claws into his arm, and all around him a great commotion was stirring, a storm rising, a wind that blew wild and frantic. A cry went up, followed by another and another, and footsteps back and forward, and someone – was it Tydi? – weeping. Dunstan tugged at Wilfrid's arm.

'What is it?' he said. 'What's happening?'

Wilfrid opened his eyes. He looked into the coffin. He looked again. He tried to speak, but some devil had its talons around his throat. He wasn't sure if what he was seeing was a vision or a demon's trick, and yet, plainly, the other brethren could see it too.

'A wonder,' someone said. 'A great wonder.'

Dunstan tapped Wilfrid with his staff.

'What is it?' he said again.

Wilfrid took a deep breath.

'It's the bishop,' he said at last. 'He is, that is, he is not...not corrupted. He is just as he was. His limbs have not turned to dust, not decayed at all.'

'It *is* a wonder,' Eadfrith said. 'Our bishop is marked by the Lord in death as he was in life.

And it was true. The Lord had laid His hand on Cuthbert so that not even the worms and maggots of the earth had dared to enter his body. He lay in the coffin as if in sleep, just as he had that day eleven years ago when the brothers placed him there, his gold and garnet pectoral cross still gleaming as though freshly polished, his shroud and headcloth still white and unblemished. Aidan's altar lay at his side.

'Bring me closer to him,' Dunstan whispered.

Wilfrid helped him to kneel down at the side of the coffin. Dunstan leaned over, reached in and with a shaking hand touched Cuthbert's face. He started back as if hit by a whip and then knelt forward again. He slowly loosened the waxed shroud and felt for Cuthbert's hand.

'It's soft,' he said. 'See here, the wrist, the elbow. The stiffness of death is not there. His joints bend as if it were only moments ago he went from this world.'

He held Cuthbert's hand in his, close to his chest. Herefrith knelt next to him, gently took Cuthbert's hand from Dunstan.

'It *is* soft,' he said.

One by one, the brethren knelt down, taking turns to touch the hand of the bishop. They milled around the coffin, whispering and shushing each other, bending over the coffin, reaching in to test the evidence of their disbelieving eyes by touching the uncorrupted, holy corpse.

But Wilfrid was cast back to Cuthbert's final hours. He looked at Cuthbert's face, the downward turn of the mouth, the strain of the hollow cheeks. All he could see was how demons had succeeded in tormenting Cuthbert to the end, how his last thoughts were of failure and despair. And though Wilfrid had sat with him as he went to his death, prayed with him and comforted him, somehow in those final hours he had never admitted, let alone atoned for his own deeds, the part he had played in the events that shaped Cuthbert's last years.

'We must tell Bishop Edberht,' Herefrith said. 'Even though he is making his holy retreat. He must be told.'

'I will go,' Eadfrith said. His eyes were shining bright as the jewels in Cuthbert's cross. 'As soon as the tide ebbs I will go to the Rock and tell him of the great wonder that will be spoken of throughout the kingdoms of this earth. And we must send word to Aldfrith King also.'

'Yes,' Herefrith said.

'Tell him we will need more cattle.'

'Cattle?'

Herefrith stared at Eadfrith. They all did. Wilfrid wondered if the miracle had unseated his mind.

'Calves, skins, I mean,' Eadfrith said. 'We will need skins and more precious pigments.' He rubbed his hands together. 'I mean to create a great work, a psalter...no...no, a gospel, a set of gospels, such a work as has not been seen before, in commemoration of this great wonder, in honour of Blessed Cuthbert that his name may live throughout the ages to come.'

The Great Wonder. There had been some miracles wrought by Cuthbert since his death – healings of bodily and spiritual afflictions – but this, the preservation of his body, intact and whole, without mark or blemish, was a wonder beyond all wonders, a sign beyond all signs that Cuthbert had been marked with the special favour of the Lord. The brethren were used to occasional pilgrims who came to visit and worship at the holy shrines of Aidan and Cuthbert, sometimes in the hope of healing, sometimes to immerse themselves deeper into God's presence by touching the relics and walking the land where the blessed had trod. But it seemed to Wilfrid that this, the Great Wonder, was a quake that would shake the whole of Northumbria, the whole land, even distant corners of the earth. The community on Lindisfarne would be transformed, and he did not think that life on their secluded island could ever return to how it had been.

Eadfrith walked back and forth, muttering to himself. A sudden shaft of sunlight streamed through the open window, illuminating him in golden light so that for an instant he looked like a radiant image from one of his own manuscripts. Wilfrid swiped away a demon sting of envy. He must not allow the devil to embitter his soul. He had not been granted the gifts of a great scribe. The Spirit did not move in his hand, and his powers of understanding were small. He thought of his own feeble tribute to the bishop, his poor scribblings still concealed in his cell. They were best left there. Eadfrith would produce a wonder work, one fitting for a wonder-worker, a bishop, a saint. And Wilfrid would offer to assist Eadfrith, preparing the parchment, the pigments, fetching, carrying, whatever was required. It was the only offering he could make.

The monks took turns to keep vigil by Cuthbert's body. The reinterment ceremony was set to take place on Easter Day and would be attended by Aldfrith King and his thegns. Directions for the ceremony were issued by Bishop Edberht through pain and gritted teeth. The Lord was slow in coming for him. He had been spared, he said, that he might witness the Great Wonder and oversee the final laying to rest of their saint, who must one day be as beloved as St Aidan himself.

A new coffin, hewn from oak, was fashioned, engraved with images of the evangelists, apostles and archangels, Latin words and runes. The holy words would wrap Cuthbert in their protection, preserve him from the worms and maggots, slaves of the devils, who now more than ever might wish to attack the Servant of the Lord, corrupt and feast on his body. The final shield would come in the years ahead when Eadfrith's Gospels would one day lie on top of the sarcophagus and give glory to Cuthbert and to God until the end of time.

At the foot of the coffin lay an array of precious objects. Gifts to honour the Saint of Lindisfarne had been arriving from across the land even before the *translatio*. From Abbess Verca of Coldingham, a linen altar cloth. From Abbot Ceolfrith of Jarrow, two tall silver candlesticks. From Iona, bound in heavy leather encrusted with tiny garnets, a copy of the *Life of St Columba*, composed by Abbot Adomnán himself. And from Whitby, only that morning, a gift from Abbess Ælfflæd. Another book. *The Life of Pope St Gregory*. Wilfrid turned the pages. Her name was not inscribed in the preface, nothing at all to indicate the work was that of a nun and not a monk. But it was hers nonetheless. Meredith's. There was the tiny curl she occasionally added to her ascenders, the little dots she sometimes placed in the bow of her *B*s – a brazen act of individual will, Dunstan would have said. She had completed her great task as she had said she would.

Wilfrid tried to remember her as she had been that night, her hands stretched out so close to his by the fire, her eyes bright, a rare smile lighting her scarred face. He recalled the shape of her hand, the long fingers blistered and calloused, nails chewed and ink-stained, and still how tender the touch of that hand had been, like the brush of a sparrow wing. And he remembered, too, her admonition to him: *Write something of your own.*

After the Night Office, Wilfrid sat at the desk in his cell and prayed. He prayed that if the Lord did not see fit to fill his head with knowledge and understanding that He might fill it with words instead. And this time he would lay the words to rest, in their rightful place. He took his manuscript from its hiding place and placed it on his desk. He smoothened out the strip of parchment, plucked a stray goat hair from it. He pared his quill and opened his inkwell. He dipped the quill and gently shook the excess ink away. He wrote the story of the Great Wonder, the final chapter.

Two

HE SCRATCHINGS of a raven's claw. Wilfrid held his manuscript up to the dawn light creeping in, slow and white, through the window of his cell. Dunstan had not been wrong all those years ago. No angels had led his hand, filled his pages with grace and light. Infested with spots and blots, misshapen letters and crooked lines, there was something strange and savage about the work, as if a raven had indeed alighted on the page and pranced with inky feet about it. But Dunstan would not see this pockmarked, patched-together compilation of words. And neither would anyone else. After Lauds he would take his completed manuscript to the church and lay it to rest. It would lie where it belonged, dead words buried with the dead.

He sat at the window and sewed his leaves of

parchment together, the pages uneven in size, the script so minuscule only a sharp-eyed young novice would be able to read it, the binding a blank piece of parchment he had stolen from the scriptorium. One day, no doubt, someone else, some noble scribe, a great scholar, would be commissioned to write Cuthbert's Life, and that, along with Eadfrith's Gospels, would be the monastery's testament to the saint.

The bell rang for Lauds. Wilfrid placed the manuscript in his pocket and proceeded towards Dunstan's cell to bring him to the church. Dunstan was not waiting at the door as was his custom. He had been slower in his movements of late, and the trembling had increased, but he refused to let anyone enter his cell. There he needed no one's assistance but God's, he said. Wilfrid stood at the door a few moments, and then, as the last of the monks filed toward the church, he knocked. There was no response. A crow perched on the roof of the cell sang lustily. Wilfrid knocked again. Startled at the noise, the crow shrieked and sprang up, flying so close to Wilfrid that its wings smacked his cheeks. Down in the church the singing of the morning psalm had begun, and still Dunstan did not emerge. Wilfrid knocked a third time and entered.

Dunstan was lying very still in his pallet, one arm hanging loosely at the side of the bed, touching the floor. The other was stretched across his breast, something small and dark clutched in his hand. Wilfrid moved closer, knelt next to the bed, put his ear to Dunstan's mouth and listened. Then he gently prised open Dunstan's fist and removed the object he had been holding, ran his fingers over the familiar leather binding. The St John pocket gospel he had made for Cuthbert many years before, the same one Wilfrid and Herefrith had read to the bishop during his final hours. Wilfrid opened it and went through the pages, each line, each border neatly and precisely laid out, each letter slowly and carefully formed, each stroke of the quill a visible meditation on God's word. Wilfrid put the Gospel in his pocket next to his own poor manuscript. He folded Dunstan's arms across his chest and blessed him. Then he went to fetch the brethren.

They buried Dunstan that same morning in the monks' graveyard next to the church, wrapped him in a simple woollen cloth and laid him in the ground. Mourning must wait, as the last remaining tasks in preparation for Cuthbert's reinterment ceremony had to be completed, though Wilfrid suspected that few would mourn the old brother who had spent his final years loudly lamenting the passing of the old days when monks were devout, novices were obedient and men avoided all that was sinful. He stayed by the graveside longer than the others, until a shout went up from the gatepost. Aldfrith King and his little son, along with a company of thegns and priests, had been spotted riding across the sands. The monks immediately made their way to the monastery gates to greet the guests. Wilfrid hurried to the church. He wouldn't have another chance.

Cuthbert was laid in the new coffin, wrapped in the linen altar cloth and clothed in a new shroud and headcloth. His old garments had been put in the silver casket and were laid at the foot of the sarcophagus into which the coffin would be placed. Cuthbert's cross had been placed neatly across his chest. At his feet, folded and scrubbed clean, was Aidan's altar. Wilfrid placed his hand on the altar, pressed his fingers against the rough lettering inscribed on it. *IN HONOREM S PETRI*. He prayed to Aidan, Peter, to all the saints, to give him strength.

His hands were steady as he untied the altar cloth and loosened the shroud, laying bare Cuthbert's thin and sunken chest. He took out his manuscript, traced the sign of the cross over it with his thumb and laid it on Cuthbert's breast. His small offering, his oblation, not a book wrought of splendid expression and magnificent illustrations, but well-meaning words written as reparation. It was all he had. He prayed a psalm of penitence, for Cuthbert, for Fergus, Laurence, his mother, his father, for Wulfi.

Domine, exaudi orationem meam ...
Inclina ad me aurem tuam ...
Percussus sum ut faenum ...
Vigilavi et factus sum sicut passer
solitarius in tecto ...
Tu autem, Domine, in aeternum permanes ...
Scribantur haec in generationem alteram.

He paused.

Scribantur haec in generationem alteram.

Let these things be written unto another generation.
He looked at his manuscript, a bedraggled thing of loose scratchings and rushed inkings. And yet, wound

within it was an account of Cuthbert's life, of the many miracles wrought by him. However feeble and humble the words, it was nonetheless a testament to God's servant. Even Dunstan had said that words committed to parchment had power, could send knowledge of the Lord's great deeds and the deeds of His labourers to the ends of the earth.

In the distance Wilfrid heard psalm-singing, drumbeats, voices raised in acclamation and praise. The solemn procession of monks, nuns and nobles was assembling. Later there would be feasting. The celebrations would last for days. From Bishop Edberht to the latest novice, from Aldfrith King to the lowliest slave, each man and woman present would come with a hunger for stories of Bishop Cuthbert, his wondrous miracles, his splendid deeds. They would sit around the fire, ears bent to the mouths of the brethren, like warriors devouring the tales of a scop. Their hunger would not be satisfied. In the days and years to come they would want more.

Let these things be written unto another generation.

A sudden rush of thoughts surged through him. Perhaps he could copy his work out again, more carefully this time, on vellum, and bind it. He held his manuscript in his hand, felt the rough grains and ridges of the parchment between his forefinger and thumb, traced the words hastily scribbled in the narrow margin of the opening page – *Vita Sancti Cuthberti, Auctore Anonymo*. He placed the manuscript back in his pocket, felt it warm against his thigh.

He went to close the shroud around Cuthbert again. He looked down at the body on which he had thought to lay his words of atonement and he remembered Dunstan's Gospel. The words of St John. Let them rest next to Cuthbert's heart instead, bind him in an everlasting hymn, sing to him throughout all ages. And he thought how that might have brought a tear to poor Dunstan's clouded eyes. He laid the gospel on Cuthbert's breast, hid it beneath the shroud and wrapped the linen cloth tightly around his body.

Outside, blackbirds sang from the church rooftop. Seals sang too, from their refuge on the sandspits. The procession was passing by the scriptorium and making its way down the path to the church. Wilfrid went to join them. He held his writing close.

Author's note

The earliest account of the life of St Cuthbert is not the celebrated version written by the Venerable Bede but one composed by an anonymous monk of Lindisfarne. Completed between twelve and twenty years after Cuthbert's death in 687, the anonymous *Life* spawned a whole series of narratives about a man destined to become one of England's foremost saints and a religious and cultural icon.

Interestingly, both Bede's *Life* and the anonymous *Life* were commissioned by Bishop Eadfrith, he of the Lindisfarne Gospels fame. Bede's version places stronger emphasis on Cuthbert's championing of the 'Roman' dating of Easter; it's possible that this was a motivating factor in the commissioning of this second prose *Life*.

Despite the fact that Bede draws liberally from the earlier version, he does not name his source. Perhaps he felt no need to do so, since everyone in the Lindisfarne community must have known who this writer was. However, for me there is a deep poignancy in the fact that Bede's reputation survives to this day while the identity of his predecessor has been lost. This was my gateway into my novel; I wanted to give Anonymous a name and a history, albeit in fictional form.

I was also interested in the Synod of Whitby; not in the arguments presented there by the opposing factions, but in the scars it must have left on the communities divided in its aftermath. At the time of Cuthbert's death, and even by the time of his exhumation, Iona and some monasteries in Ireland, Pictland and Wales persisted in their rejection of the 'Roman' timing of Easter and the Petrine tonsure, continuing to adhere to the 'old ways'.

However when Bede came to write his *Life*, circa 721, things had changed. In 716, Iona had bowed to the inevitable and finally accepted the new order. The monasteries in Pictland had 'come over' shortly before.

In writing this novel I relied heavily on stories and characters presented in the anonymous *Life* and Bede's *Life*. The degree to which these hagiographical accounts are factually accurate is a discussion for another day. Suffice it to say, medieval hagiography has much in common with historical fiction; and, like many a medieval hagiographer, I have taken liberties with the facts and shaped them to my own ends.

Over the centuries since the two Lives were

written, Cuthbert's fame and status has increased. The continuing power of his story is attested by the numbers of visitors and pilgrims who flock to Lindisfarne, to the Inner Farne Island and to his shrine in Durham. For many, these are places inhabited by a sense of sacred presence.

Cuthbert's wooden coffin, his portable altar, his pectoral cross and his ivory comb, all on view in the cathedral museum in Durham, offer a tangible connection to the past; while the Lindisfarne Gospels and the tiny eighth-century Gospel book discovered with Cuthbert's body (and now on display in the British Museum in London) are, like the Lives, witnesses to Cuthbert and the early medieval Christian world.

For readers who wish to delve further into this world, *Ecgfrith: King of the Northumbrians, High-King of Britain* by NJ Higham, *The King in the North* by Max Adams and Marc Morris' *The Anglo-Saxons* skilfully evoke the political and religious issues of the era. Kate Tristram's *The Story of Holy Island* and Magnus Magnusson's *Lindisfarne: The Cradle Island* provide an engaging record of the island of Lindisfarne itself. For details of the fascinating afterlife of Cuthbert's body, read David Willem's *St Cuthbert's Corpse: A Life After Death. The Private Lives of the Saints: Power, Passion and Politics in Anglo-Saxon England* by Janina Ramirez is a useful key to reading beyond the official hagiographic narratives.

But to gain an immersive experience of that bygone world, there is no better place to start than the texts themselves. *Two Lives of St Cuthbert* by Bertram Colgrave reproduces the anonymous *Life* and Bede's

Life in their original Latin alongside an English translation. These are rich and vivid accounts of the charismatic and holy man who became a renowned medieval saint and whose legacy endures to this day.

Acknowledgements

This novel began its life as part of a PhD thesis undertaken at University College Cork, and I am grateful for the support I received there. Sincere thanks are due to Eibhear Walshe and Mary Morrissy for their insightful feedback, guidance and support. I also wish to acknowledge Claire Connolly, Tom Birkett and Jools Gilson for practical help and advice, and Heather Laird and Sara Maitland for examining my thesis and encouraging me to move forward to publication.

For financial support I am grateful to the School of English at UCC and in particular to the Irish Research Council for the award of a postgraduate scholarship.

I am indebted to the team at Eye Books: to Dan Hiscocks for publishing my novel, to Clio Mitchell for copyediting, Ifan Bates for the cover design, and in particular to Simon Edge, whose razor-sharp editorial skills honed and shaped the book.

I owe a huge debt of gratitude to my friends Laura McKenna and Madeleine D'Arcy. Their invaluable insights, astute questions and unfailing encouragement enabled me to keep going and see the project through.

Thanks are due also to other friends and acquaintances who assisted me in many different ways, including Michelle McAdoo, Humberto Sahldana, Donal MacPolin, Imogen Robertson, Norah Perkins and Máire O'Donohue. Canon Kate Tristram of Holy Island was generous with her time and knowledge when meeting me, while the hospitality of the monks of Glenstal Abbey enabled me to enjoy a period of uninterrupted writing, while experiencing the daily routine of monastic life.

Finally, heartfelt thanks to my husband, Seamus McMahon, and our children, Ailish, Ciarán and Sinéad, who accompanied me literally and metaphorically on my writing journey, from monastic ruins to holy caves to windswept islands. Their unfailing acceptance and good humour sustained me throughout this creative pilgrimage.

If you have enjoyed *Let These Things Be Written*, do please help us spread the word – by putting a review online; by posting something on social media; or in the old-fashioned way by simply telling your friends or family about it.

Book publishing is a very competitive business these days, in a saturated market, and small independent publishers such as ourselves are often crowded out by the big houses. Support from readers like you can make all the difference to a book's success.

Many thanks.
Dan Hiscocks
Publisher, Eye Books